Master Hunter K
Book 1: Initialization

Master Hunter K series

in reading order-

From Hell

Master Hunter K
Book 1: Initialization

Translated from the Korean by
Edward Ro and Minsoo Kang.

Oppatranslations

Oppatranslations, LLC.
5110 Ravenna PL NE #201
Seattle WA 98105, USA

oppatranslations.com

Translated from the Korean by Minsoo Kang.
Edited by – Sahil Bansal, Jessie Raymond

First published by Oppatranslations, LLC 2021

© From Hell 2016
English translation © Oppatranslations, LLC 2017

Paperback
ISBN: 978-0-9992957-5-5

Send us feedback at oppatranslations@gmail.com

Our website for more novels by us https://www.oppatranslations.com/

Contents

Prologue

"No..."

Sungjin reached out toward the heaven, but strength had already left him. Somewhere, the Operator's voice filled the air.

[All players eliminated. Closing the Chapter.]

Sungjin's eyes dimmed as darkness creeped inward from the edge of his vision. Now that he faced imminent death, he had finally found peace.

"I've had enough of violence. I'm glad it is finally over."

As he let the calm envelope him, Sungjin welcomed the approaching darkness of his death. Still, the Operator's voice continued to reverberate in the background.

[You have died.]

[You were humanity's very last surviving player.]

[Benefit awarded to the last player to die is "Restart."]

At the same time, a single line of text appeared before his eyes.

Restart – Redo the hunt from the very beginning, but with current memory.

What?

Before Sungjin could mutter another sentence, he opened his eyes and saw that he was now in an entirely white room. It was a familiar room however, with perfectly square walls.

[Hunt will soon begin. Prepare for battle.]

"Restart... from scratch?"

Sungjin lifted his arms. They felt empty so he examined them closely.

"My rings are gone!"

It wasn't just the rings, all the items he had been gathering were missing. He had been brought back moments before the first hunt, to the same room where everything began.

"Haah..." Sungjin massaged his forehead as he let out a withering sigh. Before his eyes, a large bulletin board appeared.

Chapter 0 – Living Mannequin
Time Limit: 30 Seconds

Sungjin absentmindedly spoke out the next words along with the Operator.

"You will die."

[...you will die.]

Chapter 1 – Living Mannequin

One day, a mechanical but distinctly feminine voice was heard by all humans. A voice who later introduced herself as the "Operator."

[A hunt will soon begin. Prepare for combat.]

And the moment they heard the sentence, every man, woman, and child were teleported to a blank white room alone. The room itself was not large, and in the middle, a large hologram appeared.

> Chapter 0 – Living Mannequin
> Time Limit: 30 Seconds

Simple information about the enemy appeared, and then,

[Annihilate the enemy. If you cannot, you will die.]

A simple 'rule' was explained.

[For the first Chapter, just this once, you will be provided with a weapon. Select your weapon.]

> [Club], [Broad Sword], [Katana], [Hand Axe], [Long Spear], [Long Bow], [Short Sword], [Spiked Gauntlets]

When Sungjin saw this, he said out loud, "...Katana."

And that instant, a Katana appeared in his hands. It was a Japanese, curved, single-edged sword. Inspecting the weapon, he whispered to himself,

"Wow, it's been a long time since I last saw this."

Once the weapon was selected, the Operator began a countdown.

[10, 9, 8, 7, 6, 5, 4, 3, 2, 1, 0]

After 10 seconds, the billboard disappeared, and the 'enemy' described in it was summoned. An eerie doll hung on a cross-shaped wooden stand now stood before Sungjin.

The living mannequin stood there motionless.

Sungjin left the Mannequin alone and gazed at his weapon. "I have to do this... all over again...?"

Sungjin's memories flashed before his eyes. Never-ending series of battles, constant pressure to kill, and a steady stream of the deaths of irreplaceable comrades. While Sungjin was preoccupied with his thoughts, the Operator continued to speak.

[20 seconds remaining. Annihilate the enemy. If you cannot, you will die.]

Rows upon rows of sharp steel spikes appeared from the ceiling.

"I can't do this anymore...". Sungjin said and hung his head, shaking it as he stood there. The Operator spoke again.

[10 seconds remaining. Annihilate the enemy. If you cannot, you will die.]

The ceiling, which was now covered in spikes, began coming down. There was no place to hide and nowhere to run. The Operator began the countdown once more.

[10, 9, 8, 7...]

The ceiling was now low enough to touch by jumping up, but Sungjin did not move. He watched the ceiling approach closer and closer, and thought to himself.

This is it? Is this the reward for being the last human to die? I'd rather...

[6, 5, 4]

But before he finished his thoughts, he recalled a promise he'd made with someone.

"Swear to me! You must..."

[3, 2]

Sungjin frowned. And then,

[1]

He swung the Katana he held.

SHING

The blade cut through the air and drew a red line on the neck of the mannequin.

[0 You have...]

The moment the Katana cut the mannequin's neck, the Operator's voice became garbled as if bugged. The ceiling also stopped in its tracks. In a happier tone than earlier, she announced:

[All monsters eliminated. Closing the Chapter.]

Following the announcement, a hologram appeared.

```
Completion Reward: Stat Point 0
Kill Reward: Black Coin 0
```

Sungjin spoke to himself when he saw the message.

"Yeah... maybe this time it will be different."

Once Sungjin was finished, he was summoned somewhere else.

*

The place he was summoned to was an enormous hall of an unknown size. Within it, was an uncountable number of people.

Regardless of race, all ethnicities were present in the hall. The only interesting fact was that an overwhelming majority were 'adult men.' The people who were summoned looked panicked and confused.

"What's going on?"

"Where am I?"

"What is this?"

These were common questions that filled the air.

Sungjin watched with his arms folded over his chest. He'd reacted the same way as those people the first time he was there.

"Is this some sort of a reality tv show?"

"Alien abduction?"

And then, people realized that they could understand one another.

"You know how to speak Chinese?"

"How did you learn Arabic?"

"Hey, are you aware you are all speaking English?"

And the Operator's voice was heard once more, interrupting everyone's thoughts.

[Welcome!]

This time, the voice wasn't coming from inside their head, but from above. People naturally gazed upward to see who was speaking.

Above, a beautiful woman's face appeared.

[My name is Operator. I am here to welcome you all for becoming representatives of mankind.]

Sungjin smirked when he heard her words.

Welcome... what a farce.

Regardless of what Sungjin thought, the Operator continued to speak.

[This place is called 'The Hunter's Hall.' It is where the hopes and dreams of Hunters are gathered.]

[You are all here as a result of completing the Chapter 0.]

[And thereby earning the right to become Hunters who will represent all of humanity.]

The reaction from the audience was varied.

"Hunter? What does she mean?"

"Is she talking about that... that thing I just killed?"

"Did you kill that too?"

"Yes. I suppose you saw the same thing?"

Chapter 0 was something akin to a tutorial. Faced with the threat of imminent death, it was about one's ability to land the killing blow on the mannequin.

Naturally, elderly, children, and disabled were unable to pass.

"It was much harder than I thought. It kept on screaming so loudly..."

"Yours as well?"

Living Mannequins screamed for their life once attacked. Because of this disturbingly life-like behavior, those with difficulty taking a life were also eliminated from Chapter 0.

Mentally weaker men and women were part of this group.

Someone commented in hindsight, "I should have stabbed its heart first."

[Definition of Hunter:]

[Strongest representative of the entire species, living proof of the species' Strength.]

With that said, the image of the Operator changed with that of another location. This image was filled with countless men, women, children, and elderly.

[This place is Purgatory. Neither heaven nor hell.]

[Gathered here are all the people eliminated from Chapter 0.]

It was only a guess, but Sungjin felt that the image shown was probably different for every person as screams and shouts could be heard among those present in the hall once they gazed at the screen.

"Mother!"

"My love... why are you..."

"My daughter! Give me back my daughter!"

The Operator was showing everyone the people most important to them.

Sick bastards...

Sungjin swore under his breath, but he didn't become upset like the others. He was an orphan. The only 'close' people he knew were several employees at the orphanage he'd grown up at, but he didn't feel emotionally connected to them or their fate.

[Hunters who perish during the hunt will also be moved to Purgatory.]

[If someone completes all objectives and clears the challenges]

[Everyone contained in Purgatory will be returned alive.]

[However, if all Hunters fail and are moved to Purgatory]

[All of humanity will be purged.]

Sungjin doubted those words. *Purged? If that's the case, then why send me back?*

Others continued to stare blankly as the Operator continued her explanation. They had yet to understand the gravity of her words.

[Prove your power by overcoming any and all obstacles that stand in your way.]

[And with your own Strength, prove the worth of your species.]

[If you fail to do so, Humanity as a species will be made extinct.]

Whispers among the crowd grew.

"What? Extinct?"

"Us? All of humanity?"

Some were expressing anger.

"Who is this bitch?"

But the Operator's indifferent tone of voice remained unchanged by the people's reactions.

[Now, the explanations are over.]

[I pray that we will meet again.]

The hall was then completely inundated with insults and expletives.

"You fucking whore!"

"What the fuck did you say?"

"Mother fucker!"

"Fuck!"

Despite the abuse pouring out from the audience, the Operator continued her indifferent speech.

[Hunting will begin shortly. Prepare for battle.]

Despite the deafening roar of insults being thrown at the Operator, Sungjin kept his calm and planned his next move.

If things are the same as before...

Sungjin bit his lip and lifted his Katana up to inspect the sword. The blade reflected his gaze back.

Looking into the eyes reflected on the blade, he vowed to himself.

This time, I will perfectly clear every Chapter.

Sungjin fixed his grip on the Katana and prepared himself. Moments later, he was teleported away from the Hunter's Hall.

Chapter 2 – Greenskin Wildlands

A palisade could be seen in the distance, pierced all over with unnecessary spikes and nails. The tips were also filed to a point.

The meat of an unknown animal was hung over a bonfire to cook, and various sizes of skulls were placed on top of the spears to decorate the area.

The place Sungjin arrived at reeked of barbarity. And so he thought to himself,

The Chapter order is the same.

Shortly after arriving, a cube appeared and followed him. The Operator's voice could be heard from the cube.

[Welcome to Greenskin Wildlands;]

[Home of savage creatures who have gathered together to form a tribe.]

[This is the Hunter's first real challenge]

[And it is also an excellent opportunity for the Hunter to experiment with how to grow stronger.]

[The first four phases are combat tutorials designed to get you prepared.]

[However, do not lower your guard.]

[Like in real combat situation, if you take fatal damage,]

[or if the enemy is not annihilated within the time limit, the Hunter will perish.]

A billboard appeared with the enemy's information on it.

Phase 1 – Goblin
Time Limit: 3 Minutes

[Annihilate the enemy. If you cannot, you will die.]
"Kyakakakakaka~!"

A Goblin's cry could be heard from somewhere in the Wildlands. Sungjin drew out his Katana while the Operator continued to explain through the cube.

[Goblins are small creatures.]

[Typically reaching only the height of an adult's knee, or in exceptional cases, to the hips.]

[The weight of the monster is only about a fourth of an average adult, so it is not a physically powerful creature.]

[The short height causes their point of attack to be lower, along with their temperament...]

The Operator's voice stopped there, since all the Goblins were already decapitated.

[All Monsters Eliminated. Closing the Chapter.]

Following the announcement, the hologram reappeared.

Completion Reward: Stat Point 1
Kill Reward: Black Coin 1

[Use the reward you earned to strengthen yourself. With only the strength of a human...]

"Enough."

Sungjin cut off the Operator and spoke over her.

"Add the Stat Point to Dexterity."

[Dexterity rose by 1 point.]

Despite Sungjin's rude interruption, the Operator continued her explanation.

[The Black Coins can be used...]

Once again, Sungjin cut her off.

"I'm not buying."

And then once again, a billboard with the monster's information appeared in front of him.

Phase 2 – HobGoblin
Time limit: 3 minutes

[HobGoblins are stronger versions of Go...]

Sungjin did not wait for her explanation before rushing in to behead the HobGoblins. The Operator seemed to take notice of Sungjin's competency, and so she quickly allowed him to proceed.

[All Monsters Eliminated. Closing the Chapter.]

| Completion Reward: Stat Point 3 |
| Kill Reward: Black Coin 3 |

Sungjin spoke to the cube.

"Add all Stat Points to Dexterity. And I'm not buying anything."

[Dexterity rose by 3 points.]

The Operator skipped all the explanations and proceeded to the next phase.

| Phase 3 – Orc |
| Time Limit: 3 Minutes |

This time, Sungjin didn't rush out of the entryway. The Operator gave an explanation from behind.

[Orcs are powerful creatures.]

[They are as large and can be larger than an average adult male human.]

[They also wield barbaric weapons such as clubs, glaives, and axes.]

An Orc jumped out from behind the Palisade. He sported a clearly defined six pack and a well-developed trapezius muscle.

This phase was where most of the physically weaker Hunters were eliminated and sent to Purgatory.

I remember this being really hard the first time.

Recalling memories of the previous time he was in this Chapter, Sungjin could not help but laugh. *This time around, things will be different,* he thought. Sungjin had already experienced countless battles before; something as simple as an Orc did not warrant a second thought.

"Uzak Rumrum!", the Orc shouted in an unknown language and charged toward Sungjin. He aimed for Sungjin's head and swung his club. Sungjin avoided the blow by leaning back out of the strike zone.

WOOSH

The club hit nothing but air.

BAM!

It landed on the ground. The Orc stiffened up slightly upon impact. Taking advantage of his opening, Sungjin cut the back of the Orc's knee.

"Kaaaa!"

The Orc was forced to his knees, exposing his neck to Sungjin. Without mercy, Sungjin brought his blade down upon the Orc's neck.

The Orc was beheaded in a single strike. Moments later, the Operator spoke.

[All Monsters Eliminated. Closing the Chapter.]

Sungjin raised his Katana high and swung the sword, causing the blood on the Katana to fall and paint a crimson tapestry on the forest floor.

Sungjin absentmindedly cleaned off his blade as he thought to himself while examining the head of the Orc.

Now that I think of it, the last Orc was bald.

The Orc's head in front of him sported long hair.

The Chapter itself is the same... but the monsters are a little different. I'm going to have to keep this in mind.

Interrupting his thoughts, the Operator announced his reward.

Completion Reward: Stat Point 5
Kill Reward: Black Coin 5

Sungjin, once again, put all his Stat Points into Dexterity.

"All Stat Points to Dexterity."

[Dexterity rose by 5 points.]

"And I'm not..." Sungjin stopped himself before he finished saying "buying anything" as before. The next enemy was a Troll, an adversary with an amazing regenerative ability.

In order to kill a Troll in spite of his regenerative ability, fire or acid was required. The Operator also suggested the same.

[You will require fire to fight the next enemy.]

[In the first Chapter, you will be able to purchase Items from the cube.]

[Please use the Black Coins you earned to purcha...]

Sungjin cut off the Operator and spoke over her.

"How much is the Salamander's Ash?"

[It is 6 Black Coins.]

Salamander's Ash was an item that gave fire enchant to a weapon upon use. The problem was that it was a consumable item that wears off over time.

It was an item necessary for new Hunters to overcome the early Chapters, but for Sungjin who aimed for 'All Clear' and late game, it was an expense he was hesitant to make. Sungjin asked the Operator,

"How much is Moyzakui Flintstone?"

[It is 300 Black Coins.]

Unlike Salamander's ash, Moyzakui Flintstone could repeatedly be used. However, it cost 300 Black Coins. He would need to complete two Chapters before he could earn that much.

Sungjin frowned and said to the Operator:

"...Not buying."

The Operator prepared the next phase immediately upon hearing Sungjin's answer.

Phase 4 – Troll
Time limit: 3 minutes

A monster at least a head taller than an average man appeared from the palisade. When the Troll noticed Sungjin, it opened its jaws wide and roared. "Guwaaaaarg!"

From the force of its roar, long strings of mucus dripped down its jaw, clinging to its irregular and jagged teeth. Sungjin assumed his position and drew his Katana. And for the first time since returning to the beginning, Sungjin checked the timer.

...3 Minutes

***

The Troll waved his club wildly as he ran toward Sungjin.

WOOSH

WHOOSH

Sungjin watched the club carefully and dodged the two strikes before slicing the back of the Troll's knee like in the case of the Orc.

"Kurag!"

The Troll fell on his knees. Sungjin tried to cut off the Troll's head as he did with the Orc, but,

WOOSH,

The Troll swung his club toward Sungjin again. Sungjin was forced to stop as he dodged the club and backed away, creating a distance between them. The Troll stood up right away, and charged toward Sungjin. "Warrgh!"

The cut on his leg had regenerated by the time it finished screaming. If he had used Salamander's Ash, the fight would have already been over, but Sungjin wished to preserve every bit of Black Coin he could manage.

I guess the same trick won't work on a Troll.

A Troll's physical strength was massive, and with an extraordinary regenerative ability, it was impossible for a human to face off against it using purely physical attacks.

But the reason why humans could overcome the Trolls was that the Trolls lacked the ability to learn.

"Graaah!" The Troll picked up his club and charged toward Sungjin once more. Sungjin dodged the club and

WOOSH

He cut the Troll's shin and spun around, striking and severing the wrist with which the Troll held the club.

"Kragh!" While screaming in pain of losing his right hand, the Troll swung his remaining fist toward Sungjin.

Sungjin jumped back to avoid the strike. The tip of the Troll's fingers sported nails as sharp as spears.

I can't give him a chance to regenerate. Once Sungjin landed on the ground, he dashed forward to re-engage the Troll. The Troll swiped his left hand once more toward Sungjin, but Sungjin swiftly dodged and closed in on the Troll.

And all he had to do, was to draw out his Katana and hold it in the trajectory of the slash. The Troll's massive strike met the blade, and the momentum of the Troll's own attack severed his wrist effortlessly.

"Wargh!"

Sungjin got to work cutting and slashing ruthlessly at the Troll without mercy. It was a gruesome task, but Sungjin could not let up the pressure since the Troll could regenerate all of it in a matter of moments.

With both hands gone, the Troll could not retaliate against Sungjin's attacks and finally leaned forward to protect his body. The moment the Troll leaned over, Sungjin beheaded the creature.

And without a pause, the Operator announced his victory.

[All Monsters Eliminated. Closing the Chapter.]

"Haa..." Finally, Sungjin let out a sigh. "Fighting a Troll without fire... how annoying."

The fallen Troll had already regrown his right arm, along with the spear-like nails. It was an unbelievable display of regenerative ability.

But despite it all, it was a success. He had saved 6 Black Coins. The Operator announced the reward.

> Completion Reward: Stat Point 10
> Kill Reward: Black Coin 10

The reward for the Troll was double that of the Orc, which made sense. Actually, considering the difference in the level of difficulty between the two monsters, the difference in the reward amount was perhaps not high enough; in real combat, the Troll was more than twice as difficult compared to the Orc.

If the Orc was an opponent that a grown man had a good chance of defeating, then the Troll was something only a combat veteran could overcome, assuming he used the Black Coins in both cases.

I think an unimaginable amount of people will be eliminated at this stage, thought Sungjin and his guess was spot on, as many had succumbed to their deaths on this phase and were sent to Purgatory. Even so, there was no need to mourn the loss of those Hunters. In this "hunt," only the strong were allowed to survive.

In fact, the earlier the weak got eliminated, the better. Especially before the next round. The next round was not an individual round, it was a 'Raid' conducted as a team. The Operator announced this fact as well.

[Dear Hunter, you have completed this Phase faster than the others.]

[In the next Phase, you will be put into teams with other Hunters and carry out a Raid.]

[Please stand by until other Hunters complete their tutorials.]

Since Sungjin suddenly had downtime, he checked his Status for the first time since the restart.

"Operator, show me my Stats."

HP: 100 MP: 170

Strength: 12
Dexterity: 23
Endurance: 10
Magic: 14
Mind Power: 17

Unallocated Stat Points: 10

Seeing the Status window made Sungjin pause.

The Stat values are the same as last time.

From the start, Sungjin's Stat was on the high side. Before he restarted from beginning, he had asked others for their starting Stats and found that most people had averaged just around 10. This meant Sungjin was originally much stronger than an average person.

His Strength and Dexterity were 2-3 points higher than average. And although it was unclear how it was decided, he also had higher than average starting Magic Power and Mind Power. Magic Power affected the damage dealt via spells while Mind Power dictated the size of the mana pool or MP. Only his Endurance stat which controlled his health points or HP was at an average level[1].

Sungjin carefully thought about his Stat.

I began raising Dexterity which directly improved my speed, but...

He lifted up his Katana and asked the Operator a question.

"Operator, show me the specs of the sword."

Katana – Beginning the Hunt

Normal Katana – Strength C Dexterity D

Basic weapon issued by the Operator without any significant merits or demerits.

If wielded by a master, it can perform extraordinarily well.

Strength C Dexterity D...

In this "hunt," every weapon had a rating for how it affected Strength and Dexterity. Until the restart, Sungjin had used weapons rated at least an A. He asked Operator another question.

"Operator, how do ranks affect bonus stats?"

[Rank affects stats as follows.]

[Rank E – x0.1 | Rank D – x0.2 | Rank C – x0.5]

[Rank B – x1.0 | Rank A – x1.5 | Rank S – x2.0]

[Rank SS – x3.0 | Rank SSS – x4.0]

Generally speaking, blunt weapons like axes are more influenced by Strength and less from Dexterity. Swords, like the Katana wielded by Sungjin, were well balanced between Strength and Dexterity.

If he raised his Strength, the damage would increase by a large amount (in this case, by an additional x0.5), and raising the Dexterity would increase damage by a smaller (x0.2) amount. He would be trading damage for attack and dodging speed in combat.

Raising both stats had merits, but Sungjin decided to build on Dexterity first. Increasing his speed improved his ability to dodge. Instead of investing in Endurance, he opted for combat stats.

Not raising his Endurance at all was a dangerous gamble because no matter how fast he was, he could still die from one or two stray hits without investing points in Endurance.

But he paid no heed to the danger and decided to all-in on his gamble.

"Add all points to Dexterity."

[Dexterity rose by 10 points.]

Starting with the next phase, which was a Raid, points were awarded based on his merit and participation.

If I don't excel from the start, I will die in the latter half.

Sungjin's immediate goal wasn't merely survival, but to prepare for end game. So, ignoring Endurance for now, he invested solely in Dexterity. He also decided to save every Black Coin he could manage.

The average Hunter would have difficulty surviving from Chapter to Chapter without items. However, Sungjin decided that he was not going to waste any coins on consumables if possible.

[Synchronization will begin in 1 minute.]

The Operator fell silent after that last message. It appeared that there was still some time before other Hunters completed their phases. Sungjin crossed his arms and thought about the next Raid.

Killing as many monsters as possible within the time limit is a no-brainer...

It was the most basic rule, common to all Raids.

And if at all possible, I must find the hidden boss and eliminate it.

Hidden boss referred to boss mobs concealed in every map. As Chapters progressed, Hunters realized that hidden boss mobs and items existed in every map. And those secret bosses dropped 'special items.'

Problem is, I do not know where it is located.

Sungjin knew the location of a few hidden bosses in later Chapters, which was thanks to Hunters sharing the secret locations via word of mouth.

But for the first Raid, Greenskin Wildlands, nobody knew the secret location, because everyone was still new to the hunt.

In that case, I need to complete the Raid as fast as possible and search the map.

Running through the plan in his head, Sungjin pursed his lips and nodded. Finally, the Operator announced the next stage.

[All hunts have been completed.]

[Synchronizing Hunters]

The background blurred for a moment, and four people appeared in the vicinity. In addition to Sungjin, there were five Hunters now.

"What?" The other Hunters were briefly shocked upon seeing each other.

[Starting from Phase 5, the hunt will be carried out as a 'Raid' in cooperation between 5 Hunters.]

However, the moment the Operator's voice was heard, the other Hunters immediately stopped speaking. By now, they had realized that listening to the Operator was essential to their survival.

> Phase 5 – Greenskin Wildlands Raid
> Target – Hunt the Orc Chief Kamul
> Time limit: 20 minutes

[Complete your objective within the time limit.]

[If you cannot, you will die.]

The others listened carefully to the Operator's announcement. Meanwhile, Sungjin took the chance to inspect his teammates.

They were all males. Asian, Arabic, black, white; they were all from different races, and not one of them Sungjin recognized. The teammates were different from those in his previous life.

I kind of predicted this back when I saw the Orc...

Sungjin had briefly hoped that he would find the same members in his team from last time, but he knew better than to expect it. The Operator was explaining about the rewards of this Raid.

[You will be given freedom to act as you please upon completion of the Raid objective.]

[Hunt as many enemies as you can within the time limit.]

[The more you hunt, the higher the reward.]

[Loot will be distributed based on contribution.]

> Goblin – Contribution 1
> HobGoblin – Contribution 3
> Orc – Contribution 5
> Troll – Contribution 10
> Orc Chief Cunning Kamul – Contribution 50

As expected, there was no information at all about the hidden boss. The Operator only went on to explain the importance of cooperation.

[In order to complete the Raid objective, Cooperation between Hunters is essential.]

[Please discuss with your teammates, distribute your Stat Points, and purchase items as you deem necessary.]

[Raid begins in 1 minute. I wish you all best of luck.]

With that last sentence, the Operator concluded her explanation. Only the five Hunters remain. Since this was the first meeting amongst them, it was a little awkward. But finally, someone broke the ice.

"Well, since we should cooperate with each other, let's introduce ourselves."

First to speak out was the muscular black man.

"As you saw from the previous round, we need fire to beat those Trolls. How many Black Coins do you all have remaining with you? I have 7 left."

The black man wore a vest with "Police" written on it, along with a large badge. At his words, others began to speak out. This time, the tall white man, "8..."

Then the short and skinny Asian, "I have 6."

And finally, the Arabic man wearing a turban, "I also have 6."

As expected, they all had spent some coins until now. These must have been spent on potions to heal from the damage taken from fighting and the Salamander's ash which was needed to defeat the Troll.

But if they continued to burn through coins purchasing consumable items like this, they wouldn't last until the end game. Everybody had announced their number of Black Coins.

Everybody except one. They looked toward Sungjin. Finally opening his mouth, he decided to speak, "...Please listen carefully."

***

Everyone's eyes focused on Sungjin. With his eyes narrowed to a slit, Sungjin continued, "You should all follow closely behind me. I will clear this Raid quickly for you."

Sungjin's plan was simple. Finish the Raid as fast as possible, and then search for the hidden boss.

After all, his objective wasn't to simply clear the Raid. Without waiting for anyone to reply, Sungjin continued to explain, "And just in case, please go ahead and purchase Salamander's ash. You don't need potions, so don't get them."

The team continued to stare at Sungjin in shock. He added one more line.

"And as the last bit of advice, if you have any remaining unallocated Stat Points, please invest them into Endurance. Then, you will be able to survive at least a bit longer."

Once Sungjin finished, the other four men looked amongst each other. Finally, the white man spoke out first, "I mean, we don't know what's going to happen soon..."

The Arab man joined in, "He's right. We should carefully consider our options, don't you think?"

Sungjin bit his lips in frustration. But he didn't have the time nor reason to explain everything to them. And the Operator decided this was the best timing to ask Sungjin a question.

[You currently have 19 Black Coins left. Will you...]

"I'm not buying."

Sungjin answered nonchalantly, but the other four men opened their eyes wide in surprise. The black man repeated the number to verify, "19?"

The white man also asked in response, "You didn't use a single coin until now?"

The two men looked upon Sungjin with a sense of admiration, but the other two looked horrified.

The Asian man narrowed his eyes, full of distrust, and asked Sungjin, "19? You've got so many, and you are making us spend our own coins instead?"

23

The Arab man piped in as well, "19... If you have several more coins than any of us do, doesn't it make more sense for you to spend your coins?"

Sungjin massaged his forehead. He was starting to give up on the idea of trying to explain himself, "...I am unable to spend my coins."

The other four men doubted his words. Especially the Asian man, "Liar! You're just trying to save up coins to buy yourself lots of potions! So you can survive alone!"

The Arab man also butted in, "Right, to save yourself!"

Sungjin shook his head. "You don't need to help me. Just... stick together as a group and carefully hunt Goblins on the outskirts of the wildlands."

However, the Asian man pointed his finger toward Sungjin and continued to accuse him of trickery, "What is your problem? Who do you think you are? Who are you to try and teach the rest of us? You're just a teenager!"

Sungjin now started frowning. He had expected it to be difficult to explain himself, but it still felt annoying to be openly antagonized. The Operator interrupted the situation.

[30 seconds until Raid begins.]

"Okay, let's stop fighting here. Let's all cooperate. We still have thirty seconds. I shall buy one Salamander's ash to start."

The black man tried to recover the mood, but it was already beyond salvaging. The Arab man spoke to the cube, "Operator, use 6 coins and buy me two recovery potions."

The Asian man immediately followed suit, "Operator, give me two recovery potions as well."

Both men spent all of their remaining coins to buy potions. The white man began to get angry watching the two men, "What are you doing? What are you trying to do?"

The Asian man pointed his fingers at Sungjin, "You don't need to spend coins for items. He can just buy it for us if we need it."

The Arab man and Asian man continued to work together to blame Sungjin, "Yeah, who is he to be giving us orders?"

The black police officer who had been trying to rally the group also started massaging his forehead. Sungjin stared at the four men with narrowed eyes.

If this were under normal circumstances, this group would face elimination.

The first group Sungjin got into had worked together to overcome the Raid together. It was difficult, but as a result of cooperation, Sungjin was able to survive to the end and become the last remaining survivor. Groups like this, where members all argued and sought personal gain over the best interest of the group were almost guaranteed to be eliminated.

[10 seconds until Raid begins.]

Sungjin stood up from the rock he sat on and strolled to the entrance of the Raid.

"Hey, wait a minute..." The black police officer tried to stop Sungjin, but Sungjin ignored him and waited at the entrance. Soon the Operator began a countdown.

[5, 4, 3, 2, 1. Raid Commencing.]

The moment the Raid began, Sungjin dashed out toward the Wildlands.

*

After Sungjin had left, the four men didn't take a single step forward.

"Who's going to stand vanguard?"

"The weapon I picked is a spear... so I will be in the back."

"What? What are you talking about? You can stand at the front and use the range to keep enemies at bay!"

"Are you mad? It's obviously better to support from the back!"

The two who were arguing turned their sights on the black police officer.

"You... You're a police officer. You should stand vanguard."

'Protection of civilians' was now a meaningless phrase, but the other men still looked up to him and trusted him to protect them. The black police officer had no choice but to tighten his grip on the

25

club (the most similar weapon to police baton that he was used to) and stand at the front.

"Let's... uh, try to lure one or two in at a time and avoid being outnumbered."

He carefully stepped into the Wildlands. But once he was there, he couldn't help but be shocked.

"What's all this?"

In front of his eyes were a mountain of green-skinned corpses. The others also expressed their surprise.

"How is this possible?"

"Did that teenager do this all by himself?"

Just a glance was enough to see that there were more than a dozen monsters slain in front of them. The others had been going from Phase to Phase, barely winning one on one, barely holding onto their lives.

The Arab man asked, "What should we do now?"

The black policeman in the front recalled Sungjin's words.

You should all follow closely behind me. I will clear this Raid quickly for you.

The officer turned around to face the other men, "Let's follow the corpses. If we keep going, eventually we should catch up to him."

Following the corpses, the men slowly inched their way in cautiously. Suddenly, the cube let out a warning.

[Caution: Boss monster]

[Orc Chief Cunning Kamul has appeared!]

Simultaneously, a powerful roar could be heard from straight ahead.

"Kurruagh!"

The black man pointed forward, "Let's go quickly!"

But the other three were wary.

"Do we... even have to go?"

"Yeah, let's just let them be."

The black police officer shook his head in disappointment and ran toward the direction from where the roar was heard. Ahead, he saw numerous green skinned enemies, from Orcs to Trolls. But standing at the center was an Orc 1.5 times taller than all the other Orcs.

One could see in a single glance that it was none other than the Boss mob. The Boss held a massive, fearsome club embedded from tip to tip with skulls.

"What... in the world?"

Beholding the boss mob for the first time, even the brave police officer stopped in his tracks. But the teenager charged forward fearlessly.

Goblins, HobGoblins, and Orcs attempted to obstruct him, but they were cut down mercilessly. Each swing of his sword sent heads flying.

Two Trolls attacked him simultaneously, but the teenager dodged lightly, and took off an arm of one and removed the legs from both Trolls.

The Trolls who lost their legs struggled on the ground. Ignoring the Trolls who lost their mobility, the teenager rushed toward the Orc Chief.

"Kragh!"

The Orc Chief let out a fearsome roar and swung his club. The speed of his attack was unbelievable considering the Orc Chief's size. But the teenager was faster. He dodged the club as if he predicted the path and timing.

Then, he counter-attacked and attacked the chief's hands. Several fingers holding the club flew off.

"Wagh!"

The Chief cried out in pain. But no ounce of mercy could be seen in the Teenager's attack. With lightning-speed tempo, he cut the Chief's shin, chest, and shoulders all in quick succession.

The chief bit back his pain and tried to swing his club once more, but it was nowhere near as fast. The teenager easily dodged the attack and cut the chief's throat. Blood spilled from the neck like a waterfall.

"Kack... ack... ack.."

The Chief couldn't even scream out properly anymore, and after coughing up blood a few more times, he kneeled over and stopped moving. The Operator announced happily,

[Objective complete. You will be summoned back to the Hunter's Hall in 11 minutes and 32 seconds.]

The black police officer couldn't help but exclaim, "Incredible...!"

The teenager, however, had no time to rest. The Trolls had regenerated by now and began attacking the teen again. They were no match for the teen before; they were no match for the teen now. The teenager rapidly ripped apart the Trolls. It was evident that given time, the teenager would reduce them to pieces of meat and kill them. But they were interrupted.

"Help! Save us!"

The police officer heard screams of terror from behind. Two Trolls were chasing the three men he had left behind.

"What the..." There was no time for the officer to say anything. He saw the white turban of the Arab gripped by one of the Troll's hands. The black man had no choice but to run as well.

The three men ran into the hall where Sungjin was already fighting two Trolls. Sungjin turned and saw the three men run in, and the additional two Trolls that followed. The trio raced to the other side of the hall as if to hide behind Sungjin. The two new Trolls swung their clubs at him.

"Woosh".

The club split the air, and the black man closed his eye on instinct. And when he opened his eyes, each of the Trolls had lost an arm each.

"Grrrrrr"

The problem was the original two Trolls. Because of the new Trolls, the first two Trolls had an opportunity to regenerate. Sungjin, who kept an indifferent expression until now, let out his first words of frustration, "Damn it, I don't have time for this..."

The black police officer realized something from his utterance. Judging from his skill, Sungjin would win against all four Trolls hands down. But it would take considerable time since the four Trolls would each take turns regenerating.

The black man reached into his pocket and retrieved a package. It was the Salamander's ash he was forced to purchase. He scattered the ash on his club and spread it evenly on the club with his hands.

FOOF

His club lit up in flames. He got up close to Sungjin and said to him.

"Please immobilize them. I will finish them off."

Sungjin rapidly cut the Trolls. One moment, their arms were cut off at the elbows, and the next, the tendon below their knees too were cut. The Trolls who lost their arms and legs fell to the floor and flailed.

The black police officer took his flaming club and struck the Trolls in their knees. The fire burnt the wound black and prevented further regeneration. Within moments, the Trolls were killed off.

Once killing all the Trolls, Sungjin wasted no time asking the cube, "...Operator, time remaining on the clock?"

[You will return to the Hunter's Hall in 10 minutes 7 seconds.]

He had already wasted more than a minute. He had to find and kill the hidden boss in the remaining time.

***

Sungjin took a glance at the surroundings, while still holding his bloody Katana. Nothing stood out at the boss's hall. It was also improbable that both the boss and the hidden boss were placed in the same location.

Sungjin moved to leave the hall but saw the police officer. He turned toward him and asked, "Hey, what's your name?"

"Baltren. Gerald Baltren."

"Good. Listen to me, Baltren. Take the other two and try to search around here. With you three, and with that flaming club, you should be able to handle anything, even a lone Troll. Do you understand?"

The officer nodded quickly.

"And if you find anything out of place, let me know. A hidden location, or a strange-looking monster."

"But... how will we contact you when you're far away?"

"You can speak with the Operator's cube and request to communicate with the team members. It functions like a police walkie-talkie. Any other questions?"

"No, I got it."

Baltren took his club and turned around, "You heard him, right? Let's work together."

Sungjin began to walk out once more when the Asian man tried to ask him a question, "Hey, how did you find out there are secrets to search for?"

He had been shouting at and antagonizing Sungjin until just a few minutes ago so, Sungjin felt no need to acknowledge the question he had been asked.

Once Sungjin left, Baltren took the men and began to move about the Wildlands. After a few minutes,

"Kakaka!"

The men ran into a group of five Goblins.

"Get into a circle!" Under Baltren's instructions, the other two men took their place behind him with their backs against each other. Goblins were less than half a human's height, but they cooperated with each other.

The Goblins ran in first with them swinging their swords. Baltren parried the sword away and landed a strike squarely on the goblin's head.

"Kack!"

The goblin who was hit on his head collapsed on the spot. Goblins weren't a difficult foe, as expected. Baltren got more courageous and smashed the head in of two more.

The white man and Asian man also took one out each. At the end, each one of them had fought against a Troll one on one and had won.

30

Even if they were in large groups, the three men could probably overcome anything that wasn't a Troll. In fact, they could probably beat a lone Troll without much issue.

"This seems... doable."

The white man standing next to him seemed to have regained some confidence. But the problem was the Asian man, who was determined to continue to cause problems.

"Hey... is there really a reason why we need to put ourselves in danger? I thought we already completed our objectives?"

"Don't you remember the sign from the beginning? Stat Points and Black Coins per Goblin and etcetera. It's probably better to kill more monsters," said the white man.

"Ah... is that so?"

"Of course. I don't know how or why we started to 'hunt'... but we do need Black Coins for later."

Baltren, who was listening to the conversation, agreed as he said, "Yes. And that teenager said so himself. We don't need to help him, so just go around the outskirts and hunt monsters."

He recalled Sungjin's words.

You don't need to help me. Just... stick together as a group and carefully hunt Goblins on the outskirts of the wildlands.

And in the end, he had completed the boss all on his own. Baltren could tell that the teenager wasn't simply showing off; there was something more. The Asian man stroked his chin while listening and then asked, "How do points get divided? It's not like we can see drops or something."

Baltren was also curious about this point. He thought for a moment, then he noticed the cube floating around. He spoke to the cube.

"Operator."

The cube responded with the Operator's voice.

[Yes, how may I help you?]

He carefully asked the question.

"Um... How do Stat Points and Black Coins get divided?"

31

[The reward per Hunter is based on contribution during the Raid.]

"Contribution?"

Baltren asked out of instinct. The Operator answered his question anyways.

[When hunting, points for damage taken, damage done, killing blow, buffs given, debuffs dealt with, scouting, and spotting are all totalled up and divided accurately.]

The three men looked amongst themselves. Until now, they had done almost nothing. The white man whispered to himself, "I wonder what my contribution is..."

And then the cube next to him answered.

[Your contribution is 4.3%.]

The Asian man quickly asked his cube.

"What about me? How much is my contribution?"

But the cube did not answer.

"Why? Why aren't you telling me?"

While the Asian man was freaking out, Baltren calmly asked his cube,

"What is my contribution for this Raid?"

[Your contribution is 7.2%.]

It wasn't much, but it was much higher than the white man. His help in killing the four Trolls in the Boss's hall had been the cause of the difference in their contribution.

The Asian man took hold of his cube and enunciated each word carefully.

"What is my contribution rating in this Raid?"

[Your contribution is 1.8%]

He jolted in surprise.

"What?!"

He had fewer points than even the white man. Acting cowardly and avoiding action as much as possible was coming back to bite him. The white man sighed in regret, "Ahh, we should have just gone hunting as a group earlier, when that teenager told us to."

Baltren rallied the men. "There's still 10 minutes until the Raid ends. It's not too late to try and hunt and earn more points. Let's go hunting and keep an eye out for anything strange."

*

Sungjin charged through 'Greenskin Wildlands' as he kept searching.

"Eeek!"

"Cough..."

"Kack!"

He didn't stop as he cut anything down that got in his way: Goblins, Orcs, and even Trolls. It wasn't necessarily a bad thing since each kill he secured meant more Stat Points and Black Coins later.

The problem was that he could not find any clues as to where the secret boss was located. He had scoured the entire Wildlands, searching. But he couldn't find anything that seemed out of place.

"Operator, remaining time."

[You will be summoned to the Hunter's Hall in 6 minutes and 24 seconds.]

"Damn it!"

Sungjin swore out loud as he continued to run without taking a break. But there were more corpses than there were living things. In other words, he had already searched almost the entire map.

"Kurman kao!"

One Orc charged at the angry Sungjin. It was his bad luck to run into Sungjin. Before the Orc could even raise his axe, he was stabbed three times in vital points.

The Orc collapsed on the spot, bleeding out. Sungjin took a look around at the surroundings. He could not see anything other than corpses now.

Is there no hidden boss because this is the first Raid?, thought Sungjin. If this was so, then he only had one other option; wipe out the whole map.

Sungjin now began chasing down every scrap of living thing he could find. Goblins who were trying to hide from him, Orcs who were eating away at the meat by the campfire and Trolls who stupidly stumbled toward him.

Soon, he ran into the other Hunters who were fighting against three Trolls in a close battle.

Sungjin charged in like a lightning bolt and beheaded two Trolls, spraying blood everywhere.

"Th... -thank you."

The officer, Baltren, expressed his gratitude, but Sungjin replied, "So, were you able to find anything peculiar?"

"Nothing out of the ordinary."

Was there really nothing hidden? No hidden boss, or secret location? Thought Sungjin. He called over the Operator.

"Operator, what is the Raid progress?"

[95% complete.]

95%. Only the 5% reserved for the secret boss was remaining. Since no more monsters could be found anywhere, it was certain that the hidden boss existed. Sungjin wanted to move on to search again, but Baltren stopped him.

"But..."

It irritated Sungjin that Baltren was dragging out his thoughts, so he urged him on, "Yes? Please speak your mind."

Baltren pointed toward somewhere with his club, "About the palisade that surrounds the Wildlands, isn't that area a bit weird?"

Sungjin looked to the area pointed out by the club, "I had worked on traffic control before and had to put up roadblocks. The fact that those wooden barricades there overlap... seems inefficient somehow."

Sungjin immediately headed toward the wooden barricades to check. Now that he got a closer look at it, it definitely seemed strange. The rest of the wooden palisade were more or less perfectly circular in arrangement. But a portion of the wall there was indented inward. Sticking out from the wood was also something like a metal rod.

Although it looked extremely crude, Sungjin thought, *It looks just like a lever!*

Sungjin checked behind him. The three men were watching him from a safe distance. Seeing this, he proceeded to pull the lever.

RATTLE RATTLE

A sound could be heard as if something was spinning, and the palisade in front of him was lifted up.

Sungjin decided to go in.

Inside was a small area surrounded by more palisades, but it resembled the insides of a castle. And deeper inside was a dark red Orc chained up to the wall.

The fiery red skin somehow clashed with the image of "Greenskin Wildlands." Sungjin was filled with certainty that this was it.

"Grrrrrr."

The thing was emitting a deep growl while still chained. When Sungjin took one more step to check on the boss's stats, he heard a warning come out of the cube.

[Caution! Hidden Boss]

[Mad Orc Ruark has appeared!]

Sungjin gripped his Katana tightly and prepared for battle. Then, he heard voices of the three men.

"Where is..."

"What's that?"

Sungjin quickly shouted, looking back at them, "Go back! You'll die!"

And as if on cue,

"Gragh!"

Sungjin heard a powerful roar behind him. By the time he turned around, the Orc had already cut the chains and was charging toward Sungjin.

***

Sungjin gripped his Katana tightly. The Orc charged straight toward him as if it saw food for the first time after a long period of starvation.

35

Sungjin stabbed hard and fast toward the charging Orc's neck and heart.

STAB STAB

Sungjin's blade found their mark. Except that unusually, the red Orc did not respond at all. Despite aiming for vital points, there was no response from the Orc.

The Orc continued his charge and swung his arms. Sungjin was forced to jump back, and the arms missed their mark.

But, just as Sungjin was going to counter attack, he saw that the chains attached to the arms were flying toward him with a slight delay. Sungjin ducked immediately.

VOOM

Sungjin felt something metallic sail through the air above his head. When he looked up, he saw the Orc swinging his arms once again. The problem wasn't just his hands.

Each time he swung his arms, the chains attached to his arms also flew toward Sungjin like whips. Sungjin was forced to look at the chains and predict their path.

He backed away and concentrated on defense.

"How annoying."

The main boss traded speed for great power, whereas this boss had tremendous speed and reach.

It was the worst possible enemy for Sungjin, who had committed all points to Dexterity.

Because he put no points in Endurance, getting hit once or twice by the chains meant that it was game over.

"Whoa, whoa, whoa..."

As Sungjin retreated backwards while dodging and parrying, the other three men were busy escaping at full speed to avoid interrupting Sungjin's fight. To be fair, neither the main boss nor the secret boss was meant to be taken on alone.

But the others were absolutely of no help at all. Even as Sungjin slowly backed off and dodged the chains, he kept an eye out for mistakes. Once his arm became vulnerable, Sungjin took the opportunity and stabbed it three times.

PAPAPA

But as if taking no damage, the Orc continued to swing away. His nickname "mad" was probably due to his rapid and wild swinging of arms and chains. Sungjin concluded his rapid attack, and immediately switched back to defense.

Something like this guy isn't common even later on... thought Sungjin.

Even though his every Stat Point was in Dexterity, the boss moved and attacked at a comparable speed.

First, I've got to do something about those arms...

Once he established his plan of attack, he waited for a chance. He ducked from an incoming attack and then kicked the Orc's shins.

BAM!

With the sound, the Orc fell over. But despite being downed, he didn't let up the attack. He kept on swinging the chains from the ground.

Sungjin had to jump up to avoid chains coming at his feet. The chains rapidly passed by him. Once or twice, Sungjin leaped up into the air, as if playing high-risk jump rope. He embedded his scabbard into the ground between jumps.

When he jumped up, the chains from the Orc wrapped around it.

Did it work?

But after just a brief pause, the scabbard was pulled away by the force of the chains and flew across the room.

I need something heavier.

Meanwhile, the mad Orc stood up.

"Kruagh!"

The Orc began attacking with his arms and chains even faster than before. Sungjin had no opportunity to counter attack and had to focus entirely on defense as he slowly backed off.

Any way to stop his attacks? thought Sungjin as he took a look around his surroundings, but he only saw the three men trying to escape from collateral damage.

Then Sungjin noticed the policeman's weapon. It was a club made of metallic material. While dodging chains with inhuman speed, he yelled at the policeman.

"Hey, Officer! Throw me your club!"

Baltren, who was watching from a distance, panicked when his name was mentioned. Sungjin yelled louder in frustration while dodging the Orc's attacks, "Damn it! The club!"

Baltren hesitated for a moment because the red Orc's chains were destroying everything within several meters of it. But once he made up his mind, he approached the two combatants and shouted.

"Catch!"

After yelling loudly, Baltren threw his club toward Sungjin. Sungjin dodged the chains deftly by jumping backward and caught the club with his free left hand.

Holding the Katana on the right and the club on the left, Sungjin bided his time until he could kick over the Orc again. Once the Orc was tripped, he flailed wildly from the ground again.

Sungjin planted the club deep into the ground and leaped up to dodge the chains, then landed on it like some sort of martial artist from Murim[2].

When the chains came flying, it hit the club and wrapped itself around it.

CLINK!

It spun around few times and then became stuck on the club. For the first time since combat started, his arms were immobilized. Sungjin easily cut off his arm.

"Graaagh!"

Even while screaming in pain, the Orc continued to swing the chains on his remaining arm wildly. But he had not been able to land a hit on Sungjin with two chains; dodging just one was a piece of cake. Sungjin evaded the chains with ease and cut off the other arm as well.

"Kaaaa!"

The Red Orc could no longer stand nor attack due to his loss of arms. Sungjin strolled up to the Orc.

"Be at peace."

After bidding goodbye, Sungjin beheaded the Orc. Moments later, the Operator announced his victory.

[Hidden Boss Mad Orc Ruark cleared.]

[Congratulations! You have managed to complete all objectives in this Chapter!]

[Disregarding the remaining time and ending the Raid immediately.]

"Haaa..."

Sungjin let out a long sigh. He had finally found the secret location and hunted every monster.

It was Sungjin's first time fighting a hidden boss. The first time around, the top priority for each Raid had been merely survival.

After having a breather, Sungjin sheathed his sword back in the scabbard. He picked the club out of the ground and tossed it back to the officer.

Once the officer caught the club, all the cubes spoke out in unison in the Operator's voice.

[Calculating Rewards Earned.]

[Monsters Slain. Goblins: 100. HobGoblins: 30. Orcs 20. Trolls: 10. Total 390 points.]

[Boss Monster Slain: Orc Chief Cunning Kamul: 50 points.]

[Hidden Boss Mad Orc Ruark: 50 points.]

[Final point count: 490. Distributing points.]

Now each cube spoke individually, starting with the Asian man first.

[Your contribution is 0.7%. 3 Stat Points, 3 Black Coins awarded. Raid Clear Bonus 50 Stat Points and 50 Black Coins awarded. Distributing 53 Stat Points and 53 Black Coins.]

"..."

The Asian man frowned and looked around, as if not believing what he was hearing. Next up was the white man.

[Your contribution is 1.2%. 5 Stat Points, 5 Black Coins awarded. Raid Clear Bonus 50 Stat Points and 50 Black Coins awarded. Distributing 55 Stat Points and 55 Black Coins.]

And then the police officer.

[Your contribution is 5.2%. 25 Stat Points, 25 Black Coins awarded. Raid Clear Bonus 50 Stat Points and 50 Black Coins awarded. Distributing 75 Stat Points and 75 Black Coins.]

Finally, it was Sungjin's turn.

[Your contribution is 92.9%. 455 Stat Points, 455 Black Coins awarded. Raid Clear Bonus 50 Stat Points and 50 Black Coins awarded. Distributing 505 Stat Points and 505 Black Coins.]

"Whoa..."

The three men stared at Sungjin in envy and respect. But Sungjin ignored their response and calculated in his head.

Adding up the 19 Coins from before and now... 524? With this, I can get...

[And now we will distribute items.]

Once again, it began with the Asian man.

[Recovery Potion – Small x1]

A small potion bottle appeared in front of the Asian man, and he obediently picked it up from the ground, but he looked unhappily at it. "This is it?"

Next was the white man's turn.

[Recovery Potion – Small x2]

[Orc's worn cloak]

He received his items with both hands, but likewise looked fairly unhappily at them. Next was Baltren.

[Steel Shield]

[Troll's Blood x1]

A large shield dropped by the police officer's feet. He quickly picked it up. Because he was wearing a bulletproof vest, it looked just as if he was carrying a riot shield. Sungjin's turn was last.

[Yanhurat – Mad god's voice]

[Free Ark – Freeman's shackles]

[Skull Romabel – Skull crusher]

[Troll's Blood x4]

[Recovery Potion – Small x5]

A bunch of items dropped in front of him, and Sungjin bent over to pick them up. The Asian man spoke to himself, "Wow, what a contribution hog. How selfish."

It was just a complaint expressed under his breath, but Sungjin heard all of it. He frowned in annoyance, "You. If it weren't for me, all of you would have died here. Either by monsters or by running out of time. Understood?"

The Asian man didn't know when to give up and kept on complaining, "You don't know that."

His words finally pushed Sungjin over the edge. He had had enough. Sungjin drew his Katana and approached the man.

"Listen well. I will teach you a hidden characteristic of the Raid you don't know about."

"Wh... what?"

The Asian man backed up in surprise, but Sungjin swung his Katana few times at him.

SLASH SLASH SLASH

Following the sound of the blade cutting through the air, the Asian man's shirt and pants were reduced to rags.

Once the Asian man realized what was going on, he grew pale and fell over. Sungjin got right into his face and spoke vehemently.

"In Raids, there is no rule forbidding a Hunter from hunting another Hunter. Understood?"

The Asian man nodded vigorously. Sungjin stood up, still holding his Katana out. "Raids" were like this after all.

As one kills and murders, one's notion of ethics and morality fades. Sungjin was no exception.

Sungjin had long forgotten ordinary ethics and morality after participating in Raid after Raid in his previous life.

Wielding his Katana to take the man's life posed no issue to Sungjin, but he put away his blade.

With the Asian man's non-existent reward from this Raid, he would have a difficult time surviving the next one.

Once Sungjin put away his sword, the Operator resumed with the last briefing.

[Last but not least, you will be awarded with titles you've earned on this Raid.]

***

[Titles are granted based on personal achievements during Raids.]

[Variety of titles can be earned from different things.]

The Operator continued with her explanation.

[Each title has some form of effect,]

[And the Hunter can only have one title active at any given time.]

[Active titles give 100% of the listed effect, but inactive titles only give 50% of the effect.]

Sungjin closed his eyes, hugging his Katana tightly.

[Titles appear above the Hunter's head, and the other Hunters may view them.]

[I bid you achieve greatness and earn great rewards.]

[Initiating distribution.]

Once again, it began with the Asian man.

[Coward – Max HP dropped by half.]

[A red outline illuminates you to monsters, making you easier to be found.]

What?!

The Asian man, who would have complained otherwise, continued to sit where he lay, unable to move or say anything. The Operator continued on to the white man.

[Novice Sentinel – Spear damage increased by 5%]

The man's expression didn't change, as if he wasn't sure if it was a good or bad thing yet. Baltren was up next.

[Criminal Arsonist – increased fire-based damage by 20%]

"Police Officer with the title of Criminal Arsonist..." Baltren whispered to himself unhappily.

Finally, Sungjin was up.

[Master Hunter – All Stats increased by 30%]

Sungjin, whose eyes were closed until now, raised his eyebrows.

30%?!

It was an unimaginably large bonus. He had earned many titles from Raids in the past, but never a title with such advantageous bonus as this.

Titles were given based on how the Raid was conducted and it was based on merit and contribution.

Knowing exactly how the title Master Hunter was granted was unclear, but it probably had to do with clearing the Raid at 100% with overwhelming contribution percentage at close to 90%.

The Operator concluded handing out Raid rewards and addressed the Hunters.

[Your group has completed the Raid faster than other groups.]

[You will be sent back to the Hunter's Hall in 2 minutes and 37 seconds. Please hold]

Sungjin called out to the Operator.

"Operator, equip the Master Hunter title."

[Title Equipped.]

He immediately checked his status.

"Show me the status window."

> Title: Master Hunter
> HP: 130 MP: 220
>
> Strength: 15   12 (+3)
> Dexterity: 43   33 (+10)
> Endurance: 13   10 (+3)
> Magic Power: 18   14 (+4)
> Mind Power: 22   17 (+5)
>
> Unallocated Stat Points: 505

Including the Dex that he'd been raising, all other stats had risen by 30%.

With this... finishing all objectives might be possible...

Confidence surged within Sungjin. He decided to check what items he had received.

He took out a creepy necklace, which was decorated with a large eye and rows of teeth.

"Operator, what is this?"

The Operator summoned the detailed specs of the item in a hologram window.

> Yanhurat – Mad god's Voice
> Heroic Necklace
>
> Active Skill
> Zealot(III)
> For 30 seconds, increase damage by 300% and attack speed by 300%
> Once active duration ends, reduce current HP to 1/3.
> Cooldown 10 minutes.
>
> Necklace worn by the Mad Orc Ruark.
> If you put it next to your ears, you can make out a faint voice.

Forced Zealot mode...?

It was an item which had a well-defined cost/benefit. Sungjin examined the necklace carefully. The item incorporated some features of the human face into its design. Infernal staring eyes and a mouth-shaped formation of teeth were key points of its appearance. This horrifying item looked like it could have belonged in Incan or Mayan temples.

While he was looking over the necklace, he heard a voice.

"Hey..."

Sungjin felt as if someone was whispering into his ears. So he brought the necklace up to his ears. Suddenly the phrase became crystal clear.

"Kill them."

He took off the necklace off his eyes. It was an item that felt tainted.

But... I might need it someday.

Sungjin placed the necklace into his pocket. The next item he examined was a familiar shackle connected to chains. It was the weapon wielded by the boss.

Free Ark – Freeman's Shackles
Heroic Wrist Armor – Defense 28%

Active Skill
Remove Crowd Control (III)
Removes unwanted Crowd Control effects.
Cooldown: 5 Minutes

Shackles bound to the Mad Orc Ruark.
They were fairly small; it must have been extremely painful for the previous owner to have worn it.

Wait, it's not a weapon? Armor Piece?

He had spent a few minutes mindlessly dodging it, and it turned out it wasn't even an actual weapon. He held up the shackles and instructed the Operator.

"Equip."

The shackles stuck to his hands for few moments before picking an arm and locking onto his wrist. The chains wrapped around the entire length of his arm and protected him.

So this is how it works.

It was good. It was on the heavy side, but it seemed sturdy. Sungjin felt he could probably use it as a substitute shield if he ever needed it. And the Active Skill looked useful as well.

Finally, Sungjin held the club with a skull attached to it. He was familiar with it because this club was widely used by others in the previous life. It was common since it was the main boss's item drop.

Lots of Hunters could be seen using this weapon soon after the 1st Chapter.

Skull Romabel – Skull crusher
Heroic Blunt Weapon – Strength A Dexterity D

Passive skill
Illusions of Terror(II)
Weaken attack of nearby enemies by 10%

Chief Kamul's Club. He had broken many skulls with this club. It was said that he had collected skulls that did not break from bashing and had added them on to his club.

As expected, it was a great item. The special skill was nice, but even more valuable was the A rank stat booster which was extremely rare in the early game. The problem was that Sungjin had never used blunt weapons before.

It's a great item... but I should sell it.

Sungjin asked the Operator while holding the Club.

"Operator, how much can this be sold for at the Black Market?"
[50 Black Coins]

Sungjin frowned. It was extremely inefficient to sell directly to the Operator.

Well, I guess I can't help it since I don't need it.

Sungjin opened his mouth to sell it to the Operator, but then he noticed the club which the police officer was holding.

He was the only one who had sincerely tried to help Sungjin through the Raid. He called him over.

"Come here, old man."

Baltren was surprised when Sungjin addressed him again and stared at him. Sungjin had seemed like a normal teenager at the beginning. But a few moments ago, he had said,

In Raids, there is no rule forbidding a Hunter from hunting another Hunter. Understood?

When Sungjin said this, he had an expression as if he was a serial killer. Even the police were intimidated by serial killers. Baltren trembled slightly as he responded.

"Yes, what... What is it?"

"How many Black Coins do you have right now?"

Baltren answered immediately.

"76."

Sungjin showed Baltren the club and said,

"Buy this. 76 Coins."

Baltren was shocked. He didn't know that item trading was even possible. Sungjin saw his hesitation and added more explanation.

"If you intend to continue using blunt weapons, you should buy it. Selling a Heroic weapon for 76 coins is basically the same as giving it away for free."

Sungjin spoke the truth. Buying a Heroic weapon from the Black Market typically requires several hundred Black Coins.

Sungjin would be able to get just a bit more Black Coins, and Baltren would be able to obtain a Heroic weapon at a dirt-cheap price; a win-win situation.

Baltren briefly looked over the weapon and then nodded in agreement. No matter what he said, Sungjin hadn't been wrong about anything yet.

"So how does trading work?"

"Simple. Put the cubes together and declare 'trade.'"

Baltren nodded. Once the cubes were brought together, they snapped as if they were held by magnets. Sungjin spoke out first.

"Trade."

Sungjin's cube emitted a blue light. Baltren saw and followed suit. Once he did, the cubes gave out an announcement.

[Trade initiated.]

[Please declare what Item you will be trading.]

Sungjin started.

"Skull Romabel Heroic Blunt Weapon."

Baltren replied,

"76 Black Coins."

"I accept the Trade."

"I accept the Trade."

[Trade complete!]

At the same time as the announcement, the club disappeared from Sungjin's hands and appeared in Baltren's. Baltren inspected the weapon.

It was a strange weapon, decorated with skulls.

"It lowers attack power of your enemies, so... it should be useful in keeping you alive," said Sungjin.

Baltren asked Sungjin carefully, "How do you know all this?"

"...Even if I tell you, you won't be able to believe me."

Baltren decided not to pry. He felt that even if he insisted, the teenager would not be willing to give him a satisfactory response. The Operator finally gave them the status update.

[You will return to the Hunter's Hall in 1 minute.]

1 minute. Sungjin closed his eyes and held his Katana close. Baltren snuck a few glances at Sungjin.

Right now, he looked like an ordinary teenager. He even looked somewhat innocent. And to a certain extent, it even made sense why he had gotten upset earlier and made that angry face.

He slowly came to the understanding that these Raids were to be carried out by betting one's life. Having a coward and an inciter like the Asian man represented a risk to one's life.

Baltren rested the club on the ground and thought deeply on the words Sungjin had said to the Asian man.

You. If it weren't for me, all of you would have died here. Either by monsters or by running out of time. Understood?

This declaration, in truth, also applied to Baltren as well. He couldn't imagine that he could stand up to the secret boss and his wild flailing chains, the giant club-wielding Orc Chieftain, or even a small group of Trolls.

If it weren't for the teenager, he would have died. Baltren understood it perfectly. So he approached the teenager once more. He couldn't rest well without even knowing the name of his benefactor.

"Please tell me your name. Who are you?"

Sungjin stared at the police officer. Until now, he had had many comrades. And every single one of them had died.

Even if he gave this man his name, the only result it could give was regret, disappointment, and sadness. There was no point to letting people know your name. Sungjin shook his head.

"We will never meet each other again."

But Baltren persisted, "You can't know that. Please, I wish to know."

Sungjin paused for a moment and gave only the initials of his last name, "K. That is my name."

"Kei. I've said before, but my name is..."

Sungjin interrupted him, "I remember. Baltren. Gerald Baltren. Become strong. And then survive. And who knows, maybe we will cross paths again..."

With that said, the Operator began a countdown.

[You will return to the Hunter's Hall in 10 seconds.]

[9, 8, 7, 6...]

With only a few seconds left, Baltren expressed his gratitude to Sungjin, "Thank you for everything. I was able to survive because of you."

[5, 4, 3]

Baltren wanted to say a final goodbye before the time was over when he noticed the title floating above Sungjin's head. He combined the title and the name together and bid him goodbye.

"We will meet again, Master Hunter K."

[2, 1]

And with that, the Hunters disappeared from the Greenskin Wildlands.

Chapter 3 – Black Market First Shopping

Sungjin was teleported to the Hunter's Hall. The Hall was still overflowing with unfamiliar faces. He could not see the end of the crowd.

Well, numbers will thin out soon enough, he thought to himself.

This gathering of Hunters represented the top 1% of humanity's strongest individuals. It would have been impossible to clear the first Raid 'Greenskin Wildlands' without considerable individual skill and talent.

It was possible that a lucky few were given a free ride to the end, regardless of their individual merit, by overachievers like Sungjin. But those people were typically eliminated during the next Raid. No, they likely wouldn't even make it to the next Raid.

This wasn't the type of world you could survive by relying on other people. Soon the Operator began her announcement.

[Welcome back. And congratulations,]

[to everyone who successfully completed the Raid and made it back.]

The Operator's face reappeared on the screen above, but no one was shouting profanities. Most of the people were suffering from PTSD or mourning the loss of their comrades.

[As you might have experienced for yourselves in the first Raid,]

[you cannot complete the Raids with your current physical limitations.]

[Hence, raising your stats beyond human limits is necessary.]

[There are several ways to achieve this.]

Most of the crowd appeared to be exhausted, but everyone listened carefully to each and every word the Operator spoke. It was self-evident that they could not survive without listening to her tips and advice.

[First, hunt monsters and obtain Stat Points.]

[I believe you have already learned about this during the first Raid.]

[Unallocated Stat Points do not benefit you.]

[So please remember to allocate them before heading into battle.]

By now, most people should have been well aware of their stats. It is nearly impossible to have survived until this stage without putting in Stat Points.

[Second, earn Titles and get bonus Stat Points.]

[Everyone should have earned at least one title from the first Raid.]

[Equipping the title enables the selected title to perform at 100% of their listed effect, and inactive titles only provide 50% of their given effects.]

[The more titles you earn, the more advantages you'll gain. Please use the title that best suits the situation as you progress through the Raid.]

There aren't many with a title floating above their heads. Among those that do, most have titles like Scout, Orc Hunter, and Novice Swordsman.

Sungjin wore the Master Hunter title, but no one paid much attention to it. Not many understood what it meant yet.

[Third is equipment. Equipment choices are undoubtedly important.]

[They give bonus stats, and some even have special skills imbued upon them.]

Most of the Hunters were focused on the Operator's explanation, except for Sungjin. He didn't need to listen because he already knew all of it.

[It is possible to receive a piece of equipment through the Raid reward system, but they are readily available for purchase through the Black Market.]

[Explanation will continue after changing the venue.]

[You will be teleported in 10 seconds. 9, 8]

The Operator began her countdown. But Sungjin still had his arms crossed and was lost in thought.

19 Coins from the first round, 505 from the first Raid, 76 traded with Baltren. Total is exactly 600 Black Coins...

[3, 2, 1]

*

The place Sungjin was teleported was a Bazaar that had a canopy draped above.

"Welcome, welcome!"

It was a normal marketplace with vendors selling wares at the stalls. Except for one detail. The vendors were not human. To be exact, they were all demi-humans.

The axe merchant was half human and half cow- a Minotaur, the spear merchant was half human and half horse- a Centaur, the Fire Magic merchant was half human and half dragon.

For newcomers, it was a sight to behold, but Sungjin was already familiar with the place. The Operator continued her explanation.

[This place is called The Black Market. It is a Bazaar where Black Coins are used as currency.]

[Hunters may come here to obtain or sell items by trading with their Black Coins.]

[The goods are not limited to equipment; you could also purchase magic tomes which are needed to learn magic or consumables and accessories needed for battle, such as the Recovery Potion.]

The Operator continued with her long explanations covering most of the basics, although she glossed over a few important secrets of this place.

[You can no longer use cubes to purchase items, so please complete your shopping in this place before going out on Raids.]

Once the Operator's explanation finished, Sungjin began walking toward the inner part of the market.

"Dear Customer, please take a look!"

Someone tried to grab his attention, but he ignored the merchant and kept walking. His destination was a stall run by a half human half snake.

[This is the Katana shop called Last Edge, run by the merchant named Kenneth]

[You will be able to find all sorts of Katanas on sale here.]

Once he entered the stall flaps, a Naga greeted him.

"Welcome... to the Last Edge."

There was a large variety of swords hanging about in the shop, but there was only one sword Sungjin was interested in. A crimson blade hung on the wall on one side.

"May I see that real quick?"

"My my, what a great eye for quality!" the Naga merchant replied with a kind tone. "Please wait a moment. I will go fetch it for you."

The Naga handed over the crimson blade to Sungjin. Sungjin's face brightened up for the first time since the Hunt restarted.

This was the weapon he had wielded until his last moments. It was like an old friend to him. The Operator opened up the weapon status window.

Blood Vengeance – Blood's Revenge.
Legendary Katana – Strength SS Dexterity A

Active Skill
Baptism of Blood (IV) – consumes 100 HP per second from the user to increase attack damage.

According to legend, the owner of this Katana lost his family to the treachery of his liege, and carried out his vengeance against the betrayer and all the men loyal to him.

The Operator kept the window open for him, but he did not read it. He already had it memorized. Sungjin swung the sword twice to test it. He wanted to buy it immediately, but the problem was the price.

"It is worth 9700 Black Coins."

The coins in Sungjin's possession now numbered at 600. Not even close. Sungjin returned the sword to the Naga.

Right now I can't even use the active skill for more than a second anyway.

Sungjin had only come here to see his old friend. Now Sungjin headed toward his real destination. A jewelry shop located deep within the Black Market. After entering deeper and deeper into the canopied bazaar, Sungjin finally arrived at his actual destination.

[This place is merchant Meridian's shop by the name Eternal Moment.]

[Various pieces of jewelry such as necklace and rings are sold here]

"Hey there."

The merchant here was a haughty catwoman who ran this shop. Once Sungjin was inside the shop, he immediately told her what he wanted.

"I came to purchase the Heart of Gold."

"I do have the item... but it's a bit pricey for a Hunter who's only completed the first Raid."

"I already know. 500 Black Coins. I have the money, so please give me the item."

"Oh, how surprising..."

The shopkeeper's eyes twinkled as she took out the item.

Heart of Gold – Ring of the Rich
Rare Ring

Passive
Collect Interest (II)
Upon receiving Black Coin as Raid reward, gain an additional 10% more.

Famous jeweller Tarim's Ring.
It is said that he lost it while traveling across the Mage's Canyon.

A simple-looking ring with a lone blue sapphire embedded on it. It was the ring Sungjin was looking for.

"Operator, carry out the transaction."

Sungjin's cube approached Meridian and emitted a bright light.

[Heart of Gold purchased for 500 Black Coins]

The ring appeared on top of Sungjin's palm.

"Equip."

It moved on its own and fitted itself on Sungjin's ring finger. He inspected the ring on his hand. He was planning on making this item his first purchase with his first 500 Coins.

The reason was simple; it was an item with an excellent rate of return. He wasn't sure about the payout of the next Raid, but later on, there could be a possibility for him to receive more than 5000 Black Coins per Raid. In other words, the item more than paid for itself with every Raid.

Of course, Sungjin was the only person capable of taking advantage of this absurd item; it did absolutely nothing to improve his combat capability.

If a Hunter aside from Sungjin tried to invest 500 Black Coins in the early game, then their chances of survival dropped near to zero. It wasn't even likely that any other Hunter had even managed to get 500 coins until now.

Sungjin finished his shopping and left the shopping districts for the outskirts. Not too far away, he saw a small inn with an image of a bed on the sign post.

Above the entryway, a large sign read Ninety-Nine Nights. The Operator began her explanation.

[This place is an inn called Ninety-Nine Nights.]

[It is a place for Hunters to rest until the next Raid.]

Sungjin entered the inn straight away. He was already familiar with the place. The inn proprietor was a half human half owl. The Innkeeper greeted Sungjin politely.

"Welcome to Ninety-Nine Nights. My name is Dalupin, and I am the owner of this inn. I will do my best to take care of your needs. Would you like to check in?"

Sungjin sat at the nearby table and responded, "I'll check in later; please bring me some food."

"What would you like to eat? The menu is in front of you."

There was a menu placed neatly on top of each table, but he did not reach out for one; he had it all memorized.

"Medium rare beef rib steak."

After a few minutes, the owl demi-human brought a plate. On it was a seared medium rare beef rib steak. Sungjin took a fork and a knife and placed a bite-sized portion of meat into his mouth.

The meat melted in his mouth. The quality of the food here would not lose out to any famous restaurants on Earth. Sungjin enjoyed his soft and perfectly cooked meat as he asked the Operator,

"Operator, how much time until the next Raid?"

[9 hours, 3 minutes and 36 seconds]

The remaining time was free time for him to spend as he pleased. Eating and sleeping in Ninety-Nine Nights was free. Not that it alleviated the fear of death though.

Sungjin left the plate on the table once he finished eating and headed toward the room upstairs.

The bath in Ninety-Nine Nights was quite relaxing. Taking a warm bath in the tub was an excellent way to relieve his stress.

He sat inside the tub thinking. Why had the Operator revived him? Were all 'last survivors' given the reset chance? But there was no clear answer.

After all, it wasn't even understood why it was necessary to host and carry out hunts. All he could think of was that as he fights and survives, the answer might reveal itself one day.

...Since this is my second chance...

Sungjin submerged himself up to his neck.

I will perfectly clear all objectives this time... and maybe then... I will find the answers.

Chapter 4 – Ahenna's Forest

In the morning, Sungjin took a quick shower and went downstairs to the dining area for breakfast.

"Egg tart, 2 croissants, and butter."

Downing the simple breakfast, Sungjin checked his time.

"Operator, how much time is left before the next Raid?"

[15 minutes and 32 seconds.]

15 minutes...

There was one last thing he needed to complete before the next Raid began. It was allocating his stats.

"200 to Strength, 200 to Dexterity, and 105 to Endurance."

[Strength rose by 200 points. Dexterity rose by 200 points. Endurance rose by 105 points.]

"Show me my status screen."

Title: Master Hunter
HP: 1500 MP: 220

Strength:	276	212 (+64)
Dexterity:	303	233 (+70)
Endurance:	150	115 (+35)
Magic Power:	18	14 (+4)
Mind Power:	22	17 (+5)

Unallocated Points: 0

Sungjin inspected his new status window. He had spent a long time last night thinking about how to allocate his points. 200 points to Strength and Dexterity, and 105 to Endurance. With this much, his Speed and Attack Power were probably one of the best in the world, with Endurance being within top tier.

This was because it was difficult for other Hunters to earn anywhere close to 3-digit stat points from the first Raid.

I doubt I'll even take damage, though...

Raids were unpredictable; many things could happen. He might have to complete the Raid entirely alone. So Sungjin took the minimum safety measures.

A moment's slip and a small mistake could lead to death in a Raid. Confidence or not, safety should come first, and so Sungjin decided to invest for the first time into Endurance.

"Time?"

[7 minutes and 27 seconds remaining.]

"Iced americano. No syrup"

Shortly after, the Innkeeper Dalupin brought one cup of iced americano on a tray. Sungjin waited leisurely while drinking his coffee.

He downed the last bit and then was teleported away.

*

The darkness was oppressive, leaves rustled in the wind, and a half-lit moon could be seen above. In the distance, the howling of wolves could be heard.

"Aoooooo~"

Sungjin was teleported in the middle of a thick forest. The Operator began her announcement.

[Welcome. This place is called the Ahenna's Forest.]

[It is a place filled with insidious and cunning predators of the night.]

[Same as the previous Raid, the first 4 Phases will be combat tutorials.]

[If you take fatal damage,]

[or if the enemy is not annihilated within the time limit, the Hunter will be killed.]

Phase 1 – Gray Wolf Time Limit: 3 Minutes

At the same time just as the announcement ended, a Gray wolf jumped out of the trees. Sungjin took out his Katana without taking his eyes off the wolf. Unlike the monsters of the first Chapter, it bared its teeth from a distance.

"Grrrrr..."

It growled in a deep rumbling tone. Seeing the wolf brought back memories of the first time he had completed the Ahenna's Forest Raid.

I think I remember... This Raid is no pushover.

The moment Sungjin got distracted by his thoughts, the wolf took immediate notice and charged at him.

"Kyan!"

But as expected, the one that was slain was the wolf.

Completion Reward: Stat Point 5
Kill Reward: Black Coin 5

Sungjin took a look at the blood on his Katana and thought,

I don't think clearing the normal part of the Raid will pose any difficulty...

The biggest problem was the hidden boss and the secret place containing it. No matter how combat capable Sungjin was, discovering secret locations and then defeating the hidden boss within the time limit was no easy feat. Especially if done alone.

I really hope I get some good comrades this time... thought Sungjin.

Raids were originally designed to be cleared with the cooperation of five participants. Even if the teammates were unable to contribute much, at the minimum, Sungjin would need members that were able to follow simple instructions.

If any are like Baltren, it'd be superb.

But whoever one met in a Raid was a random occurrence. Luck was perhaps the most important factor in surviving the Raids.

However, this was not much of a concern for Sungjin anymore.

Pase 2 – Shadow Puma
Time Limit: 3 Minutes

[Caution: Shadow Pumas move silently in the darkness and ambush their prey.]

Despite entering the next phase, Sungjin was still lost in thought.

I had pretty good luck in my previous life. Thanks to my comrades, I was able to survive too...

Suddenly,

"Krah!"

A loud scream erupted from behind Sungjin. He didn't even turn, and threw himself to the side and tumbled. A black-colored Puma landed where he stood a second ago.

The Puma touched down noiselessly, despite being physically larger than the Gray Wolf.

Sungjin raised his Katana. The Puma, who failed his ambush, watched Sungjin with its eyes. Due to the dark-colored coat of the Puma, only its reflective amber eyes were visible in the night.

"Krah!"

The Puma charged toward Sungjin once more. It was no match for him. Sungjin waited for the Puma to get airborne before ducking out of the way and striking with his Katana.

VSZZT

The sound of flesh ripping off the bone filled the air. Straightening his clothes, Sungjin nonchalantly gazed toward the Puma. The Puma was cut from the front legs to the other side of its stomach. The cut was so severe that its intestines leaked out.

"Grr..."

The Puma, so full of life just moments before, collapsed after taking two steps and perished.

Completion Reward: 10 Stat Points
Kill Reward: 10 Black Coins

Sungjin continued to daydream about the past life.

I had some really amazing comrades. And not so great ones...

Sungjin stopped his thoughts there. He recalled a face he didn't want to remember.

> Phase 3 – Grizzly Bear
> Time Limit: 3 Minutes

"Grrrrr"

Third phase's mob was a sizable bear. It was 1.5 times taller than an average man. Its arms were as thick as a man's waist, and five claws as long as a man's arms grew on each hand.

"Grah!"

Unlike the Shadow Puma, the bear charged straight toward Sungjin. But this Grizzly Bear was unlucky. Due to the upsetting memory, Sungjin was already angry.

Sungjin's Katana flashed, illuminated by the moonlight for a split second, and the bear collapsed lifelessly on the spot.

For the majority of Hunters, this Grizzly Bear was like a gatekeeper, preventing entry into the Raid. But to Sungjin, it was more like a door flap, pushed aside at whim.

> Completion Reward: 20 Stat Points
> Kill Reward: 20 Black Coins

Although he received the Stat Points, he did not allocate them. Acting out of habit, he only swung his sword once to remove the blood on its blade.

Sungjin's Katana, whose ranks were only Strength C and Dexterity D, had cut through the bear in a single strike. The only reason this Basic Katana was able to demonstrate such power was thanks to Sungjin's oppressively high stats.

The sword was good enough for the present, but as the Chapters progressed, it would get more and more outclassed by the other weapons. Sungjin couldn't help but recall the familiar grip on his legendary weapon Blood Vengeance.

If I collect enough Black Coins...

Phase 4 – Dire Wolf
Time Limit: 3 Minute

Between the trees, a Grizzly Bear-sized pale wolf appeared. The Operator began her explanation.

[Caution: The Dire Wolf is slightly weaker than the Grizzly Bear;]

[But it can command nearby Gray Wolves.]

"Awoooooo~"

The Dire Wolf let out a long howl. And soon, three Gray Wolves appeared at its side. Four wolves including the Dire Wolf surrounded Sungjin.

Wolves were the first monsters who operated in groups using coordinated attacks against Hunters. Sungjin, who had absentmindedly progressed through the phases, gripped his Katana properly for the first time and assumed a battle position.

The reason why the upcoming Raid was so challenging was due to these wolves. The wolves, who were orbiting around Sungjin, suddenly charged toward him.

Once he saw them make a move, Sungjin charged toward the weakest one of the pack. In one smooth stroke, he severed the wolf's head.

And to follow through, he kicked the stomach of another wolf that tried to pounce on him.

"Kyan!"

The wolf collapsed on its side, whimpering like a hurt dog. The other two used that opening to attack him simultaneously.

These wolves would even sacrifice their members in an attack to out maneuver their enemy. Sungjin swiftly swung his Katana toward the larger Dire Wolf.

The Dire Wolf saw Sungjin turn toward him and stopped to dodge the Katana. Sungjin, who was facing the Dire Wolf, had to use his unarmed left arm to stop the other wolf.

"Kyan!"

The wolf bit into the chains on his left arm, causing metallic sounds to ring out but its struggle to bite through didn't last long as it quickly lost its head to Sungjin's blade. Only two wolves were left.

Even though the Dire Wolf was still alive, this fight no longer posed any challenge to Sungjin. This time, he made the first move.

The two remaining wolves tried to out maneuver him, but Sungjin's Katana knew no mercy. Within two to three swings of his blade, the wolves collapsed powerlessly.

[All Monsters eliminated. Closing the Phase.]

Completion Reward: 25 Stat Points
Kill Reward: 25 Black Coins

Sungjin examined the shackle and chains binding his left arm: Free Ark. The wolf hadn't even managed to leave a dent on it.

This is quite useful.

[You have completed all Phases faster than the other Hunters.]

[Please wait until the others complete their Phases.]

As expected, Sungjin had finished early. The environment changed once the tutorial was completed. A campfire appeared in the middle of the forest. This was where the Hunters were being gathered.

Sungjin sat by the fire and waited for the other Hunters to show up, keeping the Katana in his embrace.

[All hunts completed.]

[Synchronizing Hunters.]

Along with the Operator's words, the environment warped slightly as Sungjin watched patiently. One by one, Hunters appeared out of thin air.

***

The people that emerged in front of Sungjin were, once again, of different body physiques and races. A bespectacled young Westerner, a white-haired old man, a very short South-eastern Asian, and a tall white man.

But truth be told, their actual physique, size, or race did not matter. The more reliable indicator of their strength was the titles they had earned. Sungjin looked up and glanced at the titles.

The young Westerner had Novice Swordsman, the Southeastern Asian had Novice Scout, the white-haired old man had Lumberjack, and the tall white man had the Hooligan title. Sungjin shook his head in disappointment upon seeing their titles.

No one was particularly talented. But it was alright. As it stood, Sungjin had enough combat prowess to solo this Raid's objectives for a Full Clear. The Operator began the mission briefing.

Phase 5 – Ahenna's Forest Raid
Objective – Hunt the Wolf Queen Ahenna
Time Limit: 25 Minutes.

[Complete the objective within the Time Limit.]
[If you cannot, you will die.]
Once the Operator's briefing ended, the tall white man with the Hooligan title stepped forward and addressed the group.
"Gentlemen, gather up so we can see your ugly mugs."
The man truly embodied the word Hooligan; a tattoo covered his shoulders, and he carried himself with a subtle air of arrogance and authority.

The Novice Scout South-eastern Asian man and the bespectacled Novice Swordsman hesitated for a moment and moved closer to join the Hooligan. The Hooligan complained.

"Wow... all I get are these weaklings."

The Lumberjack old man and Sungjin maintained their distance from the campfire, watching wordlessly. The Hooligan took a note of it and addressed them.

"Hey, Old Jack, can't you hear me? Get over here. And you, Master Hunter? Get over here if you don't want to die."

The mood was just horrible, much like the first Raid.

...*I'll have to carry out this Raid by myself again.*

Sungjin gave up trying to solicit cooperation. It didn't even matter, as he did not require their help. He had enough skill and power to complete the Raid by himself. The only part that gave Sungjin insecurity was finding the secret location containing the hidden boss.

Even though Sungjin was confident that he could fight any battle perfectly, he didn't feel the same when it came to finding and defeating the hidden boss within the time limit.

In the end, the biggest obstacle is the time limit.

[The Raid begins in 1 minute.]

Before the Raid began, Sungjin called upon the Operator.

"Operator, add all Stat Points to Dexterity."

[Dexterity rose by 60 points.]

Raising Dexterity was the obvious choice. After the tutorial, he didn't feel that anything in this Raid could seriously threaten him.

He could already cut the strongest mob in this forest, the Grizzly Bear, in a single strike. Instead of raising Strength, it made more sense to invest in Dexterity to increase his speed even further.

But now that he had invested in Dexterity, he regretted investing into Endurance.

Maybe I wasted the points. I know I have to raise it at some point, but speed is more important right now.

And while Sungjin was reflecting over his point allocations,

"Hello. Hello!"

From the woods, a thin man walked out. The 6th person. Everyone's gaze was drawn toward him.

He was carrying a rucksack almost as large as his body. When Sungjin saw him, he recalled his memories from the past.

Oh yeah, he exists.

"I am the Wandering Merchant Aindell. Please purchase some goods from me before the Raid begins. Since we are way out in the boonies, the goods here will be more expensive than those in a regular shop. He he."

The Operator's cube only sold items during the first Chapter. Now the only place available to buy them was the Black Market.

But from time to time, 'Wandering Merchants' arrived at the Raid location to sell on site. The Hooligan approached him.

"Who the fuck are you?"

The Merchant smiled sheepishly. "As I explained, I am the Wandering Merchant Aindell. I sell potions and other small goods. Also..."

The Hooligan gripped him by the collar and lifted him up threateningly.

"You don't get Coins, give me all you've got, bitch"

A warning came from the cubes.

[Warning:]

[Attacking a non-hostile life form will cause penalties from the Raid Rewards.]

The Hooligan let go of the merchant immediately.

"Whoa whoa. That's no good at all. My bad, sorry about that."

"Cough cough."

Aindell let out a few fake coughs and continued.

"As I was saying, the wildlife here are afraid and weak to fire... So I recommend purchasing some Salamander's ash. For archers, I also sell fire arrows. I don't need to explain how useful Recovery Potions are, right?"

At his sales pitch, Novice Swordsman, Novice Scout, and even Lumberjack lined up and bought items from the merchant.

"Three Salamander's ash please."

"How much are the fire arrows?"

"I want three Salamander's ash, too, and three Recovery Potions."

The others quickly spent their coins earned from the previous Raid on consumables. Their actions made sense since they all just wanted to survive.

[Raid begins in 30 seconds.]

The Hooligan watched for a few moments, and then hesitantly asked,

"Hey, uh... give me some Salamander's ash too."

He was also able to purchase an item. The Merchant did not hold a grudge against the Hooligan and magnanimously sold it at the same price. Aindell directed his gaze toward Sungjin once he was done finalizing the transaction.

"Sir, do you need any items?"

Sungjin declined, shaking his head.

"Hehe, understood."

He smiled and laughed jovially. But Sungjin found that to be even more unsettling. He could not tell if this was a human or something else.

Is it like an NPC in an MMORPG?

The Operator finally began the countdown.

[Raid will commence in 10 seconds. 10...]

I guess it's nothing strange when there's even an Operator.

Sungjin pushed aside his thoughts and drew out his sword.

"Hey, I told you to get over here!"

The Hooligan tried to get Sungjin to join him, but Sungjin replied, "Be careful and move as a group. Hunt the lone wolves and bears so you won't die. Be careful about the Pumas that suddenly drop out of trees."

He suggested to them and prepared himself.

[2, 1, 0. The Raid Begins!]

At the same time as the Raid start, Sungjin dashed into the dark forest. He heard Aindell's voice from behind.

"I will remain in this location. If you need consumables during the middle of the Raid, please come by at any time!"

Hearing that, Sungjin simply thought, *There is no chance of that happening. I need to save up money and buy my Katana.*

*

Sungjin rapidly hunted every wild beast he could lay his eyes on as he charged through the forest. He hunted packs of wolves led by the Dire Wolves, as well as Pumas that silently dropped out of trees.

"Guwah!"

A grizzly bear charged at a speed unfitting of its size. But Sungjin cut it down in one swift strike. Thanks to more than 200 points invested in both Strength and Dexterity, any wildlife that came in contact with his sword was cut down like a piece of paper.

Sungjin didn't concentrate on the fights, but rather on finding anomalies in the area. Clearing the Raid was not high on his priority list.

Clearing the Chapter and having high contribution points were nice. But because Sungjin had both the Heart of Gold and the Master Hunter title equipped, missing out on a few Stat Points and Black Coins were acceptable.

The most important thing was the Item rewards obtained from the hidden bosses and hidden pieces. These items were guaranteed to be rated Heroic at the minimum. Items he would gladly spend tens of thousands of Black Coins in the market to buy.

From time to time, Sungjin saw Dire Wolves mixed within the crowd. Unlike other mobs, even he couldn't take them on lightly. They were strong, dexterous, and most importantly, cunning.

They called upon Gray Wolves to perform cooperative attacks. Of course, the side that perished were the wolves.

"Haa... Operator."

Sungjin addressed the Operator after spending a considerable amount of time cutting the animals apart to pieces.

"Time?"

[19 minutes 49 seconds remaining.]

He spent almost 5 minutes turning the forest inside out.

It should be fairly close now...

The Wolf Queen Ahenna was not in a set location. She usually appeared automatically after the number of wolves slain passed a certain threshold.

"Kwah!"

Sungjin quickly twisted his body and spun around with his Katana. Above, a Shadow Puma was cut from the neck to its armpit.

These guys always ambush just as I forget about them.

When Sungjin was about to sheath his Katana, he spotted a Gray Wolf between the trees. Sungjin drew the Katana out once more.

But, unlike other Gray Wolves, it neither attacked nor watched him. It faced the sky and let out a howl.

"Awoooo~~"

Soon, other wolves in the area joined in.

"Awoo Awoo"

The surrounding was now filled with the howl of the wolves.

"Awoooo~!"

With so many wolves, the howling continued without an end. Listening carefully, Sungjin could tell.

...She's here.

And as if to confirm his feelings, the Operator announced the arrival of the boss.

[Caution! Boss Monster]

[The Wolf Queen Ahenna has appeared!]

A moment later, a wolf twice as large as a Grizzly Bear appeared. Cunning eyes and a coat as white as snow, Ahenna looked almost divine.

But foes are foes.

Sungjin prepared himself, drawing his Katana.

"AWOOOO~"

Ahenna howled in the wind, and a dozen or so Dire Wolves appeared at her side. Each of the Dire Wolves brought with them several Gray Wolves. Sungjin quickly estimated their numbers.

Seems to about... 50 to 60 roughly...

The most difficult part about this Raid was that there was a massive numerical disadvantage.

Last time, I had great teammates, and so we were able to overcome this Boss somehow...

And while lost in thought, he was interrupted by voices coming from behind him.

"Where is she? That queen bitch?"

"I think I heard the howling from over there, sir... Wait, wha wha?"

"What the hell? That gigantic beast is a wolf? We're supposed to fight that?"

Sungjin did not turn. It was obvious who it was. He gripped his Katana tightly and bit his lips.

***

"Awo awoo awoooo~!"

Ahenna let out a long series of howls. On the surface, it sounded like an ordinary wolf's howl, but the intonation and pitch subtly changed, as if she was speaking. Upon hearing her voice, the giant wolf pack began moving as a group.

"What the hell?"

While the other three Hunters were panicking, the wolves closed in surrounding all four of them.

"Whoa whoa whoa..."

One of the Hunters who was backing up walked into Sungjin's back.

Sungjin, already out of patience, spat out a declaration to the other Hunters.

"The Boss is mine. I don't care what you all want to do, just don't get in my way."

Sungjin charged into the army of wolves toward Ahenna, as soon as he was done speaking, leaving behind the three Hunters. Ahenna, who was giving orders to the other wolves via her voice stopped and prepared for battle.

In the blink of an eye, she lunged with her claws at an incredible speed.

But Sungjin dodged her claws with an even greater speed, ducking under her attack.

It was a hundredth of a second, but Sungjin saw her eyes grow wide as if to say, "How can you dodge this?" And it was reasonable for her to be surprised as there were very few Hunters capable of evading her attack this early in the Raids.

Die.

Sungjin initiated an upward slash as soon as the paws were out of the way. Ahenna leaped back thanks to her animalistic instincts, but the tip of Sungjin's Katana still managed to reach her snout.

"Kaaa!"

Ahenna retreated, screaming in pain. Sungjin felt the feedback from the strike. It was a shallow cut.

Not enough damage.

Sungjin prepared to charge in to initiate a follow-up strike, but,

"Kao!"

A Dire Wolf charged at Sungjin from the side. Sungjin dodged it by ducking under his attack, but another charged at him.

Sungjin was forced to take a step back. And within moments, Ahenna had backed off and was immediately surrounded by a dozen Dire Wolves. Gray Wolves rushed in to encircle her completely.

Sungjin frowned.

How diligently they serve their queen.

Suddenly,

PEW!

Sungjin heard the sound of an arrow flying through the air from behind him. He saw the arrow fly in his direction. While deliberating whether or not he should knock it out of the air, he realized it was flying above his head.

What was that about?

When Sungjin checked behind him, he saw that the other Hunters were fighting for their lives.

"Fuck! Kill it!" The Novice Scout was shooting arrows randomly, missing every shot.

"Stay away! Stay away!" The Novice Swordman and the Hooligan were waving flaming weapons (imbued with Salamander's ash) wildly without thought.

Ahenna howled a command to the wolves.

"Awooawoawo~~"

The wolves upon hearing her call stopped attacking and moved as one. They orbited around the four Hunters. Although they were wolves, they were orderly and precise in the execution of their queen's commands.

Sungjin fixed his grip on the Katana and entered battle stance.

...I need to kill the leader first...

Sungjin scanned the sea of wolves. It was not difficult to find her. Snow-white fur, with an unnaturally large body size.

His gaze met hers. Ahenna was bleeding from the long cut on her face which went from her nose to her forehead. Once she looked into his eyes, she called out again,

"Aaaawoo~"

The moment her command went out, the largest of the Dire Wolves stood between Sungjin and her.

...She's smarter than I thought.

It would be difficult to complete this Raid solo. Sungjin briefly turned to look at the other Hunters. The Hunters were all grouped up together with the Hooligan shouting commands.

"Together! Together!"

Then, the Novice Swordman accidentally touched the Hooligan's shirt and lit it on fire. The Hooligan jumped up in surprise, quickly putting it out. He then cursed out at the Novice Swordman.

"Mother fucker! You wanna die, boy?"

"I... I'm so sorry!"

Sungjin shook his head in disappointment.

Wolves are better than Humans.

Sungjin felt that asking for their help would be unfavorable and might cause even more headaches. He gripped his Katana tightly; he couldn't think of a way to reach Ahenna at the moment.

Let's start by decreasing their numbers a bit.

Sungjin, changing his tactics, searched for a thinner section of the encirclement. But the first one to make a move was Ahenna.

"Argg"

With her short command, the wolves surrounding the Hunters attacked all at once.

"Fuck!"

The Novice Swordman diligently swung his sword, but the fire on the sword eventually went out.

"Uhh..."

The moment he hesitated, the hand holding his sword was ripped off. Within seconds, he was torn apart to pieces.

The Hooligan saw that the Novice Swordman's weapon went out, and understood his club would soon lose the enchantment. He searched his pocket.

But the moment he paused to reach into his pocket, a wolf pounced on him.

He hurriedly swung his club to hit the wolf, but another wolf charged from his blind spot. It jumped up and grabbed him by the neck in its jaws.

"Mother fu..." He couldn't even finish swearing before his neck was ripped open by the wolf.

The Novice Scout launched fire arrows all over the place, but his arrows only struck innocent trees. Seeing his protectors the Novice

Swordman and the Hooligan falling to their demise, he called out for assistance.

"He... Help!"

He tried to run toward Sungjin, but was bitten in the neck and killed. Sungjin genuinely felt sorry for them, but he wasn't available to lend a hand. The strongest of the wolves was busy attacking him. After exchanging a long series of blows,

"Awoawoo~"

Upon Ahenna's command, the wolves separated from Sungjin and backed off. When Sungjin looked around to search for the reason, he saw that there was a light in Ahenna's Forest.

The fire arrow from Novice Scout had started a forest fire. Ahenna and her loyal wolves backed away from Sungjin and the fire and continued to encircle him from afar.

Surrounded by wolves and the fire, Sungjin was drenched in their blood. He took this chance to look around.

So many...

He cut down the wolves without rest. But their numbers never seemed to decrease. Whenever he would wipe out a large number of wolves,

"Awooo~"

Ahenna would let out a cry, which would summon an even larger number of beasts to her. It reminded Sungjin why this place was named Ahenna's Forest. Sungjin asked the Operator,

"Operator, Time remaining?"

[14 minutes 29 seconds remaining.]

Killing the Orc Chief had taken him less than a minute, and Ahenna had already dragged out the fight for five minutes. After all, no matter how strong Sungjin was, he only had two hands and one Katana.

Recklessly charging into a well-coordinated formation of beasts was nothing short of suicide.

I really need to kill the boss first...

Sungjin searched for the Queen. She was bleeding from her snout and forehead, and only glanced at him from time to time.

She instinctively knew she was no match for him.

How annoyingly smart, thought Sungjin.

It was as if she knew that she would win by dragging out the time. Sungjin, surrounded by the wolves, couldn't help but recall the Wandering Merchant Aindell.

Maybe I should have bought a few Salamander's ash...

Sungjin had 180 coins left over. He had been so focused on saving coins for the late game that he might have penny pinched too excessively.

I should have bought some Consumables.

Now that he thought of it, he recalled that the necklace Yanhurat was inside his pocket. Keeping the wolves at bay, he took the necklace out to inspect it.

Is it time to use this...?

Yanhura's special active effect was Zealot (III).

For 30 seconds, increase damage and speed by 300%

Once the effects were over, his HP would drop to a third of what it was. But the effects were well worth the harsh penalty of the item. Sungjin, who was already abnormally powerful, would benefit immensely from using it.

But, he had seen the fate of those who had relied on the power of Zealot. Those addicted to Zealot had always met a bad end.

There were many who placed their bets heavily on Zealot's active effects. Many who swore by it, forming the core of their strategy around its usage. But those who became dependent on its effects eventually couldn't handle the penalty and faced gruesome deaths.

Sungjin held the necklace in one hand as he kept the wolves at bay. Then,

"...Kill."

He heard an ominous voice originating from his palms. Sungjin looked from the corner of his eyes toward the necklace. The Yanhurat stared back at him with a hideous smile.

The necklace continued to whisper to him to put it around his neck and to fight.

I didn't want to use this...

But as he deliberated his options, time kept on ticking by. He knew he could eventually overcome the sea of wolves and complete the objective, but the longer he took, the less time he had available to search for and defeat the hidden boss.

I will kill the queen within the next 30 seconds.

Coming to a conclusion, he swallowed his inhibitions and placed the necklace around his neck. The voices could be heard much more clearly now.

"Kill them."

Sungjin charged toward Ahenna with all due haste, ears filled with the mad whispers from the necklace. A wolf attempted to block his way. Sungjin easily cut through it.

Blood splashed onto his chin. The whispers from the necklace sped up even faster.

"Kill them, Murder them."

A gigantic Dire Wolf pounced upon Sungjin. The moment he noticed the wolf, he cut it apart with lightning speed. Sungjin's blade moved even faster than usual.

The Dire Wolf collapsed to the floor without even being able to let out a sound. Drawing blood twice, the necklace again picked up speed.

"Kill them, murder them, rip them to pieces, and end their lives!"

"Graah!"

A Grizzly Bear charged toward Sungjin, but with a single slash, the bear became slices of meat. The voices grew louder and stronger.

"Kill them! Kill them! Kill them! Kill them!"

Just hearing the necklace made his adrenaline pump wildly. His eyes felt as if they were threatening to pop out, and he unconsciously started grinding his teeth.

Sungjin made a beeline for the Queen. Innumerable beasts stood in the way to protect their Queen, but Sungjin in Zealot mode was three times faster and three times stronger. His speed and strength were like that of a hurricane, sweeping away his enemies in a rain of blood.

The beasts who came in contact with his path of destruction were cut apart like pieces of paper. He cut and cut and cut. And all the while, the maddening voice sped up without end.

"Kill! Kill! Kill! Kill!!!!!"

"Aooooooo~!"

Ahenna let out a voice full of fear, and all the wolves in the vicinity launched their attacks toward Sungjin to stop him. The sound of Ahenna's cries and the voices from the ring overlapped.

"Kill! Kill! Kill! Kill!!!!!"

And once the sounds overlapped, Sungjin couldn't help but yell toward the endless stream of wolves,

"I'll kill you all! You sons of bitches!"

***

A tree was burnt to the core and transformed into charcoal. Unable to withstand its own weight, it collapsed into a pile of ashes. Novice Scout's fire arrows had started a fully-fledged forest fire; the wind carried embers of the inferno and began to spread across the whole of Ahenna's Forest.

But not a single creature could be seen running away from the flames. Sungjin pulled his Katana out from the chest of the last wolf in the forest.

"Haa..."

Sungjin finally let out a long sigh. Behind him were mountains of corpses. Among the corpses was the 'Queen of the Forest' Ahenna herself.

Sungjin had fought in a frenzy. He had fought so wildly that he did not even recognize himself. The effects of Zealot were powerful, but it made it impossible to maintain a sound mind during the fight.

Sungjin ripped the Yanhurat off of his neck.

Kill them! Rip them to pieces!

The necklace's insane shouting seemed to continue to echo in his ears. He hadn't been hurt during the fight, but he still felt a rush of exhaustion wash over him.

"Operator, my HP?"

HP: 500/1500

His HP had dropped exactly to a third of what it was. The item activation period was exactly 30 seconds. It was fine to fight mindlessly for 30 seconds, but the problem occurred when the period ended.

Disoriented, exhausted, and with only a third of the total HP remaining, finding yourself surrounded by enemies... the same enemies you had not managed to defeat with three times the strength and speed. This was the reason why so many people who entrusted their lives to Zealot mode had succumbed to death.

Sungjin realized that in a truly life-threatening situation, unless he had the absolute certainty that all hostile forces could be eliminated during the active time, it was better not to use it.

Against Ahenna, he could have easily completed the Chapter without using it. But he was short on time.

Time.

"Operator, remaining time?"

[13 Minutes and 49 Seconds remaining.]

Not even a minute had passed since he had previously asked. Yanhurat's mind-corrupting voice had saved him lots of time.

"Operator, take out two small Recovery potions from the inventory."

The cube summoned two small potions upon command. Sungjin drank them both. The effect of the small Recovery Potion was "Fill 1/3 of the total HP."

Drinking the two potions recovered his whole HP. Sungjin now wanted to leave to search for clues about the hidden boss when,

SNAP

He heard something step on a branch, breaking it.

Was one left alive?

Sungjin looked toward the origin of the sound. Whatever had caused the sound, it was trying to hide itself. Sungjin approached the tree, Katana ready. As he grew closer toward the source, he could hear the sound of breathing growing louder. When Sungjin walked around the large tree,

"D... Die!"

A large axe came swinging at him. But it was swung at an ordinary speed. It was in slow motion compared to Ahenna's claws. Sungjin swung his sword faster than the axe to intercept it.

The Katana cut off the axe head, and the axe blade flew off into the distance, landing somewhere in the forest with a THUD.

Disarming his attacker, Sungjin inspected the assailant. It was the white-haired Lumberjack old man, who stood stiffly holding the headless axe like a sword.

"Ah... Ahhhh!"

He saw Sungjin's face and collapsed backward in fear. Sungjin stared for a moment at the old man.

...Oh yeah, I forgot about him.

Aside from Sungjin, the old man was the only person who had been acting independently from the Hooligan group.

He must have been put off by the Hooligan's arrogant behavior from the camp.

It was not a bad decision. In the end, it was what kept him alive. The Lumberjack swung his headless axe toward Sungjin and shouted,

"Stay... Stay away!"

He had no reason to approach the old man. Sungjin sheathed his Katana. But the Lumberjack added one more word.

"You... Monster...!"

What? thought Sungjin as he looked into the old man's eyes again. The old man must have seen Sungjin fight under the effects of

Yanhurat. If that was so, his reaction made sense. Sungjin decided to give him an advice.

"Hey, Grandpa. Go back to the campfire where we started the Raid and sit there. If you do so, you will be able to avoid death."

With that, Sungjin ran deeper into the forest.

*

Sungjin ran through the forest with his Katana in hand, searching for clues. But no enemies could be seen. Sungjin then realized something and asked the operator.

"Operator, Raid progress?"

[Raid is 95% complete.]

Sungjin immediately sheathed his Katana.

I guess that was all of them back there.

Ahenna's cries must have summoned every remaining beast in the forest to the fight. And every single one of them, without exception, had been eliminated by his hands. It was rather nice to know that there were no loose ends.

It was just him and the hidden boss. After roaming the forest for a while, he saw rows of trees turning black.

This must be... the boundary line.

The Raid was always conducted within a systematically enclosed area. Just because it was a forest did not mean it continued on forever. If a Hunter attempted to leave past the boundary, a terrifying warning was given.

[Please return to the hunting grounds. This area is off limits to Hunters.]

[If you remain in the restricted area after 10 seconds,]

[you will die in 10, 9...]

If this is the boundary...

Sungjin withdrew his hands from the boundary line. Then, turning around, he ran straight back perpendicularly from the boundary line.

No matter how much he searched his surroundings, he didn't see anything out of place. Soon, he returned to where Ahenna and her beasts lay strewn about the forest floor.

...Where the hell is the hidden boss?

Sungjin decided to return to the starting location. At the campfire, the old man Lumberjack and the Wandering Merchant Aindell were sitting by the fire.

"Ahh! Monster!" called out the Lumberjack.

"Oh, you were able to defeat Ahenna. Congratulations, Mister Hunter," said the merchant.

Sungjin scanned the campsite briefly.

"Go... Go away!"

"Do you wish to purchase some supplies?"

The Lumberjack begged him to leave, and the Merchant bid him to stay. Of the two, he decided to listen to the Lumberjack. He didn't have time to waste on those two anyways.

*

As time passed, the forest fire continued to spread. Ahenna's Forest was now lit as bright as day. But he didn't spot anything particularly out of place.

"Operator, time?"

[8 minutes and 39 seconds remaining.]

He had been searching fruitlessly for 5 minutes. He probed like a mad man and combed the forest. Still, the only thing he could find was the 'Boundary.'

Where is it hidden? Sungjin was starting to become annoyed when, "Hoo Hoo."

Short but unmistakable sounds of an owl could be heard from above. Sungjin looked up into the night sky. If it were still dark, it would have been hard to spot it. But thanks to the forest fire, it was easier to see.

On top of a tree, an owl was nested. The owl did not appear to be a hidden boss, but it was still suspicious. Sungjin unhesitatingly jumped up the tree, climbing it.

Sungjin's Dexterity had long since surpassed human limitations. Climbing the tree posed no difficulty for him. Once he got closer, the owl flew away.

Only the nest remained. He decided to check the nest. Within the nest was not an egg, but a round white crystal.

...*Found it.*

Sungjin reached out and lifted up the crystal. The cube began an announcement.

[Congratulations! You have obtained the Hidden Piece]

[Perfect Moonstone!]

Sungjin inspected the Perfect Moonstone. The Operator opened up a hologram for the item.

Perfect Moonstone – Crystal of the Moon.
Rare Jewel

Crystal hidden inside an owl's nest.
It is said that it contains the powers of a full moon.

There are no special effects associated with this item. In most cases, this kind of item could be sold off to the Black Market for Black Coins.

"Operator, how much can this be sold off for in the Black Market?"

[100 Black Coins]

...*only 100...*

Sungjin placed the item in his pocket for now. He left to search for the hidden boss.

Compared to the items hidden bosses can drop, 100 Black Coins was nothing. Then, he stopped. He recalled something he heard long ago in the past.

From the earlier days of the hunts, he once heard from his teammate,

"I heard that a party was able to find and kill the hidden boss in Ahenna's Forest."

Sungjin paused for a moment to try and recollect his memory.

"None of the original party members survived until now... but from what I've been told, the hidden piece found in the second forest... is not supposed to be sold."

...Not for sale?

Sungjin reached into his pocket and took out the Moonstone one more time. As the name implied, it was perfectly round, and the crystal was a perfect replica of the full moon. Sungjin looked up into the sky.

Above the burning treetops and the smoke, he could see the third quarter moon. He looked back and forth between the moon and the stone.

Half-moon... and round moonstone... that is to say, a full moon.

Sungjin, while looking back and forth between the crystal and the moon, recalled the Operator's explanation about the forest.

[It is a place filled with insidious and cunning predators of the night.]

The answer was on the tip of his tongue. All the pieces were there.

Then... just who is....

Sungjin put together the final piece. He quickly moved his feet.

***

At the campfire located at the entrance of the Raid, two individuals were conversing.

"You mean you only lived in the city your entire life?"

"Yeah. I've never even held an axe in my life before. I don't know what's going on anymore..."

Old man Lumberjack and the Wandering Merchant Aindell were having a conversation.

"I see I see. I hope you have a long life, sir."

"That would be nice... But that crazy guy from before..."

At that moment, 'That Crazy Guy' appeared, interrupting the peaceful atmosphere. Their reactions were polar opposites again. Wandering Merchant Aindell bowed, greeting him.

"Welcome, dear customer!"

And the old Lumberjack was startled, pointing his fingers at Sungjin.

"Why! You! Why are you here?"

Sungjin, for the first time, approached the two. The Lumberjack was being incredibly cautious, but Sungjin ignored him and approached the merchant instead.

"Hey, do you know anything about hidden bosses?"

Aindell tilted his head as if confused and replied, "Hidden... boss? I don't know. Is there something like that here?"

He smiled innocently for a moment, and then his expression brightened up.

"Oh! I think I've heard of something like that before. A secret boss hiding somewhere in the Raid zone. Finding it is really difficult... and it possesses incredible strength. Please be careful, Mr. Hunter, in case you ever run into something like that."

Sungjin couldn't help but smile when he heard the reply. And drawing out his Katana, he pointed the sword at the Merchant. "So you have incredible strength?"

As if not understanding his words, the merchant tilted his head again.

"What is this about, dear customer?"

The Lumberjack grasped the merchant's shoulders and said to him, "Don't listen to him, son. He's a crazed monster. You don't need to listen to him."

Sungjin addressed the old man, "Come to my side if you want to live. 'The Crazed Monster' is him, not me."

The Lumberjack seemed to be on Aindell's side. The old man stood even closer to Aindell as he replied Sungjin.

"Stop your lies... Didn't you see what happened when that Hooligan fellow tried to threaten him?"

You don't get coins. Give me everything you've got, Bitch.

The Lumberjack was probably referring to a situation from earlier that day. The Operator had definitely said at the time:

[Warning:]

[Attacking a non-hostile life form will cause penalties from the Raid Rewards.]

Sungjin knew better than anyone about this rule. There was no way he was not aware of this.

"...That only applies while he is a non-hostile life form."

But the Lumberjack refused to listen. "You bloodthirsty animal..."

He had seemed to view Sungjin as a battle-crazed maniac ever since witnessing him in Zealot mode under the influence of Yanhurat.

Sungjin shook his head in disappointment. Almost nobody had believed in Sungjin since the reset. At the very least, the old man seemed naturally distrustful.

"Well... fine. Do what you like. But, if you don't run away by the time I count to three, I can't guarantee your safety. One."

Sungjin put his hand inside the pocket and began to count.

"Two."

He gripped the Perfect Moonstone.

"Three."

At the same time he said 'Three,' he tossed the stone toward Aindell.

"Hmm? What is?" Aindell looked down at the stone he caught on instinct. In his hands, the crystal displayed the words: Full Moon.

And the moment his eyes landed on the words, his blue eyes turned amber. Sungjin knew,

...This is it.

And to confirm his suspicion, the Operator announced in an urgent tone

[Caution! Hidden Boss]

[Werewolf Aindell has appeared!]

"Graaaah!"

Aindell's short stature grew rapidly, sprouting hair all over his body, his face extending into a snout. His fangs grew out and extended past his lips.

The time it took for Wandering Merchant Aindell to transform into Werewolf Aindell was three seconds. The Lumberjack had fallen over in surprise at his transformation. Sungjin yelled at him,

"Hey, run away!"

But,

"Uh..." He didn't even have the time to scream or shout. Aindell, upon transforming, immediately turned toward the Lumberjack.

"Gah!"

The Lumberjack, who until moments ago was sharing a pleasant conversation with the merchant, had his neck ripped out by the Werewolf Aindell.

Drenched in human blood, the Werewolf let out a howl.

"Awooooo~~!"

Sungjin frowned and took out his Katana from the sheath.

I'm getting real tired of that sound now.

The Werewolf turned his gaze upon Sungjin. Sungjin clenched his teeth. Moments later, they clashed.

Sungjin swung his sword and leaned his head back as Aindell's claws cut through the air above him.

Because Sungjin had tilted his head back to dodge, he could not visually confirm the result of the first clash. However, Sungjin did not feel any resistance from the strike.

He dodged it.

Instead of launching a follow-up strike, Sungjin watched for the wolfman's next move. And just as he predicted, Aindell launched his attack toward Sungjin's unguarded left. Sungjin quickly let go of his Katana from his left hand to guard.

"Kakakaka."

Aindell's claws and the chains of Free Ark collided, sending sparks flying. If he had not equipped the Free Ark, he would have lost his hand.

...deliberate and planned attack...

Sungjin leaped back in surprise. In the previous strike, Aindell had aimed to strike Sungjin's arms to disarm him rather than go for the kill. There was no question about it. Sungjin decided to try to communicate.

"...What are you?"

And in a rough and deep voice, he replied, "You already figured me out! What an interesting Human!"

Sungjin regripped his Katana as he spoke, "I just thought it was strange, strange that the Operator would willingly throw in a random weirdo to help out in a Raid."

The Wolf gestured to the old man he killed and replied, "That man was too old; his meat tasted no good. Let's see how you taste!"

The two combatants resumed the battle. They dodged, attacked, dodged, swung... They exchanged blows at a breakneck speed. Aindell was even faster than Ahenna.

Despite Sungjin's unmatched investment into Dexterity, Aindell did not lose out on speed. The two exchanged a few more blows, and mutually took a step back. The fight suddenly came to a pause.

Aindell and Sungjin both understood that the other was a formidable foe. Aindell looked nervous. Sungjin gazed into his own reflection on the Katana.

This was designed to be difficult to clear alone.

Similar to Mad Orc Ruark, this was not a contest of strength and endurance, but of speed. The problem was compounded by the fact that the speed on both sides was roughly the same.

Sungjin considered using the Yanhurat inside his pocket; 3 times the speed for 30 seconds.

...If I use this... It'll take 30 seconds to kill... no, 10 seconds would be enough... But... I promised myself I wouldn't use it unless absolutely necessary...

For a moment, Sungjin wavered, but he made a firm decision and withdrew his hands. Sungjin decided against using it. If he wasn't strong enough to overcome a Chapter as early as the second Raid without relying on 'cheat mode,' then his future looked grim.

"Kao!"

Aindell charged once more toward Sungjin. Sungjin lowered his stance and backed off, dodging and blocking all of Aindell's attacks. Meanwhile, he calculated his next move.

If we reach that area...

Sungjin leaped back farther and farther to lure Aindell in. Being unable to land a hit, Aindell gave chase as he entered into a frenzy.

And suddenly, Sungjin stood his ground. He was standing next to the campfire. He kicked the logs up toward Aindell.

A fire attack. Aindell paused for the first time to stop the log. The moment he made contact, the fire spread to his fur.

For a miniscule amount of time, Aindell stiffened up when the fire spread to his fur. And that brief moment of hesitation was all Sungjin needed. He cut the werewolf's unguarded abdomen from side to side.

"Kaaaa!"

Aindell let out a strange scream. It was difficult to make out whether it was a scream of a wolf or a human. But Sungjin's Katana was devoid of any mercy.

Sungjin swung and slashed Aindell's legs. The werewolf's thin legs were severed without giving resistance. Sungjin had been eyeing them for a while.

Without being able to hold himself up, Aindell collapsed to the ground. He still tried to put up a fight by thrashing about from the ground, but Sungjin stomped on his stomach and simply cut off both of his arms.

"Kaaack!"

Aindell let out another cry of pain and began to pant. Even in his last moments, he glared at Sungjin with eyes filled with malice.

"How cruel..."

Sungjin held his Katana upside down and addressed him, "Yeah, that's the problem with you talkative ones."

And he thrust the Katana deep in his chest.

"Krrraahggg..."

He let out one last cry of pain and perished. Sungjin looked down at him and said his parting words.

"You said it yourself. 'Wild Beasts are afraid of fire.' What kind of idiot teaches his enemies his greatest weakness?"

The Operator soon gave out an announcement.

[Hidden Boss Werewolf Aindell cleared.]

[Congratulations! You have managed to complete all objectives in this Chapter!]

[Disregarding the remaining time and ending the Raid immediately.]

Upon hearing the announcements, he finally wiped off the sweat from his brows.

"Sigh..."

Maintaining 100% completion for a Raid, even for Chapter 2, was no easy task. Ahenna and Aindell both were extremely difficult opponents to defeat.

Will I be able to go until the end like this...?

Once he thought of it, he understood the difference between this life and his previous life. The difference was his luck with teammates. The reason why he was struggling so much despite the massive advantage granted by the 'Restart' and his unbelievable stats was due to his bad luck with teammates.

Previously, he was able to make it to the end because he consistently met reliable and rational teammates. But for some reason he had absolutely the worst luck with his teammates this time.

Of all the teammates he had met so far in two Chapters, Officer Baltren was the only one who was somewhat decent.

Sungjin paused for a moment to look up at the night sky. The half-moon was still there. Sungjin briefly thought of Baltren.

...I wonder how he's doing.

Baltren's words echoed in his mind.

We will meet again, Master Hunter K.

Meet again... The chances of meeting someone again from the previous Raid was astronomically small. Baltren was reasonably strong and had good leadership qualities. But if he got matched up with poor teammates, he'd just get killed.

And for a moment, Sungjin felt depressed. But, the Operator's voice interrupted his thoughts and brought him good news.

[Calculating Rewards.]

***

The Operator announced the rewards with her well enunciated and clear voice.

[Monsters Slain. Gray Wolf: 80. Shadow Puma: 30. Grizzly Bear: 15. Dire Wolf: 16. Total 1500 points.]

[Boss Monster Slain. Wolf Queen Ahenna: 150 points.]

[Hidden Boss. Werewolf Aindell: 150 points.]

[Final point count: 1800. Distributing points.]

Reward distribution ended quickly. Why? Because there was only one recipient.

[Your contribution is 100.0%. 1800 Stat Points, 1800 Black Coins awarded. Raid Clear Bonus 400 Stat Points and 400 Black Coins awarded. Item effect 'Additional 10% gained' activated. Distributing 2200 Stat Points and 2420 Black Coins.]

100 Black Coins remaining from Chapter 1, 60 from Chapter 2 Tutorial, and now getting 2420... Total is 2580 Black Coins.

Sungjin completed his calculations quickly and looked down at his hands. 'Heart of Gold's' Blue Sapphire glinted in the firelight.

Sungjin happily petted his ring. The ring allowed him to receive 10% extra coins this round.

[And now we will distribute the items.]

[Swift Paw – Wolf's step]

[Grand kin – Ahenna's last descendent]

[Mystery Pouch – Wandering Merchant's secret stash]

[Recovery Potion – Small X5]

[Salamander's ash X3]

Items appeared in front of his eyes and landed in a heap. Except for three items, he put all the consumables in the cube.

[Last but not least, you will be awarded titles you've earned on this Raid.]

Sungjin crossed his arms and gazed down at the cube. He wasn't expecting much. He already had Master Hunter, which had the strongest stat boost he had ever seen.

I don't think I'll need to switch out Master Hunter no matter what titles I receive from this Raid.

But Sungjin's assumptions were thankfully wrong.

[Treasure Hunter – Twice during Raids, you have the right to ask the Operator,]

[for hints about where the Hidden Piece is or the Hidden Boss is located]

"What?!"

Listening to the Operator's explanation, Sungjin immediately uncrossed his arms. He took the cube into his hands and asked the Operator once more.

"Say that again... What does the Treasure Hunter title do?"

The Operator repeated herself.

[Treasure Hunter – Twice during Raids, you have the right to ask the Operator for hints about where the Hidden Piece is or the Hidden Boss is located.]

"And... If I don't equip the title?"

[If you do not equip the title, you will only receive half of the title's effects.]

[In other words, you'll be given the right to request hints on the Hidden Piece or Boss just once per Raid.]

He had such low expectations, but he received a pleasant surprise. In fact, now he faced a dilemma.

Should he remain with Master Hunter's 30% bonus to stats, or take two hints from the Treasure Hunter?

He was only allowed to pick one title to equip for the duration of the Raid.

"Hmm... Ok understood," Sungjin decided to dwell more on it later. He could always mull over his choices while taking a bath in Ninety-Nine Nights.

Sungjin finally looked over and inspected his items. First was the boots built out of a wolf's foot.

I remember being jealous of people who wore these... How fortunate.

This was Ahenna's drop item which Sungjin had seen on a few Hunters last time around.

Swift Paw – Wolf's step
Heroic Shoes – Defense 22%

Active Skill
Swiftness (III) – When out of combat, move at 1000% of normal speed for a brief period of time. 30 Seconds Duration.
5 Minute Cooldown Time.

Shoes in the shape of a wolf's feet.
It normally has the claws hidden.

The shoes Sungjin wore now, were the sneakers he had on when he was summoned to the Hunter's Hall. Sungjin lifted up the shoes and spoke the command.

"Equip."

Moments later, the shoes were placed on his feet. It fit him perfectly. The Active Skill would be useful when searching for the hidden boss or the secret piece.

The other two items were probably drop items of the hidden boss Aindell. The first one he inspected was the small wooden carving of a wolf.

Grand Kin – Ahenna's Descendent
Heroic Summon

Active Skill
Spiritual Link (Grand Kin) – Loyal Familiar, Summon Grand Kin.

If Summon is killed, or if 10 minutes pass from the time of summoning, it disappears.

...A summon...

Sungjin threw the statue of the wolf into the air. It burst mid-air, and a normal-sized wolf emerged. The summon looked handsome for a wolf.

Fur like untouched snow, eyes as beautiful as gems; he was without a doubt Ahenna's descendent. Sungjin gestured toward Grand Kin.

"Grand Kin, come this way."

The wolf obediently approached Sungjin. Sungjin placed his hands on Grand Kin's head. The fur was soft to touch.

"...Oh yeah, I noticed that you wolves are much better than humans."

In the two Chapters he'd overcome so far, he'd had nothing but disappointing teammates. If the wolf was a faithful familiar like the Operator claimed, then he would be useful in Raids.

Sungjin spoke to himself while petting Grand Kin.

"But... Grand Kin is too long... Grand Kin... Grand... Kin... Cain? Yeah, I'll call you Cain from now on. It's okay, right?"

Grand Kin responded with a short bark. "Woof..."

It seemed as though the wolf understood all his words. Sungjin couldn't help but smile.

"Yes, nice to meet you, Cain. I look forward to working with you later."

The last item was a small rucksack. It was miniaturized, but the rucksack was otherwise identical to the one the Wandering Merchant Aindell carried with him.

In truth, this rucksack was what Sungjin was most curious about during the whole "reward' process.

Where is this used?

"Operator?"

The Operator immediately opened up a hologram to reveal information about the rucksack.

Mystery Pouch – Wandering Merchant's secret stash.
Heroic Treasure.

Active Skill
Roulette (IV) – receive one Legendary class crafting material.
Pouch Disappears after use.

Wandering Merchant Aindell's stash of crafting materials. His pouch is filled with crafting materials.

...Legendary crafting material?

Sungjin was honestly surprised. The Heroic tier he had equipped had excellent bonuses and effects, but Legendary tier items were on an entirely different scale.

With a Legendary tier item this early in the Chapters, one could almost beat the whole Chapter with just that item alone.

...Should I open it now?

While Sungjin deliberated, the Operator announced the remaining time.

[You will return to the Hunter's Hall in 1 minute.]

He only had 1 minute left.

...Well, I guess there's no harm knowing what I've got before I head into the Black Market.

Finally making up his mind, Sungjin untied the rucksack and opened up the top.

POP

With a small sound, the Operator conveyed a congratulatory message.

[Congratulations! You have obtained Ancient Stories of the East-Part1!]

"Wait... What?"

Sungjin was shocked. This Ancient Stories of the East was a very Legendary item among all Legendary items.

Its effects were extraordinary. But it was difficult to obtain because the item was divided into three parts, and only one person could own the completed item.

Before Sungjin had died, and only at the very last few Chapters, he was able to see it once or twice.

Ancient Stories of the East – Part 1.
Legendary Crafting Material.

Omnibus of ancient stories of the east.
Once parts 1, 2, and 3 are gathered, it can be made into a complete volume.

If I can just recreate this item...

If he were to obtain this item, early and mid-chapters would become unimaginably easier to complete.

"Operator, how much are part 2 and 3 of Ancient Stories of the East?"

[I am unable to give you that information.]

For the first time, the Operator did not provide the information to Sungjin. He searched in his memories for a moment and recalled that in the 'Black Market' there was a bookstore.

I'll probably be able to find some information there, thought Sungjin.

The Operator began her countdown for his return to the hall.

[You will return to the Hunter's Hall momentarily. 10, 9, 8, 7, 6, 5, 4, 3, 2, 1, 0]

*

The Hunter's Hall was still filled with a large number of people. Less than 0.1% of all humanity were present, but humans were many. Unimaginably so.

But as Chapters progressed, the numbers continued to dwindle. Sungjin recalled the past.

They kept on dying until there were less than a dozen remaining... less than...

The Operator interrupted his thoughts and announced a congratulatory message.

[Congratulations! You have all marvellously completed Chapter 2!]

Not one person celebrated the completion of the 2nd Chapter. And rightfully so; until just moments ago, they were struggling for their lives to survive.

[You, who have completed Chapter 2, are now a fully-fledged Hunter.]

Sungjin crossed his arms and stared at the Operator's face.

...and here comes the bad news.

[Chapters from now on will skip the tutorial]

[And jump straight into the Raid.]

This sentence was exactly why Sungjin was cynical about her congratulatory message.

[There will be no more 1 vs 1 Phases designed to get you familiarized with your upcoming enemies.]

[You will be entered into active combat straight away. All Hunters who have managed to survive until now,]

[are considered to be above 'able to fight 1 vs 1' level,]

[so the opportunity to safely scout out an enemy is no longer provided.]

"What...?"

Several Hunters had already figured out what kind of disadvantage this was, and let out sounds of disappointments. On the other hand,

Yawn...

Sungjin stretched as he yawned. Tutorials did not affect him one way or another. The Operator continued on and on, and Sungjin paid her no heed.

[Please do not be alarmed by the discontinuation of tutorials.]

[A note with the information about the next Raid,]

[will be delivered to the inn Ninety-Nine Nights shortly.]

The other Hunters listened to her words carefully; for them, it was a question of life and death.

Among them, only Sungjin stood crooked, arms crossed and resembled one complaining like some high school delinquent.

Shut up and send me to the Black Market.

Chapter 5 – Black Market Second Shopping

After a long and exhaustive explanation from the Operator, Sungjin was finally teleported to the Black Market.

[Once you have finished shopping, please feel free]

[to return to the Ninety-Nine Nights Inn at any time.]

The Operator continued to speak, but Sungjin had had enough.

"I got it, thank you," Sungjin waved the cube away and entered the Black Market.

...Bookstore... where was that again...?

Sungjin had been to the Black Market numerous times but couldn't recall the last time he had entered a bookstore.

There never was a really good reason to enter one. Sungjin roamed the Black Market aimlessly until he found a bookstore hidden away in a corner.

The cube presented an introduction.

[This bookstore, Dry Mouth, is run by bookkeeper Gourmet.]

[Various books and information can be purchased here.]

The shop owner was a quiet-looking goat man. He was so absorbed in his reading that he did not notice that he had a customer waiting. Sungjin eventually let out a fake cough to attract his attention.

"Cough... hmmm."

The goat man finally noticed that he was not alone; only his eyes moved as he gazed up from his book. He saw Sungjin and greeted him.

"Ah, please excuse me for not noticing you there... I hope you can understand—this is a great paragraph, you see... so, is there something you want to buy?"

Sungjin shook his head. "No... I did not come to buy a book."

He carefully took out the part 1 of Ancient Stories of the East from his vest and showed it to Gourmet. "Do you recognize this book?"

"Oh... My goodness!" Gourmet's eyes grew wide in surprise as it took turns looking back and forth between the book and Sungjin.

"This is a very precious item... where did you manage to obtain one?"

Sungjin replied matter-of-factly, "What do you mean? I obviously got it as a Raid reward."

Gourmet shook his head in disbelief and replied, licking his dry mouth, "I thought Chapter 2 just ended... how is it possible to obtain a Legendary crafting material this early on?"

"I didn't know it was possible either. So... do you carry any of the later parts of this book?"

"Hmm... Please wait for a moment." Gourmet closed the book he was reading and stood up. Behind him were mountains of books. Some were even taller than Sungjin.

He dug into the mountain and disappeared from sight. Once a minute had passed since his disappearance, the mountain seemed to collapse with books cascading down. After two major and chaotic book avalanches, Gourmet appeared holding two volumes.

In his hands were the Ancient Stories of the East Part 2 and the Ancient Stories of the East Part 3. Gourmet proudly announced:

"As I thought, I have them. So, have you come to purchase them?"

Sungjin instinctively swallowed before asking, "How much are they?"

"5000 Black Coins per volume," responded the goat man.

"What?" Sungjin couldn't believe his ears.

"5000 Black Coins per volume. Have you already lost your hearing at such a young age?"

5000 Black Coins per each crafting material; it was expensive. Far too expensive.

"That means... the final item has the component cost of 15,000 Coins..."

"In my humble opinion, the complete item is incomparably more valuable than 15,000 Coins," said the Gourmet.

Sungjin fell quiet. Gourmet was right. For now, he decided to leave the shop.

"Understood. I will come again at a later date."

He needed 10,000 Coins to purchase the two components. Haggling or intimidation did not work with vendors.

"If you want to read to pass the time before the next Raid, feel free to browse. Any book unrelated to combat is free, after all."

Sungjin waved his hands and left Gourmet's bookshop. His destination: Ninety-Nine Nights. There was nothing he wanted to purchase. There were only two items that he yearned for.

I currently have 2580 Coins. My old sword is 9700 Coins... but the remaining two crafting materials cost 10,000 Coins...

"Mister Hunter! Please look at my wares!"

A vendor shouted for his attention, but Sungjin paid no heed. He was deeply troubled by his dilemma.

Finish the book, or reunite with the old sword...

Sungjin was short by about 7500 Coins to purchase either of the two items. He would need to complete at least two more Raids to earn the required amount. Sungjin debated on which item to get first as he walked back to the Ninety-Nine Nights Inn.

*

Once he returned to Ninety-Nine Nights, he found that a familiar friend was waiting for him at the table. It was the wolf 'Grand Kin.'

"Woof." Cain barked once as if to greet Sungjin.

It was unexpected. But the Operator gave an explanation.

[Beings connected via Spiritual Link skill]

[Will be available at Ninety-Nine Nights from now on.]

Sungjin welcomed the information. He didn't feel comfortable with other people, but being able to spend time with a loyal companion like Cain had no downside.

Sungjin walked up to Cain and petted him.

"Cain... Let's go in and eat dinner or something."

Sungjin stepped into the inn and the owl demi-human Dalupin greeted him as always.

"Welcome back, Mister Hunter."

He bowed deeply until his back was nearly level with the floor.

"Ah, thanks."

"Awoo..."

Hearing an unfamiliar wolf voice, Dalupin turned his head around to look at Cain from his bowed position. Sungjiin was reminded that owl men could turn their neck around at 180 degrees.

"This wolf..."

Sungjin answered casually, "He's my ally. Please take care of him when I am not around."

"Understood, sir." Dalupin finally stood up straight and asked,

"You must be famished. What would you like for me to prepare today?"

Sungjin deliberated for a moment. "Sushi. Various kinds, about 20 pieces. Oh, and make about 5 fatty tuna."

Dalupin nodded. "Understood. I will prepare them right away."

"Ah... And raw meat for Cain. A good cut of beef around 500 grams. It's okay, right?"

Dalupin nodded once more. "Not a problem."

*

Sungjin picked up the last remaining piece of fatty tuna sushi with his chopsticks. He had been saving it for last. He dipped the tip of the rice in soy sauce before putting it in his mouth.

The soft meat of the tuna, with the perfect ratio of fat mixed in; it almost seemed sacrilegious to swallow such a perfectly prepared culinary masterpiece.

But eventually, the tuna was masticated and swallowed.

Should I order 5 more fatty tunas?

Sungjin considered his options for a while. After carefully weighing his options, he decided not to. If he overindulged on food today, it could cause problems in the Raid tomorrow.

Sungjin took a glance down once he was done eating. Cain finished his meal and licked his plate clean.

"I'll see you tomorrow, Cain."

Sungjin petted Cain one more time and returned upstairs. He asked the Operator as he took off his clothes.

"Operator, time left?"

[10 Hours 49 Minutes 21 Seconds until the next Raid.]

Until the next Raid, there were two things he had to do: distribute his stat points, and decide on a title.

Sungjin sank himself into the tub and called upon the Operator.

"What is my status right now?"

Title: Master Hunter
HP : 1500   MP : 220

Strength:	275	212	(+63)
Dexterity:	381	293	(+88)
Endurance:	150	115	(+35)
Magic Power:	18	14	(+4)
Mind Power:	22	17	(+5)

Unallocated points: 2200

2200 unallocated points after completing Chapter 2... I don't think my total Stat Points added up to 2000 after four Chapters last time, though...

It was certainly an incredible amount. It helped that Sungjin took the majority of the contribution points from both Chapter 1 and 2, as well as clearing them at 100% completion.

I guess it's because I did everything by myself...

The most important question that needed an answer now was how to distribute his stat points. After thinking about it carefully while idly splashing about in the tub, he decided to invest 700 into Strength, 800 into Dexterity, and 700 into Endurance.

The reason why such a high percentage of stat points went into Endurance was simple.

There will be mages starting with the next Chapter, thought Sungjin.

These were magical attacks that could not be dodged no matter how dexterous you were. In order to clear a Raid safely, investing in Endurance was necessary. Of course, investing so much into Endurance could lead to shortage in Attack Power, but...

If I really need to, I could always rely on Yahurat to get me through rough spots.

His next dilemma was what to do with the titles.

If I use Master Hunter, I receive bonus stats. If I use Treasure Hunter, the opportunity to find hidden pieces would increase...

It was a difficult decision. After much thought, Sungjin finally decided to keep Master Hunter for one more round.

The reason was that it was such an excellent title. Even at the final Chapter, Sungjin had never even heard of such a good title.

...I will decide on the Treasure Hunter after trying the active skill at least once. Couldn't hurt to wait and see first...

Sungjin finished his bath and wrapped up his thoughts. Fatigue from the battle today, and the subsequent relaxation at the bath, made him drowsy. He felt drawn to the bed and laid himself on its soft sheets. But...

KNOCK KNOCK

He heard a knocking at the door.

"Who is it?"

Dalupin answered from the other side, "Dear Hunter, it is the information pertaining to the next Raid."

I don't need it, though...

But Sungjin opened the door anyway. He felt it was against etiquette to refuse gestures of kindness. Especially against Dalupin, who provided him excellent meals and a place to lodge.

Once Sungjin opened the door, Dalupin handed him a piece of paper. Sungjin accepted the note and thanked the owl.

"Hope you have a restful evening," said Dalupin as he closed the door and left. Sungjin took a glance at the piece of paper. It goes without saying that there was no hint regarding the hidden piece or the hidden boss.

The information mostly pertained to terrain, the different kinds of monsters dwelling in the area, and the boss that ruled the place. Ordinary things. Everything that Sungjin already knew by experience.

Sungjin placed the paper on his bedside table. The title was illuminated by the lamp.

Information pertaining to the Greysoul Cemetery.

But he turned off the lamp. While other Hunters diligently studied the note, Sungjin laid on the bed and went to sleep.

Chapter 6 – Greysoul Cemetery

Next morning, Sungjin made his way down to the 1st floor of Ninety-Nine Nights and ordered his breakfast.

"Toast, and vanilla latte."

Right then he heard a bark and noticed Cain, whom he had forgotten about.

"Ah, that's right. Give Cain something too."

After ordering food for Cain, Sungjin took his feet out of his shoes and rested them on top of another chair. Dalupin left to prepare his breakfast.

While munching away on the toast and vanilla latte, Sungjin thought of the next Raid, Greysoul Cemetery and felt his appetite draining.

That's not really a place I wanted to return to...

Sungjin put down his half-eaten toast and left the Ninety-Nine Nights with his latte.

Cain also, as expected, followed him out. The weather was beautiful. The Black Market could be seen in the distance.

Should I buy some Holy water now?

The thought ran through his mind. But he needed to save every Black Coin he could muster so that he could purchase a Legendary item later on.

"Operator, remaining time?"

[3 Minutes 12 Seconds.]

There was still some time left before the Raid. Sungjin downed the rest of his latte and returned to the table he'd had his breakfast at. He decided to allocate his points the way he had planned last night.

"Operator, allocate 700 to Strength, 800 to Dexterity, and 700 to Endurance."

[Strength has risen by 700, Dexterity by 800, and Endurance by 700 points.]

Sungjin was now prepared mentally for the upcoming Raid. No matter how high his stat points were, it was no easy feat to finish the Chapters at 100% completion.

Especially alone.

Soon, the Operator began her countdown.

[Raid will begin shortly. 10, 9, 8]

Sungjin briefly pet familiar.

"See you in a bit, Cain."

And after a moment, he disappeared from Ninety-Nine Nights.

*

Late at night, worn-out street lamps dimly illuminated the surroundings, casting shadows upon the rows of tombstones nearby. A crow flew off of a twisted, dried-up tree devoid of leaf or life.

"Caw Caw~"

The place Sungjin was teleported to was an eerie cemetery. The Operator began her explanations.

[Hello. Welcome to Greysoul Cemetery.]

[It is a place filled with regrets and grudges of the dead.]

[As announced before, starting with this Chapter,]

[there will be no more tutorials, and the Raids will begin right away.]

...I can never get used to this place...

Sungjin took a look around his surroundings and licked his lips. It still tasted sweet from the vanilla latte.

[Synchronizing Hunters.]

The space around Sungjin blurred for a moment, and four Hunters emerged. Sungjin read the titles before even looking at the teammates themselves.

Bear Hunter, Mid-Level Samurai, Scout, Veteran Spearman.

Oh

This time there were two impressive titles. Mid-Level Samurai and Veteran Spearman.

Sungjin inspected the owners of the two titles. Anyone could tell that the Mid-Level Samurai was a Japanese man.

He looked to be about in his early twenties, maybe even younger than Sungjin. He had grown out his chin hair and had shaved part of his eyebrows to make the tips pointy. Of China, Japan, and Korea, only Japanese men would sport such a look at such an early age.

I guess he's a real Samurai.

Sungjin took a look at the Veteran Spearman. This man was completely black.

Compared to black men in America or Europe, his skin tone was of an even darker shade. It was hard to make out his features due to the dim lighting, but the whites of his eyes were prominently visible.

I think...he's African.

The last two individuals lacked anything noteworthy about themselves. The Bear Hunter was a tall westerner, and the Scout was a thin, agile-looking man. He guessed that he was probably from India.

Sungjin was checking the vibe of the group. If it was going to be awful, he wanted to tell them,

Gather as four and go hunt small mobs.

Just like he had done with the others until now. But before he got his words out, the Mid-Level Samurai stepped forward and stole the show.

"Hey, you four should group up and hunt trash. I'll go and solo the boss in a flash!"

The other four, including Sungjin, stared at the Samurai. Sungjin especially so.

The Samurai had invested well into his equipment. From top to bottom, he wore Normal to Rare items.

The Katana he held appeared fairly high spec. It was probably an item sold in the Last Edge. Sungjin couldn't help but think, *He sure bought a lot of things.*

He must have been an ace in the other Raids, carrying his team. The Scout Indian man piped in. "Well... isn't it better if we... stick together?"

"Yes, I agree. Chinese kid, no matter how strong you are, wouldn't we be stronger if we all worked together?" The Bear Hunter agreed with the Scout.

With the exception of the Mid-Level Samurai, the rest of the team seemed rather agreeable.

"Hey! Don't you see the Katana and the title? I am Japanese! Japanese! Anyway, sure, we can go together. But, when we face the boss, stand back. No matter how hard you try, I'm going to take the highest contribution."

Sungjin reflected over his actions.

Was I... like that...?

Chapter 3 – Greysoul Cemetery Raid
Objective – Hunt the Lich 'Deathmond'
Time Limit: 25 Minutes

[Complete the objective within the Time Limit.]

[If you cannot, you will die.]

[The Raid begins in 3 minutes.]

Once the Operator completed her mission briefing, the Bear Hunter said, "Well, I think we should introduce ourselves before we begin. We are going to be fighting for our lives, and trying to yell 'Hey, Master Hunter, help me!' might take too long."

The white man was looking up at Sungjin's title above his head.

"I will start. My name is Henrik Sondegaard. Since my family name is long, please just call me Henrik. What are your names?"

Henrik must have been from the Northern Europe.

"Kultu. I am from Nepal."

The man Sungjin assumed to be from India was actually from Nepal. And finally the Mid-Level Samurai.

"My name is Watanabe Hiroaki. Shorten my name and call me Hiro."

What a lively youth, thought Sungjin.

Until now, he should have been through life and death struggles, forced to kill or be killed, yet he maintained such a positive attitude. He must be like this naturally.

The only two remaining men who didn't reveal their names were the Master Hunter Sungjin and the Veteran Spearman. Once the three men stared at him, Sungjin spat out words he had prepared beforehand.

"I am K."

Henrik nodded.

"Ok. Kei."

He must have liked that his name was short. The last one remaining was the Veteran Spearman. But he only stared blankly. After he had taken turns looking at the others, he said,

"Akanna."

And thus the introductions were over. The Bear Hunter Henrik did his best to rally the team and exert leadership.

"Let's work hard together. Don't we all have a family we wish to save?"

The Mid-Level Samurai gripped his hands hard at Henrik's words. "Yes. My mother and sister are being held by them..."

Sungjin thought Hiro was perhaps not as crazy as he first seemed. The Nepali, Kultu, also nodded.

"I probably have the largest family to save. Since there are thirty members in my immediate family."

Once again, Sungjin and the African were the last ones left. Sungjin, in particular, didn't have anything to say; he had grown up in an orphanage. The people the Operator showed him as a ransom for clearing the Raids were just some orphanage workers.

They were good people, but it was nothing like a parent. No one knew what Akanna thought. He only blinked his eyes with a vacant stare. He did not speak up.

It wasn't like he couldn't speak, nor was he unable to understand. He didn't seem normal.

[The Raid begins in 1 minute.]

The Operator informed the group about the remaining time. Now, the other men became nervous.

"You read the information pamphlet, right? Arrows don't work against skeletons. I will deal with the skeletons with my axe, so please take care of the zombies and ghouls if I am busy."

"Understood."

Hiro approached Sungjin meanwhile.

"Hey, Kei, what country are you from? You're definitely not Japanese. Chinese? Korean? Probability wise, you're most likely to be Chinese, but I feel like you might be Korean."

Hiro might have been interested in Sungjin for choosing the same weapon. Sungjin continued to stare expressionlessly, but Hiro did not stop there.

"Wait, you're still using the Basic Katana! Where did you spend all of your Black Coins? And what is that shackle for? Why are you swinging your sword while being bound with chains?"

Sungjin frowned.

...Annoying.

Even though Sungjin did not give a single word in reply, Hiro continued to speak.

"I actually finished 1st place in Kendo Regional Championship in Osaka. After taking the regional title, I was preparing for the Nationals, but I ended up here instead."

That last part sounded interesting. Sungjin had also taken Kendo. If Hiro had taken first place in Osaka, he must have had considerable skill. So Sungjin gave a single word of reply.

"So... that's how you got the title of Mid-Level Samurai."

"Yeah! This Operator or whatever has good eyes. This title is awesome. It gives 20% increased damage to all attacks done by a Katana. How is it? Amazing, isn't it?"

Sungjin was at a loss for words. He wanted nothing less than to quickly kill the boss and search for the hidden boss.

"What's that title, though? Master Hunter? It sounds really cool. What are the effects?"

Sungjin sighed. "Go get it. You'll know then."

"Yeah, I'm going to smash this Raid or whatever! I'll take all the titles and all the items!"

His confidence was great. But his contribution from this particular Raid wasn't going to be high at all. Unless Sungjin decided not to participate.

How should I proceed with this Raid? Sungjin took a quick glance at the others. These were all somewhat talented individuals with potential. At their level, they should be able to survive this Chapter without protection.

Problem is contribution...

But the most important factor was 'Who are the last few survivors at the end.' There was no reason to be considerate with every random stranger he met at the beginning.

Because the chances of them surviving to the end was minuscule. The only ones who are needed to complete all Raids and objectives are the final few individuals.

To eliminate uncertainty caused by having to rely on good teammates and cooperation, he needed to be overwhelmingly powerful. Enough to finish all the Raids solo if need be.

Sungjin decided on his course of actions. And just like he had done every time, he let the others know.

"I... will go alone."

And as was with Hiro, the others turned to look at him.

"Truthfully, I am more of a lone wolf. If there is any need of my assistance, I will come to help. Please... stick together as a group of four and hunt only the normal monsters."

Henrik, who tried hard to encourage teamwork, was shocked. "What? What's wrong now? Why are you saying this?"

Kultu also chimed in. "He's right. Isn't it better to hunt together?"

Hiro was actually impressed. "Ho... Kei. How cool. Alright! It's a race!"

Finally, the Operator began her countdown.

[The Raid begins in 10 seconds. 10,]

113

Sungjin took out his Katana, and stood in front of the gates of Greysoul Cemetery.

[9, 8, 7]

Henrik tried one more time to change Sungjin's mind.

"Hey, Kei, don't do this. Let's talk about this."

But Sungjin only turned to say

"I can't. This Raid... It's like this."

Henrik's eyes grew wide. Sungjin felt pangs of guilt.

"Just... consider me a troll. You probably had one or two until now."

[3, 2, 1, 0]

And the moment the gates opened, Sungjin ran ahead. Alone.

***

Once Sungjin was gone, the remaining four people decided to work together as a group.

"Yeah, just leave it to me. I got this!"

Hiro was too talkative.

"..."

Akanna was too quiet. But regardless of their differences, they agreed to stick together to clear the graveyard.

In the front stood Henrik with his axe and Hiro with his Katana. In the middle, stood Akanna with his spear, and in the back stood Kultu with his bow.

Before entering the cemetery, Henrik and Kultu both took out the lantern they had prepared.

"What's that?" asked Hiro.

Henrik answered matter of factly. "What, this lantern? It was on the information page, you know. It says the cemetery is dark so you should buy a lantern at the Black Market."

Hiro tilted his head. "Is that so?"

Akanna also blinked with a blank expression. Henrik shook his head as he spoke,

"Mine in the front and Kultu's lantern in the back, we'll probably be okay with the lighting. Let's just go."

Henrik made his way toward the cemetery. Sometime later,

"Grrah!"

Several zombies appeared.

"Zombies!" shouted Henrik.

"Alright!" Hiro fearlessly ran ahead.

"Wait!" called Henrik. He had been planning on watching his enemies and responding defensively, but it didn't like it was possible anymore. Hesitantly, he ran forward to assist Hiro. However, Hiro proved to be better than he thought.

He wielded his blade as if possessed. Once the zombies reached his strike zone, their arms and legs were cut off and sent flying. When the zombies stumbled and fell due to the loss of their legs, they were beheaded with a lightning-fast attack before they even hit the ground.

Henrik instinctively swallowed. *I see why he's acting so cocky.*

While he was distracted, a zombie charged at him. Henrik instinctively swung his axe and cut off the zombie's wrist without resistance.

But this became a problem. A living being would have hesitated from pain, but the zombie continued to charge at Henrik, disregarding the physical harm.

Henrik, having just finished his attack motion, was in no position to defend himself. He was vulnerable to the zombie's bite. A moment of peril.

"Aho!" Akanna's long spear penetrated the zombie's head through its face and he charged at the monsters.

"Iho!"

Whenever Akanna thrust his spear, he shouted out strange words and holes appeared on a zombie's face.

The zombies hit in the face by his spear all fell powerlessly on the spot without being able to so much as wave their arms. Thanks to the spirited fighting by the two men, Henrik and Kultu did not have much to do.

"Orya!"

"Kaho!"

All Henrik and Kultu could do was provide light for Hiro and Akanna to fight properly.

"Alright, Henrik! Bring the light a little closer please!"

At least, Hiro actually needed the light to fight.

"Ahoho!"

Akanna would run into the impenetrable darkness alone, then kill the zombies on his own.

"What the hell am I watching?"

Henrik, who had lived in Copenhagen all his life, had difficulty adjusting to what he was witnessing.

But thanks to the effort of the other two men, Henrik and Kultu could progress through the Raid without much trouble.

Sometimes ghouls, which were faster than zombies, would threaten Henrik and Kultu. But whenever they were in danger, Hiro and Akanna protected them from harm.

Henrik thanked the two of them.

"Thanks to you two... I think we will be able to clear this Raid without much trouble. Of course, we will have to see the boss first to know... but from what I could see, we should be enough. The real concern is that teenager Kei from earlier. I worry about what might have happened to him."

However, Hiro's expressions were strange. He spoke as if he was put off by something.

"Yeah, I guess so... But isn't something weird here? This round?"

"What's weird?" asked Henrik.

"I mean... well, I guess something like... the number and strength of the monsters... Don't you feel that somehow it's even easier than Ahenna's Forest?"

Kultu agreed with Hiro's observations.

"I think you're right. Compared to the endless wave of wolves from the previous Raid, there does seem to be too few enemies in this

Raid. There are ghouls too... but bears were far more threatening. Is it because we haven't entered too deep inside yet?"

"Ig."

Akanna interrupted the conversation by making strange noises. Henrik looked over to him.

"What is it, Akanna? Do you have something to say?"

Akanna wordlessly motioned for Henrik's lantern. Henrik understood his gestures and obediently handed it over. But the question remained.

"Akanna, you... I thought you didn't need light to see?"

"Ig Ig."

Akanna left the other three and ran off somewhere. He then stopped and put the lantern down on the ground. The other three men opened their mouths in surprise.

"What the..."

Not far from where they had fought, there was an unimaginable number of zombie and ghoul corpses lying around. Henrik walked up to Akanna and picked up his lantern. He looked around the area with the lantern held low to the ground.

There he found not only corpses of ghouls and zombies, but also chopped-up remains of skeletons as well. Henrik murmured to himself, overwhelmed by the implications.

"What in the world..."

*

Sungjin wielded his Katana like a bolt of lightning.

"Kueueu~"

In a single strike, two zombies were cut down at once. The blood and bile splashed all over Sungjin's face.

"Krraaa Graahh" Smelling the thick scent of blood, ghouls appeared from nowhere. Their deeply bent back, jagged and uneven teeth, and rotting flesh painted a disturbing picture.

Sungjin instinctively swung his Katana. Anything that his sword touched was cut apart without resistance, spewing disgusting unidentifiable liquids everywhere.

There were largely two main complaints about the Greysoul Cemetery. One was that the enemies were smelly and gross—mostly zombies and ghouls.

The second was that these things were only dangerous when overrunning their opponents with sheer numbers. Although they did not pose any significant threat to Sungjin, fighting them was in no way hygienic.

I can't wait to clear this map.

It was already his second time, but he couldn't get used to this. Hidden piece or not, he just wanted the Raid to end.

As soon as he found a red magic circle hidden within the cemetery, he would be able to locate the boss monster, Deathmond. Kill the boss with all due haste, and search for the hidden piece. That was his plan.

"Where was that again?"

But he couldn't remember where the magic circle was located. Greysoul Cemetery was far too dark, so dark that it was hard to tell where anything was.

Last time, the five of them had roamed the cemetery aimlessly until they accidentally stumbled onto the magic circle and just barely beat the boss within the time frame.

Maybe I should have bought a lantern

Without a doubt, the information pamphlet about Greysoul Cemetery would have urged the Hunters to purchase at least one lantern.

He, once again, penny pinched too hard to save money to buy Legendary-tier items later on. Recalling something, Sungjin called upon the Operator.

"Operator."

[Yes, esteemed Hunter?]

"Take out the Salamander's ash that I received as reward last time'

A package appeared on top of the cube on command. It was a reward he had received from Ahenna's Forest. Sungjin lifted it up.

Salamander's ash
Normal Consumable item

Special Effect: Flame (I)
Flame(I) – imbues an item with a weak flame. 5 minute duration.

Ash collected from a dead fire lizard, Salamander.
It is said that there is a place in the world where Salamanders are raised on a farm to be harvested for their ash.

Sungjin rubbed the ash over his Katana. Soon, Sungjin's weapon lit up on flames, illuminating the surroundings.

Quite useful, thought Sungjin.

It was an item originally meant to be used to strengthen attack power, but Sungjin treated it as nothing more than a source of light.

His damage was already high enough. Selling the Salamander's ash only gave back a single Black Coin. With the five-minute duration, he was confident that it was plenty of time for him to find Deathmond.

CLACK CLACK

Perhaps it was due to the burning Katana that an army of skeletons was marching toward him. Sungjin preferred these guys, though; at least they didn't have rotting flesh and blood.

Instead, they each carried spears, swords, or axes. And it goes without saying that they were no match for Sungjin's speed.

Wielding the Katana in one hand and the scabbard in another, Sungjin fought as if performing two-handed sword style combat. Cutting and bashing.

No matter what Sungjin used to hit them, he shattered the bones to pieces. Once the enemies were destroyed, Sungjin paused to look up at the night sky.

The moon was nowhere to be seen. He had no sense of directions. He didn't know where he came from or where he needed to go.

I don't know where that Magic circle is. What should I do?

Sungjin pondered for a moment before coming to a plan of action; brute force everything and search as wide and as quickly as possible.

If he ran into enemies, then it was a place he hadn't been to, and if it was an area filled with corpses, then it was a place he had searched before.

Although Sungjin was sick and tired of creating mountains of zombie and ghoul corpses, he decided to swallow back his disgust and do it all over again.

*

"Did that... Kei person, do all this by himself?" Henrik asked in disbelief. Hiro replied,

"Who else could it be?"

He sounded angry.

"Well, I guess it is a good thing as long as we clear the Raid, right?" Henrik consoled him, but Hiro kept his arms crossed and remained quiet. It appeared as though he felt some sort of rivalry between Sungjin and himself.

The four Hunters fought with the 'survivors' as they searched through the Greysoul Cemetery. When suddenly,

"Eh?"

Akanna stopped on the spot. He could see far into the darkness. The others tensed up, but he put down his spear

"Amero hum manieh damondi!"

He fell to his knees and started bowing feverishly. The others looked over to see what he could be bowing to. There, they saw a person in the distance clad in a white dress.

"Eek! EEEE!" Hiro started screaming like a woman and hid behind Henrik.

"What... what's wrong?"

Hiro answered Henrik's question. "G... Ghost!"

Henrik looked over again and spotted the white-clothed person. Pale face, long hair and white dress. She was approaching them.

But her motions were too smooth. When he looked carefully, he saw that there were no feet under the hems. Henrik tried to encourage Hiro.

"We should f-fight then!"

Hiro held onto Henrik's clothes and murmured, "G... ghosts are scary!"

Akanna continued to pray and chant.

"Raome kani besemeres."

Henrik was starting to panic. The two aces of the team showed zero will to fight and were behaving strangely.

Henrik looked over to the ghost again. Even now, the ghost without legs was gliding toward them.

***

Henrik raised his axe and shouted, "Kultu!"

"I got it!"

At least Kultu was still acting sane. The ghost approached very slowly. Kultu knocked his arrow and carefully aimed for the ghost's head. Pulling back on the string, and then letting go of the arrow, he let it fly.

PEW

The arrow flew straight and true. But when it reached the ghost, it simply passed through it.

"...Damn it, what are we supposed to do...?" Henrik looked around him briefly.

"I'm so scared!" Hiro continued to cower behind him, hanging on to the hem of his shirt.

"Labeh ahondi russo oh," Akanna continued to chant and bow.

"What should we do?" Kultu stared at him, terrified. There was no one dependable. Henrik looked ahead again. The female ghost was now nearly upon them.

Henrik tightly gripped his axe. It was the only thing he could depend on. Pale face, crimson lips, bloodshot eyes. For a moment, Henrik and the ghost stared at each other.

"Huh..."

Henrik had been planning to swing his axe as soon as the ghost approached close enough. But once he looked into the ghost's eyes, he froze up. He found that he could not move.

The ghost stopped moving closer as well. She raised one arm and let out a strange noise. "Hyaaaaa..."

Come on, move!

Henrik commanded his body to defend itself, but he couldn't shake off the petrifying terror taking over his body. But after a few seconds, the ghost turned around and left in the direction she pointed.

Once she disappeared, Henrik was able to move again after a moment. Finally, he let out a sigh of relief. "Hah... what was that?"

"Is it gone?" asked Hiro.

Kultu answered Hiro's question. "Eh? It's just leaving without doing anything?"

Once the ghost left,

"Emma gordi sabath," Akanna stopped chanting and stood back up.

Everyone else turned to look at him. And for the first time, Akanna spoke words they understood.

"Thank you, blessed ancestor!"

Henrik was shocked and blurted out, "What? Akanna can speak!"

Akanna closed his mouth in response and blinked few times. Henrik was at a loss for words.

Kultu spoke up, "Excuse me, but since the ghost is gone... let's get moving again. It's been about 10 minutes since the Raid began. Shouldn't we go and clear it?"

Henrik snapped himself awake and fixed his grip on the lantern. "Y... yeah... I guess that ghost was not a monster."

The four men quickly moved from the spot. They did not wish to remain long where the ghost had appeared. But...

"Awooo~"

They heard a wolf's cry in the distance. It was a sound none of them had wanted to hear again after completing Chapter 2.

"Wait... was that a wolf?" asked Hiro.

Kultu also tilted his head and asked, "There are wolves in the cemetery?"

Henrik bit his lips. This Chapter had too many surprises. He didn't know what to expect.

*

Sungjin searched feverishly through the Greysoul Cemetery. Already 'living' monsters were becoming difficult to find.

In other words, he was running in circles. But he didn't have any other choice; it was so dark in Greysoul Cemetery that it was difficult to tell right from left.

Finally, the flame on the Katana went out; 5 minutes had elapsed. Sungjin was plunged into the oppressive darkness once more.

Wait, 5 minutes passed already? I don't have much time...!

Sungjin called the Operator out of instinct.

"Operator."

[Yes?]

"Give me..."

He was about to ask for another Salamander's ash when he remembered that he had Cain.

Ah... right...

[Please go on]

"Ah, never mind."

Sungjin reached into his pocket to retrieve a small wolf figurine. He threw it in the air.

Before reaching the ground, the small figurine transformed into a large wolf. Sungjin couldn't help but smile looking at Cain.

Wolves have superior night vision.

"Awooo~"

Cain, who made an appearance for the first time in a Raid, let out a long, drawn-out howl to announce his presence. Sungjin walked up to Cain.

"Cain, it's too dark for me to see properly so help me comb through the area. We're searching for an altar with a red pentagram. Understood? It should resemble a pile of rocks."

Cain let out short barks to convey that he understood.

"Search for corpses... not the unmoving ones on the ground, but the ones that are still moving. Seeking out surviving enemies should lead us to the boss."

Sungjin tried to explain in detail, but Cain had already begun his search. Sungjin followed behind Cain's wagging tail.

After a while, Cain stopped and bared his teeth letting out a warning.

"What did you find, Cain?"

CREAK CLICK

Sungjin caught up with Cain, and from afar heard the sounds of ghouls and skeletons. Enemies. The numbers were great. Cain must have growled to warn Sungjin of what was ahead. Sungjin drew out his Katana.

*

"Sigh... No enemies..."

Hiro complained about the lack of enemies to fight. Henrik agreed with him.

"Yeah..."

Henrik preferred safety over recklessness, but Hiro was right. Once in a while, the group would run across some bones or rotting tissue, but they were always found to be ripped apart to pieces.

And while wandering around bored, the four Hunters heard another strange noise.

SHING! WOOF! KAACK

It was a sound of conflict. The Hunters gazed toward the source. Henrik looked at each of the other Hunters and asked, "Should we go check it out?"

No one refused. Since the run-in with the ghost, they had not seen a single enemy alive. They headed toward the source of the conflict.

"Peerless Warrior."

Akanna said his second coherent sentence. The Hunters raised their lantern high and continued to walk toward the commotion.

And soon, they were able to see Kei fight. He, who wielded his Katana with a speed and power that rivalled bolts of lightning.

Each swing of his blade cut apart three or four zombies.

Ghouls attempted to launch surprise attacks from his blind spot from time to time, but Sungjin seemed to have eyes on the back of his head; he would stop them with his scabbard and bisect them with his Katana's follow-up attack.

"Krrruughaaggg."

In the face of Sungjin's mighty blade, ghouls were cut away like pieces of paper.

A skeleton attempted to stab Sungjin with a spear, but Sungjin dodged it easily by leaning back.

Cain followed up with a charge knocking the skeleton down. The skeleton struggled for a moment on the floor, but the wolf ripped it apart with its claws.

"Wow..." Henrik whispered in awe. Hiro was good, but only when judged as a human being.

What he witnessed in Kei's fight was beyond the level of a mere human being; it was like watching a War God of Old.

Hiro. Henrik remembered Hiro and turned to look at him. Hiro was watching the fight with his mouth agape as well.

I wonder what he's feeling right now.

And by the time he finished his thoughts, the commotion ended. The sound of fighting stopped, and Henrik looked over to Sungjin. He was surrounded by nothing but corpses.

Kei frowned as he wiped off the blood and gore from his Katana. The wolf next to him turned to look at them briefly before barking.

"Awo."

Kei finally turned to look at the four Hunters. "Ah... You've come."

But,

"Grrr"

The wolf next to him bared its fangs threateningly. Kei noticed and chastised the wolf.

"Hey, don't do that, Cain. These Hunters are not enemies."

At his words, the wolf relaxed and walked in between Sungjin's legs. He was tame and loyal to his master. After telling off his wolf, Sungjin looked up.

*

Sungjin quickly did a mental head count.

One, two, three, four

Evidently, no one had died. No one seemed particularly injured. He didn't have a chance to see, but most likely the Veteran Spearman and the Mid-Level Samurai had protected the group well.

It is a rather talented group, thought Sungjin.

Unbeknownst to him, the main reason for their safety was that nearly all the monsters had been annihilated by his hands. The European standing at the front approached him and began to speak.

"That was amazing back there, Kei."

Sungjin welcomed him. "I am glad that all of you are fine."

"I can't believe how skilled you were... Enough to survive alone," continued Henrik.

"Ah, thanks." Sungjin glossed over his praises. There were more important things to discuss. He pointed out the pile of rocks forming an altar and spoke,

"So... I am about to go for the boss... What would you like to do?"

It was the Magic Summoning circle used to summon Lich Deathmond. It had been discovered by Cain while searching through the darkness.

The European man saw the altar and tensed up. The Japanese boy next to him stepped forward.

"What do you mean? We fight."

The African man behind them continued to stare with a blank face.

The Nepali behind the whole group seemed anxious. Sungjin directed his words to him.

"Well, I won't ask you not to participate. But even I can't fight and protect at the same time. If you don't feel like you can handle it, please feel free to drop out of the fight. In fact, it'll be okay if you don't participate at all; I can clear the Raid for us."

The boss, Lich Deathmond, was a troublesome enemy; he used magic attacks. Many strong individuals had met their sudden demise by his magic.

At his words, the European, Henrik, and the Nepali, Kultu, stepped back. Only three remained.

Sungjin, Hiro, and the African, Akanna. Sungjin quickly glanced over them.

Well... at the very least they're not at a level where they would do more harm than good.

Sungjin stood in front of the altar. On top, a satanic pentagram was drawn.

Arranged at its center were ribs and pelvic bones emitting blue lights.

"Hey, Samurai, there should be some blue glowing bones laying around. Go get them for me."

Hiro silently gathered the bones as Sungjin asked. Sungjin also searched and found three blueish bones.

Right femur, right humerus, and the skull. The Samurai brought the left humerus and the left femur. Sungjin pointed toward the magic circle and explained.

"Arrange those on the pentagram over there. The body forms the center, so place those two bones on the left side. You understand, right?"

And as instructed, the Samurai placed the bones on the left side of the ribs and pelvic bone.

Sungjin followed suit and placed the right femur and humerus on the pentagram. He paused for a moment before turning to the other two Hunters.

"Get ready, Mid-Level Samurai and Veteran Spearman."

The two men nodded slightly. Sungjin placed the last piece, the skull, on the pentagram.

The red magic circle lit up, casting shadows all around. The bones began to reattach themselves to each other. The Operator gave out an announcement.

[Caution! Boss Monster]

[Lich Deathmond has appeared!]

***

With the ribs and the pelvic bone at the center, the skull, scapula, humerus, and femur attached themselves to the existing skeletal structure.

Once the bones settled in their proper locations, smaller bones such as the fingers and toes came to attach themselves to existing pieces, soon forming the shape of a human.

Blue strands emerged from the skull and entangled the bones, and a staff emerged from the top of the altar and flew into its hands. The jaws began to move.

"Come, those who are fated to die."

As soon as he spoke, Sungjin who had been waiting with his Katana drawn, charged at him.

Lich Deathmond was a mage. To combat enemies who used magic, it was essential to attack them with all due haste before they could complete their incantations.

Seeing Sungjin move, the Lich lifted up his left hand and shouted, "Frozen wall, to me! Ice Shield!"

A blue crystal wall appeared in front of Sungjin. But Sungjin cut down the wall without hesitation.

The wall of ice split in half and fell apart. The Lich quickly tried to swing his right arm holding the staff but, Cain leaped up and bit the staff, holding on. Taking advantage of the opening created by Cain's surprise attack, Sungjin quickly swung his blade.

Caught off guard, the Lich's left arm was cut to pieces and sent flying.

The Lich floated up slightly and leaped back. Sungjin wanted to press in to continue the attack, but the Lich began chanting.

"Push away my enemies! Gust!"

The Lich's short incantation was followed by a powerful gust of wind. There was no damage, but Sungjin, who was in the air, was carried by the wind and pushed away from the Lich.

At the same time Sungjin landed on his feet, Hiro launched his attack on the Lich's right arm.

"Ice Shield." The Lich summoned another ice wall. Hiro tried to cut through the block of ice like Sungjin had before him.

With a crack, the Katana clashed with the wall, but the cut was too shallow. Hiro's Katana stopped halfway through the ice.

"What?" Hiro shouted out in surprise.

The Lich took the time to cast another spell. "Piercing spears of ice! Ice Lance!"

The Lich's staff formed three icicles in the air around it. Once they took shape and solidified, the icicles flew toward Hiro, who was still struggling to free his Katana from the Ice wall.

Hiro hastily pulled his Katana free from the wall and deflected the icicles. He knocked one out of the air, and then another, and then...

"Kuh!"

Hiro didn't manage to block the third icicle and was stabbed in the stomach, falling over.

But Hiro's actions were not in vain. While he was dealing with the Boss's magic attacks,

"Ho!" Akanna appeared from the darkness and shattered the Lich's right arm holding the staff. Upon losing both the arms,

"Gust!" The Lich called forth his wind magic once more to push Akanna back.

"Defy gravity! Flight!"

The Lich then lifted up into the sky. And with the three Hunters watching, the legs fell off from the hips and attached themselves to the elbows.

It was a strange sight to see: arms replaced by legs, with feet where hands used to be. The staff flew up from the ground and placed itself between the toes.

"Cold which burns, blade that severs! Scythe of Ice!"

Upon his incantations, a large blade formed on the tip of the staff, like those of Grim Reaper.

Cain began to growl upon seeing the Lich's scythe.

2nd Phase... alright.

Sungjin fixed the grip on his Katana.

"Uho!" Akanna turned his spear around and readied his combat stance. Hiro gulped down a potion as quickly as he could.

Once the Lich was done transforming, it returned to the ground. Sungjin, Akanna, and Hiro all charged at the Lich simultaneously.

The Lich moved back as it swung the scythe. Due to the staff's length, the length of its legs, and the length of the humerus, the reach of the Lich's attack was enormous.

And because the Lich continuously swung his scythe, no one, not even Sungjin could easily approach him. Taking advantage of the Hunters' hesitation, the Lich recited an incantation.

"Spreading death, Orb of Ice"

A small spherical orb appeared on the Lich's hands and started floating toward the Hunters. The orb was moving even slower than it looked.

It was doubtful whether it would hit anyone who was paying attention. Then, Sungjin recalled something from his past.

I've seen that before...

And the moment he recalled just what it was, he shouted as he threw himself onto the floor.

"Get down!"

The orb exploded and scattered shrapnel everywhere. Sungjin braced himself. There was no way to avoid all the debris.

But, Sungjin felt no pain after the explosion. When he raised his head, he saw a whimpering Cain standing over him bleeding; pieces of shrapnel were embedded all over his body.

Wrath took Sungjin's heart, and he leaped to his feet, infuriated. Hiro and Akanna both were hurt and couldn't move properly. Sungjin charged at the Lich alone.

The Lich swung his scythe like a whip, but Sungjin dodged every swing and moved closer to the Lich. Once Sungjin got close enough, the Lich hurriedly recited an incantation.

"Ice Shield."

But the ice wall could not hold up to Sungjin's blade guided by anger. The wall crumbled away to nothing. In moments, Sungjin bisected the Lich's arms (made of leg bones).

"Gust!"

The Lich, who was now without arms or legs, retreated after reciting the incantations. Just the skull and the torso were left. Sungjin dashed forward to finish off the boss.

"Oryah!"

"Oh Ho!"

Behind Sungjin, Akanna and Hiro got up and also charged together. The Lich saw the three Hunters and began an incantation.

"Cold which obstructs! Frostbite!"

Ice pillars emerged from the ground and froze the Hunter's feet to the ground. The Lich attempted to use the opportunity to shout an incantation, but,

"Free Ark!"

The shackle on Sungjin's arm gave off a brilliant light, and the ice holding his feet gave way without resistance.

Freeing himself of the magical bindings, Sungjin sped toward the boss like a bullet. The Lich, who assumed the Frostbite would last a bit longer, called out,

"Wind which freezes all, ice which rips everything apart!"

Because Sungjin had freed himself in an instant and charged toward him, he wasn't able to complete the spell.

"Blizzard Sto—"

Sungjin, in his extreme anger, cut the Lich from the bottom up; Starting from the tailbone and reaching all the way to the jawbone, he cut the boss monster in half.

[Objective complete. Returning to Hunter's Hall in 17 Minutes and 52 Seconds.]

The cube announced victory, but Sungjin was not happy at all. He walked up to Cain, who was laying on the ground.

Cain was bleeding out and dying. Shortly after, he disappeared with a BANG and returned to the form of a wooden carving. Sungjin picked up the figurine.

"Thank you, Cain... You worked hard."

After a moment, Sungjin placed the figurine in his pocket.

*

[Objective complete. Returning to Hunter's Hall in 17 Minutes and 52 Seconds.]

Once they heard the announcements, Henrik and Kultu came back to see the other three men.

"Good work, all of you. Are you alright though?" asked Henrik and he was right to be worried. Akanna and Hiro were dripping with blood. Shards of ice still pierced their skin in many places, and small and large cuts covered their bodies.

Only Kei was left devoid of cuts and bruises. Kei swung his Katana few times and then turned to leave. But,

"Kei... No. Kei Sama."

Hiro stopped Kei. Kei turned to see what Hiro wanted. Hiro got down to the ground and gave a deep bow on his hands and knees.

"I, Watanabe Hiroaki of 20 years of age, have been shown new heights of greatness. I wish to make you my sensei, so please accept me as your pupil."

Kei looked uncomfortable... no, he looked alarmed. "What are you talking about? We're going our separate ways after this Chapter..."

But Hiro was insistent.

"Please accept me as your pupil anyway. You never know if we will meet each other again in another Chapter."

Kei returned his sword to the scabbard and replied, "Even if you say that, there is no option other than to become stronger on your own."

Even though the Chapter was completed safely, Sungjin looked distraught. Suddenly he called to the Operator.

"Operator, how much time left?"

[You will return to the Hunter's Hall in 17 Minutes and 24 Seconds.]

After asking for the time, Sungjin turned to leave. Hiro, who had his forehead touching the ground, looked up and stood up to follow.

"Sensei, where are you going? I will go with you."

The other two people, Henrik and Kultu, looked at each other. The Boss monster had been killed, but there was bound to be more undead mobs remaining somewhere.

In other words, the safest place right now was standing close to Sungjin.

"Let's go too."

The two men understood each other without communicating. They, too, followed Sungjin. Akanna briefly wiped the blood off of his face and followed behind the others.

The other Hunters followed Kei like a shadow. Hiro stayed close to Kei and continued to try and make conversation with him.

"Sensei, please give me one word of advice. How can I become powerful like you?"

Sungjin finally broke the silence and half-heartedly gave a response. "The Operator already said how. Increase your stats, get good items... And stuff."

He recited a textbook answer.

133

"Do you have no comment about my Kendo skills?"

Sungjin bit his lips for a moment and pondered, but he gave another half-hearted answer in the end.

"Just do a lot of fighting. Forget everything you learned at the Dojo."

"Excuse me?"

Sungjin explained himself. "We're not fighting humans. We fight monsters. Real combat experience here is more important."

"Ah... Thank you for your teachings, Sensei."

Sungjin shook his head at Hiro's words and continued to comb through the area. And along the way-

"Sensei? Where are you headed to anyway? Don't go too far. There's a ghost that may appear somewhere ahead."

Sungjin, who had been responding in a half bored and half annoyed manner, changed his tone of voice. He stopped in his tracks and turned to interrogate Hiro.

"What ghost?"

Seeing Sungjin's sudden spike in interest, Hiro excitedly explained what he knew.

"Well, you know, a female ghost like those you see in scary movies. With pale skin and blood dripping from the lips..."

Sungjin took hold of Hiro's shoulders and spoke once more.

"Where did you see it?"

"Way over there! Right before we saw the boss. It was flying around that area. You know, it's pretty hard to tell where we were, though..."

Sungjin glanced at Kultu and Henrik. The two men shook their heads. He returned his gaze to Hiro.

"That ghost... is it very noticeable?"

"Very. She wore a white dress and seemed to glow slightly. She should be visible from far away."

Sungjin suddenly turned his head.

"Hidden..." He muttered something under his breath and suddenly shouted, "Swift Paw."

Sungjin's boots suddenly grew claws. And before the others recovered from the surprise, he began running away at an incredible speed.

No, it was beyond incredible. It was completely outside the boundary of human limitations.

Although Henrik and Kultu stared with their mouths open, Hiro yelled,

"Sensei! Wait for me!"

Only Hiro chased after Sungjin in the darkness.

***

Sungjin blazed through Greysoul Cemetery, searching. Swift Paw – Wolf's step's effect was stronger than anticipated.

Because it gave ten times the normal movement speed, Sungjin was actually forced to slow down. But the result was magnificent; it effectively reduced the time spent on searching to a tenth.

Sungjin thought of what he had just heard moments before, as he continued to search between the many tombstones.

Well, you know, a female ghost like those you see in scary movies. With pale skin and blood dripping from the lips...

A hint came from an unexpected source.

...I am certain that the ghost has something to do with the hidden boss or the hidden piece, thought Sungjin.

Now that he thought of it, he had heard some rumours of a ghost in Chapter 3. Hunters from the previous life sometimes gossiped about it.

And here I thought that I should have used the Treasure Hunter active skill right after the boss...

Sungjin saved his active skill for now. He had already gotten a hint about at least one of the two things, and there was a possibility that the hint the Operator would provide was on the same subject.

There was not one undead remaining in the entire Greysoul Cemetery. Most were wiped out during his search, and the stragglers were hunted down by the other four Hunters.

...Ghost... where are you?

Sungjin checked his surroundings as he sped through the Cemetery. And finally, his speed gradually started decreasing.

It's been 30 seconds already? I haven't located the ghost yet...

Soon Sungjin was back to running at his normal speed. He paused for a moment.

He was surrounded by an indistinguishable sea of tombstones.

Damn... Sungjin turned his head while swearing, and just then he saw something white floating in the distance; a woman in a white dress.

There! Sungjin sprinted toward the ghost.

*

"Sensei!" Hiro tried to keep up with Sungjin, but it was impossible. The latter ran at impossible speeds, and Hiro lost sight of him in mere moments.

He paused and stared toward the general direction Sungjin had disappeared to. Anyone else would have given up at this point. But not Hiro.

"Holy cow! Sensei is so amazing!"

After taking a quick breather, Hiro continued with his chase.

After about two minutes, he spotted the ghost he had seen earlier.

"Eek!" Hiro stopped immediately. In fact, he subconsciously took a step back. He was alone and without Henrik, Kultu, or Akanna.

Hiro was not afraid of skeletons or zombies, but the ghost scared the wits out of him. Then, he spotted Sungjin next to the ghost.

"What should I do...?"

Hiro nibbled on his nails and began to fret. He was in a dilemma due to the forces of attraction and repulsion being gathered in one spot.

I am a man of martial arts. I need to overcome my fears.

Hiro finally made up his mind and approached Sungjin and the ghost. Once he got within earshot, Sungjin turned to look at him. "Hmm? What? How did you catch up?"

Moments later, the ghost turned to look at him as well.

"Eee!"

Being stared at by a ghost with an ashen face and completely black eyes, Hiro wanted to run away. But, Sungjin stopped him.

"Don't worry. This ghost is... non-hostile."

Sungjin was right. The ghost never showed intentions to attack anyone. But Hiro still could not approach the apparition.

Hostile or not, the appearance of the ghost was enough to inspire fear in a man's heart.

And while Hiro was keeping his distance from the ghost, the ghost looked toward Sungjin. And in a similar manner, as she had done with Henrik, she raised her hands to point far in the distance and let out a strange noise. "Hiiiiii..."

Sungjin was completely unafraid of the ghost. He simply stroked his chin.

"This thing... I think it's trying to say something..." was all he said. Suddenly, the ghost began to float away toward the direction she had pointed out moments ago. Sungjin followed her without another word. Hiro watched for a moment.

"Sen... Sensei!" He called after Sungjin, but Sungjin did not respond. Hiro had no choice but to follow the two, albeit a few steps behind.

After a long while, the ghost stopped again and let out a strange noise. "Haaaaaa..."

Sungjin stopped next to her.

"Hmmm... Is there something here?" He mused to himself before calling the Operator.

"Operator. Salamander's ash."

He took out a Salamander's ash from the inventory. Hiro was familiar with that item. He'd used it in Chapter 1 to hunt the Trolls, and against the wolves in Chapter 2.

Kei opened the package and spread the ash across his Katana.
FOOF

The Katana lit up on fire and illuminated the area. Using the Katana as a torch, he checked the immediate surroundings. And exactly under the ghost,

He spotted a stone crypt door engraved with an image of two identical girls, standing back to back.

"Twins." Sungjin spoke to himself and sliced the door open with his Katana.

"Kahaaa~"

The Ghost screamed out loud. It was still layered with an unholy cadence but, this time, it seemed... happy.

She spun in the air once and then flew into the stone entrance. Sungjin and Hiro peeked into the opening in the stone doorway.

It was difficult to see what was inside. Once Sungjin inserted the inflamed Katana between the crack, a large pile of bones came into view.

"Hiiie!" Hiro gasped in terror again. On the other hand, Sungjin moved to enter the crypt fearlessly.

Hiro grabbed his shirt and pulled him back. "Sensei, are you not afraid of ghosts?"

Sungjin looked back toward Hiro and said something Hiro didn't quite understand.

"I've already died once. Why would I fear ghosts?"

Before Hiro could respond, Sungjin entered the crypt. The entryway was too small and dark. Hiro made an excuse for himself.

"I can just wait for Sensei out here..."

He sat down in front of the crypt. What Sungjin just said moments before: *I've already died once*, was completely and utterly ignored.

*

Sungjin entered the Columbarium alone. Using the Katana as a torch, he illuminated different parts of the room. The Columbarium was damp and narrow. Despite it all, Sungjin entered confidently, taking no mind to the environment.

For him, it was beyond a doubt that this place was what he had been searching for all along. At the end of the narrow walkway, a small space opened up.

And within, the female ghost who led him here was waiting for him. Standing inside of a crypt surrounded by bones, looking up at the bloodied ghost, Sungjin thought ... *Yeah I think I can understand why people might be afraid.*

"Hyaaa..." The ghost let out a strange noise and once again raised her hands. When Sungjin saw her hands, he thought it was different from before.

Her hands were not in a grip and were held in their natural state with the fingers slightly curled. But Sungjin thought she had her pointer finger raised slightly higher than the rest, as if gesturing toward something.

What is she pointing to? Sungjin followed the direction of her finger. She was pointing at one of the walls of the Columbarium.

Sungjin slowly moved toward the wall. Upon closer inspection, he noticed that one of the bricks was slightly pushed out compared to the rest of the bricks of that wall.

He carefully gripped the brick and pulled it out gingerly.

The brick came out much easier than expected. And inside of the wall, Sungjin could see a wrapped object.

What is this? Sungjin reached in and pulled it out. The wrapped object slid out easily, its frame resembling that of a sword.

Once he had it all the way out, the wrappings unwound themselves and a sword sheathed in an extremely shabby and worn scabbard revealed itself.

The grip was so weathered that it looked as if it would break if pulled too hard from the scabbard. Sungjin gently grasped the handle of the sword and drew the blade.

"Holy..." Sungjin couldn't help but exclaim out loud. Hidden within the worn-out grip and scabbard was a pristine blade, giving off a soft blue glow.

Once the blade was drawn, the ghost next to him disintegrated into a cloud of smoke and was sucked into the blade.

"Kyahaaa~"

Without fail, the ghost managed to let out a strange noise. Once the ghost was gone, Sungjin heard the Operator's voice.

[Congratulations]

[You have found the Hidden Piece]

[Moon Spectre – Possessed Sword Obtained.]

"Good." Sungjin grinned as he inspected his sword.

Moon Spectre – Possessed Sword
Legendary Katana – Strength S Dexterity A Mind Power B

Passive Skill
Soul Absorption (II)
Recover 2% of the total mana per hit.

Active Skill
Deathly Wail (IV)
A ghost will induce fear to all nearby creatures. Cooldown 10 minutes

A Katana imbued with the power of ghosts. It is unknown if the vengeful spirit was originally the owner of the Katana, or if the soul became vengeful upon being slain by the Katana.

"...Legendary?"

He had received a completed Legendary item. It was unbelievable. He wished he had known about such an easy to obtain Legendary-class weapon the first time around.

Sungjin glanced over to the specs. The most eye-catching stats were obviously the S-rank Strength and A-rank Dex bonus damages.

"Operator, what was the bonus per ranks again?"

[Rank affects stats as follows.]

[Rank E – x0.1 | Rank D – x0.2 | Rank C – x0.5]

[Rank B – x1.0 | Rank A – x1.5 | Rank S – x2.0]

[Rank SS – x3.0 | Rank SSS – x4.0]

Sungjin had not come across an enemy yet that he could not kill in a single strike with his Strength C Dex D Basic Katana. And yet, he just received an S and an A grade Legendary Katana, effectively raising his damage by four times.

Well... I guess for the next few Chapters, all the enemies are basically going to be made of wet paper mâché... Sungjin mused over his stats as he read the notes for skills. Deathly Wail (IV) seemed fairly useful.

There was also the Rank B bonus damage from Mind Power. This meant that raising Strength by 1 would increase his damage by 2, but raising Mind Power would also provide 1 bonus damage.

Putting Mind Power stat damage boost on a Katana... means...

Furthermore, it also had a passive skill 'Soul Absorption (II)' as well.

In other words, this is a sword designed for a magic swordsman, concluded Sungjin.

The base stats were great, but he needed to think about this one.

I'll come back to it another time.

Sungjin finally put the sword back in the scabbard.

SHINK!

The blade let out a crisp sound as it slid into the scabbard. Sungjin left the Columbarium, with the Moon Spectre hanging from his side.

***

Zombies, skeletons, and ghouls charged at Sungjin from all sides. Sungjin swung his Katana and with each strike, dozens of enemies fell where they stood. But whenever Sungjin would cull their numbers,

"Rise of the Dead!"

The Necromancer would call forth more and more undead from their graves. The ability was similar to Ahenna's, but this was far worse.

It was impossible to gauge how many more undead would emerge from the ground, especially in the Cemetery where graves continued as far as the eyes could see. Soon, the sheer volume of the enemies forced Sungjin into a stalemate.

"...Kill..."

Yanhurat beckoned Sungjin, but he did his best to ignore its temptations.

Meanwhile,

PEW

Kultu's arrows came flying at him. Instead of deflecting the blow with his weapon, Sungjin snatched it out of the air with his bare hands.

Kultu wordlessly drew another arrow and knocked it on the bow. If he were a human, he would have hesitated due to surprise at Sungjin's overwhelming display of Strength.

Are the undead... unable to feel fear?

Sungjin paused to think about his Moon Spectre and the active ability Deathly Wail.

It's worth a try. And while Sungjin was contemplating, the Necromancer cast another spell.

"Frenzy!"

The undead began to ramp up speed. When Sungjin saw them, he instead returned the sword into the sheath.

...SHING... CLICK

And when the masses of undead had completely enveloped him, Sungjin pulled it out of the sheath and shouted, "Deathly Wail!"

The moment the sword left the sheath,

"KYAAAAA!"

An unbelievably loud and otherworldly screech filled the air.

Immediately, the ghouls, skeletons, and zombies which had surrounded him scattered. The same enemies who had fought apathetically, disregarding their lost limbs or his display of strength, escaped as fast as their legs would carry them.

They trampled each other in their haste to get away from Sungjin. Bones broke, limbs were lost, they clamored to climb over one another; it was sheer pandemonium. Soon, the Cemetery was bare save the Gravekeeper Oryx.

He, too, trembled in fear, backing off slowly, holding his shovel defensively. "You... That sword..."

It looked like there was something the Gravekeeper wanted to say, but Sungjin did not care. He did not want to listen. Sungjin walked up to him and

SHING

Along with the sound of the blade slicing through the air, Oryx was beheaded.

And the moment his head separated from his shoulders, the undead dropped down in unison, like marionettes cut from their strings. Nothing stirred in the vicinity.

[Hidden Boss Gravekeeper Oryx cleared.]

[Congratulations! You have managed to complete all objectives in this Chapter!]

[Disregarding the remaining time and ending the Raid immediately.]

Once the hidden boss was cleared, the Raid completion suddenly became 100%. It seemed that killing the necromancer simultaneously killed all the remaining undead as well. Sungjin took a glance at his sword Moon Spectre again.

That worked better than expected.

Never mind the undead, it had even paralyzed the boss. With this much effectiveness, it was undoubtedly a very potent ability.

Excellent. Sungjin smiled and re-sheathed his sword.

"Ahhh!"

Suddenly he heard a scream. Looking around, he saw Henrik laying on the ground trembling in fear.

It was probably due to Moon Spectres' Deathly Wail. Sungjin also saw Hiro disappearing in the distance, running away.

So it's also effective against humans.

It was a good opportunity to learn what Deathly Wail was capable of; the Legendary weapon lived up to its name. Sungjin scanned his surroundings since the fight was now over.

Close by, Akanna and Kultu's corpse lay mangled on the ground. Seeing them, Sungjin bit his lower lip.

...I didn't want for this to happen.

If he had not summoned the hidden boss, they would not have died. Sungjin closed his eyes and hung his head to give them a moment of silence; he felt pity and remorse for the dead.

Meanwhile, Henrik had recovered enough to approach Sungjin and offer some kind words.

"Don't let it get to you, Kei. According to the Operator, they didn't die; they were just sent to Purgatory. They'll all be revived along with the others once the Raids are complete."

Henrik was right. At this point, the only thing Sungjin could do for them was to complete the Raids.

If he could manage to do that, then the two men would be revived along with everyone at the end. Of course, if he failed, none of them would ever see the light of the day again. Hiro, who somehow managed to make it back offered his words as well.

"Sensei, with your skills, you will definitely see the Raids to the end. The two people that died today would have believed in you as well."

Their words eased Sungjin's sense of guilt. He looked at the corpses again.

Please believe in me.

He gathered his hands and closed his eyes. He didn't have a religion, but he felt that he had to offer them prayers. The Operator interrupted him with an announcement.

[Calculating Rewards Earned.]

[Monsters Slain. Zombie: 120. Skeleton: 60. Ghoul 40. Total 2400 points.]

[Boss Monster Slain: Lich Deathmond: 300 points.]

[Hidden Boss Gravekeeper Oryx: 300 points.]

[Final point count: 3000 Points. Distributing points.]

Henrik's cube began the distribution. The person with the lowest contribution always went first.

[Your contribution is 6%. 180 Stat Points, 180 Black Coins awarded. Raid Clear Bonus 800 Stat Points and 800 Black Coins awarded. Distributing 980 Stat Points and 980 Black Coins.]

Hiro's cube was second.

[Your contribution is 18%. 540 Stat Points, 540 Black Coins awarded. Raid Clear Bonus 800 Stat Points and 800 Black Coins awarded. Distributing 1340 Stat Points and 1340 Black Coins.]

And finally, Sungjin's cube spoke up.

[Your contribution is 76.0%. 2280 Stat Points, 2280 Black Coins awarded. Raid Clear Bonus 800 Stat Points and 800 Black Coins awarded. Item effect 'Additional 10% gained' activated. Distributing 3080 Stat Points and 3388 Black Coins.]

3080 points and 3388 coins

Sungjin memorized the numbers for now.

[And now we will distribute the items.]

First to receive the items was Henrik.

[Skeleton's Scimitar]

[Recovery Potion – Small X3]

Followed by Hiro's brief item reward payout.

[Skeleton's Bone Armor]

[Spell Book – Frostbite]

[Recovery Potion – Small X4]

Finally, it was Sungjin's turn.

[Sael's Breath – Mantle of Freezing]

[Manyata – Master's Bell]

[Ring of Deathmond – Lich's Finger]

[Spell Book – Frostbite]

[Spell Book – Rise of the Dead]

[Recovery Potion – Small X4]

By now, everyone was familiar with collecting their loot. Sungjin put everything, except for his three equipment pieces, into the cube.

[Last but not the least, you will be awarded titles you've earned on this Raid.]

Of course, first person to receive again was Henrik.

[Guide – The path to the boss monster becomes visible.]

Henrik became disappointed. "I'll probably just die if I get to the boss, what's the point of this...?"

Next was Hiro.

[Undead Hunter – deal 30% bonus damage to undead-type monsters.]

"There's going to be more undead in the future? Fueee..."

Finally Sungjin.

[Elite Samurai – increases damage dealt by Katana-type weapons by 40%.]

"Wow..."

Sungjin didn't have to respond; Hiro was exclaiming loud enough for both of them.

"That's so amazing, Sensei!"

On the other hand, Sungjin listened quietly.

Elite... At least it's the highest tier...

Damage increases to 1.4 times the normal and 1.2 times while unequipped. It was an amazing spec to have.

But, ever since Sungjin obtained the S-grade Moon Spectre, he already had enough power to one-shot any non-boss enemies for the next 2-3 Chapters.

This title was like pouring oil onto a raging inferno.

Well, I suppose it will come in handy in the late game.

Sungjin quietly and nonchalantly accepted his new title. Once the distribution of rewards was over, Sungjin called over the Operator.

"Operator, will there be debriefing once we reach the Hunter's Hall?"

[No. There will be no debriefing. You will be sent to the Black Market directly in 6 minutes and 32 seconds.]

Sungjin nodded.

My memories were correct.

Although he'd had an easier time compared to the earlier two Chapters where he didn't have the proper items to face the monsters, confronting the undead had tired him out mentally.

Sungjin couldn't wait to return and get a good rest at the Ninety-Nine Nights. Right then, Hiro ran up to him and asked, "Sensei, please... What are hidden bosses?"

Sungjin looked at Hiro carefully. "That's..."

Should I tell him or not...

Sungjin deliberated for a moment. Hidden bosses were always stronger than regular bosses.

In fact, even regular bosses were supposed to be difficult to clear for an average Hunter. Being greedy and carelessly attempting hidden bosses was the surest way to get eliminated. Sungjin shook his head in response.

"No. It's too difficult for you."

"But... I've never seen three Heroic items drop from a single Raid. I want to become strong like Sensei."

Sungjin shook his head. He had countless experiences behind him, overcoming obstacles and death. He did not wish to unwittingly send a child younger than himself to his own death.

"You saw earlier what happened to Akanna and Kultu. Do you still want to know?"

Hiro could not be dissuaded. "Yes, I wish to know, sir."

Hiro was making a serious face for the first time.

Sungjin struggled in his mind for a while and finally responded. "To be fair... There's nothing for me to tell you at all. The only thing I can say is that every Chapter also hosts a hidden boss, and that the hidden boss is incredibly powerful. You probably figured it out by now, right?"

"What do you mean?"

Sungjin answered Hiro's question. "That I am also figuring things out as I go, and I don't have all the answers."

"...Is that so?"

"Yes." Sungjin nodded.

"Then... I guess I should start searching for them starting next Chapter," said Hiro.

Sungjin waved his finger in response. "Ah... that's exactly why I didn't want to tell you about it earlier. Hidden bosses are stronger than regular bosses. So if you do ever want to challenge a hidden boss..."

Sungjin swallowed before continuing his explanation.

"Only attempt to search for it if all five members of your party survived the regular boss. Only attempt the hidden boss if your team has great synergy and you feel confident that your team can overcome even the hidden boss. Otherwise, you're just going to get everyone killed for nothing."

At Sungjin's serious response, Hiro fell quiet again.

Sungjin watched him and thought to himself. *He wouldn't carelessly put himself into unmanageable danger with this much warning, right?*

Even 'Killing the boss with all party members intact' was no easy feat. A few seconds later, he finally responded.

"I understand, Sensei."

With the remaining time, Sungjin decided to inspect the three items he had received.

Ah... I didn't even check what these items do.

Due to his conversation with Hiro, Sungjin hadn't even had the opportunity to inspect his new equipment. Sungjin lifted one up to check it...

[Returning to the Black Market in 10 seconds. 10, 9, 8...]

The Operator began a countdown. Hiro bid him goodbye.

"Then, Sensei, I promise that the next time we meet I will be much stronger."

Sungjin responded to Hiro's farewell. "Well... If you don't get stronger, you won't survive very long anyway."

And it was the truth. Hiro was gifted with talent, but he was still very likely to die before reaching end game. The final few Chapters were impossible to survive without having the skill and luck of 'The Chosen Ones.'

Henrik, who was stuck between the two men, awkwardly gave his farewells. "Oh... I was able to survive thanks to you two. Thank you very much."

"Yes, you worked hard too, Henrik. Take care," said Hiro.

And thus the farewells concluded, and the three of them disappeared to the Black Market.

Chapter 7 – Black Market Third Shopping

Once Sungjin materialized in the Black Market, he walked until he reached a street-side tea shop. He entered the shop and took a seat. The Operator began an explanation.

[This is a street side tea shop run by shop owner Xiu Ran, First Drop.]

[You can enjoy various flavors of tea for free here.]

A large Panda demi-human approached Sungjin.

"What would you like to drink, dear Hunter?"

"Black tea, royal blend please."

"Understood. Will be right out."

Moments later, the shopkeeper handed Sungjin a Chinese-style tea. The aroma filled the air. Tasting the tea, Sungjin took out his equipment to inspect it.

He needed to know which items were worth keeping so he could decide to sell them or not.

First up was a cape which had the consistency and appearance of a jellyfish's skin. It was extremely thin, billowed easily in the wind, and was partially opaque. Parts of it were frozen.

Sael's Breath – Mantle of Freezing
Heroic Mantle
Damage reduction 5%

Passive Skill
Protection from Flame (III)
Reduce damage inflicted by fire-based attacks by 60%

Active Skill
Solidify (IV)
Mantle instantly freezes, briefly reducing damage taken by 99%.
Cooldown 5 minutes

Mantle once owned by Ice Queen Sael. She, who froze a large number of people around her due to her inability to control her magic, learned to control her power thanks to the love and effort by her younger sister.

...99% damage reduction...

It would definitely come in handy when facing enemies with un-dodgeable attacks–like the Lich's Orb of Ice. The passive was also very helpful.

Sungjin held up the mantle.

"Equip."

The Mantle left his hands and attached itself to his back, then swayed in the wind. He was pleasantly surprised by the near weightless feel of the cape; save for the slight chill he felt on his back.

The next item was a strange-looking hand bell. It was small and had minuscule engravings.

Manyata – Master's Bell
Heroic Accessory

Active Skill – Call of Madness (IV)
Owned Summons become invulnerable for 10 seconds and raises Damage and Speed by 400%. Cooldown 10 minutes

Gravekeeper Oryx's Bell. He used this weapon to drive his subordinates like a slave.

The bell was well suited for the Necromancer.
Mmm... Summons... Summons, eh? Where can I get one...?
Now that he thought about it, he remembered he had Cain.
If I use this on Cain... Hmm I'll keep it on me for now.
Sungjin placed the bell inside his pocket. The next item he checked was a long skeletal finger.

Ring of Deathmond – Lich's Finger
Heroic Ring

Active Skill
Lich's Beckoning (III)
Absorb mana from corpses. Recovers 75% of the total mana. Cooldown 10 minutes

Boost Magic (II)
The next magic cast by incantation becomes doubly powerful and costs twice the mana. Cooldown 5 minutes.

Lich Deathmond's finger bones. His finger caused many hearts to freeze over.

This was the main boss's regular drop, so it was rather common. During his last life, many magic users had kept this ring around.

It was because both the active skills on it were extremely advantageous for a mage.

Magic...

Sungjin had been purely a swordsman in his last life.

His primary weapon Blood Vengeance had SS Strength and A Dexterity bonus stats. So he had raised Strength for extra damage, Dexterity for combat speed, and Endurance for the preservation of his life.

Surviving Chapter to Chapter was always a struggle, so raising Intelligence or Mind were avoided entirely. Naturally, he never had an opportunity to use magic.

So whenever he received a mage-type item, he would trade with other Hunters or sell it off at the Black Market to buy potions. But, things were different now.

I think this time I should invest in trying out magic as well.

He had invested a significant amount of points into Strength, Dexterity, and Endurance to get through the first three Chapters, but investing in magic for late game was a good idea. Trying to beat later part of the Raids with purely physical attacks had its own limitations.

Since he had a title which raised all Stat Points by 30%, he could afford to try investing somewhat into Magic Power and Mental Power. Investing into becoming a Magic Swordsman would definitely prove to be advantageous later down the line.

It would be preferable if there was an actual mage, though...

He couldn't help but recall memories of his past life.

"Leave your back to me."

Sungjin shook his head. He could not trust anyone. It was great if they were helpful. But he had to prepare for moments when others were not dependable. Sungjin lifted up the Lich's finger and said,

"Equip."

CREAK

The Lich's Finger moved to his left ring finger and made uncomfortable noises as it formed a ring around his hand by curling up. Judging purely by its appearance, it was an extremely unattractive ring.

After Sungjin had examined his three equipment pieces which he'd received from the round, he called the Operator.

"Operator, give me both of the Spellbooks I got this round."

The Operator gave Sungjin two Spellbooks from the cube. On the cover, the name of the spells was written.

Spell Book – Frostbite
2nd Circle Blue Magic

The ground freezes, binding (rooting) enemies to the ground.

I don't know when I'll ever use it...

Since he opted to try magic this time, he decided to try the spells he had obtained. Sungjin lifted up the book and shouted, "Memorize!"

The spellbook, Frostbite, emitted bright blue lights, and spontaneously combusted. The Operator gave an announcement.

[Spell – Frostbite memorized.]

[Incantation for the spell is 'Binding Frost!']

The Operator explained expressionlessly about the spell.

"...Ok." Sungjin looked over at the other spell he had received.

Spellbook – Rise of the Dead
4th Circle Black Magic

Revive fallen enemies as undead summons to use in combat. 10 minute duration.

There was no question about how this spell would be used. The only problem was how much utility he could squeeze out of revived monsters. Sungjin shouted without hesitation, "Memorize!"

The spellbook, Rise of the Dead, emitted black light and burst into flames.

[Spell – Rise of the Dead Memorized.]

[Incantation for the spell is 'Awaken and become my slave!']

And so Sungjin was now able to use two magic spells.

I don't think I'll have any trouble clearing the next few Chapters with just the sword... but I might as well try the spells out in the next round.

Once he'd finished inspecting all his new items from the last Raid, Sungjin wanted to stand up and leave. But he was reminded that there was yet another Item which he had received from the Raid.

It was the Moon Spectre hanging from his side. Sungjin pulled the sword out of the scabbard to inspect it.

Moon Spectre – Possessed Sword
Legendary Katana – Strength S Dexterity A Mind Power B

Passive Skill
Soul Absorption (II)
Recover 2% of the total Mana per hit

Active Skill
Deathly Wail (IV)
A ghost will induce fear to all nearby creatures. Cooldown 10 minutes

A Katana imbued with the power of ghosts. It is unknown if the vengeful spirit was originally the owner of the Katana, or if the soul became vengeful upon being slain by the Katana.

Deathly Wail. It was much more powerful than I expected.

The effectiveness of the skill was awe inspiring.

It caused fear to all beings (even undead) within twenty meters. It was like obtaining another 'ace in the hole card' like Yanhurat.

And this... doesn't even have a side effect...

It was a skill well suited for a Legendary-class item.

The stat boost on this sword was slightly lower than the Blood Vengeance, but Sungjin already had an extremely high number of points invested in Strength and Dexterity compared to the Chapter he was in, enough that even boss monsters were in danger of being instantly-killed by so much as grazing them with his sword.

The B-rank damage boost attached to Mind Power was quite good. Especially if Sungjin started using magic spells, he will need to raise Mind Power; being able to improve damage by boosting Mind Power was definitely a big advantage.

The passive 'Soul Absorption' was also great.

Legendary sure deserves its reputation.

After taking a moment to appreciate the blue glow of the Katana, Sungjin emptied his teacup and stood up. "Thank you for the tea."

The Fat Panda Xiu Ran came to see him out. "Be careful now."

Sungjin left First Drop and headed toward the Last Edge.

"Welcome, dear Hunter." As always, Naga Kenneth greeted him.

Sungjin asked, "Let me see that crimson Katana... Blood Vengeance again."

"Understood, dear Hunter." Kenneth entered deeper into the shop and retrieved the 'Blood Vengeance' for Sungjin.

"Here is the sword you requested."

Sungjin gripped the handle of his beloved sword. The handle felt nostalgic.

"But... I don't think I can use you this time." Sungjin apologized to the sword as if it was his lover. He already obtained a Legendary-class sword Moon Spectre; Purchasing Blood Vengeance was too inefficient to justify.

It would have been great if Sungjin was able to dual wield, but he was not able to do so. Sungjin was right handed; even if he were to hold a weapon in his left hand, it would become nothing but a useless accessory.

Sungjin returned the Blood Vengeance to Kenneth. "I'm sorry I'm just looking without buying anything."

Kenneth obediently accepted the Katana from Sungjin and replied, "It is no problem at all. Do you have any other requests for me?"

At the Naga's words, Sungjin thought of what other requests Kenneth could complete for him.

"Hey, Operator?"

[Please go on.]

"Give me the Basic Katana."

Sungjin extracted the first Katana he received from the first Raid.

"I want to sell this."

"Understood. The Basic Katana can be sold for 10 coins. Do you really want to sell it?"

Sungjin nodded. Kenneth handed Sungjin 10 Black Coins. Once his business was complete, Sungjin bid Kenneth goodbye.

"I hope to see you again, esteemed Hunter," responded the shopkeeper.

Sungjin put the ten coins away into the cube and called for the Operator, "Operator, How many coins do I have?"

[Currently, you have a total of 5978 Black Coins]

5978 Coins... I need 4022 more to complete it.

He no longer had any dilemma about which item to buy first; there was only one choice left.

Sungjin decided to use Moon Spectre rather than Blood Vengeance this time. As he walked back to the Ninety-Nine Nights, Sungjin thought to himself,

I will obtain 4022 Coins and complete the book with the next Chapter.

*

"Awoo~"

When Sungjin returned to the Ninety-Nine Nights, Cain came to greet him. He was healthy, without a trace of injury caused by the Lich's attack. Cain circled around Sungjin few times, expressing his joy.

Sungjin embraced Cain by his neck. "Hello, Cain. You did well earlier. Thank you."

Cain gave a short bark as if he didn't mind.

Sungjin and Cain proceeded to enter into Ninety-Nine Nights and like always, the Innkeeper Dalupin greeted them.

"Welcome back, esteemed Hunter."

Sungjin nodded back before taking a seat.

"For today's dinner..." He quickly ordered the food that came to his mind immediately.

"One slice of cheesecake, please. Raw lamb for Cain too."

"Understood."

Moments later, Dalupin returned with a radiating dish of cheesecake, and a bleeding slab of lamb meat.

Sungjin picked up his fork to eat, but Dalupin handed him a piece of paper and said, "Ah... this is the next Raid's information."

Sungjin cut the edge of the cheesecake with his fork and placed it into his mouth before giving a reply. "Put it on the table. I will take a look after dinner."

"Understood."

Dalupin placed the piece of paper down next to Sungjin's plate. Sungjin glanced at the paper.

Information regarding Giant's Canyon.

He only checked the title,

The order is still the same.

And resumed eating his cake. The cake melted in his mouth, and each bite spread the delicious, cheesy flavour and aroma across his taste buds.

Chapter 8 – Giant's Canyon

The next morning, Sungjin came down from his room earlier than usual.

The ever present innkeeper greeted him. "Good morning, sir, did you sleep well? You're up much earlier than usual."

Sungjin nodded towards him as he responded, "I slept well."

"What would you like for breakfast?" asked Dalupin.

"Baguette made into a sandwich with vegetables and bacon. One cup of americano espresso and something for Cain as well."

"Understood."

Dalupin acknowledged Sungjin's request with a bow. But before he returned to the kitchen, Sungjin interrupted him.

"Ah, before you get me breakfast, would you mind getting a pen and some paper for me please?"

Dalupin obliged and brought him the needed stationary.

"Thank you."

After receiving the writing tools, Sungjin asked the Operator, "Operator, show me my status window."

The cube displayed a hologram in front of Sungjin.

Title Master Hunter
HP: 10600   MP: 220

Strength:	1186	912 (+274)
Dexterity:	1421	1093 (+328)
Endurance:	1060	815 (+245)
Magic Power:	18	14 (+4)
Mind Power:	22	17 (+5)

Unallocated Points: 3080

Sungjin wrote at the top of the page.

3080

After writing down his available Stat Points, he wrote the totals of his current Strength and Dexterity.

1186, 1421...

These numbers represented his allocated points plus the 30% buff due to the Master Hunter title. In truth, with these stats, he would have no trouble clearing the next 2-3 Chapters.

His stat points surpassed a thousand, plus with the S-rank (x2.0) damage boost to Strength and the A-rank (x1.5) damage boost to Dexterity from Moon Spectre, and effects of the Elite Samurai title.

Sungjin already had enough damage to one-shot even hidden bosses, and enough speed to dodge every strike. It was proven in the previous Raid against the Gravekeeper Oryx.

Well, advantage is advantage... thought Sungjin. He wrote the following next to both Strength and Dexterity.

+1000

He didn't need them immediately, but there were stronger enemies the further he progressed through the Raids. There was a need to invest into his Strength and Dexterity regularly and consistently.

Even if he started using magic, swordsmanship was the basis of his power; he needed to maintain its power at absolutely domineering levels.

The next stat he looked at was Endurance. He didn't need this immediately at all. Sungjin had never needed it so far.

There was only one case where he was hit, and even then, Cain had blocked most of the damage for him.

The only time he had lost any significant HP was due to the side effect of Yanhurat's 'Zealot' mode.

But...

He wrote the following next to Endurance.

+500

Sungjin had fought every boss until the very end and knew how to deal with all of them. But he had not even seen most of the hidden bosses yet.

There was always a chance that any one of them could attack using dangerous magic or abilities he'd never seen before; he needed to have some form of failsafe put in place ahead of time.

The remaining points were now 580. As a test, Sungjin decided to invest these points into Magic Power and Mind Power.

The main reason for getting up earlier than usual was so that he could write out the stats on paper and think carefully about them. Especially the two stats related to magic.

Sungjin spoke to the cube, "Operator, how is mana consumption calculated?"

[Spell's Circle level x Magic Power]

The information matched what he had heard from other Hunters. For example, if he wanted to cast 2nd Circle magic Frostbite, its cost would be calculated as 2 X 18. The total cost of mana was currently 36.

The root of the problem was that he needed to figure out a good ratio between Magic Power and Mind Power.

If his Magic Power was significantly lower than Mind Power, he could use the spells many times, but at very weak levels of effectiveness. Inversely, if his Mind Power were significantly lower than Magic Power, the effectiveness of each spell would be great, but he could only use it a limited number of times.

The problem was that because Sungjin had never used magic before, he didn't know what the optimal allocation of stats was.

Since this is my first time...

Sungjin decided to try out the magic in the next Chapter to get a feel of its power.

I'll start out with 1:1 ratio and try out different combinations later. I might have to readjust stat distribution once higher-circle spells are unlocked.

Sungjin decided to write '+290' next to Magic Power and Mind Power.

Once he was finished writing, he noticed the sandwiches set in front of him. He had been so focused on the stat distribution that he had not noticed Dalupin come by.

Sungjin picked up the Baguette sandwich and took a bite. While chewing on the sandwich, he began speaking to the Operator.

"Operator. Put 1000 points on Strength, 1000 points on Dexterity, 500 on Endurance, 290 on Magic Power, and 290 on Mind Power."

[Points have been allocated.]

"Show me my Status window"

Title: Master Hunter
HP: 17100 MP 3990

Strength:	2486	1912	(+574)
Dexterity:	2721	2093	(+628)
Endurance:	1710	1315	(+395)
Magic Power:	395	304	(+91)
Mind Power:	399	307	(+92)

Unallocated points: 0

So with Stats like this...

Sungjin picked up the pen one more time and began to write.

Frostbite will take 395×2, or 790 mana per shot. Rise of the Dead takes 395X4 for 1580. Since total mana is 3990, I can cast Frostbite five times, or Rise of the Dead twice without refills.

It was enough for trying out magic for the next round. And if he wanted then he could use Lich's Finger and Moon Spectre to recover lost Mana if need be.

For now, it was more important to get used to casting spells than checking the spell's effectiveness. When Sungjin finished his calculations, the Operator gave an announcement.

[Raid will begin in 30 minutes.]

Sungjin spent the remaining time leisurely enjoying breakfast in the inn. Soon, he was teleported away, to Giant's Canyon.

*

The sun was setting in the west, its crimson lights dyeing the world red. The tall canyon walls stood on either side, with rays of lights falling down the middle, illuminating the dry, cracked ground.

The place Sungjin was teleported to was an enormous canyon. The Operator began her announcement.

[Welcome to Giant's Canyon]

[Where races of Giants gather and live together.]

[Please be warned: Giants are as dangerous]

[As they are large.]

Sungjin looked around without much care. The Grand Canyon in America would probably look something like this. Although he'd never actually been there himself.

[Synchronizing Hunters]

To be fair, Sungjin no longer worried about who his teammates were going to be; he had enough Stat Points to clear the next three Chapters alone safely within the time limit.

"Haa…hh," Sungjin let out a yawn. Waking up earlier than usual to do the stat distribution made him drowsy. Blinking away the tears that came out, Sungjin checked the titles first.

Guardian, Assassin, Mid-Level Spearman.

The titles were all somewhat decent; only the strong could move forward and survive.

Sungjin was reading the titles with half closed eyes. But, the last title caught him by surprise.

Elite Sniper

What?! Sungjin's eyes grew wide and his head snapped down to look at the owner. And he was surprised once more; the Elite Sniper had shoulder-length hair.

A woman?

It was impressive for anyone to have achieved the rank of Elite Sniper already. And a woman at that. Furthermore, she was a beauty.

The Asiatic trademark of straight black hair ran down slightly past her shoulders. She wore no makeup over her pure white face.

Sharp eyes and a high nose with a cool visage, as well as a slender body devoid of excess fat, she exuded feminine beauty. It went without saying she must have regularly exercised to achieve such a healthy and athletic body conformation.

Sungjin stared at her for a moment. *Where have I seen her before?*

For some reason, she looked familiar.

The other three Hunters also stared at her. Starting from Chapter 1, there existed an extremely low number of women who could survive until now.

Among the group, the Asian Mid-Level Spearman approached and addressed her.

"Excuse me... Serin Han, right? Archery Gold Medalist Serin Han?"

"Ah..." Sungjin finally recalled her. Archery Gold Medalist Serin Han.

She had attended the Olympics and won the Individual Gold in Archery. She got additional coverage for her exceptional beauty, even appearing in 'Sexiest Olympic Star' rankings, becoming famous overseas.

She even appeared in various street signs and TV commercials for makeup, so even Sungjin who didn't regularly watch TV was familiar with her.

Mid-Level Spearman extended his hand to her and greeted her. "I am... A huge fan. My name is Xian Wang. I saw you often appearing as a cosmetic model in China."

But Serin crossed her arms, ignoring his outstretched hands, and gave a short response with a nod, "Ah ok."

Cold, thought Sungjin.

It wasn't like he couldn't understand her. The Raids were barbaric, anarchistic business. There was no guarantee her own teammates wouldn't turn against her during Raids.

Just like there were no rules against killing other Hunters, there were also no rules protecting Hunters from each other in 'other' ways.

But, if she attained the rank Elite Sniper, there shouldn't be too many men who could easily take her down.

Sungjin looked around with that in mind. The last two teammates were dark skinned, but were also quite different.

The Guardian held a club embedded with nails and held a large shield; like Kultu, he looked like he was from India. While the 'Assassin' who held a dagger looked South American.

[Raid will begin in 3 minutes]

Xian Wang clapped his hands upon the Operator's announcement.

"Come now, let's group up. Let's discuss a strategy on how we're going to proceed."

Not a single person responded to him. Not Sungjin Master Hunter, nor Elite Sniper Serin Han, nor Guardian, nor Assassin.

Sungjin glanced at the other members. *It's a collection of social recluses. I think I like it this way better, though...*

No matter who his teammates were, Sungjin's objective had not changed.

Find the hidden piece, hidden boss, and gather rare loot.

Now that he thought of it, he had another objective.

Ah, and also practice casting magic.

Sungjin briefly extracted his Moon Spectre out of the sheath before sliding it back in.

CLICK

It had such a satisfying ring to it. Then, he felt someone's gaze fall upon him. It was Serin Han. She must have seen the otherworldly blue glow on the blade of the sword attached to the world's most

165

beaten-up sword handle and sheath. She stared at the sword, transfixed for a moment.

When Sungjin turned to look at her, their eyes locked onto each other. And after a brief stare, she turned away. He didn't know if it was because of her pride, but she seemed even more unapproachable.

Sigh... I'm not going to do anything to you, no need to act so cold.

Sungjin instead turned his sights to the sunset in the distance. Raising his arms high, he stretched.

"Haa...hh"

He couldn't help but yawn again. Sungjin twisted his neck and began stretching the rest of his body. There were only three minutes left until the Raid began.

***

> Giant's Canyon Raid
> Objective – Hunt Ogre Mage Pach and Cho'Roch
> Time limit: 1 Hour.

Despite the Operator's mission briefing, the Hunters continued to stare among themselves wordlessly. The mood was stiff. Xian Wang clapped his hands one more time to gather their attention.

"Let's introduce ourselves at least. I'll start. My name is Xian Wang, Chinese. I am 30 years old, and I use a spear in fights."

Again, no one responded. This time, Xian asked Serin to help him out.

"Miss Serin, could you please introduce yourself? I already know, but most people here still don't know who you are..."

Addressed directly, she finally opened her mouth.

"I am Serin Han. Korean."

With her short reply, the other two men also introduced themselves. Beginning with the shield-wielding Guardian.

"Raj. Indian."

And the 'Assassin' with a dagger.

"Santiago. Mexican."

Santiago took his dagger and cleaned his nails. When the sleeve of his shirt slid down, an intricate tattoo could be seen on his arm.

South American Drug Cartel?

Sungjin kept him in mind. In the late game, he had seen many individuals with extremely dark pasts.

After all, violent individuals were better suited to survive and adapt to danger.

While Sungjin was thinking about this, the rest of the Hunters turned to look at him.

"I am K," said Sungjin.

At his response, Xian Wang asked, "Kei... Kei...? Are you Japanese?"

Sungjin couldn't help but smile before replying, "Nationality... why does that matter at all?"

Xian Wang answered, raising both his hands up, "Ah, well... I guess it doesn't. Ok, then, let's talk about how we're going to fight from this point forward. I use a spear... and I can fight enemies from some distance away."

The Guardian spoke up. "I have invested heavily into Endurance. And I spent all the coins I've received on armor. I should be able to provide a sturdy shield wall."

On his belt were several Recovery Potions. He must have done lots of tanking until now. The next was Santiago.

"I am... experienced with slashing throats with a dagger. I've noticed that all monsters... also have throats."

There was something incredibly threatening about him. Next was Serin Han.

"You've probably heard already, but I am an Archery Gold Medalist."

Last was Sungjin. He thought about what he should say for a moment, but he got a fun idea.

"I am a mage."

Everyone looked at him incredulously.

I should try one spell before Raid begins, thought Sungjin.

He aimed away from the Hunters and recited an incantation.

"Binding Frost! Frostbite!"

Sungjin's hand emitted a bright blue light, and then a 10 meters squared area of the ground that he indicated froze over. Sungjin inspected the effects of his spell.

It didn't freeze over much at all. Compared to the Chapter 3 Raid boss Lich, the effective area was tiny.

I guess it's because the Magic Power is still fairly low.

But even though Sungjin thought so,

"Wow..."

One of his teammates was amazed. It was likely Xian Wang's first time seeing a Hunter use magic. The average Hunter was not in a position to use magic by the start of Chapter 4.

Well... I think at least 'one other' should have been able to already by this point...

An old teammate from his past life came to mind. Sungjin withdrew the hand he cast the spell from and addressed the others.

"As you can see, I am a mage. I can cast a few spells to assist the team."

"I see! Then...what about that sword?" Xian Wang pointed at Moon Spectre as he asked.

Sungjin lifted up his sword as he replied, "I just picked this up from the ground along the way. I thought I should have something in my hand just in case."

It wasn't completely a lie. It was true that he had picked up the sword along the way. Xian Wang nodded, accepting Sungjin's explanation.

Moon Spectre looked so shabby on the outside that nobody doubted him. Xian Wang clapped yet again as he tried to gather attention.

"Ok good. We have an Archery Gold medallist and also a Mage. The team looks really strong this time."

Everyone turned to look at Sungjin. Only Serin Han gave him disapproving looks, as she was the only one who had witnessed the blue glow of the Moon Spectre.

"Let's avoid useless deaths and get to the end together."

The Guardian nodded in agreement. "Got it. Let's all work hard together."

Sungjin debated on running off by himself from the start, but he decided to participate with the team at first.

He didn't care about anyone else, but he wanted to see the skill of Elite Sniper Serin Han with his own eyes.

Since the Raid is an hour long... spending a few minutes watching them fight shouldn't pose a problem.

Serin took out a hair band and tied up her hair in a ponytail. It appeared that it would get in the way of her archery. She seemed very professional somehow.

If she's really that good... she should have been able to make it to the end last time.

There was only one of two explanations for why Sungjin had not seen her before: lack of skill, or bad luck.

The cube soon gave a countdown.

[Raid will begin in 10 seconds. 10, 9, 8, 7, 6, 5, 4, 3, 2, 1, 0]

The Raid began, and the five of them entered the Canyon together. At the front stood Raj, and next to him, Santiago.

In the center stood Xian Wang, and at the back stood Serin Han with Sungjin right behind her.

Serin gave him odd looks.

"The mage is supposed to be at the very back," said Sungjin.

"Liar," replied Serin before walking away. Sungjin wasn't sure if she meant he was lying about being a mage, or that mages stood in the far back.

In the end, he still followed behind the other four Hunters.

"Here they come! Brace yourselves!" called out Raj.

A large Ogre appeared from afar, wielding a giant hammer. Guardian Raj banged on his shield with his club to attract attention.

"Here! Here! Come and get me!"

The Ogre took his hammer and brought it down upon Raj. Raj pretended to block it with his shield, but took a step back, out of the way of the hammer.

Meanwhile, Xian found an opening to stab the Ogre's arm with his spear. However, the Ogre was tougher than he looked.

The monster grasped the spear and pulled it out of his arm. Then he lifted it up in the air, along with Xian, who held onto the spear.

"Uhh... Uhhhhh..." While he panicked

PEW

Serin let loose an arrow. The arrow embedded itself in one of the Ogre's eyes.

The Ogre was not stationary; she had hit a moving target on a living thing in the middle of combat. It was amazing accuracy.

She certainly has the skill worthy of a Gold Medallist, Sungjin thought to himself.

"Kraaaah!" The Ogre covered his eyes in agony and let go of Xian's spear.

Then, out of nowhere, Santiago appeared from behind the Ogre, on his back. He cut open the carotid artery.

"Kaa..." The Ogre finally dropped his shield and grasped his bleeding neck. Blood gushed out from between his fingers. It was a bad move.

He was now defenseless. Raj and Xian charged the Ogre. After several strikes, the Ogre finally fell.

"Graah!"

But two more Ogres appeared in the area and began to charge at the group from afar. The Ogres seemed enraged by their comrade's death and ran rapidly towards the Hunters.

I'll contribute a little too.

Sungjin chanted the incantations.

"Binding Frost! Frostbite!"

The spell was very effective against the Ogres. The Ogres were rooted in place, unable to move forward.

Serin pulled her bow far and aimed up, then recited the incantations.

"Rain of Arrows."

She let go. She had let loose a single arrow, but it started duplicating itself and rained down upon the Ogres en masse.

The Ogres were unable to move away from the arrows and were forced to protect their heads with their bare hands; despite protecting their head, the Ogres still took significant damage from the rain of arrows and became bloodied.

"Whoa..." Xian Wang exclaimed with his mouth agape.

"What are you doing, all of you?" Serin's shout snapped them awake.

"Let's... Let's go!" called out Xian and charged towards the two Ogres. Guardian Raj and Assassin Santiago followed suit. The Ogres were frozen in place and with arms turned into pin cushions from the arrows.

They were surrounded by the three men and eventually succumbed to their constant attacks. Once the Ogres were finally killed off, Xian took a look around.

Xian was checking to see if any other Ogres were coming to take revenge, but he didn't spot any enemy reinforcements. Finally, he let out a long sigh.

"Haa... It is great that the team is so well balanced this time."

Raj happily agreed. "Yes, with that Gold Medallist lady and that mage, I think this Chapter will be a breeze."

Serin Han walked up from behind. She glanced at the fallen Ogres and frowned. And in a barely audible voice, she commented, "...Monsters... Disgusting."

While everyone else was commenting on the fight, Santiago finally spoke up.

"So... Where is the mage?"

The other three people looked around to see where the mage had been a few moments ago. He had disappeared without a trace.

*

At that moment, Sungjin was charging deeper and deeper into the canyon.

This Chapter, Chapter 4 – Giant's Canyon, was inherently different from Chapter 2 or Chapter 3's dark and open-ended map; the layout was very simple to follow.

If he just followed the one and only path through the Canyon, he was guaranteed to run into the bosses Pach and Cho'Roch at the other end of it.

Swift Paw's sharp claws allowed Sungjin to run past monsters before they could even respond to him; he sprinted through the canyon at unbelievable speeds.

I will kill the boss first, and then search for the hidden boss and hidden piece in the remaining time.

That was his plan. While running through the canyon at breakneck speed, he briefly thought about Serin Han. About the incredibly accurate Rain of Arrows she had fired.

That was definitely an active skill attached to a Heroic or higher-class weapon, he concluded.

Sungjin didn't know if it was a Raid reward, or if it was purchased with Coins, but he was certain that her bow was an extremely powerful weapon.

And rightfully so; if she was confident in archery, investing everything into a good bow was the right decision. In any properly functioning party, there should almost never be a situation where the archer had to face off a monster at melee.

While Sungjin was running through the canyon, his running speed suddenly decreased. Thirty seconds had passed.

Because Sungjin slowed down, a nearby two-headed Ettin came running after him.

"Uuuuwaaaagg~"

Seeing the Ettin charge towards him, Sungjin drew the Moon Spectre.

I am a mage

He couldn't help but smile at his earlier lie. And before he had even finished his thoughts, the Ettin was already split in half, falling apart.

And as was his habit, he swung his Katana in the air to throw the blood off of the blade. The canyon continued on straight ahead.

Ahead of him, he saw countless Ogres, Ettins, and their smaller minions. But Sungjin preferred this.

I love this Chapter for being so straightforward.

Sungjin charged ahead, Moon Spectre drawn and ready.

***

Serin pulled the bow to its limit. And while everyone's gaze was focused on the arrow tip, she let loose the shot.

PEW

The Arrow flew off to the distance with a satisfying sound.

STAB

It pierced through one of the two heads of an Ettin.

"Graah!"

The remaining head scanned its surroundings and then spotted the four Hunters. It came charging towards the Hunters in anger.

Xian Wang shouted in response. "Pulling successful. Brace yourselves!"

Raj stood in front of the other Hunters and shouted while banging on his shield.

"Here! Come at me!"

The Ettin, overflowing with rage, swung his club down as he charged.

I can't dodge this.

Raj made a judgement call and decided to raise his shield and shout,

"Iron Wall of Anvil!"

The lion-shaped runes etched into his shield grew bright, and the shield doubled in size, as if hiding Raj behind a castle wall.

When the Ettin's club collided with the wall, the blunt weapon shattered into pieces after a loud CRACK

Raj flinched slightly, but most of the momentum had already been cancelled out. Xian Wang stabbed the Ettin, who stood stunned for a moment from the recoil in the chest.

"Gaaa..."

And Santiago passed by Xian, muttering the words,

"Slice and Dice."

The daggers in his hands began to spin on their own, resembling a drill. Santiago dashed towards the Ettin and violently stabbed the monster.

The Ettin stepped back in response to Santiago's savage attack.

PEW

But the remaining head was hit by an arrow, penetrating deep into its skull. The monster collapsed on the spot.

"Amazing..." Xian Wang held the spear with his armpits and applauded his teammates. The others in his party were extremely strong.

Raj, who was in charge of the defense of his team, had an excellent shield, good Endurance, and a high number of Recovery Potions.

Santiago was agile and seemed to wield a pair of Heroic tier Daggers.

And nothing needed to be said about the Gold Medallist Archer Serin, who controlled the start and the end of every fight with her incredibly accurate sniping.

Despite the fact that the mage, Kei, had run off alone without a trace, the Raid proceeded without a hitch thanks to the other three Hunters.

Xian Wang was able to reach this Chapter thanks to being carried to the end of each Raid by exceptionally powerful individuals, but it appeared that teammates in this Chapter were better still.

Once the fight was over, Raj stood up with his regular-sized shield and asked, "Hey, Operator, what's my current HP?"

[HP: 7932/9200]

"Alright, alert me when it drops below a third of the total health so that I can drink potions."

[Understood.]

Xian Wang was shocked. "Your health is over 9000!?"

Raj shrugged as he gave a response. "I mean... If you're going to fight as the vanguard, then I think having high health is standard. In exchange, my offensive power is pretty low."

Serin glanced at him and suggested, "Please make sure you max out your HP before facing the Boss monster. You never know what will happen."

"Sure thing, pretty lady." Raj pretended to stroke his moustache and stole glances at Serin's figure. Xian didn't know if the person in question noticed, but he did.

Xian didn't like it, so he decided to change the subject.

"By the way, I wonder where that mage has gone off to."

Santiago twirled his dagger skilfully as he responded, "Who knows, maybe he got scared and ran off."

Xian looked back at the direction they had come from. He didn't see anybody. The only thing he saw were piles of dead bodies.

The canyon was straight as an arrow. The mage was neither ahead nor behind them. He was nowhere to be seen.

"I'm fairly sure we will be fine at dealing with the normal monsters, but... will it be alright fighting the boss mob with just four of us?"

Xian had raised a reasonable concern, to which Raj replied, "Well... We won't know until we butt heads, right? It's not like we can just run away because we don't think we can do it. You know what this tin can always says."

Raj tapped the cube following him.

"Complete the objective. Or you will die."

Santiago laughed with a high-pitched snicker. Serin didn't respond.

Xian let his shoulders drop. "I guess... you're right after all. Then let's get going."

Ahead, an Ogre could be seen standing alone.

Once again, everyone's eyes were on Serin's bow and arrow.

PEW

Serin's arrows flew off into the distance and landed in the Ogre's head. The Ogre turned with the arrow still stuck in his head, glaring at the Hunters. Filled with rage, he charged towards them. Raj stepped forward to deal with him.

"Bring it on you beast!"

Raj taunted the monster to draw attention while the other three worked together to kill it. Using this strategy, the four Hunters made their way through the canyon, slowly and steadily.

*

"Grah!"

The Ogre angrily swung its mace.

WOOSH, WOOSH

The mace which was swinging in the air sounded quite threatening. Even Sungjin, who had invested many points into Endurance, would be reduced to a bloody pulp if he took several hits.

IF it hits, that is.

Sungjin was no longer at a level where a normal mob could hit him with a simple attack. He easily dodged the mace and swung his Moon Spectre twice while evading the attacks.

The Ogre's blood spewed out of an X-shaped cut on his chest, and it fell on its back.

"Krah!"

Two more clubs came at Sungjin. One was swung by a two-headed Ettin, and the other was swung by a hairy Giant Trogg.

Sungjin crouched and covered himself with Sael's Breath before shouting,

"Solidify!"

The moment his command was uttered, the mantle froze in place. The clubs landed on him, but,

DONG

A dull sound rang out as if the clubs had hit a thick steel plate. The attack did not hurt Sungjin at all.

That's useful.

Sungjin stood up and faced the enemies. The Sael's Breath resumed fluttering in the wind.

"Kuaaa!"

"Uraa!"

The two giants lifted their clubs again, but Sungjin's blade flashed twice.

WOOSH

WOOSH

And the arms holding the clubs, each the thickness of a man's waist, were cut off without resistance.

The now disarmed monsters tried to swat Sungjin, but it was in vain. They were unable to land a blow on him. In just a few seconds, the two giants let out a deep groan and collapsed.

The combat ended, and so Sungjin hopped on top of the Ogre's stomach with one leg and surveyed the area.

In the distance, he could see the main boss Pach and Cho'Roch. Sungjin checked behind him. He saw nothing but a field of corpses littering the canyon. Sungjin called to the Operator.

"Operator, time?"

[39 Minutes 58 Seconds remaining.]

I already got to the main boss and still have about 40 minutes left... I guess I am in no rush to use the Treasure Hunter title anytime soon.

Sungjin hopped off the stomach of the Ogre. He held his hand out towards the corpse and shouted an incantation.

"Awaken and become my slave! Rise of the Dead!"

The Ogre stood up as if nothing had happened and took his place behind Sungjin. Sungjin looked up at him for a moment. It was the first time Sungjin had ever used this spell.

He turned and spoke to his cube, "Operator, how do I control him?"

[Undead monsters raised by Rise of the Dead will respond to verbal commands.]

Sungjin decided to try it out.

"Follow me for now"

"Kraa..." The Ogre responded in a lower and flatter tone than when he was alive.

It followed Sungjin. Very. Slowly. Sungjin looked back and saw that he was walking sluggishly towards him.

"What the... Why is it so slow?"

Sungjin walked back towards the undead Giant. He took a look around. Once he confirmed that all the enemies were dead, he spread his arms wide.

"Hit me."

"Grah~"

The Ogre lifted up his club and swung down. Of course, the movement was extremely slow.

WOOSH

Sungjin slightly tilted his body and easily evaded the strike. The Ogre seemed several times slower than when it was alive.

...I guess my Magic Power is too low.

His spell was nowhere near as powerful as 'that person' from his previous life.

When 'that person' cast Rise of the Dead, the resulting undead revived stronger than the original. Sungjin looked over to the boss Pach and Cho'Roch.

I can't even use it as a meat shield at this level.

Sungjin pointed at the giant.

"Go back to being dead."

"Gaah..."

The Ogre zombie fell over again, unmoving. Sungjin stared at the Ogre for a moment.

"Ah, right..." He recalled that he had a strange-looking bell in his pocket by the name Manyata. Sungjin took it out.

"Operator, does this item affect revived undead as well?"

[It does.]

I should try it next time.

He put back the bell.

"Current mana?"

[MP: 1090/3990]

Frostbite and Rise of the Dead cost 790 and 1580 respectively. He had enough for a Frostbite, and was a little short to use Rise of the Dead.

He had nearly reached the boss without considering his MP level.
I should try to be better at managing my mana in the future.

Sungjin pointed at an Ettin's corpse and said, "Lich's Beckoning"

The Lich's Finger, which was previously wrapped around his ring finger, slithered its way up to his knuckle and beckoned twice. A blue, mist-like light emerged from the corpse and was sucked into his outstretched finger. Even though the process was meant to help Sungjin recover lost mana, he felt slightly uncomfortable.

"Operator, Mana?"

[MP: 3990/3990]

"Mmm. Ok."

Sungjin walked towards the hall where the boss was waiting.

Pach and Cho'Roch was an Ogre with two heads like that of an Ettin. The boss saw the approaching Hunter and yelled at him simultaneously.

"Come, Human!"

"It's a Human!"

[Caution! Boss Monster]

[Ogre Mage Pach and Cho'Roch has appeared!]

The cube rang out with an announcement.

"Mage? What do you mean? I am a warrior!"

"I am a powerful mage!"

The head holding a large club yelled in anger, and the skinnier head on the left nodded happily.

Sungjin could not differentiate between 'Pach and Cho'Roch'. But momentarily, they looked at each other and yelled at the same time.

"What are you talking about? We're a warrior!"

"What the hell are you talking about? We're obviously a mage!"

"You should listen to your elders!"

"What do you mean? I am older one!"

"What?"

"It's obviously me who's older. My head came out first!"

Sungjin shook his head.

They're exactly the same as last time... Loud and annoying.

He drew out his blade. The boss brothers finally turned their attentions to him and said the same thing for the first time.

"You dare challenge us?"

"I'll kill you! Puny Human!"

"I'll kill you! Puny Human!"

***

"Gruah!"

The Trogg brandished his axe. Raj easily blocked the attack with his shield when,

SMACK

A stone came flying, hitting him straight on the head.

"Ack!" Raj cried out in pain and fell over. Santiago, who was attempting to flank the Trogg as usual, noticed that rocks were flying his way as well and backed off.

When the Hunters turned to see where the rocks were coming from, they saw two Troggs throwing fist-sized stones towards them.

Serin quickly changed her aim and launched an arrow at the Troggs.

"Kaa!"

The arrow pierced the hand of the Trogg who was about to throw another stone. The Trogg involuntarily dropped the rock which landed on its feet.

"Kaaack!" the creature cried out in pain.

Disabling the Trogg, Serin nocked another arrow and aimed for the other one. However, the Trogg threw a rock at Serin before she could react.

The large piece of rock came flying at speeds comparable to her arrow. Serin lowered the bow, but it was too late to move out of the way.

"Miss Serin!"

Xian Wang quickly stood in front of her and tried to deflect the stone.

POW

The stone broke into smaller pieces, and the shards embedded themselves deep into his skin.

"Ah..."

Xian Wang was brought to his knees. Serin took the opportunity to nock another arrow. The Trogg hastily stooped down to pick up another stone, but she was faster with her bow.

"Kuraah!"

Serin's arrow pierced through the Trogg's head.

The Trogg who had dropped his stone bent down to pick up the rock again, but Serin unleashed two rapid shots back to back; one through the neck and the other through the heart, killing the target. Only the first Trogg remained.

"Iron wall of Anvil!"

"Slice and Dice!"

The last enemy was killed with the cooperation of Santiago and Raj. Raj, who was still bleeding from his head, suggested:

"Let's take a break for a moment before we continue further."

The cube announced

[Your HP is now under two-thirds.]

Xian, who was also bleeding all over, agreed.

"Yes, that's a good idea."

The plan was to take the enemies down one by one, always as a group of four versus one. But because pairs of enemy reinforcements would appear without warning, it had become difficult to make good progress.

Raj uttered a complaint as he drank his potion. "Just where the hell are those pairs of reinforcements coming from?"

Xian answered while uncorking his own. "I thought... I saw them climbing out of some sort of tunnel under the ground."

However, as they were speaking, the cube suddenly let out an announcement.

[Caution! Boss Monster]

[Ogre Mage Pach and Cho'Roch has appeared!]

"What?!" Raj chugged the rest of his potion and stood up, readying his shield.

"Boss?" Xian also quickly finished his potion and picked up his spear. Santiago got up from his seat taking out his dagger; he scanned the surroundings.

Serin quickly placed an arrow on the bow and took a look around. But nothing, not even minions, could be spotted.

The four Hunters tensed up and anxiously looked around, but nothing came to attack them. After five seconds, Xian finally grumbled,

"Boss appeared? But... where?"

*

"Fight me, human!"

The warrior shouted loudly to goad Sungjin. The sheer volume of the voice might have intimidated an ordinary person. But Sungjin fearlessly charged towards the boss.

I don't know who's Pach and who's Cho'Roch, but... mage first!

Sungjin dashed towards the Ogre on the left holding the staff. The mage shouted an incantation.

"Move like the wind! Haste!"

Thanks to the magic, the Ogre moved three... no, four times faster than ordinary Ogres. By the time Sungjin reached the Ogre within melee range, the Ogre had twisted his body to face him with the right side brandishing his weapon.

Sungjin swung his Katana, but the warrior moved just as fast to block all his attacks.

CLANG, CLANG, CLANG!

After three rapid strikes, the Ogre spun around a full rotation, and the mage on the left side charged at him with the staff; an unexpected tactic.

Sungjin leaned far back to dodge the attack. But the warrior Ogre followed up and immediately launched another strike. Sungjin had no choice but to leap back.

Immediately Sungjin retreated, the mage raised the staff and recited an incantation.

"Incinerate everything in your path! Fireball!"

A gigantic ball of fire came flying towards Sungjin.

BOOM

He leaped back again, but he wasn't able to get far enough away from the heat wave resulting from the explosion. Sungjin crouched and covered his body with the Ice Queen's Mantle.

Most of the flames were nullified by the frozen mantle, but Sungjin had lost hit points to an enemy for the first time since the restart. Pach and Cho'Roch laughed at Sungjin, mocking him.

"You think you can take us on alone?"

"Stupid! Idiot!"

Sungjin bit his lower lip.

A perfect pair...

The enemy attacked with a staff and a club independent of each other, so predicting their attack was difficult. Adding magic attacks on top of that made it even more so.

It's definitely hard to defeat it alone.

So Sungjin took out 'Grand Kin's Wooden Figurine' and threw it in front of him.

"Cain, come out."

The figurine transformed into a large wolf and took its side by Sungjin. Pach and Cho'Roch laughed again at the new development.

"What a cute puppy!"

"So adorable! ADORABLE!"

Sungjin paid them no mind and spoke to his familiar.

"Cain. Get the left head."

Upon hearing Sungjin's instructions, he dashed towards the right to fight the warrior. Cain leaped towards the left head as instructed. But Pach and Cho'Roch were not going to take this standing still.

The warrior raised his club to counter Sungjin, and the mage recited an incantation.

"Burn, membrane of flames! Fire Wall!"

Almost instantly, a wall of fire appeared in front of the Ogre. But, Sungjin had moved in faster than the casting of the spell and was already engaging the warrior. Cain, on the other hand, was unable to make it in time and was stuck outside.

Sungjin swung his Katana towards the right side but,

"You little...!"

The warrior swung his metallic club to block his attacks. As expected, the mage joined in by swinging his staff as well. Sungjin dodged and shook the bell he had prepared in his left hand.

DING

The small bell rang once, and Sungjin shouted, "Cain!"

Instantly, Cain came bursting through the firewall and launched himself towards the mage at an unbelievable speed.

Both arms of the Ogre had been extended towards Sungjin and they were without defense for a moment.

Cain easily found the opportunity to bite and hold onto the mage's neck. The mage desperately called to the other head for help.

"Pach!"

"I know!"

Now Sungjin knew who was who. Warrior Pach swung his club to bat Cain away, who was holding onto his throat.

And at that moment, the warrior had let Sungjin free to act as he wished. The Hunter attacked without mercy.

As always, Sungjin aimed to disarm the enemy first; Pach's hands were cut off.

"Ahhh!!! Cho'Roch!"

Pach desperately cried out to Cho'Roch for help.

Cho'Roch frantically waved his staff to ward off Sungjin, but there was no way he could face him alone.

Sungjin easily dodged the staff and counter-attacked, wounding the boss in the chest.

"Ack!"

"Kaa!"

Both heads screamed out loud as they stumbled backward. Sungjin prepared to finish them off.

"Wind! Push away my..."

"Rawr!"

Cho'Roch attempted to cast a spell, but Cain once again leaped up and bit him in the throat, preventing him from finishing his incantations. And using the opportunity, Sungjin cut the Ogre in half.

"Grauuu..."

"Grauuu..."

Pach and Cho'Roch let out strange noises as they fell to the ground, defeated. The cube announced victory with a jubilant voice.

[Ogre Mage Pach and Cho'Roch defeated!]

[Raid Cleared! Returning to the Black Market in 36 Minutes and 32 Seconds]

"Haa..." Sungjin let out a sigh and instinctively wiped his brow.

The boss was much harder than he had thought. No matter how high his stats were, trying to beat a boss designed to be fought by five people was no easy task.

"Awoo~"

Cain let out a howl as if asking for attention. Sungjin obediently turned his gaze onto him.

"Ah, Cain, you did a great job."

Sungjin put his hands around Cain's neck and checked his sides. Specifically, where he was hit earlier by Pach's club.

"Are you alright?"

Cain gave a short bark to show he was fine.

Master's Bell had Invulnerability built in. Cain had greatly benefitted this time. Not a single hair was harmed on his body.

Now that he thought of it, Cain had leaped through a solid wall of fire earlier, like some circus lion act. But he had emerged unscathed. Sungjin pet Cain on the head.

"Fire must have been scary to jump through as a wolf... You were really brave, my friend."

Happy from being praised, Cain let out a long howl.

*

[Ogre Mage Pach and Cho'Roch defeated!]

[Raid Cleared! Returning to the Black Market in 36 Minutes and 32 Seconds]

The other Hunters stopped in their tracks.

"What?"

"The hell...?"

Something strange was going on. The Hunters were right to be confused. While hunting normal mobs, the Operator announced that the Boss 'had appeared' and now it announced that the Boss was 'defeated.'

The four people couldn't imagine that the 'Mage' Kei had cleared the boss single-handedly; it was against common sense and good reason. Raj double checked with the Operator.

"Wait, Operator, did you just say that we cleared the Raid?"

[Yes, that is correct. You will return to the Black Market in 36 Minutes and 24 Seconds.]

Everyone frowned at the Operator's words.

Xian Wang pointed forward with his spear and said, "We didn't even get a glimpse of the boss, and yet it was defeated... I don't know what happened, but we should go a bit further."

But, the Hunters were even more shocked once they entered deeper into the Canyon. In front of them was an entire stretch of canyon floor covered with corpses of giants as far as the eyes could see.

"Whoa..."

Xian looked back at his team. Even the normally calm and collected Serin looked shocked.

Raj and Santiago exchanged a word between themselves. Xian asked the other three Hunters, "Just what is going... on?"

"Come over for a second." Raj beckoned Xian to come closer.

Xian walked over to Raj and Santiago. Once he got close enough, Raj spoke quietly.

"Well, we don't know what happened... but the Raid is apparently done and... we got plenty of time. What do you say, wanna have some fun?"

Fun?

Xian tilted his head, unsure of what he meant. Raj glanced over to Serin as he continued.

"It won't be easy, but if we three work together... Hmm?"

Once Xian realized what he was suggesting, he was taken back. "What the hell are you?"

But he didn't even finish his sentence when

STAB

He heard a noise from below. When Xian looked down, he saw Santiago's dagger embedded deep into his side.

***

Sungjin sheathed the Moon Spectre. Since the boss had been slain, it was time to begin the search for the hidden pieces.

However, Sungjin was in a dilemma.

Assuming that the secret place and the hidden boss both exist... when would it be best to use the Treasure Hunter active skill?

Sungjin did not know which would be more difficult to find, and therefore more 'worth it' to use the title effect for. However, he was interrupted by Cain's howling.

"Awooo~"

Cain was howling towards the direction of the canyon they had come from.

"What's wrong, Cain?"

Sungjin asked the wolf. Cain flicked his ears as if he was listening to something in the distance. Sungjin stayed silent so that Cain could concentrate. Moments later, Cain looked up at Sungjin and yelped.

He started moving and began to lead the way. Cain seemed to be in a hurry as if it was urgent. Sungjin chased after him quickly.

"What's going on?" Sungjin tilted his head in confusion.

Did he... spot a hidden piece?

Just in case, Sungjin gave him the command.

"If you found something, go ahead and show me. You can run as fast as you can manage, I'll keep up."

At his command, Cain stopped holding back and bolted off, sprinting ahead.

He let out a long howl before running at full speed. Without question, Cain was much faster than Sungjin.

"Swift Paw"

Sungjin used the power of his wolf claws to catch up.

*

Xian unsteadily stepped back. With the dagger still embedded in his abdomen, he swung his spear.

BANG

His spear was blocked by Raj's sturdy shield.

Serin finally noticed that the men had begun to fight amongst themselves and glanced over. "Excuse me, what's going on?"

Santiago brandished his other dagger.

STAB

He stabbed Xian a second time. Serin had fought all this time not batting an eye while killing countless monsters, but once she saw teammates getting hurt, she covered her mouth and gasped, "What the..."

Xian waved his spear wildly. "Miss Serin... Run!"

He tried to warn her, but it became his last words. Raj smashed his club over his head, killing Xian.

Once Xian collapsed to the ground, a red light illuminated Raj and Santiago's body for a moment, and a warning blared out from the cube.

[Allied Hunters attacked. Entering 'Troll' state.]

[Hunters in Troll state receive 10% penalty to Raid Rewards.]

[And in the event that the Troll is killed by other Hunters,]

[It will not inflict the 'Troll' state on the attacker.]

"Eh? Is that so?" Raj responded back to the cube's announcement. But Santiago gave it no mind.

He was already charging towards Serin.

"Why..." Serin panicked upon seeing Santiago charge towards her and readied the bow.

PEW

The arrow landed in his shoulder, but it did not faze him; Santiago continued to run with the arrow sticking out of his shoulders.

The distance between them rapidly decreased. Serin knocked and released another shot, but he was already within arm's reach.

PEW

Santiago easily evaded the shot and attacked with his dagger; he aimed for her wrist holding the bow.

However, his dagger collided with her bow instead. Serin quickly pulled back her arm, but her bow was knocked away from her.

Serin pulled out the dagger she kept on her back, but she was no match for Santiago in a knife fight. She aimed for Santiago's chest and stabbed, but,

"Clang!"

With one strike, he knocked the dagger out of her hands and grabbed her by the wrist. Serin tried to put up resistance by hitting Santiago with her bare fist, but it was futile.

Santiago took his dagger and stabbed Serin through the hand.

"Kyaa!" Serin let out a cry of pain.

Santiago followed through with the attack and embedded the dagger deep into the ground, pinning her hand. Once he prevented the use of both of her hands, his eyes betrayed the perverse intentions behind them as he licked his lips.

"Just kill me, you disgusting animal." Serin spat insults at him, but he paid her no mind.

Using the other dagger, Santiago deftly ripped open Serin's clothes, as if he was very familiar with the process.

"Let me go, you bastard!" Serin wriggled to try and free herself, but due to the dagger, it only caused her to bleed more.

Raj stood from the back and spoke as if Serin belonged to him. "Hey hey, don't make too many scratches; I don't like damage."

Santiago finished up with Serin and began taking off his own clothes. Suddenly

"Roar!"

A wolf appeared out of nowhere and slammed into Santiago; he was caught completely unaware. Santiago was knocked far away by the impact.

"What?"

Raj shouted out, alarmed. Meanwhile, someone spoke from behind him.

"Whoa whoa, what's all this?"

Raj jumped up in surprise at the sound of the voice. He looked around. Behind him was the Master Hunter Kei who had gone missing for the entire duration of the Raid.

Sungjin looked at the red outline on Raj and Santiago and commented, "Troll state?"

That was all he said. He saw Xian's corpse, and the now naked Serin on the ground.

"Ah... well, I guess something like this is inevitable," Sungjin spoke to himself and grabbed his extremely shabby-looking Katana handle.

"Hmm... It doesn't suit me to act like a knight in shining armor, but I also don't want to run into trolls like you later down the line."

Anyone who was not an ally was an enemy. Raj quickly made up his mind and attacked Sungjin. Since Sungjin was a 'mage,' Raj

191

wanted to take the initiative before the other party had a chance to cast a spell.

"Die!"

He swung his club at Sungjin. It should have been easy to take down a mage with brute force. It should have. But.

WOOSH

Raj's arm was cut off with a single lazy swing by Sungjin.

"Ahhh!"

Raj grabbed his arm by the elbow and backed off. He held up his shield worth 600 coins and retreated backward.

Despite losing one arm, he kept on concentrating. He had tanked for four Chapters now.

Endure it. I will drink potions and outlast him...

But interrupting his thoughts, Sungjin ran towards Raj. Raj hastily activated a skill.

"Iron Wall of Anvil!"

Raj's shield grew in size and covered him. But, Sungjin cut the shield in half with a single strike.

"What is going on?" Once his trusty shield was cut down so effortlessly, Raj instinctively backed off as he began stuttering. "You... Mage... You..."

Sungjin's sword knew no mercy. He walked up to the hunter and swung his Katana.

Raj was wearing an intricate chain mail armor, but the Katana cut through all as if they didn't exist.

CHI-CHI-CHI-CHANG

Along with the chains being cut apart, his skin and bones were cut away as well.

"AHHHHHHHH!" Raj let out a loud cry of pain. It was only one blow, but,

[Warning! HP is below 10%]

The Operator rang out with a warning.

Raj opened his eyes wide in disbelief as he continued to step back. "My HP is almost 10,000..."

Sungjin couldn't help but grin. "So what? I probably have almost 20,000. Isn't that right, Operator?"

[Your maximum HP is 17,100.]

Raj's eyes grew even wider. The stats were incomparably different. Raj continued to stare, unable to act.

Sungjin spun his Katana around as he spoke, "I don't like seeing human blood... but it looks like you guys killed that Chinese guy. You understand that you guys spilled human blood, right?

Sungjin was about to finish off Raj with his Katana, but,

PEW

An arrow came and pierced through Raj's skull between his brows. Raj died before he even realized he was hit.

*

Sungjin lowered his Katana and looked behind him. Serin was holding her bow, with a pitiful, pathetic expression on her face.

"Why would you anger a scary lady...?" Sungjin complained as he took a look around. There was one other troll. But, he was nowhere to be found.

Where...?

Cain stood a bit further away, waiting for him. He had ambushed the other troll earlier, but was alone for some reason.

Sungjin approached his familiar and asked, "Cain, where did he go?"

But Cain did not answer. Instead, he faced somewhere off in the distance and growled.

Something was wrong. Sungjin inspected Cain's body. When he looked closer, he saw that there were small cuts around his neck. The wound was not red, but a strange hue of purple.

"Paralysis poison," concluded Sungjin. He got up in anger and looked around. But there was no trace of the troll. The troll must have poisoned Cain with Paralysis and ran away.

Cain was stuck, unable to move and deeply in pain. Sungjin whispered into Cain's ears,

"You did well, Cain. Go rest at the inn. I'll catch up."

And standing up, he uttered a command.

"Unsummon."

Cain returned to the form of a small wooden figurine. Sungjin placed the figurine back in his pocket and approached Serin.

Serin was trying to cover herself with the remainder of her clothes while crying. Although she didn't make any noise, hot tears streamed endlessly down her cheeks.

Sungjin returned the Katana to the sheath and asked her, "Are you okay?"

Serin wordlessly glared at Sungjin, as if to declare that all men were the same. Sungjin raised his hands to show he meant no harm.

"Ah, I have no interest in you. But... I have to go searching for something, so I have to leave this place. That guy got away, that Assassin guy. So leaving you alone here is a little..."

Once Sungjin mentioned Assassin, her eyes instantly teared up. It was inevitable; just moments ago, he had almost managed to rape her.

Sungjin scratched his head and continued. "Well... yeah... To make a long story short, I'm going to go and look for something, so I can't stay here. If you want to follow, I will protect you. You should come with me if it's not too much to ask."

Sungjin headed back towards the canyon. A few steps away, he looked back.

Serin wrapped herself with a ripped shirt and was wordlessly following him. Seeing her, Sungjin thought to himself,

The consequence of exceptional beauty... Most likely... she didn't manage to make it last time because...

You cannot survive to the end with just skill; that was how the Raid worked.

Concluding his thoughts, Sungjin resumed his footsteps, searching for the hidden piece.

***

Sungjin continuously scanned his surroundings as he progressed through the Canyon. He was searching for the hidden piece while keeping an eye out for the Assassin.

And once in a while, he looked back to check on Serin, who followed from behind. Her cheeks carried traces of tears, but she looked much calmer now.

Of course, because of her earlier 'experience,' she kept her bow and arrow at the ready, but she was regaining her usual haughty demeanor.

Sungjin stopped to speak to her. "Excuse me, but..."

Serin bit her lip without replying. She was still extremely wary of Sungjin.

"Did you happen to see anything weird or out of place on your way here?" Sungjin asked Serin carefully.

"Weird...?"

"Yes. Anything is fine... Did you see anything like that? Something that shouldn't be there, something that seemed odd... Like a concealed location..."

Serin answered as if Sungjin's question was puzzling. "What do you mean by that? This whole place is filled with nothing but strange things."

"Excuse me?"

"Hairy monsters, pot-bellied beasts, two-headed giants."

"I mean..."

She was technically correct, so Sungjin didn't have much to say in the way of a reply. He decided to change his question instead.

"I don't mean it in that way. I meant especially strange things. An abnormally powerful beast among beasts, weirder things among weird things. Something that stands out even in this place."

Serin shook her head. "I don't know. I hate being around these monsters; I just wanted to get out of this place as soon as possible. So I focused on nothing but shooting arrows into their heads."

"I see." Sungjin nodded. In truth, he didn't expect much from her anyway; even by Chapter 10 most people were unaware that hidden pieces existed at all.

Should I use the Treasure Hunter's active skill?

Serin then interrupted Sungjin's thoughts and asked a question.

"Kei... That's a fake name, right? What country are you really from?"

Sungjin shook his head.

"It doesn't matter. Think what you want," Sungjin answered half-heartedly. He didn't want to get close to someone who was most likely going to die in the near future.

It always hurt less when a stranger died compared to when a friend did. That was the reason why Sungjin called himself 'K.'

"It has to be between China, Japan, and Korea," speculated Serin.

Sungjin didn't plan on answering. Then,

"Between Kimchi Jjigae and Doenjang Jjigae, which is your favourite?"

Sungjin instinctively and unintentionally 'thought' of the answer. Serin's sharp eyes did not miss his slight change in behaviour.

"You must be Korean," said Serin.

"What?"

"If you were Chinese or Japanese, you probably would have first asked what those were."

Sungjin thought of saying *I've been to Korea before.*

And stopped himself.

She's a smart one.

Sungjin turned his head halfway and replied, "I said this before, but what difference does nationality make here?"

"It is only right that the one who is saved remembers the name and nationality of the one who saved her," came Serin's response.

"What?" Sungjin turned his head all the way back to look at her.

She finally replied, "I wanted to say thank you earlier."

Now that he thought of it, it was the first time she had thanked him. A faint smile appeared on her face, as she slightly lowered her head towards him.

Sungjin was battle hardened and emotionally vacant, but even his long-cold heart was shaken by her beautiful smile.

"Ah well, got it." Sungjin intentionally looked away. He then called to the Operator.

"Remaining time?"

[32 minutes 49 seconds]

...If I don't find it within twenty minutes, I will use the Treasure Hunter Active skill.

Sungjin resumed combing the Canyon.

*

A long time after, Serin called out to Sungjin.

"Hey."

Sungjin stopped on the spot. He turned and looked at her. "What is it?

Serin pointed with her thumb somewhere before continuing, "Isn't that suspicious?"

Sungjin looked over in the general direction she was pointing towards. There was an ordinary canyon wall. "What's strange about it?"

"Its appearance... Have you ever been to the Grand Canyon?"

Sungjin shook his head. He was an orphan. Poor even among the poor. He had never been out of the country his entire life; not even to China or Japan.

"I have. Twice. I lived in America as a child," said Serin.

Sungjin nodded. He recalled a news article from the past.

Beautiful Archer Serin Han. Born into money and privilege; her father was a major player in the American finance industry.

"The canyon walls are formed by compacting earth and sediments layer over layer over long periods of time. So, typically, there are varieties of colors present on the canyon wall. But over there..."

Sungjin looked over to the canyon wall again, listening to her explanation. Now that she mentioned it, he too noticed the strangeness of that particular part of the wall.

To the left and the right of it, the walls were layered horizontally in a uniform pattern. Only this portion of the canyon wall was different.

At the center, the layers were narrow, and the colors shifted within the layer. The variance of the color within the layer became worse closer to the center.

The way the canyon face was shaped, it stuck out in some parts, and it was indented inward at others. On this portion of the wall, however, the outs and ins were too straight, as if designed and cut with precision tools.

"Wait... this looks like..." Sungjin tried to touch the canyon wall. The moment his hand touched the wall cracks appeared on it, and a slick white surface became visible.

What is this, some slime? He thought for a moment. But in the middle of the white surface, a large black pupil rotated to look at him.

"Eye?!" Sungjin cried out in shock. And at the same time, the earth shook tremendously. The Operator gave out an announcement.

[Caution! Hidden Boss]

[King of Giants Cyclops has appeared!]

"What does she mean, 'Hidden Boss'?" Serin asked from behind, but Sungjin didn't answer. One side of the canyon wall rose up, and a hand emerged from within.

Serin looked up at the gigantic hand and gasped. "My goodness..."

The gargantuan hand grasped the top of the canyon wall.

RUMBLE

The ground began to shake again. Along with the earth-shattering rumble and quake, the hidden boss began to show itself.

The boss's stature made the Ogres, Ettins, and Trolls look like little children's toys.

Just looking up at the boss, it was easily as tall as a ten-story building. Sungjin had seen many gigantic bosses in later Chapters, but never one as tall as this.

The giant stood up by leaning on the canyon cliff wall and blinked its huge eye a few times. It looked down upon Sungjin and let out a mighty roar.

"Kruuuuah!"

The earth itself trembled at its monstrous bellow.

PEW

A familiar sound rang out from behind, and he saw an arrow zip through the air. Serin shot an arrow up towards the giant's head. Of course, the target was the lone eye.

Taking out its eye would make the hunt comparatively easy. But once the arrow reached about its chest height, the giant slapped it out of the air.

The height of the Giant was about 25-30 meters. No matter how large the Cyclops' eyes were, it was a difficult height to reach with the arrow.

Serin complained under her breath. "Just what the heck is that thing?"

She looked discouraged. That was probably the normal reaction for this moment. Even though she had overcome large wolves, undead monsters, and other nightmarish creatures, she had never seen anything so seemingly unsurmountable.

Sungjin drew out his blade and shouted, "Stay back for a bit!"

And charged at the giant.

Let's test the waters.

The Cyclops raised its foot when it noticed Sungjin run towards it. A huge shadow appeared on and around Sungjin.

Sungjin quickly moved out of the shadow of the colossus. Its speed was nothing extraordinary, but due to its enormous size and mass, improperly dodging would result in becoming an instant pancake.

BOOOM

The foot landed where Sungjin had stood moments before. Turning around, Sungjin swung his Katana at one of the toes in front of him.

"Graagh!" the creature cried in pain as the strike landed on him.

Each time it cried out, the earth itself shook along with it.

Is it taking any damage? Sungjin asked himself. Another shadow appeared on top of Sungjin. He tumbled backwards.

BOOM

A large fist punched the earth where he had been moments before. Sungjin prepared to counter attack when the fist opened up, and the giant tried to catch and grab Sungjin.

Sungjin couldn't avoid it. He quickly wrapped the Mantle around himself and shouted, "Solidify!"

CRACK! SHATTER!

Sael's Breath shattered upon contact with the Giant's hand. Having blocked the Giant's attack with the Mantle, Sungjin spun around and swung his Katana towards the hand.

"Kaaaa!"

The middle finger was cut deep by the Katana. It evidently hurt a great deal. The Cyclops began stomping the ground chaotically in anger. Sungjin rapidly dodged the indiscriminate attack with great dexterity. Even while doing so, he thought to himself,

It's not a boss I can easily kill even with high stats. It's going to take more than one or two shots.

And that was the truth. No matter how powerful Sungjin and his Katana was, it was only as large as a needle in comparison to the massive giant. The only parts of its body Sungjin could destroy in one hit were its fingers or toes.

Climb the thing and make a lethal strike.

Sungjin made up his mind and began to put his plan into action. He approached the giant to lure an attack. It first raised its foot.

Feet are no good.

Sungjin dodged the foot for now. And as a follow-up, a slightly smaller shadow appeared around Sungjin.

Without a doubt, this was the fist. Sungjin intentionally dodged it by a hair.

BOOM!

The fist landed on the ground close by. Instead of swinging his Katana, he jumped up and held onto the hand.

And without realizing that Sungjin had hitched a ride on his wrist, the giant raised his hands as normal.

Along the way up, the Cyclops turned his attention to his hand. The two stared at each other.

Danger.

Sungjin felt threatened, and quickly stabbed Moon Spectre deep into the giant's hand.

"Grrrr~" The giant cried out in pain as if it was stung by a bee. It angrily waved its arms about, to throw Sungjin off of him. Sungjin was thrashed about violently.

It was a dangerous moment for him. If he let go of Moon Spectre, then he would be flung off far into the distance like an ant. The giant only increased the intensity it applied in swinging its arm.

If this keeps up...

While Sungjin was flailing in the air, he heard someone calling for him.

"Kei!"

Despite the shaking, he still looked towards the source of the voice. Serin had climbed to the top of the canyon cliff and was aiming towards the giant with her bow and arrow.

She let loose an arrow aimed at its eye.

"Rain of Arrows."

The arrows multiplied in the air and flew towards the giant's face. Every single one of them hit the mark; it was inevitable due to the large size of her target.

In just a moment, dozens of arrows embedded themselves deep into the giant's face.

"Graaagh!"

The Cyclops screamed out in pain and instinctively used its hands to cover its face from the arrows. And with it, Sungjin was brought to his target.

Sungjin pulled out the Moon Spectre from the wrist of the Cyclops and held it in both hands. And once he grew close enough, he pushed himself off from the hand, launching himself towards the head.

"Yargh!" Sungjin yelled out loud as he sailed through the air, Katana pointed straight at the eye. And just like that, Sungjin impaled the Moon Spectre deep into the Cyclops' eye.

***

Sungjin held onto the Moon Spectre and dragged his blade through the Cyclops' flesh—from the giant's lone eye, through the nose, past the jaws, and until it sliced through and emerged from the underside of the chin.

Once Sungjin had separated the giant's face in half, he impaled the blade into the Cyclops' chest and continued to carve up its body as he made his way down.

"Graaagh..."

The Cyclops let out cries of agony through its now separated mouth. Once Sungjin reached its abdomen, the cube announced their victory.

[Hidden Boss King of Giants Cyclops Cleared!]

However, Sungjin did not retract his blade just yet; he was still too high up to jump down safely. Controlling the Moon Spectre's depth in the giant's flesh to adjust his falling speed, Sungjin slowly made his way down the giant.

Once he was at a reasonable height, Sungjin pulled the sword out of the giant and leapt off. After a few rotations in the air, he landed on the canyon floor safely. The giant slowly collapsed over the side of the canyon wall.

RUMBLE RUMBLE RUMBLE RUMBLE

Along with a deafening sound of shattered canyon wall, large volumes of sand and dirt rained down from above. The cloud of dust which followed obscured the vision and blocked the airways.

"Cough! Cough!"

Sungjin couldn't help but begin to cough. Covering his nose and mouth with his hands, he slowly walked out of the area. Meanwhile, the Operator announced

[Raid 100% complete!]

[However, there is an active 'Troll' in the party.]

[Raid reward will be postponed until the Troll, or the other members, are eliminated]

[or if the timer runs out.]

Sungjin, who had relaxed his guard once the hidden boss was eliminated, quickly realized his oversight.

The Assassin!

Even up until the boss showed himself, he had been on alert for the assassin, but once the fight began, he had completely forgotten about him. Sungjin pulled the Moon Spectre out again and walked through the dust cloud.

As time passed, the sandstorm settled down. Little by little the air cleared up, and he could see again. In the distance, he heard Serin's voice.

"Kei!"

It was hard to hear through the dust, but she sounded nervous. Sungjin made his way towards the source of her voice.

"Se... Serin! Serin!"

In the distance, he could see someone standing. Sungjin made his way towards the figure, but Santiago's voice stopped him in his tracks.

"Hey, mage. Stop right there, or I will kill this girl."

Sungjin had no choice but to stop.

Once the dust settled a bit more, he was able to see what was going on.

Santiago held a dagger to Serin's neck and was glaring at him. "I guess I should call you swordsman instead. I saw everything. Drop your weapon."

Sungjin paused to take a look at Santiago, and then at Serin who was held hostage. He took a moment to think. *What should I do?*

Seeing that Sungjin still held onto his Katana, Santiago threatened him further. "No tricks. She's one slice away from death. I've made sure of that."

There was one dagger impaled into Serin's side. She was bleeding out from the wound.

Sungjin yelled to calm Santiago down. "I got it I got it. I'll put down the sword. Please let her go."

Slowly and cautiously, Sungjin placed the Moon Spectre back into the scabbard. And he untied the scabbard from his side. Pretending to drop it, he rapidly drew the blade out and shouted, "Deathly Wail!"

The Moon Spectre glowed bright blue.

"KYAAAAAAAAA!"

A hell-like screech filled the air, reverberating all around the canyon. Sungjin immediately charged forward.

"Uhh... uh..." Santiago lost his grip on Serin and took an involuntary step back. Sungjin rushed towards him. Santiago waved his dagger towards Sungjin wildly, but,

CLANG CLANG!

In just two swings, Santiago's daggers were knocked away from his hands. Sungjin kicked his undefended chest.

POW

Santiago fell on his backside. Sungjin stared at him. Santiago's eyes were filled with terror, for one reason or another.

"Ahh... Ahh..." Without getting up, Santiago tried to crawl away as fast as he could. Sungjin walked up to him and cut off both of his feet.

"Ahhh!" Santiago let out a long cry of agony but, Sungjin remained unfazed.

"This is for Cain." Sungjin pointed his sword towards Santiago as he walked over.

Now certain that he was going to die, Santiago began to beg for his life. "Mercy... Mercy! Please!"

Santiago begged while holding his hands together in a prayer. This helped Sungjin see the fancy tattoo covering Santiago's arm.

Sungjin held up the Moon Spectre towards his face and said, "I know scum like you. On Earth, before we were sent here, you probably did these kinds of things without hesitation. Of course, looking at things from 'this' angle."

Sungjin did not attack him with his sword and kept on talking.

"You probably looked down at your victims, who were helpless and begged for mercy. I could have killed you many times over by now. The reason why I am waiting..."

"Anything but my life," Santiago continued to beg.

"This is it. I wanted you to experience this. The terror you inflicted on your victims until now."

Sungjin counted to five in his mind. Santiago tried to escape, but his feet had been cut off. He was able to crawl away slowly with his hands, but it didn't get him far.

"I think that's enough for introspection." Sungjin took a single step forward and swung his sword.

"Die."

SHING

Santiago's head flew off and landed some distance away. As was his habit, Sungjin swung his Katana once to fling the blood off of the blade.

Santiago's blood splattered on the ground, and Sungjin returned the blade to its sheath. Turning around, he left to attend to Serin.

Serin was trembling while tightly holding herself. If anything could be described as a side effect of Deathly Wail, it was that it also affected allies equally.

Sungjin approached her and tried to calm her down, "Don't be afraid, Miss Serin. It's okay. That thing was not real... it's fake."

Serin looked up towards Sungjin and asked, "And... him?"

Sungjin tilted his head towards where Santiago's corpse lay. She uneasily turned her gaze towards the direction he indicated. In the distance, she saw Santiago's severed head.

Serin returned her gaze to him and said, "Thank you... Really, thank you, Kei."

Sungjin nodded to acknowledge her expression of gratitude and moved away from her to give her some privacy. The cube broke the silence.

[All 'Trolls' in the party have been eliminated.]

[Distributing Raid reward]

He hadn't found the hidden piece yet, and the distribution already began. It was okay, since he could still go off to search once the distribution was over.

[Calculating Rewards Earned.]

[Monsters Slain. Ogres: 30. Trogg: 20. Ettin: 10. Total 3200 points.]

[Boss Monster Slain: Ogre Mage Pach and Cho'Roch: 400 points.]

[Hidden Boss King of Giants Cyclops: 400 points.]

[Final point count: 4000 Points. Distributing points.]

First up was Serin.

[Your contribution is 29.5%. 1180 Stat Points, 1180 Black Coins awarded. Raid Clear Bonus 1000 Stat Points and 1000 Black Coins awarded. Distributing 2180 Stat Points and 2180 Black Coins.]

Her contribution points were enormous compared to the points Sungjin's former teammates had received. But it made sense, since she had landed almost every shot she'd fired, and the other three perished during PvP. Next up was Sungjin.

[Your contribution is 70.5%. 2820 Stat Points, 2820 Black Coins awarded. Raid Clear Bonus 1000 Stat Points and 1000 Black Coins awarded. Item effect 'Additional 10% gained' activated. Distributing 3820 Stat Points and 4202 Black Coins.]

Sungjin thought to himself. *4202... I almost didn't make it.*

He needed 4022 coins to complete the book. Without the Heart of Gold passive, he would have fallen short.

[And now we will distribute the items.]

Of course, it began with Serin since she had fewer contribution points.

[Eye of the Cyclops – Strength of the Giants]

[Recovery Potion – Small x4]

Next up was Sungjin. Despite having been through this process numerous times, Sungjin still looked forward to seeing what he'd earned.

[Manta – Cho'Roch's Staff]

[Kamram – Ring of the Siamese Twins]

[Recovery Potion – Small x3]

[Spell Book – Fireball]

And it ended there. Although it usually gave out three Heroic Items.

Why? Why did I only get two?

Sungjin complained internally. But the Operator was not done.

[Congratulations! You obtained a Legendary item 'Kamram – Ring of the Siamese Twins'!]

Legendary Item?!

The Operator always announced each Legendary item loot that was received. Sungjin instantly forgot about his complaint and eagerly picked up the ring that appeared before him.

At the center of the ring were two crimson gems, stuck together like Siamese twins.

What is this? He wanted to ask the Operator, but the distribution was not over.

[Last but not the least, you will be awarded titles you've earned on this Raid.]

One more time, Serin was first.

[Head Hunter – When striking the enemy on the head with an arrow, increase damage dealt by 40%]

It was a great title. If you considered her skill, it was no different from having permanent 40% damage boost at all times. Next up was Sungjin.

[Adjudicator – When killing party members who entered the 'Troll' state, obtain two of their equipped items.]

Huh?

He hadn't ever imagined that such a title existed.

Is it because I killed two trolls in one Raid?

In Sungjin's previous life, he had had exceptionally good luck with teammates. He almost never encountered a 'Troll,' so this title would have been impossible to earn for him.

He also never saw anyone walking around with it. To be fair, this was a hard title to justify equipping.

In a Raid where your life was always on the line, there was no reason to keep this title equipped just because there was a chance for a troll's appearance.

No, if a troll were to appear, it usually meant the party would be wiped out.

Well, since it's being given to me, I'll accept it gratefully.

Once the rewards were distributed, Serin approached Sungjin.

"Good work, Master Hunter K. Your skill lives up to your title."

Sungjin nodded. "Serin, you too... well, good work on overcoming this Chapter, you know, after everything that happened."

Sungjin kicked himself inside for mentioning 'that.' It would have probably been better not to have mentioned it at all.

But luckily, Serin seemed to take it well.

"It's okay. To be fair... something similar happened to me in the last Chapter as well."

Listening to her frankly say that, Sungjin was at a loss for words. There was a reason why so few women survived to later stages of the Raids.

"At that time, I took care of the situation with my bow, but this time... Anyway, thank you so much, Kei."

Sungjin wordlessly nodded. He felt saying anything now to her was improper. The Operator informed them their remaining time.

[Returning to the Black Market in 28 Minutes and 48 Seconds.]

There was still lots of time left. But there was one more thing Sungjin had to do: searching for the hidden piece. Sungjin told the Operator,

"I want to use the Treasure Hunter active skill. Please tell me the hint about the hidden piece on this map."

***

The Operator recited a verse.

[Wandering merchant from far away land]

[Crossing the canyon, treasure in hand]

[Caught by giants and hung by his toes]

[Giants know not of the value he towed]

['Eating' is the most valuable thing that they know]

Sungjin deliberated over the verses. The verse hinted at a hidden location, but there was no direct hint about where that might be.

"Tell me again."

After the second time, Sungjin figured out that there were two hints about the location. "Hung by his toes" and "Eating."

Upside down... for eating.

Somewhere the Giants would cook... Somewhere suitable to make food. Sungjin searched his memories.

Oh wait a minute... Now that he thought of it, he recalled seeing a cook-pot. One large enough to fit someone in it.

Where was that again?

It was somewhere within the Canyon; he was sure of it.

Sungjin asked Serin, who stood next to him. "Miss Serin, do you remember seeing a gigantic cook-pot?"

"A cook-pot?"

"Yeah, not a normal-sized one, something large enough for a grown man to fit in. Something really large."

Serin shook her head. "No, I don't remember seeing something like that. If I saw something that strange, I would remember."

Which means that I had seen it in the later half of the canyon, deduced Sungjin.

Serin had probably only been halfway through the canyon. She couldn't possibly have seen anything that appeared in the later portions of the canyon.

Once he made up his mind, Sungjin turned to search for the cook-pot. But Serin stopped him to ask, "Kei, where are you going?"

"Ah... that..."

Sungjin hesitated. He didn't feel comfortable telling her about the existence of hidden pieces. After mulling over it for a second he decided to go through with it. "I have something to find. A hidden element."

She was already extremely grateful to Sungjin for saving her. He believed that she would not request anything unreasonable of him even if they did find the treasure.

"Hidden elements?"

"Yes. Just like the secret boss we just fought, there are also secret treasures hidden on each map."

"Really?" Serin's eyes grew wide with surprise.

"Yes. So I am going to go and search for it. You are welcome to stay here and rest until you return to the Black Market. We already hit 100% Raid completion, so there are no more mobs to be found on the map."

Sungjin wanted to turn and leave as soon as he was done with his explanation, but Serin replied, "Let's go together. I don't have anything better to do anyway... and staying with that corpse alone feels... bad."

Serin indicated towards Santiago's corpse, which was lying a slight distance away.

Ah... Yeah, that would be bad for her. Sungjin nodded slightly and respected her decision. Either way, having two pairs of eyes searching for the hidden item was better than one.

She had already proved useful in finding the hidden boss. Sungjin and Serin began to walk deeper into the canyon one more time.

They walked for a while without speaking. But surprisingly, it was the proud Serin who broke the silence.

"Excuse me are hidden bosses... in every round?"

She became chattier.

"Yes," responded Sungjin.

"And you hunted them each time?"

"Yes."

"How?! Finding them is one thing, but didn't you fear death? Don't they scare you?"

Sungjin shrugged. "As you can see... if you can't grow stronger in these Raids, you can't survive. So... I have to work harder and push myself further; to be stronger."

"Kei, you're already plenty strong, though."

Sungjin did not reply. He didn't want to tell her that later Chapters fielded terrible monsters.

Instead, he decided to give her a warning.

"Miss Serin, please get as strong as you possibly can be. That's how you get to live longer."

"I am trying my best each round... so does that mean I should be trying to find and defeat the hidden boss each round?"

"That's..." Sungjin was caught in a dilemma, just like in the case with Hiro. Telling her 'yes' entailed too many risks.

"A decision like that... make the call after you've seriously considered your situation."

"Like how?" asked Serin.

"You should only consider attempting the hidden boss if all of the following are true: All 5 party members are exceptionally powerful and talented. Your team works together very well and stays coordinated. No internal strife has occurred after killing the final boss. Only if all of these are true, can you consider attempting the hidden boss. Otherwise, everyone is going to die."

Sungjin told her something similar to what he had said to Hiro.

Serin carefully considered his words. "Thank you for letting me know. But..."

Her words trailed off. Sungjin understood why. She even said she had experienced 'something similar' in previous rounds.

Her exceptional beauty was interfering with her chances of survival.

Ah... that's right. Sungjin suddenly recalled something and decided to tell her. "Um... In the Black Market, you can find a mask shop."

"Mask... shop...?"

"Yes. If you go there, you will be able to purchase masks that temporarily changes your appearance. Please go there. In my opinion, you are..."

Far too beautiful.

Was what Sungjin wanted to say, but he felt bashful and changed his words. "... going to find it useful."

Serin nodded. "I understand. Thank you for all your help, Kei."

And with her words of gratitude, she gave a radiant smile quite unlike her usual cold self.

"Sure." Sungjin intentionally replied back half-heartedly. And he stole a glance at her.

This lady... if luck would allow, could be a strong candidate for the final party members...

They were nearing Chapter 5. The initial stages of the Raids were going to be over soon, and Sungjin was slowly making plans to prepare for the future.

The last surviving team; Final 5.

Being included in the final five was beyond a doubt for Sungjin. He became greatly overpowered thanks to the 'Restart.'

The problem was the other four individuals.

No matter how strong an individual was, there was no way one person could complete the Raid all alone. These Raids were designed to be beaten with the cooperation of five people.

Cooperation, as Chapters continue, becomes increasingly important in making meaningful progress. It was a good idea to start considering who had the potential to become the final team members from now on.

There are two main factors in becoming one of the final five. One is exceptional skill, and second is unbreakable trust.

Sungjin had no doubts as to her skill. She had won the Gold medal in Olympics; it proved that she was one of the top archers among humans. And Sungjin saw her skills first hand.

And unlike her initial cold demeanor, she was a respectable and upright human being. Most importantly, she already deeply trusted him. Thinking thus far, Sungjin continued to speak.

"As you might have noticed... as the Raids continue to progress, an incredible number of people will perish along the way."

Serin's face expression hardened immediately, and she nodded nervously.

"So... even though the Raids began with all of humanity participating, the number of people will..."

Sungjin was about to say "continue to dwindle until there are only five people remaining," but he changed his verbiage slightly.

"Probably dwindle until there are only five people remaining at the end. You understand this much, right?"

Serin nodded slightly. "Yes... That would make sense if these Raids continue without an end."

"If that time comes and only five are remaining, it is best if all five are dependable people, in skill and in trust, right?" continued Sungjin.

"I think so. I get how people with great skill might be able to survive until the end, but isn't it impossible to guarantee that each person in the end is trustworthy?" questioned Serin.

Sungjin thought of what she had said. It was technically correct. But...

If I wanted, I could 'pick' at least few of the members of the Final Five.

Sungjin knew he had some level of control over the membership; he had overwhelming advantage of skill, information, and Stat Points above other Hunters.

Manipulating not only the outcome of Raids but also the process was possible to a certain extent. While Sungjin was lost in thought, Serin said, "Look!"

Sungjin stopped and looked towards where Serin had pointed. There was a large pot boiling in the distance.

Sungjin had tunnel visioned on his way to kill the boss and had overlooked the pot. He then asked Serin, "Please step back a bit."

"Why? Are you... thinking of tipping it over?"

"Yes."

"Let me do it. I know you're strong and all, but tipping over a boiling pot of water with nothing but a sword... Is probably dangerous, right?"

She was right. Sungjin stepped off to the side to let her have a clear shot at the pot. The only question was, did her arrow have the penetrating power to pierce through the pot?

But when she pulled back her bow, she spoke: "Strength of Giants"

For a brief moment, her Pearl Ring illuminated brightly.

Ah...

It was the ring she had received as the Raid reward. She must have already checked the stats on the ring and equipped it. It reminded Sungjin of "Kamram – Ring of the Siamese Twins" in his pocket.

I didn't even check what I have... I suppose I could check it along with the hidden piece reward.

Sungjin decided to indulge in joys of checking out his equipment a bit later.

PING!

The arrow she shot flew off towards the pot, making a far more threatening noise than ever before. In one strike, the arrow passed through the pot.

BUBBLE GURGLE GURGLE GURGLE

Water gushed forth the hole she had punched through the pot. She looked down at her ring and said,

"It's quite useful. Although X2 bonus on Strength only has a 3-second duration, so I can't use it more than once..."

He nodded to her comment. Her Rain of Arrows was a great AOE skill suitable for multiple enemies, and now, she had obtained a powerful lethal shot she could use for bosses.

The two of them stared at the pot for a while. But there was nothing inside. The Operator remained quiet.

"What's going on?"

Sungjin was confused for a moment.

Did I misunderstand the verses? Or...

His thoughts were interrupted.

"Kei, isn't that thing suspicious?"

Serin said, grabbing his attention. Next to the pot was a large corpse of an Ettin, and a small tent built right up to the cliff wall.

Sungjin walked over to it. The first thing he noticed was the Ettin. He didn't recall killing it, but the wounds on it suggested it was him who had killed it.

I guess I just ran by while mindlessly killing them.

Passing by the corpse, he entered the tent. Inside the tent, he didn't notice anything out of place... Except,

There's a wall in the back of the tent? Why?

Finding it extremely suspicious, he approached the wall. Upon closer inspection, he found a place where the wall was slightly separated from the tent fabric. There was an empty space beyond.

No light passed through from above, and a slight breeze blew out from the gap. Around him, filling the tent, was a large pile of dissected animals and meat.

This is the giant's refrigerator.

But then

"What... Wait, a Human? Please! Save me!"

He could hear voices from the other side. Sungjin searched between the gap. He saw there, in the dark, a half-rat demi-human hanging by his feet upside down.

The cube cheerfully rang out with an announcement.

[Congratulations! You have discovered]

[Hidden Vendor Wandering Merchant Ruff Han!]

***

Sungjin gazed up at the Ratman hanging from the ceiling.

Another demi-human? Are all the vendors like that...?

Even Wandering Merchant Aindell was a demi-human. Half human, half wolf. Sungjin approached the Ratman. The Ratman shouted at him from his tied up position.

"Hey, Human! Help me! If you give me a hand, I'll make it worth your while!"

Serin entered the cave from behind. "Wow... I didn't know there was such a place here."

The Ratman also yelled at Serin.

"Hey, Human girl! Help me!"

"What's up with him?" asked Serin.

Before Sungjin had a chance to reply to her question, the Ratman interrupted by shouting,

"I said help!"

Sungjin used his fingers to plug up his ears.

"I got it, I got it. Please stop. Stop it."

He looked over to Serin.

"Serin, please shoot him down. I'll catch him."

"Ok."

She immediately let loose an arrow.

PING

The rope which held him was cut with a snap and Sungjin easily caught the falling Ratman.

Ugh...

For one reason or another, the stench on the Ratman was terrible. Sungjin immediately threw the Ratman away.

The Giants really planned to eat this thing...?

The Ratman finally got to his feet and took a breather. "Haa... I thought I was going to die. You have my thanks, Humans!"

The Ratman smiled at them, exposing his yellow teeth. Sungjin felt no desire to become friendly with him; skipping all the small talk he asked, "So, how are you going to make it worth our while?"

The Ratman made a curious smile and replied, "Ah, that... I can't do it now. Later on..."

"What?" Sungjin raised his eyebrows.

The Ratman didn't catch on to the mood and continued while shaking his head, "I said I will make it worthwhile; I never said it was going to be right..."

WOOSH

Sungjin pulled out Moon Spectre and brought it up to the Ratman's neck.

"So, you're going to go back on your word, is it?"

Once he saw the naked blade pressed against his neck, the ratman's demeanor changed instantly. "No, I mean... listen..."

Sungjin waited patiently for him to continue. He was the Hidden Vendor after all; he must have something special with him.

"My treasure... I had hidden it before I was caught. I have to go find it first."

Sungjin replied to him frankly. "Tell me where it is then. I will go find it myself."

"The Treasure is hidden beyond the 'Boundary.' You know that, right? You'll die if you leave the boundary for more than 10 seconds! Bada boom!" exclaimed the ratman.

Sungjin considered his words. The merchant's words had no credibility, but there was no way to disprove him either.

There were sometimes merchants who valued their goods over their own lives; ones that would never spill a secret no matter the cost.

What should I do?

Sungjin continued to hold the Moon Spectre against the creature's and thought of his options. It was then the ratman changed his mind.

"Instead... Instead, let me... Let me give you something I do have on me."

Sungjin used the sword to raise the Ratman's chin and asked, "What is it, exactly?"

If it was something ordinary, he planned to reject it. But he didn't expect Ruff Han to say the following.

"Wandering Merchant's Mystery Pouch."

"What?" Sungjin was shocked. It was the same item that had given Sungjin Ancient Stories of the East – Part 1.

Ratman Ruff Han took out a pouch from his vest and handed it to Sungjin.

"Here, take it! And let me go! I don't want to lose another second until I go searching for my stash!"

Sungjin quickly took the pouch and asked the Operator.

"Operator, explanation, quick."

The Operator quickly brought up the information screen at his request.

Mystery Pouch – Wandering Merchant's secret stash
Heroic Treasure

Unique Skill – Roulette (IV)
Roulette (IV) – receive one Legendary class crafting material.
Pouch disappears after use.

It was definitely the same item as before.

This... is totally acceptable. Sungjin returned the Moon Spectre to its sheath.

Now free from the threat of violence, the ratman reached into his pocket and took out another pouch and tossed it over to Serin as well. "Thank you very much as well, pretty lady!"

He threw her a wink. Sungjin couldn't see her face, but he couldn't imagine her looking very happy.

"I have settled my debt with this, Humans!" The ratman fell on all fours and dashed away towards an exit on the other side of the cave; an exit too small for a human being to fit through.

"And I'm not a liar! I'll see you again in a future Raid! If you're able, that is!"

'If you're able...' probably meant 'you'll most likely die and so we might not see each other'... It wasn't exactly a positive farewell.

Once the Hidden Merchant Ruff Han left, Sungjin took a look at the pouch.

If Ancient Stories of the East Part 2 or 3 comes out of here...

"Roulette..."

Serin was staring at the screen for the pouch as well. It was most likely her first time seeing this type of item.

"This is an extremely good item; It gives a Legendary crafting material," explained Sungjin.

"Ooh..."

"Well, there's no point hoarding it for later... so I'll go first."

"Please go ahead."

Sungjin breathed in deeply to prepare himself and then shouted, "Roulette!"

The ribbon tying up the pouch released automatically and the content revealed itself. Although he had no creed, he still prayed.

Please!

The appearance of the treasure was,

A Book!

Sungjin quickly picked it up to check the screen. Now as long as it was not Part 1, he was golden. However,

> Ancient Stories of the Middle East – Part 2
> Legendary Crafting Material
>
> Omnibus of ancient stories of the Middle East. Once parts 1, 2, and 3 are gathered, it can be made into a complete volume.

Middle East?!

It was an entirely wrong line of books. With the component cost of 5000 coins per book, an item you could only equip one at a time, there was no reason or need to craft multiple books of this kind.

...Damn... Sungjin massaged his forehead wallowing in regret. But then,

"Roulette." Serin also used her Roulette. Once the pouch unveiled itself, the item that appeared was,

Another book!

Serin lifted up her item. "Operator... What is this item?"

The Operator opened up an information screen for her. And on it displayed the item Sungjin had been wanting; Ancient Stories of the East – Part 2. Sungjin forgot himself and immediately grabbed her arm.

"Wah!" Serin jumped up slightly in surprise; she had never seen Kei react to anything before like that.

"Why? Is it a good thing?" asked Serin.

Sungjin held onto her hands and responded, "Miss Serin, please, let's trade these two books."

"Excuse me?" Serin's cheeks turned slightly rosy.

Oh, right... Noticing the change in her behavior, Sungjin continued after letting go of her hands.

"This book is one of the materials required to complete a single item: an Ancient Omnibus. This Omnibus grants enormous power," said Sungjin.

Serin understood quickly. "Yes, and?"

"And so... I already have Ancient Stories of the East – Part 1. So... I need Part 2 of the same series."

Serin nodded. "Okay, then. I'll just give you this, as thanks for protecting me this Raid."

"Ah, wait, that's..."

Sungjin hesitated. But within moments, he made up his mind; only one person could own a single book at a time.

Of course, if he accepted the book now and sold it on the Black Market later, he could get 500 Coins, but it was far too inefficient to do so.

Trade was the right course of action. Especially if she had the potential to become one of the Final Five. So Sungjin explained to her,

"No. We should trade these; my Ancient Stories of the Middle East – Part 2 to your Ancient Stories of the East – Part 2. I suggest that you collect all three parts to the Ancient Stories of the Middle East and craft the complete book. If you manage to do so, it should be enough to keep you alive for at least several Chapters."

The Operator gave an announcement.

[Returning to the Black Market in 10 Minutes]

Time was running out. Serin nodded. "I understand, Kei."

Sungjin and Serin put their cubes together to trade. Once it was done, Sungjin had finally obtained Part 2 of the book he wanted.

Now all I have to do is buy the final part from the bookstore.

While Sungjin was thinking about that, Serin took a look at her new item. "Ancient stories..."

Sungjin decided to ask, "Miss Serin, how many Black Coins do you have right now?"

"Black Coins? Including what I just got from this Raid, around 5000."

She hadn't spent too much; with the exception of her bow, she probably hadn't spent her coins elsewhere. Sungjin told her,

"When you go back to the Black Market this time, please go to 'Gourmet's Bookstore.' Ask about the book... and if you are able, make the complete item."

Serin nodded.

Sungjin continued, "And... I don't know the name, but please visit the mask shop run by a Raccoon merchant. Okay?"

"Okay."

Once Sungjin was done, he placed the book into the cube. Not too long after, the Operator announced

[You will return to the Black Market in 1 minute.]

Serin, who had kept quiet until now asked Sungjin,

"Kei... Will we be able to see each other again?"

Sungjin answered,

"Raids are designed in such a way that survivors will meet each other again. And as you can tell, I am very strong. I will survive until the very end. So...if you can keep yourself safe and survive Chapter to Chapter, we will eventually be able to see each other again. I promise."

At his words, Serin nodded bravely.

"Um... Before we go our separate ways... Can you please tell me your real name?"

Sungjin hesitated.

[You will return to the Black Market in 10 seconds. 10]

Once the Operator's countdown began, Sungjin said to her, "If we meet each other again, I promise I will tell you my real name."

[9, 8, 7]

Serin nodded helplessly. "Ok, it's a promise."

[6, 5, 4]

Sungjin couldn't help but tell her one more time out of his concern for her. "Mask shop, bookstore. You got it, right?"

Serin nodded. She was intelligent. She would not forget.

[3, 2. 1]

In the last moments, she bid him goodbye.

"Let's meet again, Kei."

Sungjin wanted to reply to her. But,

[0]

The countdown finished, and the Hunters were teleported away from the Canyon.

Chapter 9 – Black Market Fourth Shopping

Even as he was teleported to the Black Market, Sungjin had tried saying words of farewell. But he had missed his chance.

We will probably never see each other again..

But that was also too heart breaking to say. It was a mistake allowing himself to let her get under his skin; while cooperating and working together, he had ever so slightly opened his heart to her.

Sungjin looked around. He located the teashop First Drop and walked over to inspect his reward.

Once Sungjin sat in the same seat as last time, the Panda man welcomed him. "What should I get you today?"

"Iced tea... and something to snack on," said Sungjin.

"Understood, coming right up."

Once the shopkeeper left, Sungjin took out the 'Kamram – Ring of the Siamese Twins' for inspection. One ring with two gems; it was a strange-looking ring.

Just what does it do?

Without having to ask, the Operator opened up the detailed screen for him.

Kamram – Ring of the Siamese Twins
Legendary Ring

Passive Skill
Dual Weapon Mastery (V.)
Copies 100% of the proficiency of the dominant hand over to the other hand.

One will, two talents.
The pinnacle of martial prowess.

Sungjin was stunned. While he was reeling from shock, Xiu Ran set down iced tea and some rice cakes in front of him.

After a while, Sungjin grasped the cold tea cup. Once he had downed the entire content of chilled tea, he felt recovered enough to process what he had just received.

Does this mean?

Sungjin decided to test out the effects of 'Kamram' immediately. "Equip"

The ring readjusted its size and settled itself over Sungjin's right ring finger. It was a strange sensation; Sungjin felt slightly disoriented for a moment, but also somehow more sensitive than before.

His eyes refocused, and his hands trembled. He wanted to test it out right away. But now that he thought of it, he didn't have a second Katana.

I shouldn't have sold the Basic Katana, thought Sungjin.

If he had kept it, it would have been perfect for practice. But he already sold it for mere ten coins.

What should I do?

Then, he remembered he actually had another weapon. The Manta – Cho'Roch's Staff.

Sungjin took one rice cake and chewed on it as he put his hand on top of the cube.

"Operator, give me the Manta."

The lid on the cube opened up, and an extremely long, metallic staff emerged from within.

It was a staff in name only; it looked more like a piece of rebar. Sungjin inspected the rod-like staff.

Manta – Cho'Roch's Staff
Heroic Staff – Strength B Dexterity D Magic Power C

Passive Skill
Red Magician (II)
Improves the effects of offensive magic by 20%

Magic Swordsman (I)
Each magic cast improves weapon damage by 10%
Each attack by weapon improves magic damage by 10%
Max 3 stacks

Staff of the Powerful Mage, Cho'Roch.
Became a mage due to losing the bet on a coin flip against his younger brother.

It was better than expected. The bonus weapon damage and the 20% increase in spell effect was already quite good, but the 'Magic Swordsman' passive made it a lot better. Even more so, because Sungjin had already decided to try the Magic Swordsman route.

Taking the staff in hand, Sungjin briefly left the shop. And using the left hand, he tried swinging the staff around. He was able to wield it perfectly well. Then, taking out the 'Moon Spectre,' he tried to swing the sword around. It felt as natural as if he was using his right hand.

Have I become ambidextrous now? While he was thinking so,

"Whoa, Whoa, Mr Hunter"

Sungjin heard someone speak to him from behind. When he turned around to see, it was a half-dog demi-human. The demi-human approached him and said, "Please do not wave your weapon around in public."

The clothes the demi-human wore was reminiscent of a police outfit. The security in this place was rather tight.

Sungjin nodded and replied, "Ah, I was just experimenting, testing things out. I wasn't trying to harm anyone."

"Okay, understood."

Sungjin returned to the shop and took his seat. From the earlier test, he was certain;

I can wield Moon Spectre and Blood Vengeance at the same time.

Upon thinking that, Sungjin couldn't help but get hyped. But there was still a roadblock to this.

"Operator, how many coins do I have?"

[You have 10180 Black Coins]

'Stories of the East – Part 3' would take 5000 Coins, and Blood Vengeance was 9700 Coins; with the current amount of coins, he would have to pick one or the other.

By the time the next Raid is over.

Sungjin returned to the same dilemma he had been in during his last visit to the Black Market.

Do I complete the book, or buy the Blood Vengeance?

But unlike last time, it only took 3 seconds to make a decision.

I'll make the book. With it, I won't have to exert myself much during combat.

Buying Blood Vengeance after practicing with Manta was probably a good idea anyway. Kenneth's Last Edge wasn't going anywhere. He could get the sword at any time.

Once Sungjin was done gathering his thoughts, he finished off the rest of the tea and the rice cakes and stood up. He immediately headed out to Gourmet's bookstore.

"Ho, young Master Hunter, so did you prepare the coins?"

Sungjin confidently nodded. "Five thousand Black Coins. Please give me the last volume of 'Stories of the East.'"

Gourmet looked up at Sungjin and asked, "Hmm? What about Part 2?"

"I obtained the 2nd part. In the Raid."

Gourmet formed an 'o' with his mouth in surprise. "Ohh, what a lucky young man!"

"Things worked out somehow."

"Okay, just a moment, then." Gourmet turned around.

Sungjin thought Gourmet would enter a mountain full of books again, but Gourmet soon turned around to present him the book; it seemed that he had it prepared and waiting for Sungjin's return.

"Operator, after payment, please take out 'Stories from the East' Part 1 and 2 from the inventory."

[Understood.]

As requested, the cube completed the transaction and gave him the other two parts of the book.

Sungjin held the three parts of the book in order with both his hands and raised them above his head.

"Combine!"

With his shout, the three components floated into the air, and let out bright illuminations.

"Ooh!" The goat Merchant Gourmet watched the light show from over his spectacles.

*

"Hey, another donut please."

"Understood."

The black police officer Baltren was sitting in the donut shop, inspecting the club he had received from the previous Raid.

Manmu – Pach's Club
Heroic blunt – Strength S Dexterity C

Passive Skill
Stun (II)
Each strike against the same enemy increases the chance to stun it by 20%.
Max 3 Stacks.

Powerful Warrior Pach's club.
Winning a coin flip against his older brother, Pach decided to become a warrior.

Hmmm...

He was in a dilemma. There was a weakness in this club compared to the club he had received in Chapter 1, the Skull Romabel.

Skull Romabel is great for defense... and this one is ideal for offense. What should I do? Should I carry both and switch them according to the situation?

But he was interrupted by a strange noise coming from the cube.

[Attention please]

It was the first time he had heard this from the cube. Baltren put down his club to look at the cube.

*

"Haa..."

Hiro looked up at the sky, still holding his Katana.

"Where could he have been? That hidden boss..."

He was lucky last round, all four of his teammates had been excellent. Using great teamwork, they had been able to successfully hunt Pach and Cho'Roch safely without losing anyone. They had even had 15 minutes left.

"It was perfect... Just where was he?"

They had combed the entire canyon, but had failed to find the boss. Hiro briefly recalled his sensei.

"Sensei... He managed it last time, so he probably did it this time too... right?"

"Ramen's ready!"

Meanwhile, his ramen was done. Hiro first picked up the bowl and drank the soup.

"Mmmmm~"

It was hot and well-seasoned. It was great that he was able to find this ramen shop in the market. Hiro took a long strand of ramen and took his first bite.

But, the cube let out a sound he had never heard before.

[Attention please]

"Hmm?" Hiro cut the noodle short and stared at the cube.

*

"Aww, why? Why does a pretty girl like you want to hide your face behind a mask?"

Serin smiled slightly and answered. "Well... I think I'll need it... for the Raid..."

"Ahh what a shame! I know... 'Consequence of exceptional beauty'...! What a horrible thing! But...! Since our life is so short anyway, isn't it better to live our short lives looking beautiful? Don't you think so?"

The Racoon Mask Merchant was an overly talkative old lady.

Serin replied, "So... anything you'd recommend? How much of my appearance can you change?"

"Appearance? All of it. Age, gender, race..."

It could even change gender. How convenient.

"Ah... ok."

"The only thing you can't alter are things which affect combat. For example, longer arms... The mask shop is forbidden from selling things related to combat."

"So, is there anything you'd recommend?"

"Try this on." The Racoon merchant handed Serin a mask. She was about to put the mask on when she was interrupted by the cube.

[Attention please]

"You'll see if you put it on, how..."

Serin stopped the merchant. "Wait, please."

The merchant immediately shut her mouth. The cube continued with the announcement.

[Master Hunter has succeeded in completing the Legendary Ancient Omnibus Romance of the Three Kingdoms]

[All other copies will be destroyed, and the owners will be refunded by 500 coins.]

*

Hunters, all in their own instance of the Market, heard the announcement. Most did not know of this Master Hunter, but a few were able to guess who it referred to.

229

Baltren thought to himself, *"That teenager..."*

Hiro shouted towards the sky. "Wow! Sensei did it!"

Serin, still holding the mask, thought of the man she had been with until moments ago.

"Master Hunter... Kei".

***

Sungjin raised his hands towards the sky. The book basked the room in blinding light and gently settled on top of his hands as it dimmed.

The goat Merchant Gourmet let out a tsk with his tongue and commented, "Chapter 4 just finished... and you have already completed the Ancient Omnibus... What on Earth..."

Sungjin read the front cover. Without a doubt, it was Romance of the Three Kingdoms. He turned to Gourmet and thanked him from the bottom of his heart.

"Thank you for the trade. I will head out now."

"Okay, see you around. If you ever need to see me again, that is."

Sungjin thanked him once more and then left the shop. As he strolled through the market, he flipped through the pages of Romance of the Three Kingdoms. Last time, this book had been in another Hunter's possession.

Ancient Omnibus was a unique item which only one Hunter could own at a time, so he could only watch as others used them in his previous life.

Romance of the Three Kingdoms – Ancient stories of the East
Legendary Ancient Omnibus

Active Skill
Declamation (V)
Read the novel. Reading different parts of the novel causes different effects.
1 use per day.

A tale among tales, a classic among classics; an Omnibus which systematically deconstructs the ups and downs of human and national relationships for the reader.

I can't believe I'm reading this now.

It was a whole new level of satisfaction. The effects were considerably advantageous even in the later Chapters, but obtaining it in very beginning was nothing short of over-powered.

I'll have to test it as soon as possible.

Sungjin carefully placed the book into his vest and left for Ninety-Nine Nights, where Dalupin and Cain were waiting.

*

Once he returned to the Ninety-Nine Nights Cain greeted him first with short barks as usual. Sungjin checked his neck. There was not a single mark on him; his injuries were healed, and not a single scratch remained.

Any wounds and injuries sustained during the Raids were reverted once the Raid was over with the Hunters being returned to the Black Market.

Sungjin brought his face close to Cain's ears and whispered, "You worked hard, Cain. Thank you."

"Wooo~" Cain affirmed with a cry.

"Okay, okay." Sungjin briefly bent down and hugged Cain by his neck. However, he felt that something was odd.

His arms felt a little short. Sungjin stopped for a moment and stared at Cain.

Did he... get fat? Taller?

"Cain, did you get bigger?"

Cain let out a short bark. Sungjin could not discern the intention.

"Well... ok. Anyways, good work, let's go eat."

"Woof!"

This was easily understood. Once inside, Dalupin greeted Sungjin as usual. "Welcome back, esteemed Hunter."

"Prepare a meal for us please."

"What would you like to order?"

"Hmm..." Sungjin thought for a moment. The first item that came to his mind was,

"Pizza."

"Traditional Italian style? Or American franchise style?"

"Eh... Korean franchise style? Modified American style? Either way, with tons of cheese."

"Understood. Any requests for toppings?"

"Bacon, pepperoni, black olives, bell pepper, and garlic, please. Also, lamb meat for Cain."

"Understood. Please wait for a moment. I will go prepare your food."

Dalupin bowed deeply and returned to the kitchen. While Dalupin was gone, Sungjin recalled the Spellbook he had obtained in the last Raid and decided to take it out.

I should memorize it quickly before the pizza is done.

"Operator, give me the Spellbook please."

The cube wordlessly obeyed, spitting out the Spellbook. Sungjin opened the crimson Spellbook.

> Spellbook – Fireball
> 4th Circle Offensive Magic
>
> Launch a large fireball. The fireball explodes on contact, and the flames spread out dealing collateral damage in the vicinity of the blast.

This was a standard fire-type magic. Most mages would have used this spell at one point or another. Sungjin did not hesitate.

"Memorize."

The red cover of the Spellbook lit up, illuminating the inn.

[Magic – Fireball was memorized.]

[Incantation for the spell is 'Incinerate everything in your path! Fireball!']

Once Sungjin was done memorizing the spell, Dalupin returned with the pizza. Of course, along with a sizable lamb meat.

"Eat lots, Cain."

Sungjin patted Cain on the head before taking the first slice to eat. The cheese stretched into long strands as he took the slice.

Sungjin cut the cheese with his fingers before stuffing the slice into his mouth.

"Mmmm."

The thick flavour of the cheese cooked on top of soft bread, with pepperoni and bacon mixed in; it was an overwhelming and succulent first bite. Perfectly cooked bell pepper and garlic also gave a refreshing aftertaste, as well as controlling the greasiness. The pizza highlighted the skill of a master.

Sungjin stared at Dalupin.

"Anything else you need?" Dalupin tilted his head at Sungjin's stare. As if proving his half-owl status, his head tilted more than sixty degrees. Sungjin wordlessly gave him a thumbs up.

On understanding what he wanted to convey, Dalupin lowered his head and answered, "Ah, thank you."

Title: Master Hunter
HP: 17100 MP: 3990

Strength:	2486	1912	(+574)
Dexterity:	2721	2093	(+628)
Endurance:	1710	1315	(+395)
Magic Power:	395	304	(+91)
Mind Power:	399	307	(+92)

Unallocated Points: 3820

"Hmm..." Sitting in the warm bath, Sungjin furrowed his brows as he pondered over his stats.

I should continue to invest into Strength, Dexterity, and Endurance... right?

Even if Sungjin was going to experiment with becoming a magic swordsman, the basis of his power was still that of a swordsman. Even though he had begun investing into Magic Power and Mind Power, he couldn't afford to forget this important fact.

I must continue to maintain overwhelming physical superiority, and raise Magic Power enough to be helpful, he thought.

Sungjin reserved 1000 points each for Strength, Dexterity, and Endurance.

And then 820 points remain.

He didn't get much of an opportunity to utilize his magic in the previous Raid.

Ah... I had even filled up my mana right before the fight with Pach and Cho'Roch and totally forgot to try using spells on them.

He was still not acquainted with using magic. When in danger, he fell back to swordsmanship. Anyone would have probably acted the same.

It was human nature to fall back to familiar things unless there was a certain margin of safety and time to explore new things. On top of that, his spells were weak compared to his swordplay.

If I'm not going to be using it often... I'll try making Magic Power stronger to make it worth the while.

Sungjin concluded his thoughts.

Even considering the 4th Circle magic Fireball, there shouldn't be a pressing need to increase the mana pool too much.

Thus, Sungjin planned out his Stat Points as follows

With 3 to 1 ratio for Magic to Mind Power, raising 615 points and 205 points respectively should do it.

Sungjin tried to calculate the points out.

304 plus 615 is 919, taking into consideration Master Hunters effects.

Annoyed already at the calculations, Sungjin called for the Operator's help.

"Operator, what would be the resulting total points if I were to increase Magic Power by 615?"

[1195]

"And if I raise Mind Power by 205?"

[666]

The MP would become 6660. Using 4th Circle magic with 1195 Magic Power would allow him to fire the spell at least once.

If I ever need mana, I could always use Lich's Finger, and Moon Spectre's passive to recover it.

Sungjin decided to try to min/max the magic; he wanted to see what it was like.

"Operator, raise Strength by 1000, Dexterity by 1000, and Endurance by 1000. Add 615 to Magic Power and 205 to Mind Power"

[Applied.]

Once the distribution was complete, Sungjin dipped himself deeper into the tub. Chapter 4 had been eventful.

Trying magic for the first time, meeting Serin Han, fighting a building-sized Cyclops, killing two player-killing trolls, running into the Wandering Merchant Ruff Han. And completing an Ancient Omnibus.

So many things in just a few hours.

"Sigh..." Sungjin closed his eyes and let the thoughts wash over him as he pondered over them.

At this point... I've pretty much cleared every Raid perfectly.

Sungjin tried to think back to his previous life.

[Spell Master has succeeded in completing the Legendary Ancient Omnibus Romance of the Three Kingdoms]

Let's see... what Chapter was that again?

Even a vague and generous estimate put it at about seven or eight Chapters from now. Sungjin was able to complete Romance of the Three Kingdoms in four Chapters, so he felt that he was off to a great start.

Compared to blindly trying to complete the Raids like the last time, he was already several times stronger. Now, Sungjin was confident that he would have no trouble with the Raids for a long while.

Of course with the exception of extenuating circumstances. That reminded Sungjin of the past. *Why did you do that?!*

Extenuating Circumstances. Sungjin couldn't help but mutter a name that resurfaced from the past.

"Spell Master Ed..."

He still had no clear answer for what had happened back then, but it was all in the past.

No need to complicate myself.

Sungjin got up from the bath.

Even if trolls get in my way, even if there is not one dependable ally, even if I have to go on alone, I will see it to the end.

In the middle of the living room was Moon Spectre and Romance of the Three Kingdoms resting on top of a table. With these two items, Sungjin was more than ready to handle anything and everything for at least some time.

Especially once the next Raid was completed and once he got his hands on the Blood Vengeance.

Sungjin wiped down the moisture and dressed himself.

KNOCK KNOCK

Sungjin heard knocks on the door. There was only one possible person who could knock on the door this late at night.

"Please come in."

As expected, it was Dalupin. "Dear Hunter, here is the information page for the next Raid."

Sungjin accepted the sheet.

Dalupin bowed as he said, "Then I bid you goodnight."

He excused himself and left the room. Once Dalupin had closed the door, Sungjin checked the top of the information sheet and only read the title.

Information concerning Kutan Desert.

Still the same order. Sungjin discarded the paper and threw himself on the bed. It had been a long day. Soon after closing his eyes, he was fast asleep.

Chapter 10 – Kutan Desert

[One hour left before the Raid commences.]

Sungjin woke up to the Operator's voice.

Mmm?

When he came to, he was laying on top of the bed in Ninety-Nine Nights. Sungjin normally set an alarm two hours before Raid start, but tonight he had allowed himself to sleep in. Sungjin thought for a moment.

Did I remember to distribute points?

Yes, he recalled the bath last night. Sungjin closed his eyes again. Everything urgent had already been taken care of. It would not take him longer than 50 minutes to get ready.

"Operator, remind me in 10 minutes."

[Understood.]

But, 5 minutes later,

KNOCK KNOCK

Dalupin came knocking.

"Sir?"

Sungjin had no choice but to get up. "Yes?"

He answered as he opened the door. Outside, Dalupin stood waiting, holding items in each hand. One was a waterskin, and the other was a long piece of cloth.

Oh yeah...

"You usually get up earlier... but since you were taking your time this morning, I decided to deliver this to you myself. These are supplies provided to all Hunters. As you have already found out, the Raid will be taking place in the Desert, so..."

Sungjin nodded. Dalupin first handed over the water.

"This waterskin contains cold water. It is constantly refilled by magical means, so feel free to use it as much as you like."

Sungjin accepted the waterskin. "Thank you."

"And this long cloth..."

"I know. I'll eat first, and I'll make sure to take it with me before the Raid begins, so please wait for now."

"Understood. I have prepared a variety of clothes which..."

"I know. Later."

Dalupin bowed deeply and excused himself. "Understood."

He closed the door and left. Sungjin went to take a quick shower and checked the closet.

The closet was mostly full of large muslin cloth that Arabians are often seen wearing. For the second time ever, Sungjin wore the muslin clothes. It did not suit him, but he had no other choice.

[10 minutes have elapsed.]

The alarm from earlier went off.

"I got it, I got it."

Sungjin tapped the top of the cube and climbed down the stairs to the first floor.

"Woof!"

After greeting Cain, Sungjin ordered Cain's food first.

"Please give Cain the best cut of beef. In the future, please provide him three meals a day, something Cain would like, and in enough quantities."

"As you wish."

"And for me..." Sungjin paused for a moment to consider his options for breakfast and said the first thing that came to mind.

"Korean meal, with Doenjang Jjigae as the soup."

Once he was done ordering, it occurred to him that this was a topic recently.

Where was it again?

It didn't take long until he recalled who it was.

'Between Kimchi Jjigae and Doenjang Jjigae, which is your favourite?'

Sungjin couldn't help but grin. Dalupin soon brought over the bubbling hot soup and few side dishes to go along with the rice.

While Sungjin was enjoying some fruit punch after the meal, the Operator gave out an announcement.

[Raid will commence in 10 minutes.]

He had just finished eating moments ago.

I guess I'll have to digest food while hunting.

Turning to his host, Sungjin put in a request, "Hey, Dalupin, please do that now."

"Ah, yes."

Sungjin stood up straight in his chair. Dalupin brought out the long cloth from before and wrapped it around Sungjin's head into a turban.

Sungjin turned his head left and right. It was his second time, but he was still not used to it. But he tolerated it since it was essential this time.

Sungjin picked up the waterskin he had received that morning and opened it up. He took a quick swig from the waterskin.

"Mmm..."

It was almost cold enough to cause brain freeze. But it is perfect since the water is meant to be used in the desert.

Once he was ready, Sungjin stood outside the doors of the Ninety-Nine Nights and stretched. Soon after, he was teleported into the Raid.

*

The intense rays of sunlight blinded the eyes and burned the skin. The hot tan sand formed heat waves, causing things in the distance to shimmer. Following the contour of the landscape, dry winds blew, scattering sand and altering the dunes.

The place Sungjin was teleported to was a hot scorching desert. The Operator began her explanation.

[Welcome to the Kutan Desert.]

[It is a barren land of death where few survive.]

[Please be warned; the few that are able to endure the blistering heat and deadly winds]

[are extremely tough and violent.]

Sungjin frowned and looked up at the sky. The sun was too hot; he didn't want to stay here for long.

[Synchronizing Hunters.]

Sungjin stood with his arms crossed and watched his teammates appear one by one. High-Level Guardian, Zealot, Gladiator, High-Level Scout. Most of the titles were excellent this round.

After four rounds, most of the weak and mediocre Hunters had been filtered out, and now only the strong remained. This time, Sungjin looked at his teammates with more scrutiny. The High-Level Guardian was an Asian wielding an enormous shield and mace.

Despite being an Asian man, the High-Level Guardian was bulky in size, like a sumo wrestler.

He doesn't look like a Korean man... is he Chinese?

Just at the last Raid, he had had Xian Wang in the team, but considering the enormous population of China, it wouldn't be strange to have at least one Chinese Hunter in every round.

The Zealot was a tall black man. Not only was he tall, but his muscles were also considerably large. He held an axe in both hands, with each emitting a crimson light. His appearance was very fearsome.

Dual-axe Zealot... how apt.

The Gladiator was a sharp-nosed white man; one could almost cut paper on his nose. Although his body size looked relatively normal, the tight muscular structure of the man was visible even through his clothes; he must have lifted weights regularly.

He carried a sword somewhere between the length of a short sword and a long sword. On his left arm was a round shield that covered his entire arm, which gave him an appearance akin to a Roman Gladiator.

This man is strong.

Sungjin examined the man carefully. Behind him was the experience of overcoming countless battles.

Just looking at him and reading his demeanour, Sungjin could sense that the man was extraordinarily powerful.

Last was the High-Level Scout. He was a long-bearded Arabian. He was tall and thin, and his weapon was an expensive-looking crossbow.

Serin was like that too... ranged Hunters sure invest a lot into expensive weapons.

There were a variety of races, but everyone was wearing a turban on their head. Only the Arabian man was able to carry the look. And each individual seemed strong.

All four men probably had their strengths and weaknesses, but all four men had probably taken a majority share of the contribution points in each of their Raids.

Everyone carefully glanced at each other. By now, they all probably understood that getting a good grasp of the nature and strength of their teammates would help them survive.

At some point, Sungjin realized that all four men were staring at the title floating above his head.

[Master Hunter has succeeded in completing the Legendary Ancient Omnibus Romance of the Three Kingdoms.]

It was probably due to this message. Everyone had been given this announcement while shopping and resting in the Black Market.

Who is Master Hunter? Must have been their thought.

And then during the next Raid, they had found a Master Hunter in their team, so the logical progression of their thoughts was *Is it him?* Sungjin pretended not to notice the stares.

Titles were not unique to a person, so just because he held the title did not guarantee that he was the same person as the one mentioned in the announcement. Although, getting the Master Hunter title was nearly impossible.

The awkward silence continued for a good long while, but eventually it was broken.

"Okay, I think that went on long enough. Let's introduce ourselves."

It was the black Zealot. He began with his self-introduction.

"I am Ralph, an American. I look forward to working with you gentlemen."

And one by one the Hunters introduced themselves. The Asian High Level Guardian answered, "I am Bukitai, Mongolian."

Sungjin nodded. *Ah, so he was a Mongol... I thought he was too large compared to other Asian men.*

Next was the sharp-nosed white Gladiator. "Igor Janović, Russia"

The cold voice fit his image well.

Next was the Arabian High Level Scout. "Munir Yusef. Please call me Munir. I am Algerian."

Last was Sungjin's turn. "K... Chinese."

He half-heartedly answered. He didn't want to reveal his nationality, but he didn't want anyone to complain again that he had not revealed his country of origin.

When he declared himself Chinese, the other men accepted it without any question.

The only person here who could potentially tell Asian men apart by nationality was probably the Mongol, but he didn't seem interested in prying.

Instead, he was busy drinking water from Dalupin's water-skin. His massive frame was already drenched in sweat.

The Zealot banged his axes together as if he was clapping and announced, "Let's cooperate and overcome this Raid together."

Munir agreed. "Yes, let's do that."

Even the Gladiator nodded. The only ones that did not respond were the two Asian men.

The Mongol was too busy spraying his entire body with cold water, and Sungjin was daydreaming about when would be the best time to utilize the power of Romance of the Three Kingdoms.

Should I try it on the boss? Or should I wait until the hidden boss, since they are usually stronger?

He looked far off into the distance at the endless desert. This Chapter was not ideal for him. Limited the area may be, the content was a featureless desert for as far as the eyes could see.

Although it was fundamentally different from Greysoul Cemetery, it felt the same; he still couldn't tell the locations of objects. Sungjin thought to himself.

The Raid boss is one thing... How do I find the hidden boss in the middle of this desert?

Kutan Desert Raid
Objective – Hunt the King of Lizards- Basilisk
Time Limit: 2 hours

The Operator's mission briefing popped up. The time limit was much longer than most previous Raids at two hours, but that actually signified that this Raid was going to be very tough on the Hunters.

Sungjin looked up at the sky once more. Just standing for two hours in this sun would be enough to cause someone to go unconscious.

He was already dripping with sweat, and only a few minutes had passed. Sungjin uncorked the water-skin Dalupin had handed him and drank a few gulps of water.

Monsters were one thing, but resisting the scorching heat caused extreme fatigue.

The American, Ralph, and even the Russian, Igor, were drenched in sweat, looking exhausted even before the Raid began; Bukitai's state wasn't any better. Only the Algerian, Munir, looked fine.

Uninterested in the Hunter's circumstances, the Operator began the countdown in an apathetic voice.

[Raid will begin in 10 seconds. 10, 9, 8]

Sungjin licked his lower lip and put his hands over Moon Spectre. And he thought to himself,

Hidden boss or whatever, I'm going to end this Raid quickly.

***

[3, 2, 1, 0 Raid commencing]

Along with the signal, the Hunters began moving into the desert cautiously. Sungjin decided to stick with them for the time being although he had no intentions of participating in hunting as a group with the rest.

The difference in ability was absolute. It made more sense to hunt alone and clear the Raid quickly before beginning the search for the hidden elements.

It was just that he was curious about the skill level of his teammates. Especially the Gladiator Igor.

I'll just watch for few minutes before heading off to kill the boss.

As one would expect, the High Level Guardian Bukitai took the vanguard position. Next was the Gladiator Igor, followed by Zealot Ralph and Master Hunter Sungjin.

High Level Scout Munir stood at the back with his crossbow. The formation of the Hunters was predetermined by the characteristics of the weapons they wielded.

Sungjin strolled along, moving together with the other Hunters, when a Giant Scorpion emerged from the far side of the sand dunes.

It was about five meters in length, sporting two gigantic claws and the iconic poisonous stinger poised two meters above its body.

SSH SSH SSH

Three or four bolts were fired in quick succession from Munir's crossbow. The Giant Scorpion, however, sensed that something was flying its way and raised its claws in defense.

Munir's bolts could not penetrate the claw's thick plating and bounced off harmlessly.

The scorpion moved its many legs and slid down the dunes, rapidly charging towards the Hunters at an alarming rate. Bukitai at the vanguard nervously readied his shield.

However, before the scorpion reached the Hunters, Munir put down his crossbow and raised one hand.

"Binding frost! Frostbite!"

Mmm? Sungjin stared at him. To be fair, it wasn't too unusual. Frostbite was a 2nd Circle magic which could be obtained from the

Lich. With a little investment in one's stats, the magic was possible to cast.

The problem was its effectiveness; his stats were probably geared towards the use of his crossbow, meaning the spell effect would probably be weak. Lo and behold, the affected area of the spell was smaller than Sungjin's own attempt from back in the fourth Chapter.

His spell only managed to slightly slow down the speed of the monster. But it was still better than nothing.

"Yaa!" Thanks to his spell, Bukitai was able to get the courage to pick up his shield and charge ahead. The Giant Scorpion wildly flailed its claws.

Bukitai used his giant shield to skilfully block the blows from the claws. Meanwhile,

"Tail!" Munir yelled from the back. While Bukitai was distracted with the claws, the scorpion had poised its tail for a strike.

Too late, Bukitai saw the tail and attempted to raise his shield to protect himself. But before he managed to,

BANG!

Gladiator Igor blocked the tail with his shield. Not only that, he moved at incredible speed to swing his sword and severed the tail.

"Ooh..." Sungjin puckered his lips and nodded. With that much Speed and Attack Power, never mind his equipment, the Gladiator had considerably high stats; he must have maintained an overwhelming contribution level until now.

With the tail already gone, the claws were cut off by the combined attack of both Bukitai and the Zealot Ralph.

SSH SSH SSH

Munir's triple crossbow shot landed on some of the more thinly armoured parts of the scorpion's body. The four Hunters managed to kill their first enemy without much problem.

Munir puckered his lips and whistled.

Ralph turned around to the other three men. "I think we'll be okay like this."

Something was wrong. There were only 'three others,' one was missing.

"Where's the Chinese guy?" Igor looked around searching for him.

Only Bukitai, who had grown up in the wide open plains, was able to get a glimpse of Sungjin in the distance. But only for a moment.

Sungjin disappeared from sight utilizing Swift Paw.

Bukitai squinted his already narrow eyes to see, but Sungjin's form was lost between the shaky waves of heat.

*

Sungjin paused for a moment after covering a large distance to pour water over his head with his magic water-skin.

"So hot!"

He didn't run with an objective in mind. Like Ahenna, the Basilisk would appear by itself once enough enemies were slain.

He just did not wish to share contribution points with others.

All four of them looked strong, so they shouldn't face anything that can kill them.

Sungjin began hunting solo in the desert. He saw a large Desert Lizard in the distance. The body itself was already four meters long, and with the tail, the lizard was about six meters in length.

It lay as still as a corpse in the distance. This was a characteristic of the lizard; it was silent and still, but once it decided to move, it ran with amazing nimbleness.

He took out Moon Spectre and approached the lizard. The lizard continued to lay still.

Stop acting.

Sungjin thought of just running in and slashing it with his sword, but,

'Binding Frost!'

He recalled Munir's spell and changed his mind. He transferred the Moon Spectre to his right hand, and holding up his left hand he said, "Binding frost! Frostbite!"

The effects were amazing. Despite the desert heat, the immediate surroundings of the lizard froze and became solid. The affected area was much larger than the last time he had tried. He definitely saw the benefit of having higher Magic Power.

Once the feet were frozen stiff, the lizard stopped pretending to be inanimate and began trying to break free. It was no easy feat breaking free. Sungjin quickly ran up to the lizard.

CRACK

The lizard's hide was extremely tough, but it could not stand up to Sungjin's absolute stat superiority. Its head fell from its body. Sungjin lifted up his sword and thought,

It's still one shot one kill.

Just then

WOOSH

A large tail came swinging towards his face. Sungjin quickly swung Moon Spectre and cut off the tail.

What?

When he checked his surroundings, he saw the headless lizard thrashing about mindlessly.

Ah... I forgot.

Even if the head was cut off, the body would still stay alive for a little bit. Of course, it couldn't launch any intentional attacks without a head, but being careful around it after beheading it was probably a good idea.

Calming his heart, he took a deep breath when two Giant Scorpions came charging at him. Looking carefully, he saw a third behind the first two.

A total of three monsters. Not bad at all. It was not like normal mobs were capable of hurting even a single hair on his body.

Quick, come, come.

Sungjin charged towards the scorpions. He cut through the claws of the first one, cut the side and the tail off the second, dodged an incoming claw attack, cut, evaded, cut, cut... The enemies quickly met their demise.

Easy... Too easy, thought Sungjin.

He nimbly moved his body and killed the first two scorpions before the third arrived. It was time for a one on one attack.

Two scorpions were no match for him; one had no chance. Sungjin fixed his grip and waited for the last one to arrive. However, his field of view lowered as the sand started to sink rapidly.

"What?"

A hole appeared between his legs, and the sand rapidly drained into it.

Sungjin climbed up the sand and jumped out of the sinkhole. In the place he had stood moments before, the grotesque, vortex-like jaws of a Sandworm appeared from below.

Only the teeth were visible, yet the diameter of the mouth was easily six to seven meters wide. The Sandworm chomped the air twice where Sungjin had been standing and disappeared back underground.

If Sungjin had stood in place, he would have been eaten feet first.

Sungjin didn't have time to sigh in relief; the scorpion was upon him.

He prepared himself to fight, but his feet sank into the sand again. Without hesitating, Sungjin immediately jumped away from the spot.

A hole indicated where the sand would soon be sucked in, followed by the rapid sinking of the sand.

So annoying.

He just barely got out of the area again. Ignoring the cascading sand, the scorpion ran along the slope of the sand and continued to charge towards him.

In Sungjin's case, he preferred this; it gave him the opportunity to take care of the scorpion first. Once he cut off the claws and the tails, he climbed on top of the scorpion.

The scorpion was completely disarmed and was helpless; it couldn't put up any resistance to him as he rode it. Soon, the sand beneath the scorpion began to sink.

It has come.

249

Sungjin stabbed Moon Spectre deep into the scorpion's body.

CRACK!

The sword easily passed through the scorpion and ended its life. When the scorpion's death throes stopped, the sand rapidly got sucked into a vortex and rows of jagged teeth appeared from the sand.

Sungjin jumped straight up from the scorpion's back. The Sandworm rose out of the sand and bit into the scorpion instead.

CRUNCH CRUNCH

It utterly crushed the shell of the scorpion, devouring it in a few bites. The Sandworm showed signs of wanting to retreat into the sand, but before it had the chance, Sungjin aimed his hands towards the giant Sandworm and chanted, "Incinerate everything in your path! Fireball!"

A gigantic fireball flew into the Sandworm's mouth. Moments later,

BOOM

An explosion went off inside the Sandworm's body, and flames violently billowed out of the ground. Fireball was a destructive spell such that even after the explosion, it also covered the area in flames.

And this very spell exploded from within the monster's body. It most likely couldn't have survived such an attack. Seeing the inferno raging on the sand due to the aftereffect of the attack, Sungjin finally took a sigh of relief.

"Whew... I had forgotten all about him..."

Sungjin had been moving through the Raids based on his memories of the past, so enemies and elements of the Raid he had forgotten about would occasionally surprise him.

If I had just read Dalupin's information sheet, I wouldn't have been caught off guard like that... I'll start reading it from now on.

Sungjin reflected over his actions as he moved his feet. Due to his overwhelmingly superior stats, normal mobs couldn't hope to face him alone. The only problem he faced in the Raid was his arrogance.

*

Each of the four Hunters stood a distance away from each other, watching each other nervously. They were all sweating.

"Uh... Oh? Me... It's on me!" Bukitai's feet began to sink. He tried to climb out of the hole, but his feet sank faster than he could climb out.

"Catch!" Munir threw his turban as a makeshift rope for Bukitai to grab. Bukitai put the shield on his back and grabbed onto the cloth.

Bukitai barely climbed out of the hole with Munir's assistance. Shortly after, rows of jagged teeth appeared within the vortex, and a Sandworm finally showed itself.

"Now!" Munir yelled as he fired his crossbows.

PI PI PIT

The bolts embedded themselves deep into the Sandworm's skin.

"Uoooh!" Zealot Ralph jumped high up and brought down his axe upon the worm. Meanwhile, Gladiator Igor mercilessly slashed and stabbed away at the Sandworm's body.

"Kyoooo~" The Sandworm let out a strange cry of agony as it began thrashing about, twisting its body. The Sandworm came out of the ground and swept around in a large circular area.

Munir was already far away, so he was able to get out of the way in time, but Bukitai and Ralph were hit straight on by the sweeping body of the thrashing Sandworm and sent flying. The only one who was able to counter attack was Igor.

He found an indent in the ground and jumped into the depression. Laying in the sand, he held his sword up in the air.

The Sandworm, thrashing about wildly in pain, ran into the waiting blade; half of its body was cut away by the sword.

"Kyooo..." The Sandworm fell into a heap and died. It had attacked five or six times before the Hunters had managed to take it down. Munir wiped the sweat off his brows.

"Whew... scorpion and lizards are hard enough, but this..."

And finally, he yelled after the two men who had been flung away by the Sandworm's attack.

"Hey, all of you, are you alright?"

The Hunters raised their hands to show they were fine. Although they had taken damage, it wasn't anything lethal.

While the two Hunters drank Recovery Potions, Igor scanned their surroundings, wary of any enemies that might be approaching.

In the distance, he saw dunes shifting rapidly despite no winds blowing. Igor called out to Bukitai.

"Hey, Mongolian, what's that over there?"

Bukitai gazed into the distance by squinting his eyes. And before he was about to report what he saw, the Operator beat him to the punch.

[Caution! Boss Monster]

[Basilisk has appeared!]

Everyone was alarmed by the Operator's announcement. Ralph spoke first, "Hmm? Didn't the information sheet say that the boss only appears after 75% of the monsters were killed?"

Munir opened his eyes wide in surprise upon realization.

"We've already killed 75% of the mobs? It's only been 20 minutes..."

***

"Incinerate everything in your path! Fireball!"

Sungjin threw another fireball into a Sandworm's mouth.

BOOM

Flames erupted from the Sandworm's mouth, and the worm collapsed into a heap.

Geez, so much pain.

He wiped the sweat off of his brows; he was throwing a fireball in the midst of murderous heat. But at least the effects were good.

Spell attacks such as Fireball were useful in taking out troublesome enemies like Sandworms from afar. And after using it a few times, Sungjin felt his mana starting to run low.

Sungjin's Magic Power was 1195, and MP was 6660. Fireball was a 4th circle spell, so it cost 4780 units; in other words, each cast consumed more than half the mana pool.

Due to its enormous mana consumption, after just a single cast of Fireball, he had to diligently cut away enemies using his Moon Spectre.

Trading reusability for firepower.

If the Magic Power was too high, the spell's power improved at the expense of mana cost. If Mind Power was too high, the spells could be cast often, but at weaker effectiveness. Finding the proper proportion was important.

Mana... Got to refill mana.

Sungjin pointed his left ring finger towards a flaming Sandworm.

"Lich's Beckon."

The bones wrapped around his finger moved automatically to absorb mana on his behalf. While waiting for the mana restoration to finish, he held the magic water-skin upside down over his head to take a shower.

Even though he had drenched himself, in just a minute or two he was sure the water would evaporate off of him. After all, this was the desert.

"Ohh!" He had moved the water-skin to the back of his neck and involuntarily gasped to the rush of cold water running down his back. It was at this moment that the Operator gave an announcement.

[Caution! Boss Monster]

[Basilisk has appeared!]

"Mmm?" Sungjin looked around in surprise, but he couldn't locate the Giant Lizard Basilisk.

He asked the cube, "Operator, Raid progress?"

[75.8%]

The other Hunters must have pushed the Raid progress past the 75% mark while Sungjin was busy cooling himself down. If that was the case, the boss had probably spawned close to the other Hunters.

Sungjin looked back at the direction he came from. The path was strewn about with corpses of monsters he had killed, but he could see no sign of the other four Hunters nor the whereabouts of the Boss Monster.

If he let it go unchecked, a similar situation to what happened in Grey Soul Cemetery could occur.

What should I do?

Sungjin considered his options for a moment and came up with a solution.

"Cain, come." Sungjin summoned Cain.

Cain took a look around his surroundings; he seemed unaccustomed to the desert scenery. Sungjin spoke softly into his ears.

"Cain use everything you've got, smell or sound... find the Hunters. Got it?"

"Woof."

And within a moment, Cain barked twice looking off into the distance.

"So it's that way!" Sungjin looked towards the direction Cain had indicated.

"Swift Paw!"

He deployed the wolf claws and prepared to run alongside Cain when he found his familiar had stopped moving.

Sungjin paused to look at him. "What's wrong?"

Cain was in an unnatural state. The wolf stared at Sungjin with his tongue hanging out.

"Ah..." The cause of his behavior was obvious; even with Arabic clothing, drenched in water, and with a turban over his head, Sungjin was suffering from the dreadful heat. For Cain, who sported a lush winter coat, it must be beyond the level of torture.

Forget running; he looked in pain just sitting there.

"Yeah I don't think this is right. Go back, Cain. Unsummon."

Sungjin transformed Cain back into a wooden figurine. Then, looking in the direction Cain had shown him, he began running. Alone.

*

The four Hunters quickly raised their weapons. The boss Basilisk made its appearance in the distant sand dune.

It stood at an imposing height, double that of the other lizards. If ancient dinosaurs had still existed, it would have probably been of a similar size.

"Kuuoo!"

It bellowed, and the whole desert reverberated with the echo of the Boss's cry. The Hunters exchanged glances.

Igor spoke up. "As you all saw in the information sheet, looking at the eyes causes Petrification. Munir, you fight it from behind and don't look at its face. Watch out for the tail."

Munir nodded. Igor continued.

"Ralph... is Zealot or whatnot ready?"

He had somehow taken the position of the leader among the Hunters, and they accepted it without question.

The three others were all skilled in their own ways, but after a few hunts they knew Igor was on a different level altogether.

"It's ready to go at any time. It's just... once I use it, my HP drops to half. Look." Ralph raised his axe up for them to see.

Thorfinn – Zealot's Axe
Heroic Axe – Strength S Dexterity C

Passive Skill
Rampage (II)
Each strike against the same enemy increases damage by 20%.
Max 3 Stacks

Active Skill
Zealot (II)
For 30 seconds, increases damage by 200% and attack speed by 200%
Once active duration ends, reduces current HP by half. 5 minute Cooldown

Everyone read the information on the Axe.

"As you can see... it's quite a useful active skill, but in return when the timer's up, it becomes extremely dangerous. So... Please protect me," said Ralph.

Igor scanned the item one more time and replied, "I'll give you a sign when I think it's safe, or if there is a good opportunity to use it."

Ralph bit his lower lip and nodded. Igor addressed the tank, Bukitai, last.

"Bukitai, try to keep its attention on you without looking at its eyes."

Bukitai responded, blinking blankly, "But... how do I block the attacks without looking up?"

"Watch the ground. With that size, you should be able to predict its movement by watching the shadows."

Bukitai dropped his shoulders in dejection. "That's easy to say..."

"Just try to survive. I'll be helping as well," said Igor.

Bukitai nodded at his reassurance. Once the strategy meeting was over, Igor tilted his head towards the Boss and said, "Ok, then, let's go"

Bukitai walked forward, using his shield to block out the Basilisk's eyes. After covering some distance,

"Kuuwargh!" The Basilisk let out a mighty roar, and the earth began to tremble, shifting the sands.

Igor shouted out, "It's coming! Brace yourselves!"

Bukitai tried to peek ahead of him. Upon seeing the Basilisk's giant legs moving towards him, he tensed up.

Shadows... watch the shadows.

But it was no easy feat trying to predict an enemy's motion relying on nothing but shadows. He didn't make any attempt to look up and kept his eyes glued on the feet.

Right leg, left leg, right leg, left leg. Soon its shadow covered the area surrounding Bukitai. The boss kicked using its right leg, and Bukitai positioned his shield to block.

BANG!

The Giant Basilisk's claws collided with Bukitai's shield, and he was pushed back. Despite it all, he shouted, "Quickly! Attack!"

From afar, Munir shot his crossbow bolts.

SSH SSH SSH

"Uryah!" Ralph's battle cry rang out. But Bukitai did not turn to look around, afraid that he might accidentally look into the Basilisk's eye.

WOOSH

The Giant Lizard kicked him again. From the right, and then left, and then right again. Watching the shadows, Bukitai continued to block the lizard's attack. He shouted once again to the other Hunters.

"I won't last long, my HP is running out!"

It was at this time.

SLITHER

Something slimy and gross wrapped around his body and lifted him up in the air.

Caught by surprise, Bukitai looked up to see. The elongated tongue of the Basilisk had wrapped around him.

"Wha..." Once lifted up into the air, he began thrashing about to get loose. But by accident, he looked into the Basilisk's amber eyes.

"Ack!" Bukitai instantly became rigid. He was still conscious, but he was like a vegetable.

Move... I've got to move!

The Basilisk brought Bukitai closer to swallow him. Then,

WOOSH WOOSH WOOSH WOOSH

A round shield flew like a frisbee and struck against the Basilisk's tongue.

"Kaaooo~!" The Basilisk's tongue was cut halfway through, and Bukitai dropped to the ground like a stone. Even after reaching the ground, he was unable to move.

But he could still see. The round shield which cut the Basilisk's tongue continued to fly for a bit, and returned back into Igor's hands. It was a normal-looking round shield, so Bukitai had no idea how such a feat was possible.

"Wa..." Meanwhile, he discovered that he could speak again. Quickly, he tried to move his arms and legs and found that they were beginning to respond to his will. The paralysis lasted only about three to four seconds.

Bukitai lifted his shield up and tried to block the Basilisk's legs again. But the Basilisk stepped out of the way and ran past him.

The Boss was now chasing Igor, who had cut his tongue. And meanwhile, there was an unintended collateral damage.

"Ack!" Ralph the Zealot had accidentally looked into the Basilisk's eye while slashing away at the monster's side. Stunned in place, he was kicked and flung away by the lizard.

And there was another casualty. Munir.

"Help! Save me!" He had been caught by the Basilisk's tail and was hanging in the air.

It's all my fault... I didn't do my job correctly. Bukitai blamed himself as he made his way towards the Basilisk. But then, he heard a familiar voice.

"So, I wasn't too late."

Even before he turned to see, the speaker continued,

"Let me borrow your shoulder, friend."

Someone stepped on his shoulder. Bukitai naturally gazed up. The missing member, Master Hunter Kei, stood on top of his shoulder and jumped off.

The Master Hunter leapt towards the Basilisk's head. However, while Sungjin was in mid-air, the Basilisk seemed to have sensed something approaching and turned to face its assailant. The Basilisk's eyes met with Sungjin's.

Bukitai shouted out in spite of himself. "No!"

Looking into the monster's eyes was a death sentence. But Master Hunter got a full view of both.

"Damn it!" Bukitai ran forward to rescue the Hunter. But he heard the Master Hunter shout,

"Free Ark!"

And with the shout, Sungjin plunged his sword deep into the Basilisk's eye.

"Kaaoo!"

The Basilisk shouted louder than ever before. Sungjin spun in the air and landed in front of the giant lizard. "Stupid lizard and your annoying beady eyes..."

The Basilisk reflexively used its legs to kick Sungjin.

WOOSH

It was an incredibly fast attack. But somehow Sungjin easily dodged it. Only sand remained in the place where he had stood moments before.

While Bukitai was staring with his mouth wide open, Sungjin snuck to the side of the Basilisk. He raised his hands high and shouted an incantation.

"Incinerate everything in your path! Fireball!"

His eyes were facing towards the ground, but the Fireball from his hand landed squarely in the Basilisk's other eye.

"Kaaaa~!" Basilisk cried out in agony. Bukitai took a look around. The Basilisk, now blinded, was thrashing wildly with its legs.

This should be easy now. Bukitai was filled with newfound courage and charged towards the Basilisk. He heard Igor shout out as well.

"Ralph! Now!"

And from afar he heard Ralph's voice.

"Kill... Kill! I will kill you, fucking lizard!"

The four Hunters, now five now along with Kei who had been missing all this time, simultaneously poured their attacks against the blinded Basilisk.

***

"Baaak!" Boss "Basilisk" let out a cry of pain as it collapsed on the spot. The Operator soon gave out an announcement.

[Boss 'Basilisk' defeated.]

[Raid Cleared!]

[You will be returned to Hunter's Hall in 1 hour 29 minutes and 44 seconds.]

Bukitai yelled out loud, "Hey! Are you all alright?"

"I'm alright." Igor responded from next to him. He was drenched in sweat, but not a single injury marked his body.

"I'm... also ok." Ralph replied, whilst laying on the floor, he raised his axe. He was exhausted after pouring a long chain of attacks on the boss under the effects of Zealot.

He looked fatigued, but otherwise had no major injury on him. Last was Munir, but he was nowhere to be seen.

"Alhamdulilah," Munir was on his knees praying to the heavens. He had been caught by the tail and flung in the air, but he also appeared to be well without any life-threatening injury. All three of his comrades were okay.

"Whew..." Bukitai let out a sigh of relief. For one reason or another, he assumed the role of a tank in the Raids, but whenever someone died, it felt like it was his fault, even when it wasn't necessarily true.

Meanwhile, he heard a voice coming from above.

"Well, since everyone looks like they're alright..."

The Hunters looked up at the speaker. Kei, who'd been missing the entire Raid, was standing on top of the dead Basilisk.

"If you all will excuse me, I'll get going, then."

He hopped and slid down the tail of the Basilisk as if skating and then took off, running into the distance. He ran as if his life depended on it.

Bukitai muttered under his breath upon seeing him leave. "Where is he going? Raid is already over..."

That man was full of mystery. But it was alright. The Raid was over, and the Hunters were no longer in a rush. They could rest and take it easy.

Thanks to the large body of the Basilisk, it provided shade from the desert sun. The remaining four Hunters sat together under the shade. Ralph tapped the side of the lizard with his axe and asked, "Anyone see its eyes? I couldn't move when I saw it."

Bukitai nodded. "Yes, the paralysis was terrifying."

Munir replied, biting his lips. "I thought it was over for me when it grabbed me with its tail, especially when I fell on the ground. Thank Allah it was sand and not hard earth... Otherwise, I would have been sent to the Almighty."

Bukitai remembered something and turned to Igor. "Ah, that's right. Thank you, Igor, you have my gratitude. You saved me back there. Thanks to your boomerang-like shield."

Unlike the three other men who were gossiping about the earlier battle, Igor simply nodded to Bukitai instead of speaking up.

How did you do that with the shield earlier? Bukitai wanted to ask. But he couldn't. Igor did not look happy, despite the Raid being complete. Bukitai passed that off as just being Igor's quirk.

Since Russians are naturally cold people.

However, Igor soon opened his mouth. "Hey."

Everyone turned to look at him. But the target of Igor's attention was not a man, but the Operator's cube.

"Operator, what's my current Raid contribution?"

[Your Contribution is 10.3%]

Now everyone was staring at Igor's cube. Igor's face twisted immediately in both anger and disappointment. He looked side to side at the others and said,

"Quick, check your contributions too!"

One by one, the Hunters did as he bid.

Zealot Ralph:

[Your Contribution is 6.3%]

High-Level Scout Munir:

[Your Contribution is 5.9%]

Last, High-Level Guardian Bukitai

[Your Contribution is 7.1%]

All the Hunters were shocked at their levels of contribution. Ralph was first to comment.

"How can this be? I have never earned less than 20% contribution in any Raid. Especially ever since I received this axe..."

Bukitai snorted and added, "Hmm... Since Chapter 2 I was always in the first place..."

Munir stroked his beard as he replied, "Me too..."

It was an unbelievable situation. Each of the four Hunters had always maintained a minimum contribution level of 20% per Raid, and yet all four combined now reached just 29.6%. Slightly short of 30% of the total. There was only one possible explanation.

"That Chinese man..." Igor whispered. The others stared at him. Kei had disappeared once more into the distant desert landscape.

Ralph stared off into the distance and commented, "No wonder the boss just randomly appeared..."

Igor suddenly stood up and addressed the other men.

"Listen all, let's use whatever remaining time we have left to hunt monsters. What are we doing here, resting? Let's go try and secure even one more point."

The remaining three Hunters glanced at each other. And without complaint, all three stood up. They realized that this was the best course of action.

In any given Chapter, earning even a single additional Black Coin meant having an easier time in the future Chapters. The Hunters picked up their weapons and began to move back into the desert.

*

Meanwhile, Sungjin was dashing through the desert dunes. There was only one reason why he was running; he was searching for the hidden piece. The scorching sun and the heat were intolerable. He wanted nothing more than to finish quickly and return to Ninety-Nine Nights for a nice bath and rest.

But the damnable desert seemed to never end. He had been searching ever since he had killed the Raid boss, but he hadn't even run into the boundary line. The only thing breaking the monotony were lizards who from time to time ambushed him from blind spots.

So annoying.

It only took a single swing of his blade to deal with the reptiles. After a while, Sungjin stopped for a moment.

He surveyed his surroundings while showering with the magic water-skin. But nowhere did he find anything of interest as far as his eyes could see.

"Haa... Where is it?"

He couldn't help but be tempted to activate Treasure Hunter, but he restrained himself.

There was no way to know how things would progress later. He decided to continue searching for a little longer.

"Operator, is Swift Paw off cooldown?"

[It is available for use.]

He had used it earlier when searching for the boss, and the cooldown had already ended. Sungjin activated Swift Paw and began combing the desert.

During his search, he found something peculiar in the distance. In the endless ocean of sand, there was an area with a bluish glow.

Oasis! Sungjin, filled with renewed vigour, ran towards the oasis. There was no doubt in his mind that the Oasis would hide a hidden piece or a hidden boss.

But after running for a while, the oasis disappeared from view. "Wait."

Mirage. It was a phenomenon that occurred due to light bending over long distances above hot terrain. Sungjin was aware of such an occurrence, but now that he was seeing it for real, he couldn't help but be disappointed.

Sungjin took a look around. This time, the oasis was located behind him. He ran towards it again.

And soon, he began to run slower and slower. The Swift Paw active time had run out.

The timing.

Now he had to wait for another five minutes before Swift Paw was available for use. Furthermore, at Sungjin's dismay, the same thing happened where the Oasis would disappear and appear behind him.

Whenever he would get close to the oasis, it would disappear like a wisp of smoke. The water and green plants growing by the water's edge would dissipate into sand dunes without a trace.

Sungjin felt like he was under some illusion spell.

Damn it!

But he couldn't give up. Once more, he searched for the oasis. This time, it was in the distance off to the side.

I don't even have Swift Paw.

But he had no choice. Sungjin diligently climbed the dune and made his way towards the oasis. And once again, the oasis disappeared before he got there.

Nothing but sand dunes remained. Sungjin was now utterly frustrated and annoyed. He had chased nothing but illusion three times now and felt like someone was toying with him.

He faced the sky and shouted at the top of his lungs, "Fuuuccck!"

It was then that he saw something flying towards him from a distance. It had a lion's body with a Human face, sporting a giant pair of wings on its back.

"A Sphinx?" Sungjin prepared to fight. He must have discovered a hidden boss by coincidence. In one hand he prepared his 'Moon Spectre,' and with the other, he pointed towards the Sphinx.

Once it reached his targeting range, he began the incantation.

"Incinerate everything in your path!"

[Warning.]

The Operator began an announcement. He knew the next words.

Hidden boss has appeared.

But,

[Attacking a non-hostile life-form will cause penalties from the Raid Rewards.]

Unlike what he had been expecting, he had gotten an entirely different warning message. Sungjin hastily cancelled the casting of the spell. Not too long after, the Sphinx landed in front of Sungjin.

The Sphinx wasn't as large as he had thought. The body was about the size of an elephant. It was just that the wings were twice as long as its body, so it greatly exaggerated the size of the Sphinx.

Sungjin looked up at the Sphinx's face. It was only after their eyes met that the Sphinx began to speak.

"Young wanderer in the desert, what do you seek?"

Sungjin answered simply. "The oasis."

"I see. I will take you to the oasis if you are able to answer my riddle. How about it? Would you like to try my riddle?"

Sungjin nodded. His behaviour seemed to upset the Sphinx. It asked again.

"Answer with your words. Young wanderer, will you try to answer my riddle?"

It was another strange character. Without understanding why he was insisting on a verbal reply, Sungjin decided to comply with its wishes.

"Yes of course."

"Good. Here is the riddle. What is the creature that walks on four legs in the morning, two legs at noon, and three in the evening?"

It was a question he had heard many times in the past. Sungjin already knew the answer. "The answer is Man."

"Why is that so?" asked the Sphinx.

"Man crawls on all fours as a baby, then walks on two feet as an adult, and then uses a walking stick in old age."

"That is correct. But of course, this is only common sense. I was only testing your common sense. Now I shall give you the real riddle. Are you prepared?"

Sungjin frowned. The Sphinx did not appear to be an honest and forthcoming character. But unlike the Wandering Merchant Ruff Han, it didn't seem like a character he could threaten at the sword point.

Noting that Sungjin did not answer, it asked him again.

"I ask again. Are you prepared to receive the true riddle?"

It appeared that the creature just loved asking questions. Sungjin decided to act in accordance with its wishes. "Yes, I am prepared."

Finally, the Sphinx told Sungjin the actual riddle.

"Good. Now, listen well, and answer carefully."

Sungjin focused his attention to the Sphinx and watched its lips. The Sphinx spoke out the riddle.

"What is the first cut, the proof of ties? This, owned by all, is utterly useless, and yet without it, you cannot exist. What is this?"

***

Sungjin briefly thought about it for a moment. *First cut... proof of ties...*

And in less than ten seconds, he came up with the answer. Sungjin looked up at the Sphinx. It was watching him, full of anticipation. It seemed like waiting for an answer gave the Sphinx quite a thrill.

Sungjin gave his answer. "It's the belly button."

The Sphinx's expression changed dramatically. "Eh? Why?"

"First injury that everyone has... belly button. Proof that we were once connected to our mothers, so in many ways it is a proof of our

266

ties. I couldn't have been born without a belly button... but it has no uses anymore, so it is useless."

"..."

The Sphinx stared at Sungjin with an indecipherable expression. Sungjin rested his hand on the handle of Moon Spectre. It was possible that the Sphinx might rapidly change its behaviour unexpectedly like in the case of Wandering Merchant Aindell.

If that's the case... the Sphinx would be the hidden boss.

But

"Correct. How did you get the answer so quickly?" That's all the Sphinx wanted to know.

Sungjin didn't reply.

"I thought you would take at least 10 seconds... no, even 30 seconds to consider the answer. Why were you so confident about your answer?"

"Okay, that's enough. Take me to the oasis," answered Sungjin.

The Sphinx replied looking down at Sungjin. "Yes, a promise is a promise. Can you ride on my back?"

Sungjin hopped on its front paws and climbed on top of its back. The Sphinx addressed him once he got on.

"Grab on tight. If you fall off before you reach the oasis and die, it'll be a shame, right?"

As soon as he spoke, the Sphinx took off into the air without waiting for a reply. Sungjin got the high-altitude view of the desert from the Sphinx's back.

Once they climbed higher, he could see the oasis off in the distance. The Sphinx flew towards the oasis with a powerful beat of its wings.

*

Meanwhile, the others were roaming the map. They were combing the desert for any monsters that remained so that they could get their hands on even a single more coin.

Two Giant Lizards came charging at the group at the same time.

Bukitai shouted from the vanguard, "Here they come! Get ready!"

"Blinding frost! Frostbite!" Munir slowed the advance of one lizard, and the four Hunters focused and fired on the other lizard. Of course, the one leading the charge was Bukitai.

But even before he reached the first lizard, the ground began to shift.

Bukitai shouted out, alarmed, "Sandworm! There's a Sandworm!"

The Hunters immediately backed off from the spot. Even the lizards quickly got out of the way. Moments later-

"Queh~"

A giant Sandworm emerged from the ground and burrowed itself again.

"Spread out! Make room!" Igor shouted. This was the standard procedure for fighting Sandworms. The Sandworms could only create one tunnel at a time.

Standing apart from each other meant only one person could be targeted at a time.

When the hole emerged from underneath one person, others could rescue him while focus firing on the Sandworm once it emerged. Using this strategy, the Hunters had killed several Sandworms already.

The problem was, that there were also two lizards in the mix, complicating things. One of the lizards charged Bukitai and swung at him with a paw.

Bukitai lifted up his shield to block the attack, but he wasn't able to devote his attention to the enemy. He was distracted by the thought that the Sandworm might appear beneath his feet. To make matters worse, the other lizard also charged at him and targeted him.

"Munir, can you use magic?" asked Bukitai.

"I am out of Mana!"

...*damn.* Bukitai swore under his breath. If he had to face the Sandworm and both Lizards at the same time, he would be in grave danger. But he heard shouts from the back.

"Uh... It's on me! Me!"

It was Ralph's voice. Bukitai couldn't help but let out a sigh of relief.

While he held off the lizards, the other two could rescue Ralph, defeat the Sandworm, and then come to his aid.

"Help me! Igor! Munir!"

It was unfortunate that Ralph became the target, but he should be okay since he had capable teammates such as Igor and Munir. However,

"Ahhh!"

He heard Ralph cry out in pain. Bukitai was surprised. He wanted to look back to check, but he was under the combined attack of two Giant Lizards. He couldn't look away from the fight.

He continued to swing his mace and block with his shield as he shouted back, "Ralph? What happened?"

There was no answer from Ralph. All he heard was

SSH SSH SSH

Munir's bolts

WOOSH WOOSH WOOSH WOOSH

Igor's flying shield.

"Keeeee~"

And the sound of the Sandworm's death throes. He didn't know what had happened, but they were able to kill off the Sandworm. Bukitai took the time to shout back while facing the lizards.

"Ralph are you alright? Munir, Igor, give me a hand."

But there was no response. If they had managed to kill the Sandworm, Igor should have come running in with his sword, along with Munir's covering fire.

Bukitai backed off from the lizards to take a look behind him. Seeing the scene, he froze for a moment.

Next to the dead Sandworm was Ralph, missing his lower half. And standing with their weapons down were Igor and Munir, who were just watching him.

Bukitai shouted at them. "What are you doing? Help me!"

He had looked away for too long. One of the lizards managed to land a strike on his side with its long claws.

"Ack!"

Bukitai, pierced by claws, swung his mace to strike the lizard's hand.

"Kaa..." The lizard cried out and retreated its claws. But the other lizard came to strike at him.

"I said help me!" Bukitai shouted, but neither of them took up their weapons. Bukitai fiercely put up resistance with his weapon, but he couldn't outlast the two enemies.

One lizard pierced his shoulder with long claws, and the other knocked the shield out of his hands.

Disarmed, Bukitai was ripped apart to pieces by the lizards. Until his final moments, Bukitai stood even as he was shredded by the lizards, staring at Munir and Igor who watched him die, whispering,

"Munir... Igor... Why...?"

Once Bukitai died where he stood, Igor finally spoke. "I'll take the right, distract the left."

Munir nodded. "Got it."

As instructed, he pointed towards the lizard on the left.

"Binding frost! Frostbite!"

While the lizard was slowed, Munir began firing upon the lizard.

"Kaa!"

The lizard cried out in agony as the bolts found their target. Meanwhile, the other lizard began a fight with Igor. He calmly blocked the claws with his shield as he surgically wielded his sword, removing the lizard's foot, tongue, tail, and finally the head.

Incredible... Munir thought as he continued to snipe the remaining lizard from afar.

After turning into a porcupine from Munir's crossbow bolts, the lizard was beheaded by Igor without having a chance to properly attack even once.

Once the combat was over, Munir walked up to Igor. "Good work."

Igor did not respond to him. He only asked the Operator, "Contribution?"

[Your Contribution is 20.7%]

Munir also checked his own contribution.

[Your Contribution is 11.4%.]

Each of their contributions had doubled from before. Munir let out a toothy grin as he offered his hands in a handshake with Igor. "It was good doing business with you."

Igor also smiled and grasped his hand. "Yes, it was."

When Igor returned the handshake, Munir asked Igor, "Why did you pick me, though? Why not offer the same to someone else?"

Igor answered while shaking his hands. "First of all... because you had the lowest contribution amongst us. I thought that you would not refuse."

Munir nodded. "That seems logical. Anything else?"

"Second... You are the weakest. I am certain I can win in 1 on 1."

"Excuse me?" While Munir was confused, Igor took his sword and cut off Munir's hand which he had been grasping.

"Ahhh!" Munir stepped back, holding the stump of his hands. "You..."

Igor calmly walked up to him.

Munir quickly shouted, "Blinding frost! Frostbite!'

The magic took hold and held Igor in place. Igor was unable to move for a moment. Munir shouted at him. "You said there's penalty for direct attacks against others!"

But Igor's expression could not possibly get any colder. Penalty or not, Igor had decided to kill him. Once Munir realized this, he began to run away.

CRUNCH CRUNCH CRUNCH

He could hear one foot crushing the ice.

CRUNCH CRUNCH CRUNCH CRUNCH

Now he heard two feet walking on the ice. Igor had begun his chase. Munir turned around and cast the spell again.

"Blinding frost! Frostbite!"

Igor was rooted in place again. But, this time, the Operator gave out a warning.

[Low Mana. Less than 10% remaining.]

Not enough mana.

Munir had lied to Bukitai earlier, but now it was for real. He only had one shot left. He had to run away as far as he could and hide until the Raid ended. In the long run, he held the advantage if he could get some distance between them, since he originally came from a desert country. With this in mind, he climbed on top of a large dune. But...

WOOSH WOOSH WOOSH WOOSH

Igor's shield came flying and hit Munir's calf.

"Ahh!" Munir fell, holding his leg. Unfortunately, he tumbled down the side of the dune towards Igor.

Igor freed himself from the spell and continued to walk towards Munir. Out of mana, missing his primary arm, Munir had no choice open to him except to beg for mercy.

"Igor, you told me yourself you'll receive a penalty if you kill other people! Why are you doing this?"

But Igor did not respond, stabbing Munir with his sword instead. He held the sword in place until Munir died.

[You have killed your fellow Hunter. Entering 'Troll' state.]

[Hunters in 'Troll' state receive 10% penalty to Raid Rewards.]

[And in the event that the Troll is killed by other Hunters,]

[It will not inflict the 'Troll' state on the attacker.]

After listening to the Operator's explanation, Igor told Munir, who lay bleeding on the desert sand, his reason.

"Even taking on the 10% penalty, killing you is more profitable."

Of course, Munir was unable to hear him.

*

At that moment, Sungjin was sailing through the air, riding on the back of the Sphinx. Once the oasis grew close enough to see clearly, the Sphinx addressed him.

"Hold on tight, Human. It would be a shame to die after coming all this way, wouldn't it?"

The Sphinx suddenly initiated a high-speed dive. Sungjin had no choice but to hang on for his life.

...Couldn't he just fly slower?

But even before he was done complaining, the Sphinx touched down close to the oasis.

BOOM

The Operator let out a congratulatory message.

[Congratulations! You have discovered the hidden Oasis 'Suleman'!]

Jumping off the Sphinx's back, Sungjin complained. "Hey, couldn't you just descend slowly?"

The Sphinx looked Sungjin square in the eye and answered, "Next time, answer slower. Otherwise, it's no fun for the person giving the riddle, no?"

"So you did that on purpose?" Sungjin bubbled in anger and reached for his sword.

"Well then goodbye. See you later if we ever have another chance." The Sphinx quickly returned to the sky and flew away. Sungjin stared after him for a moment.

You appear again?

He didn't want to meet the creature again if he could help it. Once the Sphinx had disappeared far into the distance, Sungjin turned his gaze towards the oasis. In the end, he had, in fact, managed to reach the secret location.

Sungjin rubbed his hands together in anticipation as he began to look around the oasis.

Let's see... where could the treasures be hidden?

***

Sungjin walked around the oasis alone. The water in the oasis was dirtier than he had imagined.

273

In movies or cartoons, characters were usually depicted running into the water to swim or drink from it, but Sungjin felt no such inclinations.

Maybe if I was dying of thirst, he thought.

Sungjin held the magic water-skin above his head upside down as he walked in circles around the oasis. The oasis covered a small area; it took less than a minute to walk the circumference of it.

He couldn't spot anything special about it; he had been hoping for clues about the hidden piece, but there was nothing.

So... what now? Sungjin thought to himself as he gazed into the water. And then, suddenly, something sparkly caught his eyes. Sungjin stared at it.

In the center of the oasis stood a large palm tree. And on top of the tree sat a grimy old lamp.

Found it! Thought Sungjin, and he stepped into the oasis. However,

FOOF

Something popped out from within the murky waters. Sungjin jumped back in surprise. It was a crocodile. An extremely large one at that.

Crocodile? In the desert?

Sungjin checked the cube. It did not say anything. It wasn't a hidden boss.

Sungjin shifted his gaze back to the crocodile. It was preparing to launch a follow-up attack after its failed ambush, but nothing except the hidden boss could possibly give Sungjin trouble.

"You surprised me, dumb animal!"

Nevertheless, the crocodile died with just a few slashes. Staying alert, in case there were more crocodiles waiting, Sungjin cautiously made his way deeper into the oasis.

The oasis was shallow enough to walk into it. And there didn't appear to be any other crocodiles. Without further trouble, Sungjin was able to reach the palm tree growing in the center of the oasis.

Once he was within arm's reach of the tree, Sungjin returned the Moon Spectre back into the sheath and climbed the tree.

Hmm... I should try to learn some sort of flight spell.

Being able to fly would be extremely helpful getting around, and aid in searching for the hidden boss and the hidden piece.

I'll have to remember to look around the Black Market.

Making a mental note for himself for later, Sungjin arrived at the top of the palm tree. There, the lamp lay gently enshrined in the center of the palm leaves.

Worn-out Lamp
Normal Ornament

Active Skill
Rub (I)
Rub the lamp. Effects are unknown.

A lamp, worn out due to age and weathering.
Though, it would have been a work of art at the time of its creation.

Hmm... The part about 'Effects are unknown' caught his attention. Sungjin placed the lamp into his pocket and slid down the palm tree. He walked out of the oasis and inspected the item.

The lamp was caked with dirt and was extremely ancient looking. But, in between the scum built up over the years, the sun's reflection he saw from underneath the grime gave proof of its golden material.

I wonder what it'll do.

Sungjin first checked his surroundings, and then began to scrub away at the lamp. Soon, smoke emitting a dim, blue light began to billow out of the lamp.

Sungjin recalled the folklore: the Legend of Genie in the lamp granting wishes.

"Wish... Hmm... What should I wish for?" Filled with anticipation, Sungjin watched the smoke build up. But... the smoke continued to billow out for a long while.

Come on... Come on...

The lamp continued to smoke for what felt like an eternity.

What... What's that? Sungjin looked up at the sky and jumped back in surprise. High above, a large gathering of clouds formed the figure of a giant. Only his upper body was done forming, and already it was as tall as a five-story building. He was gargantuan.

Sungjin stared up at the giant.

Yeah... Bigger means he can grant better wishes, right?

*

After killing all of his teammates, Igor called out to the Operator.

"Operator, what is my contribution now?"

[Your contribution is 26.4%]

It was as he had planned. Munir had 11.4% before he died. Igor had received exactly half of Munir's contribution upon his death.

The other half had most likely gone to the Chinese man. Igor rubbed his sword and shield together. And for a moment he looked up at the sky. The sun continued to cook his body.

I even took desert simulation training... but the reality is much worse. Wait... is this even real?" thought Igor.

He lay against the side of the lizard and closed his eyes. But...

Igor Janović! You must train harder for the sake of our Motherland!

A voice inside his head woke him up. Looking up at the sky, he spoke to himself. "Why does the Motherland matter in this situation? Does the Motherland even exist anymore?"

However, his superior officer was not here to listen to his complaint. He thought to himself. *Would he be fighting too? Somewhere in this world?*

He would have most likely survived. In the Federal Security Service of the Russian Federation (FSB) where Igor had received his military training, every man and woman were professionally trained for survival.

And the instructor who mentored Igor was a specialist among specialists in survival skills and tactics. Unless, of course, he was very unlucky. No, even if he were unlucky with his teammates, he would have still survived somehow.

He would have killed all his teammates, like Igor, to take all the reward for himself. Igor asked the Operator for the time.

"How much time do I have left?"

[1 hour and 5 minutes left in the Raid.]

1 hour and 5 minutes...

The current Raid progress stood at 92.7%. With the exception of the mysterious 5% he could never locate, there was still 2.3% left in the Raid completion. Igor stood up again.

Perfection, or the closest thing to it; his training demanded it of him. Igor moved back into the desert to fulfil his due diligence.

Occasionally Giant Lizards or Giant Scorpions came to attack Igor, but he could defeat them 1v1 without much difficulty.

Of course, he did not find it easy when two or three appeared at the same time. But, animals were still animals; these monsters were simply larger and stronger than the earthen kind. Their intelligence level was still low.

Simple tricks he had learned in the Spetsnaz scattered the enemy, and he could resume facing them one by one with brutal efficiency.

After hunting for a long while, he could not see any more enemies. All he could see intermittently were corpses lying in pieces, scattered about. Upon close inspection, all of the corpses showed signs of cuts made by a Japanese Katana. The culprit was most certainly the mysterious Chinese man.

...Chinese...

He asked the Operator,

"Raid Completion level?"

[94.2%]

Igor thought for a moment. *Again... 5% is missing.*

He did not understand why he could never fill the completion level to 100%. Even when he made sure that there was nothing left alive, there was always 5% remaining. But that did not stop Igor.

He may not have understood the requirements to fill the last 5%, but he would try until the very end. That was his training and his philosophy.

After combing the desert for a good long time, finally, he found a lizard aimlessly roaming around, lost and alone. After killing the lizard,

[95%.]

He had finally reached 95% completion. He knew there were no more monsters left to find. After several Chapters, he had confirmed this as the truth.

Just where is the last 5%?

And while he was pondering, somewhere in the distance,

RUMBLE

He heard something strange. It was familiar, but something he'd never expected to hear in the desert.

Lightning storm?

Igor stared off into the distance. Very far away, he could see that a large cloud had formed. Under it, he could also see a spec of green.

Oasis?

He had been planning on resting after hunting the last lizard, but he immediately made his way towards the oasis. He felt convinced that whatever was happening over there held answers about the mysterious 5% which had eluded him thus far.

Igor slapped his shins and spoke a single command.

"Forced March."

The armor on his shins folded outward, clanging away until it covered his feet completely. And with enhanced speed, he ran towards the oasis.

*

The giant who emerged from the lamp looked down upon Sungjin and asked, "Who has awoken me?"

Filled with anticipation, Sungjin answered, "Me! I have!"

"Really?" The giant stared for a moment and began his introduction.

"I am the most powerful mage to have ever lived in Kutan, Soldamyr."

Sungjin nodded. He predicted the follow-up phrase.

Make a wish. I shall grant you anything that your heart desires.

But he was completely wrong. What he heard was, "I shall test you to see if you have the right to become my master."

The cube, which had stayed quiet when the Sphinx and the Crocodile appeared, suddenly let out an announcement.

[Caution! Hidden Boss]

[The Great Genie Soldamyr has appeared!]

"What?!" Sungjin threw away the lamp in surprise and pulled out his sword. But the Genie Soldamyr had already began casting his first spell.

"Murderous thunder, jump from foe to foe!"

Bright balls of light gathered in his hands and soon poured out towards Sungjin.

"Chain Lightning!"

Sungjin tumbled away, but the lightning landed on the oasis, and also struck Sungjin.

"Ack!" Sungjin couldn't help but cry out. Even though he had dodged the main body of the spell, it was still a powerful strike.

But why? Sungjin thought for a moment. Now that he looked at himself, he saw that he was still dripping wet.

Getting electrocuted despite dodging the spell was probably due to that. Sungjin quickly moved away from the oasis.

Soldamyr changed his spell. "Incinerate everything in your path! Fireball!"

The Genie's fireball was at least twice as wide in diameter. Sungjin retreated while wrapping himself in Sael's Breath and shouted, "Solidify!"

BOOM

279

The fireball exploded and lit the surroundings on fire. It was a powerful boss and was incomparable to the previous bosses he had fought.

Sungjin quickly took out the Romance of the Three Kingdoms from his vest. He had been saving it all this time to try it out on the hidden boss anyway. It was a great time to test it.

But Soldamyr continued to shout incantations. "Lance which pierces all! Lightning Bolt!"

Sungjin quickly tumbled away and dodged the spell.

BOOM

The sand where it landed was scorched black.

I need an opportunity to read the book.

The only weakness with the books was that like magic casting, it required reading time. Sungjin thought of using Cain, but he had already summoned and unsummoned Cain.

What should I do? Sungjin considered his options. The crocodile corpse came into view.

"Lance which pierces all! Lightning Bolt!"

Another chant came and Sungjin tumbled away.

BOOM

He accidentally held the Moon Spectre too close to the strike zone, and his right arm went numb. Sungjin gritted his teeth against the pain, then, pointing towards the crocodile with his left hand, he shouted an incantation.

"Awaken and become my slave! Rise of the Dead!"

The crocodile came back alive and began to move. At the same time, Sungjin took out and rang Manyata – Master's bell.

RING RING

Along with the sound, the crocodile began to move rapidly. Sungjin's attempt was successful. Under the effect of Manyata, the crocodile zombie moved with incredible dexterity.

"Discard your fangs and become a tame sheep! Polymorph!" chanted the Genie turning the crocodile into sheep.

Even though it was instantly countered before it could launch even a single attack, it gave him the time he needed. Sungjin opened the book.

The book was designed to automatically open to the most relevant page. Once the book was open, Sungjin read out loud the content of the book. Quickly, and accurately.

"Cao Cao's great army pursued deep into the night and reached the fields of Changban. But he stared down at the army while blocking the bridge. Shaking his lance and glaring most threateningly, he shouted."

***

"I am Zhang Yide!"

Sungjin enunciated and pronounced each and every word carefully until the end. The book closed itself and flew into his arms. This was proof that the 'Declamation' had successfully activated. The Operator gave out an announcement.

[Seance of Zhang Fei Yide activated!]

The books always armed the user with the perfect skill for the circumstance. Sungjin grasped the Moon Spectre and charged towards the Genie immediately.

[Passive skill – Enhance Attack (III), Swift (III) applied.]

Sungjin didn't pay attention to the Operator's announcements, but he felt his strength increase and his movements speed up.

"Baa~"

Soldamyr, who was busy turning the crocodile into a sheep, returned his attention back onto Sungjin, who was rushing towards him.

Sungjin was moving even faster than before; the same guy who could, even in normal conditions, dodge bolts of lightning. Soldamyr decided to turn him into a sheep as well. He began to recite the incantation rapidly.

"Discard your fangs and—"

However, Sungjin heard the Operator's voice while charging towards the Genie.

[Active Skill Shout of Changban (I) is available for instant cast]

Sungjin did not know what Shout of Changban was, but

"—become a tame sheep!"

He didn't have time to think it through. The spell was nearly complete. Sungjin wasted no time activating the skill.

"Shout of Changban!"

His mouth moved on its own after,

"COME AND BATTLE ME TO THE DEATH!"

A voice loud enough to tremble the earth burst forth. Following the superhuman bellow, the Genie was unable to continue the incantation.

Sungjin didn't know for sure, but it seemed to have a spell cancellation effect. Soldamyr attempted to stop Sungjin using his hands, but Sungjin easily cut away the fingers.

Sungjin leapt to his arm and began carving up the Genie's body.

Without magic, the mage Soldamyr was unable to put up resistance to Sungjin's blade properly; he severely lacked in physical offense or defense.

[Effects of Seance over in 10, 9]

The operator began a countdown, but

[8, 7]

When about 7 seconds were left, the Genie's body suddenly turned into smoke along with a 'pop' and was sucked back into the lamp. Left alone mid-air, Sungjin spun around in the air a few times and landed on the sand safely.

The Operator's cube announced his victory soon after.

[Hidden Boss the Great Genie Soldamyr Cleared!]

Sungjin returned the Moon Spectre to the sheath. And then let out a sigh of relief. "Whew"

"Grr," right then the zombie crocodile came running towards him after the polymorph spell ended.

"Oh my goodness," Sungjin had been surprised by the Crocodile twice now. He had forgotten that he had reanimated the Corpse using his magic.

"Grr," the crocodile circled Sungjin as if searching for something to attack.

"Whoa, whoa, ok I got it, it's over. Return."

Responding to Sungjin's gestures, the crocodile returned to being a corpse. Finishing the combat, he opened the magic water-skin and poured the water onto his head.

"Ha.."

It had not been an easy fight. Soldamyr had lived up to his name as the greatest mage in Kutan's history; his spells were incredibly powerful.

Without Romance of the Three Kingdoms and Seance of Zhang Fei, it would have been an extremely difficult and drawn out fight. Sungjin asked the Operator out of curiosity.

"Operator, what's the actual effect of Shout of Changban active skill?"

The Operator opened up an information screen.

Active Skill – Shout of Changban (Innate skill of Seance of Zhang Fei)[3]

Make a thunderous shout

All things within a 300-meter radius, including the caster, are unable to cast abilities for 10 seconds

---

This was most definitely a 'hard counter' for any mage character. The true strength of the book was not just from the spell effects, but the fact that it picked the spell based on the situation; the book would call forth the perfect hero from the story using Seance.

When I have to face other mages... I might need it again.

Sungjin organized his thoughts as he corked the water-skin and returned it to his belt. Now that he took a look at himself, he saw that a portion of his clothes had been burnt off. It probably happened while he was dodging the bolts of lightning.

Sungjin spoke to himself absentmindedly. "This is probably the first time I lost so much HP... right, Operator?"

The Operator responded even to his ramblings.

[This is correct. You have lost a total of 4724 HP. This is the highest recorded HP you have lost so far.]

Sungjin's HP was approaching 20,000, but for 'normal Hunters,' taking 4724 was nearly lethal.

I didn't even take a single hit straight on... what amazing power.

Sungjin thought as he stretched himself. After the Genie had disappeared, all that was left was the intense rays of the sun. He couldn't help but think of the cool balcony of Ninety-Nine Nights.

When I go back this time... I should have chilled noodles. Yes... Chilled. And sherbet ice cream for dessert. Hmm, I wonder if there are still mobs left. It's not going to start handing out Raid reward yet, is it?

Sungjin turned to the Operator. "Operator, are there any hidden elements left? If there is, please activate Treasure Hunter now."

[There are no more hidden elements left in this Chapter.]

It must be because the secret place held the hidden boss, rather than an item.

Hmm... I see... Sungjin nodded to himself as he was thinking, but the Operator continued to speak.

[Raid 100% complete.]

Sungjin looked at the cube in surprise. *What?*

The other Hunters must have finished hunting the rest of the monsters. Sungjin celebrated internally. *That's great! Let's get the rewards and go home.*

But the Operator wasn't done.

[However, there is an active 'Troll' in the party.]

[Raid reward will be postponed until the Troll, or the other members are eliminated]

[or if the timer runs out.]

"Hmm?" Sungjin stared at the cube. "Troll?"

Something must have happened between the other four Hunters. Sungjin gazed into the distance. Tanned sand continued endlessly towards the horizon.

Just roaming the desert was torture, but trying to find the troll hiding in the middle of this vast desert within the time limit was nothing short of impossible. Sungjin considered his options.

What should I do?

But it was at that moment

WOOSH WOOSH WOOSH WOOSH

He heard something from behind.

*

While Igor was running towards the oasis, the Operator gave out an announcement.

[Caution! Hidden Boss]

[The Great Genie Soldamyr has appeared!]

Igor turned to look at the cube with the corner of his eyes.

Hidden boss? There are hidden bosses?

It only took him a moment to accept it, since he could visually confirm the existence of the hidden boss from afar. Seeing the form of the giant hovering over the oasis, he was certain.

The secret behind the missing 5%... that must be it.

Not too long after, Igor was able to reach the oasis. The battle had already started by the time he arrived.

"Incinerate everything in your path! Fireball!" came the shout of the Genie.

Igor hid himself behind a dune and watched the fight. The Genie wielded unbelievably powerful magic.

It was incomparably stronger than the mage bosses of the past, such as the Lich or the Two-headed Ogre. Igor quickly calculated in his head.

The teenager currently had 73.6% of the total contribution. If he gets killed by the Genie, Igor would get all of it automatically. Problem was

"Solidify!"

The teenager's skill was also incredible, being able to face off against the Genie alone on equal terms. Igor theorized three outcomes.

First, if the teenager was killed, Igor would leave the oasis before the Genie discovered him. The Genie was probably an extremely dangerous foe.

Second, if the teenager won without much problem, he would, again, leave the oasis. No matter how he thought of it, the teenager's skills were above his own. He didn't forget the fact that he, as a troll, could be killed by others without any penalty.

Third, in case the fight was close and the teenager pulled off a narrow victory... Igor looked down at his sword and shield. *If that's the case, I will finish it myself.*

He was already in the 'troll state.' There was nothing to lose by getting more blood on his hands. Planning his next move carefully, Igor slowly made his way into the tall grass of the oasis and hid himself.

He was confident in camouflage and ambush. He was also confident that he could avoid detection without a camo suit.

Hiding in the bush, he watched the fight. The Genie appeared to have the upper hand.

"Lance which pierces all! Lightning Bolt!"

The teenager seemed unable to deal with the Genie's rapid spell attacks properly. But the tables turned suddenly.

"I am Zhang Yide!"

It was after the teenager read out of a book. An ancient Chinese warrior appeared and hovered behind him like a guardian spirit.

And the teenager dashed forward, even faster than before. Igor thought, *Is it... some sort of buff spell?*

But the book effects did not stop there. Opening his mouth suddenly, the Teenager bellowed.

"COME AND BATTLE ME TO THE DEATH!"

It was an unbelievable shout, done in unison with the guardian spirit behind him. From the moment he bellowed, the giant from the lamp became mute, unable to cast any spell and unable to put up a fight.

And finally, the giant turned back into smoke and disappeared. Once the battle was over, Igor inspected the teenager.

Because the fight had just gotten over, the teenager seemed unaware of Igor. Igor had to make a decision now.

Second, if the teenager won without much problem, he would, again, leave the oasis.

Third, in case the fight was close and the teenager pulled off a narrow victory.

Igor was trying to decide if it was the second case or the third, but he heard the Chinese teenager talk to himself.

"This is probably the first time I lost so much HP... right, Operator?"

And the Operator answered his question.

[This is correct. You have lost a total of 4724 HP. This is the highest recorded HP you have lost so far.]

Igor quickly considered his options. He had monopolized all the points from the very start.

I don't know how he obtained such powerful items... but there should be little if any difference in stats.

Considering stat allocation needed for Strength, Dexterity, and Endurance, 4724 was not a small amount of HP to lose. Even more so considering the teenage was also using magic.

His total HP should be about 10,000... no, it's most likely less than that.

The Lightning spell attack from earlier must have dealt a great amount of damage. Igor made up his mind and looked down at his shield. That Chinese teenager was without a doubt stronger than himself.

But if he was below half health, or farther below that, then Igor stood a chance. Especially if he took the first strike in an ambush. It was then,

[Raid 100% complete.]

[However, there is an active 'Troll' in the party.]

The Operator gave an announcement.

"Troll?" The Chinese teenager came to find out about him.

At this moment, Igor decided. *If I don't get stronger now, I will die later.*

He immediately threw his round shield.

WHOOSH WOOSH WOOSH

Igor drew his sword and charged towards the teen.

***

Sungjin turned. A round shield was flying towards his neck. He quickly tilted his head.

WOOSH

A violently spinning bladed shield flew past him. Meanwhile,

"Uwooo!" Gladiator Igor came running towards him with his sword drawn.

"Haa!" Igor swung his blade. He was quite fast, but it was nowhere near fast enough for Sungjin. Sungjin drew his Katana and easily parried the strike.

SSSH

But from behind him, he could hear the shield returning. Igor prepared for another attack which was a front to back pincer strike.

Sungjin opened his eyes wide. *Is this what he was aiming for?*

Sael's Breath was still under cooldown. Sungjin removed his left hand from the sword and parried Igor's attack with Moon Spectre held only by his right hand, and blocked the shield with Free Ark on his left.

BANG! CLANG!

Four metallic objects collided at the same time. Sungjin thought that he had deflected the shield away with his wrist, but

"Haa!"

When Igor reached out with his arms, the shield returned to his hands. Since he didn't shout an incantation, it wasn't magic. It was most likely a skill built into the shield as an innate ability.

Sungjin shook his left arm, which had numbed, and gazed at the shield.

A ranged, self-returning shield.

He had known from the very first moment when he laid his eyes on Igor that this man was strong. He could tell with how fast Igor was able to move. Sungjin had no idea how he managed to scrape together so many Stat Points, but his Dexterity was extremely high.

And that strange shield... it couldn't be anything less than a Heroic tier item. Which meant, Igor was likely concealing other high-rank items that Sungjin didn't know about.

Sungjin quickly returned the Moon Spectre back into the sheath. He was preparing to use Deathly Wail. Since he had tested the effects against the rapist, Sungjin knew that the Deathly Wail was extremely useful in duels against other people.

Sungjin kept the Moon Spectre on standby as he asked Igor a question. "So... is this the way you have chosen to become stronger? Backstabbing your teammates?"

Igor nodded. "It's simple math, isn't it? Giving up just 10%, and taking the other 90%. In some ways, isn't this just like how the world works? Competing over limited resources? This game is structured this way; work together until you clear the Raid, and then..."

Igor drew his finger over his neck. "Kill. Take the contribution points by force. This is a far more profitable outcome. I realized this from the very start. And I acted upon it. I have monopolized each and every point from every Raid."

Monopolized each and every point.

Igor's strength made sense. Even if he hadn't found a single hidden element of the Raids, he still had access to a considerable amount of stats and coins using this method.

Sungjin replied, "Yes... You're not technically wrong. But you will never know what it's like to receive 100% contribution points."

Sungjin was done speaking. There was nothing more that needed to be said. Putting his hand on the hilt of the 'Moon Spectre,' he charged towards Igor. Igor threw his shield one more time.

WHOOSH WOOSH WOOSH WOOSH

Sungjin did not fear the shield that he could plainly see flying towards him. He lightly dodged the shield. It would eventually return, but probably not in time.

Because Sungjin finally drew his blade.

"Deathly Wail."

Along with Sungjin's commands

"KYAAAAA!!!"

An unearthly screech reverberated and filled the air. It was such a horrifying sound that even the hair on the back of Sungjin's neck stood up.

Igor did not retreat or run away, but he did take few steps backwards.

It's over. Sungjin thought, swinging his blade as he dashed forward. But,

"Cleanse," Igor shouted.

CLANG

Igor picked up his sword and parried Sungjin's strike.

"What?" Sungjin was surprised. *He instantly countered Deathly Wail!*

Sungjin saw a necklace shine on Igor's neck. It must have had a similar effect as the Free Ark. While Sungjin was shocked, Igor made his move.

"Haa!" With his gesture

WHOOSH

Sungjin could hear the shield begin to return. He could be attacked from both sides shortly. Sungjin tumbled off to the side and decided to dodge the shield for now.

The shield returned to Igor's hands. Sungjin stared at him. He was no easy foe.

Sungjin considered his options. But the only thing he had was '2nd circle magic' and Yanhurat.

If I use Yanhurat here... I'll eventually become addicted to its effects. I'll start with magic first.

But now that he thought of it, he had another option. He immediately acted on it.

"Operator, give me Manta."

The long staff 'Manta' emerged from the cube and flew at him. Sungjin grabbed the staff and held it in his left arm.

"Swordsman... suddenly equips a staff? And in the off-hand? Trying to use magic?" Igor dashed forward this time. "You won't get a chance!"

Magic... ok, you'll see. Sungjin watched him come, and he swung his sword and staff together.

He intentionally aimed at two different spots, and timed his strike to hit simultaneously. Igor had to block the Moon Spectre with his shield and the 'Manta' with his sword. But that was only for a moment.

WOOSH

VOOM

Sungjin began a rapid combination of attacks utilizing weapons in both hands. Igor was unable to do anything but defend.

How... Igor couldn't understand how this was possible: using two very different weapons in a dual wield and been able to use them effectively in combat.

Most dual wielders often attacked with their primary hand and defended with their off hand.

Igor had observed many instructors fight with various weapons, from east to west. But not even the Grandmasters of their various weapons could pull off such a feat.

Astonished and pushed back by Sungjin's vicious attacks, he decided to finally use his ace in the hole.

"Haa!" He threw the shield towards Sungjin at close range. Sungjin had already easily dodged the shield before, and dodging it from close range was just as simple.

But using this as a chance, Igor turned and hastily retreated.

So... he chooses to escape, thought Sungjin.

He wouldn't be able to go far. Sungjin's Swift Paw was already off cooldown. And, he had magical spells available to him.

Sungjin chanted, "Binding frost! Frostbite!"

Igor's feet froze in place. Igor could no longer run. Igor even threw his sword in a last-ditch effort to make a stand.

WOOSH

There was no way Sungjin wouldn't be able to dodge the sword.

So he abandons his only weapon. Looks like he's given up. Sungjin calmly walked up to him.

But, Igor spread his arms wide and shouted, "Haa!"

It was now that Sungjin noticed his gloves. At the center, the gloves had what appeared to be a circular opening. It was now that he realized.

It wasn't the shield! Sungjin quickly turned around.

WOOSH

SHING

The shield and the sword were both flying towards him. If he only had Moon Spectre, it could have been a dangerous moment. But, he also had Manta in his other hand.

CHING!

CLANG!

The sword and shield made loud noises upon contact and were deflected off, returning to Igor's hands.

I can't let him buy any more time. Sungjin charged towards Igor. He was still unable to move due to the frost. Sungjin resumed rapidly attacking Igor with both of his weapons. Finally, Sungjin managed to knock the sword out of his hands.

CLANG!

"Haa!" Igor attempted to call the sword back to him, but he got distracted from blocking with his shield for a split second. It was the slightest of cracks in his defence, but that was sufficient.

Sungjin thrust his sword to the right of the shield, between Igor's body and the shield, and cut off Igor's shield arm. Igor, having lost his arm, took a few steps back. Despite losing his arm, he didn't cry out in pain.

What a monster, thought Sungjin.

But no matter what, Igor's arm was permanently lost; it would not return like his sword and shield. Sungjin first swung the Manta and followed up quickly with the Moon Spectre.

Igor parried the Manta, but had his sword arm cut off in the process. He was completely disarmed.

"Umph..." He finally let out a groan. Rather than responding to bodily pain, it seemed to be a response to having been defeated. Sungjin approached the unarmed Igor.

He was a far stronger opponent than Sungjin had first thought. His stats were superb, but even more amazing was his ironclad will which could endure the pain of having limbs chopped off, and the clever ways he fought and laid traps.

Before finishing him off, Sungjin couldn't help but whisper, "If only you weren't a troll... you would have made a great ally."

Igor heard him and replied, "Kill me. I accept that you are stronger than me, and I will not beg for my life."

Sungjin stared at him. Unlike the rapist, he was no coward. Sungjin lifted the sword above his head. But before he took the final blow, Igor added one more thing.

"Kill me, and continue forward. Survive to the end and save us from our imprisonment. Please, bring salvation to mankind."

Sungjin couldn't help but freeze in place. Igor must have figured out how the Raids would proceed. And as if he was in his final confessions, he continued, "I was trained by the Spetsnaz. Even if my methods were violent, I had firmly believed that I must do anything, including monopolizing all the points through murder, to rise to the top. But not even in my dreams could I have imagined I could run into someone as strong as you."

Finally, his face relaxed, as if he was prepared to face death.

"Back in the Hunter's Hall, I saw the image of my beloved, my parents, all caged within Purgatory. You are capable of bringing it all to an end, right? Please, make it stop. With your own hands, please rescue us from this hell. And finally, save us. All of us."

Igor begged Sungjin. But he was begging Sungjin not to spare him, but to kill him.

Sungjin hesitated for a moment, but he swung his blade and fulfilled Igor's final wishes. Standing respectfully in front of the corpse before him, Sungjin whispered, "I have accepted your last wishes. Must be nice... to be able to push off your responsibilities to someone else..."

Sungjin wanted to cry. But the desert wind blew against his face and dried up whatever tears that would have formed.

Sungjin gazed up. The burning sun hung in the sky. This dry, accursed desert didn't even allow tears to drop. The Operator made a cheerful announcement without caring about what Sungjin was feeling at the moment.

[All 'Trolls' in the party have been eliminated.]

[And now]

Sungjin used every fiber of his being to swing the Moon Spectre and attacked the cube.

BANG!

It let out a loud noise, but not a scratch formed on the cube.

The Operator continued to speak, ignoring him.

[Distributing Raid reward.]

***

[Monsters Slain. Giant Lizard: 40. Giant Scorpion: 20. Sandworm: 10. Total 4000 points.]

[Boss Monster Slain: Basilisk: 600 points.]

[Hidden Boss the Great Genie Soldamyr: 600 points.]

[Final point count: 5200 Points. Distributing points.]

Reward calculations ended quickly this time, since there was only one recipient.

[Your contribution is 100.0%. 5200 Stat Points, 5200 Black Coins awarded. Raid Clear Bonus 1500 Stat Points and 1500 Black Coins awarded. Item effect 'Additional 10% gained' activated. Distributing 6700 Stat Points and 7370 Black Coins.]

An incredible amount of points and coins were awarded to Sungjin, but he didn't feel all that happy.

[And now we will distribute the items.]

[Soldamyr – Sealed Great Magician]

[Bayram – Basilisk's Eye]

[Al Zard – Magic Carpet]

[Recovery Potion – Medium x4]

[Spell Book – Chain Lightning]

[Spell Book – Polymorph]

The distribution finished, and the Operator cheerfully congratulated Sungjin.

[Congratulations! You have obtained the Legendary item Soldamyr – Sealed Great Magician!]

Sungjin got down to pick up the items that fell in a heap in front of him. The first item he grabbed was obviously the golden Legendary lamp.

The appearance of the lamp was identical to the worn-out lamp he had rubbed earlier, but it was now clean without a single smudge or blemish. It almost seemed to radiate with a golden aura.

While Sungjin was lost in the golden exterior of the lavish Legendary lamp, the Operator continued to speak.

[Last but not least, you will be awarded titles you've earned on this Raid.]

[Inquisition – When hit by spells cast by others, gain 10% increase in speed and damage.]

[No stacking limit.]

Sungjin glanced at the cube. It was a familiar title. Many Hunters had kept this one active due to how powerful this title was.

The Operator must have awarded him the title due to being hit a few times by Soldamyr's spells. Sungjin wanted to check the items he had received, but another object popped out of the cube.

[Title Adjudicator activated.]

[You obtained Telkron – Jester's Gloves.]

Uh...

Sungjin picked up the item that had just dropped. It looked like an ordinary pair of leather glove. Except for the fact that there was a strange circle drawn at the center of it.

When Sungjin peeked at Igor's corpse, the gloves were missing from his hands. Turning his attention back to the gloves, he checked the details.

Telkron – Jester's Gloves
Heroic Glove – Defense 12%

Active skill
Pa – Throw the weapon or shield in hand.
Haa – Thrown weapons return to the hand it was thrown from.
The weapon's flying speed scales off of the total weapon damage dealt. Cooldown 20 seconds.

The previous owner, who had been relying on the gloves rather than his own skill, was chased out of the circus when he had lost it.

As I thought... the gloves were the cause.

The defence rating was fairly low; it was mainly an offensive-type item. Sungjin had no gloves, so he immediately equipped it.

"Equip." The leather gloves covered his hands, and they felt good. Sungjin lifted up the Moon Spectre and said,

"Pa."

Despite not having thrown the weapon, the Moon Spectre flew out of his hands at great speeds. Once it reached a certain distance, Sungjin said,

"Haa."

The Moon Spectre spun rapidly in midair for a second before turning around and eventually returning to his hands. *Hmm... It's nice...*

Igor had used this item with very high proficiency. All Sungjin had to do now was practice and get better at using it. Doing so would significantly improve the range of actions he could take with his weapons.

I'll need to practice it as soon as I can.

Making a mental note to himself, Sungjin returned the Moon Spectre to its sheath. The next item he wanted to check was the Legendary lamp. Sungjin lifted it up for inspection.

Soldamyr – Sealed Great Magician
Legendary Summon

Active Skill
Spiritual Link (Soldamyr) – Loyal Familiar, Summon Soldamyr.
If summon is killed, or if 10 minutes pass from the time of summoning, it disappears.

Soldamyr, once the strongest magician to have ever lived in Kutan sealed himself into the lamp in exchange for eternal life.

Sungjin rubbed the lamp. The bluish cloud billowed out of the lamp and formed the shape of a man. It was large, but far smaller than earlier.

It was only about twice the height of a normal adult male. Once the form stabilized, it began to speak.

"Greetings. I am Soldamyr, and I humbly apologize for my earlier behavior. Since you have overcome my test, I formally acknowledge you as my new master."

They had only just finished crossing blades, and yet the Genie was very polite.

"Nice to meet you. So, how will you help me? If you don't mind me asking," said Sungjin.

"Murderous thunder, jump from foe to foe! Chain Lightning!"

The Genie shouted out a magic incantation. Then, he explained himself.

"If you summon me, I shall cast appropriate magic on your behalf. Of course, within the limit of my mana supply."

"Cast magic... on my behalf?"

"Yes. Of Blue, Red, Green, White, and Black magic types, I can cast any spell within Blue, Red, and Black magic type under the 7th circle."

Sungjin tilted his head. He knew that Kutan referred to the desert, but he didn't know the history of the land very well.

"So the strongest mage to have ever lived in Kutan... can only cast three of the five schools of magic, and can only cast up to the 7th circle? And you also have mana restrictions?"

"Ah... I had voluntarily sealed myself in the lamp. Thanks to the extension of my life, I was able to spend an eternity studying and researching various forms of magic... But in return, my abilities have greatly diminished. I hope you can understand," explained the Genie.

While Sungjin was feeling deeply disappointed, Soldamyr crossed his arms and reflected over his past.

"Before I was sealed, I was often compared to two legendary mages who came before me... the great Dark Flame Mage."

Using his finger and with the help of magic, he created an illusion of two men. Sungjin didn't know who they were, but Soldamyr continued with his explanations,

"And the only magician to have attained perfection, the Blue Sky Mage. I have been judged to be the closest one to crack the last inner circle since the 'Blue Sky Mage.' If I had not sealed myself, I might have been able to obtain the tenth circle, the 'Circle of Perfection.'"

He kept spouting nonsense. The Genie seemed to be starved for conversation after being imprisoned in the lamp for so long.

"Ok... got it. Well, see you next time, then," said Sungjin.

"Understood. If you have any question about magic, please don't forget to consult me. I may have less Magic Power and mana compared to before, but my knowledge has grown by leaps and bounds."

"Sure. Unsummon."

Instantly, the Genie turned into a puff of smoke and got sucked into the lamp. Since he could cast spells on Sungjin's behalf, he could prove to be useful. The next item to inspect was a necklace with a yellow eye as an ornament.

Bayram – Basilisk's Eye
Heroic Necklace

Active Skill
Snake Eye (III) – Paralyze enemies for 3 seconds. Cooldown 10 minutes.

Giant Lizard Basilisk's eye. He who gazes into this eye momentarily experiences nightmares.

Sungjin recalled the moment when he had looked into the real Basilisk's eye. He was able to free himself using Free Ark, but he had gotten paralyzed for a moment.

He understood its effects after experiencing it for himself, and so now all he had to do was find the right time to use it. The last item he received was a carpet all rolled up.

Al Zard – Magic Carpet

Active Skill
Flight (III) – Can fly for 20 minutes. Cooldown 1 hour.

Far, far away in the middle of the desert, a wondrous place. A place where anyone would want to go at least once.

That explanation seems familiar for some reason.

Sungjin spread open the carpet and took a look at it. It was a little small. It was just large enough to accommodate two adults sitting on top of it.

He sat upon it and tested the carpet.

"Flight."

The carpet began to float up away from the ground. Sungjin sat for a moment, pondering,

How do I drive this?

He looked over to the large palm tree at the oasis.

I want to go over there.

The carpet flew up rapidly and brought him over to the palm tree.

"Oooh." Sungjin had been planning on buying 'Flight' after this Chapter and memorizing the spell, but with this carpet, it wasn't immediately necessary.

It also didn't cost any mana or anything; there were no demerits to using it to get around. Sungjin flew higher, riding the magic carpet. He heard the Operator speak from the cube following him from behind.

[You will return to the Hunter's Hall in 10 seconds. 10, 9, 8]

Sungjin continued to fly around the Kutan desert while ignoring her. She continued her countdown.

[3, 2, 1, 0]

Her countdown completed, and Sungjin disappeared from midair.

*

"Haa... Haa.."

The black cop Baltren looked around. There was nothing but the desert as far as his eyes could see.

Did I lose them?

He was running in the desert, sweating like a fountain. He wiped his sweat off his face as he whispered, "Crazy bastards..."

It had looked like this Chapter was going to end safely. Everyone had worked together and coordinated in killing the Basilisk; everything was going smoothly.

Although one of the Hunters had died during the hunt, the Raid had gone well overall. But the problem arose when someone decided to ask, "What is my contribution?"

It turned out that the person on the team with the highest contribution was Baltren.

Baltren had thought that it was due to the fact that he had effectively tanked for the team and protected the others.

But, one of the Hunters expressed displeasure. "Why am I getting so little?"

And so the teammates started blaming others and arguing. Before anything could be done, they began drawing blood, fighting each other.

And they even attacked Baltren who was standing by the side. The reason? Because he had the most.

If he had not used the item from the last Raid Manmu – Pach's Club to make the other Hunters faint, he would have been forced to fight for his life.

Troll... how did this happen?

He was a cop, but there was no law to defend here. He kept his watchful eye on the surroundings. Eventually, the Operator gave an announcement.

[You will return to the Hunter's Hall in 10 Seconds.]

He took a deep sigh of relief. He had never been so happy to hear the announcement.

Finally, being chased by people who were even worse than monsters was over.

Chapter 11 – Black Market Fifth Shopping

Sungjin sat on the floor with his legs crossed, still holding onto his sword.

The place he was sitting was the Hunter's Hall. It was an unimaginably immense hall lined endlessly with pillars.

After a short while, other Hunters were also teleported to the same place. Sungjin looked up at the others. Everyone was drenched in sweat and covered in sand.

Once the crowd of Hunters grew large enough, the Operator's face showed up as a hologram above the pillars.

[Congratulations!]

[The Hunters gathered here have all successfully cleared five Chapters thus far.]

Not many were happy despite her announcement. The Hunters had been fighting and struggling for their lives until just a moment ago.

[The current number of surviving Hunters is 637,024.]

[The Raid began with a total of 7,310,067,613 Hunters.]

[Less than 1 out of 10,000 of the original is remaining.]

Sungjin tried to recall the past. He did remember that once the 'Kutan Desert' was cleared the Operator gave an announcement about the total number of surviving Hunters, but he couldn't recall the exact amount.

Well, based on luck, I bet it would fluctuate greatly... While Sungjin was lost in thought, the Operator continued to speak.

[Everyone present here is part of the top 0.01% of the rankings.]

[You have all proven your own self-worth.]

Sungjin briefly thought of Serin Han and Igor. He also remembered the 'Coward' from the first Chapter. It was possible that he had survived until now... although the chances were extremely slim.

[Please continue to grow and become stronger.]

[And clear all the Raids.]

Briefly, the Operator disappeared and was replaced by an image of people. Sungjin decided to look away and observe other people's faces.

Everyone had deep frowns and angry faces: they were most likely being shown images of their friends and families.

[To remind you]

[Once the final Raid is beaten,]

[Everyone trapped in Purgatory will be revived.]

Someone muttered under their breath. "Fuck... How are we supposed to believe that?"

Someone else commented, "They're holding everyone hostage... this is basically extortion!"

The Operator continued regardless.

[Starting from this Chapter onward, at the center of the Black Market]

Despite grumbling just a second ago, once the Operator began an announcement, the Hunters stopped speaking immediately; the Operator's words were absolute when it came to survival in the Raids.

[A new area will appear.]

[It is very useful in increasing your chances of survival, so I would recommend visiting it at least once.]

[You will be sent to the Black Market in 10 seconds.]

Sungjin could hear people murmur around him.

"New area? What's that?"

"It's probably useless without using tons of coins."

Sungjin couldn't help but think, *You don't need it at all!*

[3, 2, 1, 0.]

Along with the countdown, the people gathered in the Hunter's Hall were scattered to their own instances of the Black Market.

*

Sungjin immediately began walking once he arrived. His destination was the one and only; Kenneth's Katana shop. Once

Sungjin was close, he asked the Operator for the amount of Coins he carried.

"Operator, how many Coins do I have?"

[You have 12550 Coins.]

Sungjin nodded and then entered the shop. And as always, Kenneth welcomed him inside.

"Welcome back, Mister Hunter."

"Hey, Kenneth, sorry but... Can I... see the Blood Vengeance again?"

This was already the third time. Kenneth smiled brightly and replied, "Of course you can, don't be sorry."

And for the third time, Kenneth brought Blood Vengeance to Sungjin. Sungjin held the sword in his hands. Then, he held the Moon Spectre in the right and Blood Vengeance in the left and tried swinging the sword with the sheath on. The swords smoothly sailed through the air.

SSSH SSSH

Kenneth hissed while clapping.

"I have seen a multitude of customers wield a sword... but it's the first time I've seen anyone handle two swords so proficiently."

Sungjin was also very happy with himself. The Moon Spectre and the Blood Vengeance; he was now able to field both swords simultaneously. With these two swords, he wouldn't need to purchase any other weapon.

Sungjin lifted up the Blood Vengeance and said, "Please let me buy this. Operator, pay."

The cube came forward and completed the transaction.

Kenneth bowed and thanked Sungjin. "9700 Coins received for one Blood Vengeance. Thank you for your business."

To her sincere and polite gesture, Sungjin replied in kind by also bowing his head.

"Thank you as well. Take care now."

Sungjin hung the Blood Vengeance on his belt. He had finally become a Dual-Wield Swordsman.

Sungjin was going to go straight back to the Ninety-Nine Nights, but he thought of something. *Ah... That's right.*

At the newly created area, there was a business he had to attend to. Sungjin passed many shops to make his way to the center of the Market.

In a previously empty lot, a circular stall had sprung up which was run by three pig demi-humans.

"Do you have anything you wish to sell?"

"Or is there something you'd like to buy?"

"Whichever it is, please come!"

Sungjin walked over. The Operator began her explanation.

[This is the Achi Brother's Time is Money Plan.]

[Hunters can put up items for auction at this shop, which can then be purchased by other Hunters.]

Sungjin walked up to the smallest of the three pig brothers and then called for the Operator.

"Operator, give me Manta."

Receiving Manta from the cube, Sungjin handed over the staff to the pigman. "Please put this up for auction."

The pigman replied, "Oh, this is a Heroic tier item. The minimum payout for Heroic tier items is 2000 coins. If someone makes a bid for the item, the item will remain available until sundown for another bid."

"I know. Start the auction price at 3000 and set the instant buyout at 6000 coins." Sungjin knew the general prices of items thanks to his experience.

Rare was between 500 and 2000, Heroic between 2000 and 5000, and Legendary was between 5000 and 50,000.

Unique Legendary items were priceless, but they were typically unavailable due to the advantage they offered in the Raid.

That was why Sungjin had no intentions to auction Romance of the Three Kingdoms.

"Understood." The Pigman took the item and placed it inside a larger cube at the center of their shop. "If it gets sold, we will send the earnings to Ninety-Nine Nights."

Sungjin nodded. To be honest, items with magic enhancements like 'Manta' weren't likely to be sold. It was because most Hunters were not ready to fight exclusively with magic until after Chapter 7 or 8.

But as long as he kept the item available in the shop, someone was bound to buy it. The item itself was not bad at all. Another Pig demi-human approached Sungjin.

"Anything you would like to buy?"

Sungjin shook his head, but he thought he might as well ask.

"Well... Any Legendary-Tier items available for sale?"

"There are no Legendary items for sale currently."

Just as he thought. It was too early for Legendary items to be in the surplus. Since Sungjin had no interest in anything less than a Legendary tier item, he left the market without worry.

"Okay, I'll have to check back in another time."

Sungjin immediately headed off to Ninety-Nine Nights. He had already decided on tonight's menu.

*

SLURP

It was the cold noodles, in a bowl with chilled soup. Sungjin drank directly from the bowl that Dalupin served the noodles in. It was so refreshing after the torturous desert Raid.

"You look much better now, Master," Soldamyr said, sitting across the table. Thanks to 'Spiritual Link' he was able to stay at Ninety-Nine Nights along with Cain.

"Of course. Kutan Desert is the only desert I've been to. That being said, don't you need to eat something?"

"No, I only need to absorb mana from the atmosphere."

"I see..."

SLURP SLURP

Cain was busily wolfing up the chicken meat.

Sungjin petted his head. "Good good, eat a lot, Cain."

Cain was definitely bigger now. Last time it hadn't been too noticeable, but now Sungjin was absolutely certain. Cain was growing at a very fast pace each day.

Does this even make sense?

Sungjin wondered, but he quickly dismissed his thoughts; time itself flowed strangely in the Black Market.

The Raid always began in the morning, but by the time they returned, it was late afternoon. It wouldn't be strange if several days passed while Sungjin was participating in the Raid. Once he was done with his meal he got up to return to his room.

"See you later, Soldamyr. Bye, Cain."

Facing the innkeeper, Sungjin thanked him.

"Thank you for the meal, Dalupin."

Sungjin left and returned to his room. He was fatigued due to the desert heat.

He filled the tub and lay in the bath as he always did.

"Haa..."

Sungjin couldn't help but sigh. He had known it would be a tough Raid, but it was far more difficult than he had anticipated.

Kill me, and continue forward. Survive to the end and save us from our imprisonment. Please, bring salvation to mankind.

The Raid was physically taxing, but after killing Igor with his own hands, he felt an internal turmoil.

Once the final Raid is beaten, everyone trapped in Purgatory will be revived.

He had forgotten somehow but, Igor and the Operator had reminded him of his mission. Very likely, the salvation of mankind rested on his shoulders. It was a heavy burden to take.

Sungjin raised his gaze to the ceiling. *But... this isn't something I can clear on my own.*

If he could complete every Raid by himself, it would be perfect, but that was impossible. The way the Raids had been designed, cooperation with several teammates was necessary to clear it.

The further along in the Raids he progressed, the more important his teammates became. It was not only about having strong teammates, but having teammates he could trust. But often it was difficult to find both qualities in the same person.

It was true in the 'real world,' and it was especially true in the Raid. He couldn't help but recall Igor's words.

In some ways, isn't this just like how the world works? Competing over limited resources? This game is structured this way; work together until you clear the Raid, and then kill. Take the contribution points by force. This is a far more profitable outcome.

He wasn't wrong. The design of the Raid seemed to encourage troll activity. It would be extremely rare to be able to find kind-hearted yet strong individuals, especially in a system that rewarded team killing.

So... does this system favour evil over good? thought Sungjin.

If that was true, then something needed to be done, considering his 'previous failure.' Sungjin lay back in the tub and thought to himself. He recalled Serin and Igor's case.

If I really intend to complete the final Raid... I can't be the only one to grow stronger... I need to overcome the system and be able to influence the Raid as a whole.

And then he thought of something. *Overcome the system.*

There was a place where that might be possible. Sungjin got up from the bath and wiped himself down with a towel.

KNOCK KNOCK

Dalupin appeared as if he knew when Sungjin might be done with the bath.

"Please come in."

Dalupin greeted him politely and then handed over a piece of paper. "It is the information brochure on the next Chapter."

Sungjin accepted it and asked Dalupin, "Dalupin I have a special request for tonight."

"Go ahead and ask."

"Please wake me up at... At 4:20 am... no, make that 4:10 am."

"Four in the morning?" The owl demi-human stared at him quizzically, not understanding what this was about. Dalupin blinked a few times.

Sungjin answered, "Yes. You sleep during the day anyway, right?"

There was not an instance where Dalupin ever refused.

"Understood."

After he had left, Sungjin went straight to bed. He had to sleep earlier tonight. He had to wake up at 4:10 am to make it to the hidden market, which opened at 4:30.

***

KNOCK KNOCK

Sungjin opened his eyes. Soon,

KNOCK KNOCK

He heard the knock on the door again. Sungjin turned towards the door and said, "I'm awake. Thank you very much, Dalupin."

He didn't hear anyone from outside anymore. Sungjin got up and stretched. After quickly washing his face, he dressed up and went out the door.

Dalupin was watching Sungjin while blinking.

Sungjin looked towards him and said, "I'll be going, then."

"But... where are you going at this hour?" asked Dalupin.

Sungjin stopped to turn and look at him. "Are you asking because you really do not know?"

Dalupin fell silent.

Sungjin turned his body to face him. "Don't be like that, Dalupin. I don't want to come to resent the man who shelters and feeds me."

He was curious as to what expression Dalupin had on his face, but Sungjin left the door.

Cain who was watching him from the outside let out a short bark. He wanted to follow Sungjin.

"Ah... Cain. Don't... don't come this time."

Cain barked twice in response. It seemed he wanted to come anyway.

Sungjin stared at him for a moment before replying, "Ok, do as you like."

Sungjin led the way into the Black Market. Cain followed closely behind him. The market was dead quiet at night.

The Black Market existed for the sake of providing service to a single Hunter. If the Hunter was asleep, there was no reason to continue operations. With the exception of a single shop.

Sungjin was searching for a lone shop. It was hidden deep within the Black Market; it was one of the most difficult shops to locate.

It should be around here.

But he couldn't see it. Sungjin asked the Operator.

"Operator, what time is it?"

[It is currently 4:32 am.]

I got here a little early.

Sungjin squatted for a second to look at Cain in the eye.

"Cain, the place where I am going... I mean, the person I am going to meet... He's someone dangerous. I do not know for sure, but... that's what I feel. So you have to remain calm, okay?"

Cain replied with a short cry.

Sungjin was playing with Cain's fur when he saw the light blink on and off.

Sungjin turned to look. Then he saw that it wasn't the light that blinked, but the surrounding, which was suddenly growing darker. There was a shop covered in darkness. It was the darkest place in the entire market, darker than anywhere else.

That must be it. Sungjin swallowed and then tried to go into the shop, but his familiar suddenly started whimpering.

Cain was acting unlike himself and was very fearful.

"Cain, if you don't want to come, I'll go alone. Go rest at Ninety-Nine Nights."

Cain paced around restlessly and then sat down.

I guess he can't help it.

"Okay, just wait there, Cain. I'll be back."

Sungjin entered the darkness. Within the shop was a stairway leading down to the basement. If not for the sensation of his feet touching the stairs, he wouldn't have been able to tell there was anything there, due to the sheer darkness.

Sungjin slowly and cautiously made his way towards the basement. Once the stairs ended, there was a small candle lighting up in what appeared to be a bar.

There was not a single customer inside. Save for an individual seated in the back corner in the dark.

What a terrible taste... thought Sungjin.

The Operator gave an announcement.

[This place is the hidden shop, Darker than Black.]

Sungjin glanced at the cube. The explanation ended there. Normally she would continue by saying,

"This place sells a variety of Katanas."

"You can enjoy various flavors of tea in this shop for free."

But there was no such explanation for this place.

Well... I guess that makes sense. How fitting that there is no explanation about the purpose of this shop.

Sungjin walked over to the man sitting in the corner and sat across from him. Finally, the man opened his mouth to speak.

"He who searches for answers finds questions, and he who searches for questions finds answers. Welcome, young one. What do you seek?"

Sungjin was trying to see the man across the table. He couldn't make out the details due of the darkness.

The man opened his mouth and said, "Do you wish to see my face? Let there be light! Illuminate!"

A small orb of light emerged from his hands and floated above the table. Sungjin was now able to see the man. He was a Human.

All the other vendors were demi-humans mixed with animals. But this man was 100% Human. He didn't look particularly weird, but it was strange.

His facial features gave off the feeling that he was Asian, and yet at certain angles, he looked western.

"But why does my appearance matter?" said the man and then his face transformed; it was now Igor's face. Sungjin was shocked. The man continued to speak as his face continuously shifted. This time it was Serin.

"Something like,"

Hiro's face.

"Appearances,"

Baltren's face.

"Have no value."

And after the last phrase, his face returned to normal. The man continued, "If you have questions, ask, if you have something you need, request. I exist only to fulfill those things."

Sungjin was about to say something when he was cut off.

"With compensation. I will do, or answer anything with appropriate compensation."

Sungjin hesitated for a moment before asking, "It exists, doesn't it? An item that lets you move to Raids in other instances."

*

Sungjin lifted up his coffee mug. After taking a sip, he looked into the content of the cup. Black coffee. It was black, but nowhere near as black as the darkness that had surrounded him.

What an apt name, Darker than Black.

Thinking so, Sungjin picked up a green book he had laid on top of the table.

Spell Book – Polymorph
5th Circle Green Magic

Transform the target into a sheep. Duration depends on the Magic Power. If the poly-morphed target is hit, the spell is undone.

Soldamyr began to speak needlessly. "It is a great spell. When you face multiple enemies, it is useful for poly-morphing one or two until you finish the rest."

Sungjin had seen the effects first-hand, and so he knew it was a good spell. He lifted up the book higher and said, "Memorize."

The spellbook burnt up with a green light.

[Spell – Polymorph memorized.]

[The incantation for the spell is 'Discard your fangs and become a tame sheep! Polymorph!']

Next, Sungjin picked up a blue book.

Spell Book – Chain Lightning
6th Circle Blue Magic

Fire a bolt of lightning that hits the target and jumps on nearby enemies.

Each successive enemy hit by the lightning reduces the damage for the next target.

Once again, Soldamyr piped up. "This is my signature skill. I cannot count the number of enemies that I have defeated using this spell."

Boasting and reminiscing about your past is your signature skill, thought Sungjin. He was about to put the Genie back in the lamp when the Genie spoke again.

"One thing to note is that if you previously used Polymorph on an enemy, attacking other enemies with this magic may unintentionally strike them and undo the spell. Please keep this in mind as you use the two spells you have learned."

Sungjin thought his explanations made sense. He nodded. "Understood. Thank you for your tips, Soldamyr."

Sungjin lifted up the book and shouted, "Memorize."

The spellbook burnt up with a blue luminescence. Since he was done memorizing the spells, it was time to raise the stats.

"Operator," Sungjin called for the Operator. He told her the stat distribution he had thought of.

"Increase Strength by 1500, Dexterity by 2000, Endurance by 1000, Magic Power by 700, Mind Power by 1500."

[Applied.]

"Show me my stats."

The Operator displayed his stats on the hologram.

Strength	5736	4412	(+1324)
Dexterity	6621	5093	(+1528)
Endurance	4310	3315	(+995)
Magic Power	2105	1619	(+486)
Mind Power	2616	2012	(+604)
Unallocated Points: 0			

What he had learned from the previous stat allocation, was the importance of Mind Power. After raising Magic Power to a high level, he found that he was unable to use magic when he needed to.

Sungjin initially thought that he would increase his Magic Power slowly over time, but as he saw during the Kutan Desert Raid, the effects were quite powerful, and it was very comfortable fighting against monsters with spells.

Incinerate everything in your path! Fireball!

Without that spell, killing Sandworms that popped out of the ground would have been much more annoying. Sungjin stared at the modified status window for a second.

At the current state, there should be no problem with magic... I think I have more than enough stat points.

Sungjin considered his dilemma. There was no longer a shadow of a doubt that he could beat the Raids with his current stats alone. There was only one issue he needed to make a decision on.

Should I try the next Raid with the Treasure Hunter?

He didn't think that there would be any problem. Almost every Chapter had turned into a treasure hunt for Sungjin anyway.

With every Chapter, Sungjin had grown so powerful that clearing it posed no challenge anymore. So, the most obvious choice of action was to test how it would be to keep Treasure Hunter title active.

"Operator, change my title to Treasure Hunter."

[Applied.]

Sungjin finished all his preparations, so he picked up the sandwich sitting next to his mug of coffee and took a bite.

The bread was soft and the lettuce crisp. The folded piece of ham perfectly complemented the rest of the sandwich. While enjoying the sandwich, he read the sheet of paper in front of him.

Information on Count Dimitri's Castle Ruins.

Sungjin asked the Operator without looking away from the sheet, "Operator, how much longer until the Raid begins?"

[36 minutes and 24 seconds.]

Plenty of time.

Sungjin slowly read the content from top to down on the information sheet. He was more nervous than usual.

By the end of this Raid, he was planning on buying 'that item,' which would allow Sungjin to intervene in other Raids.

Unlike other times, Sungjin focused on the details written on the information sheet. What caught his eye was the section about the boss himself.

Boss Count Dimitri's special ability is 'Drink Blood.' If he succeeds in drinking blood, then he regains health and is empowered. Protecting your allies is the key to success in this Raid.

Protecting...I'm not very good at this.

And while reading through the information page, he was teleported away, to Count Dimitri's Castle Ruins.

315

Chapter 12 – Count Dimitri's Castle Ruins

"Heee~" The sound of a horse's neigh could be heard from the distance. And outside the shaking carriage window, a tall tower could be seen. The moon hung low over the tower, and unknown beasts were flying in the moonlit sky.

KLOPP KLOPP KLOPP KLOPP

The shaking of the carriage matched the sound of the horse's hooves. The place Sungjin was summoned to was inside of a shaking horse-drawn carriage. More specifically, a carriage headed towards the Castle Ruins.

[Welcome. This is Count Dimitri's Castle Ruins.]

[It is the ruins of a castle built thousands of years ago.]

[Please be warned: the inhabitants of this castle]

[Have lived here since the time it was built.]

The Operator gave an announcement, and the carriage stopped just as she finished. The carriage was parked outside a large door. A creepy droning voice came from the outside. "We have arrived, sir Hunter."

Sungjin finally opened the door and emerged from within. In front of the door, the carriage driver was waiting for him. The driver was missing his head. This was Sungjin's second time seeing him, but it still creeped him out.

I don't like this place... Sungjin walked over and stood by the entrance.

"Haaam," He couldn't help but yawn. It was because he had woken up very early in the morning.

[Synchronizing Hunters.]

Sungjin blinked and watched the people as they emerged. And as was his habit, he checked their titles first.

Armored Soldier.

Guard.

First-Class Marksman.

It was then that he noticed. Sungjin thought he hadn't seen clearly, so he rubbed his eyes and squinted. *Wait... am I seeing this correctly?*

He had not mistaken. Tall stature with a shaven head, strange tattoos all over; it was a monk with blue eyes. He had an appearance that would stand out anywhere.

Sungjin already knew his name.

"Mahadas!" Sungjin shouted out the name before he could hold himself. It was the first time that he had run into someone from his previous life since the restart. Above the monk's head read Elite Pugilist.

The monk turned to look at Sungjin. "Have we met?"

Yes. Yes, they had. He was one of the few that had survived until the end. When only a few dozen people are left, you often ran into teammates from previous rounds.

Although he wasn't lucky enough to make it to the final ten, he had partied up with Sungjin on three occasions. They had struggled together for survival.

And now they ran into each other during this life very early on.

What a small world... Sungjin couldn't help but hold his hands and shake it.

Mahadas blinked a few times and stared at Sungjin, surprised. "How did you come to know me?"

Thanks to having met three times in Raids, Sungjin already knew his background fairly well. He was originally a professional Tae Kwon Do fighter from Canada. Once he earned the championship for North America, he was recruited into the MMA scene.

His toughness was legendary, as was the reach of his punches. And with his training in Tae Kwon Do, his kicking skills were ranked very high. With a perfect physique for fighting, the MMA scene eagerly anticipated his debut match.

However, during a practice match, a close friend and fellow athlete had died after an accidental kick to the face.

So he put aside his multimillion dollar contract and entered into a Buddhist Monastery in Korea. Gazing at Sungjin with his shocking sky blue eyes, he said, "If you know who I am, you must be Korean... But I am nothing more than an ordinary monk now. Please forget about my past."

Then, someone else in the group recognized Mahadas: Armored Soldier. He raised his face plate and said, "Ah, I think I recognize you too. You've shaved, but... you were some sort of a fighter, right? MMA or something?"

His facial features suggested that the man was of South American descent. Perhaps from Mexico.

"That's all in the past." Mahadas turned away, feeling uncomfortable for being recognized.

It was then that the tall Guard decided to speak up, "Hey, it's okay getting to know each other, but let's include everyone, alright?"

And the last person there also piped in. The short, Asian First-Class Marksman.

"Yeah. I don't know if the tattooed monk is famous or not, but let's first make preparations to beat the Raid."

Sungjin finally let go of the monk's hands. The two Hunters were right, and this was Mahadas's first time meeting Sungjin. Acting friendly and familiar more than this would probably be unwelcome.

It was then that the Raid Objectives popped up.

> Count Dimitri's Castle Ruins Raid
> Objective – Hunt the Thousand-Year Count 'Dimitri'
> Time limit: 1 hour 30 minutes

[Raid will begin in 3 minutes.]

At her announcements, the Hunters gathered up and began preparations. The Guard began with his self-introduction.

"I am Dominic Spencer. I am from England, and as you can see, I use the spear."

He held up his spear for others to see and then he added. "I am trying out some magic spells too. Mainly offensive spells. Either way, it's fire-based magic."

The Armored Soldier twirled his moustache as he spoke up. "My name is Giovani. I was from Mexico... No, I am from Mexico."

He seemed to be hiding something.

"Is he an illegal immigrant? Not that it matters right now," thought Sungjin.

If he were anything like Santiago, it would be problematic. The Asian man holding a bow was Chinese.

"My name is Peng Long. Chinese. I mostly use the bow, but I am also trying out magic."

Mahadas gathered his hands together in a prayer and answered, "My name is Mahadas. My nationality... I am Canadian, but... it doesn't matter now. Before entering the monastery, I had been taught Martial Arts... and that is what I use to fight."

Sungjin glanced to his side. Because there was actually a Chinese man on the team, it would be difficult to lie. So Sungjin revealed his true nationality. "Kei. Korean."

Guard Dominic Spencer took the lead. There was almost always one in a group of five that was able to rally the team effectively. "Let's discuss what we're going to do. I assume everyone here has read the information page. The boss is a vampire that can suck blood and empower himself..."

"So... if he sucks blood he gets several times stronger?" said Giovani as he continued to rub his moustache into a point. It seemed to be a deeply ingrained habit.

Sungjin had experienced it before, as well as read up on the information sheet. Once he sucked someone's blood, he got fully healed and his stats increased by several times.

In the previous Raid, there was a case where one of the team members had gotten bit. And so the Raid was just barely cleared before time ran out.

It would be great if it was possible for me to go alone and just solo the Raid...

Sungjin gazed up to look at the Castle Ruins. This Raid was different from all the previous ones.

Unlike the previous Raids, this zone was not designed to be traversed solo. That was, until the Raid boss was defeated.

It wasn't yet clear if the hidden boss or hidden piece could be hunted alone, but until the Raid boss was cleared, Sungjin was forced to tag along with his team. He glanced at his teammates.

They were planning their positions in a formation.

"Since Giovani is a tank, please stand in the front... followed by martial arts monk and the Korean swordsman... and me. Then Peng Long in the back. Does this work for everyone?" said the Guard.

"Fine by me. Also... I noticed that at first the weapons and roles were randomly distributed, but as time progressed, it now looks like the system assigns us to teams according to roles, don't you think so?" asked the 'Armored Solider' Giovani.

"I think you're right. 1 tank, 3 DPS, and then backline support. This setup started about... 2 Raids ago? Something like that," said Peng.

He would have to wait to see their individual skill, but no one appeared to be of poor character yet. And since Mahadas was on his team, Sungjin could relax a bit.

While the four men continued to talk among themselves, Sungjin was thinking by himself.

First, buy the Item from Darker than Black using the Raid reward... and starting with the Raid after that... I will start to influence Raids other than mine.

He already had 3 Legendary items. He even owned the Unique Legendary item Romance of the Three Kingdoms. Raids no longer posed any challenge to him. It was time to start thinking of the big picture.

Search through other Raids and help those with good moral character, and those who aren't... Kill them... And handpick the 'final ten' myself.

This was Sungjin's new plan of action as a result of the 'Igor event.' He was more than strong enough to affect as many Raids as he could within the limit of his power; he needed to exert his influence over the overall Raid as much as possible.

The end goal was to create the final ten survivors who were all incredibly talented as well as those he could trust. People upon whom he could depend on with his life. Only then would it be possible to clear the final Raid.

Last time, the final ten were all unbelievably powerful individuals. Befitting to be called 'Those Chosen by the Gods.' But because of this, they had bickered and argued with each other without a good sense of cooperation and camaraderie until they were all wiped out.

The Raids were impossible to clear with simply strong individuals. He knew that from experience.

Within the Raids, I will rise as a new God to rewrite the rules and take control over everything.

While he was thinking so,

"Hey, Korean teenager!" The Guard Dominic was addressing him. "What do you think?"

Sungjin didn't know how to respond for a moment. He hadn't been paying attention to the conversation. Now that he noticed, everyone was looking at him.

Giovani realized that Sungjin was spacing out and complained. "Hey, what are you thinking? This is a matter of life and death. How can you be so irresponsible?"

They must have been making quite a strategy among themselves while Sungjin was daydreaming. This party appeared to be very cooperative. At least for now.

What should I say? Sungjin considered his options for a moment while he pursed his lips. But he decided to answer truthfully. He had to work with these people for the time being.

"Um. Honestly, I don't need something like strategy. And...the same goes for the rest of you."

Everyone's eyes grew wide at his claim. Dominic narrowed his eyes out of suspicion and questioned Sungjin. "What do you mean?"

Sungjin answered, "You'll see. Just follow me."

Instead of answering, he put his right hand on Moon Spectre and the left hand on the Blood Vengeance. Before he could unsheath his two swords, Peng Long commented, "Two... Two swords? Dual Wielding?"

Martial arts expert Mahadas commented as well. "That... shouldn't be easy to fight with."

This wasn't something that Sungjin could easily explain in a short time. Pulling out the two swords, Sungjin put on a fancy display of martial prowess before the others.

WOOSH WOOSH WOOSH WOOSH

The two swords glistened in the moonlight. The others who had thought just a moment ago 'we might have a troll' were left speechless.

And meanwhile, the Operator announced the time remaining.

[The Raid will begin in 10 Seconds.]

***

[3, 2, 1, 0, Raid commencing.]

At the same time,

CREAK

The iron gates automatically opened inward. But no one was moving. They were watching Sungjin's sword dance in a daze.

Sungjin held the Moon Spectre and Blood Vengeance in a cross and tilted his head towards the entry way.

"Let's go."

Sungjin stood at the vanguard. Followed closely by Giovani, Mahadas, Dominic, and finally Peng Long. With the exception of Sungjin, it was the original formation.

Inside of the iron gates was a large garden. Even though it was called a garden, it wasn't like it was full of life. Dried and cracked pots, broken pieces of glass, long dead flowers, and twisted trees: the garden was full of death.

"Woof! Woof woof!" A dog's barking could be heard from the inside. Two dobermans showed themselves, but they did not look like any ordinary dogs.

Past the rotten cheeks, their teeth were visible with missing eyelids, showing the entirety of their eyeballs; they were zombie dogs. The Hunters tensed up at their grotesque appearance. With the exception of Sungjin.

Sungjin slowly made his way forward. The zombie dogs backed up to keep a distance from him, barking all the while.

"Snarl! Woof woof!"

They continued to threaten him. Ignoring them, Sungjin continued forward. Eventually, the dogs charged towards Sungjin.

"Kaa!" Heavily decayed with nearly non-existent skin, the zombie moved much faster than a live doberman.

WOOSH WOOSH

But, with a flash of Sungjin's two swords, the dobermans were bisected instantly. Sungjin continued to walk up to the front door without any sense of caution or urgency.

He felt that something was missing. Looking behind him, the Hunters were all standing with their mouth agape. Only Mahadas was looking at the doberman corpses. Sungjin shouted out to them, "Aren't you coming? Come quickly; we have to go together."

At his words, the Hunters came running towards the castle entryway. In front of the gates, there were five strange-looking stones.

"You all read the information sheet, right? Let's stand on top of each stone," said Sungjin.

Obediently, the Hunters followed his instructions. And once all five took their place, a bell was heard ringing in the distance.

DING! DING! DING!

And the Hunters heard a voice coming from above.

"Ah, welcome! It's been such a long time since we last had guests!"

The Hunters all looked up towards the sky. A cloud of bats flew together and formed a single figure on top of the tower. It was in the form of a man with a long cape.

"How do you do? I am the master of this castle."

The man whose face was whiter than the moon politely bowed to them. "I am Count Dimitri."

He opened his mouth and smiled, his sharp fangs on display. Everyone was taken aback by his fangs, but Sungjin had other thoughts. *Wait... Wait a minute... hold on.*

"I have prepared a fun recreational event for our dear guests on each floor."

Sungjin quietly spoke to the cube. It was barely audible. "Operator, get me Al Zard."

The magic carpet emerged from within the cube at his request.

"I have spent a long time preparing these fun little entertainments, so you should have lots of fun. Enough that you won't want to leave ever again. Hu hu hu hu..."

The Thousand-Year Count Dimitri let out a strange laughter. The Hunters watched him completely absorbed. But Sungjin was distracted; he was coming up with a plan.

If I take Al Zard up to him and kill him now, wouldn't the Raid be cleared? Thought Sungjin.

"I hope you enjoy your stay."

At the same time as the Count's farewell,

CREAK

The gates began to lift, letting out rusty noises of moving gears. Before the Count stood back up from his deep bow, Sungjin threw Al Zard forward and shouted, "Flight"

The Magic Carpet opened itself.

PEW

But, Peng Long's arrow flew first. Sungjin watched the arrow fly in surprise. The arrow made it all the way in front of the Count's nose, but with a 'pop' the Count reverted back to a large cloud of bats.

"Hahahahaha," His laughter filled the sky.

Damn Sungjin chased after the bats using Al Zard. He could hear the Count's voice coming from the mass of bats.

"You can only play with me after you've finished with the other little recreations I have prepared for you. Please come to the top of the tower. Then, I will do my best to entertain you personally."

I don't have time for that.

A high-speed aerial chase ensued. Sungjin chanted an incantation while chasing the bats.

"Murderous thunder, jump from foe to foe! Chain Lightning."

A ball of lightning gathered in Sungjin's right hand and shot out of the Moon Spectre like a bullet. But, a small portion of the bats separated from the main mass and prevented the main body from being harmed.

The bats that were hit by the lightning fell to the ground, but the masses of bats continued to escape. Once the bats reached the other side of the castle, they flew towards the moat. Sungjin began to recite a different spell.

"Incinerate everything in your..."

But while he was doing so, the bats began to enter the sewer built on the inside of the moat. Sungjin quickly finished off the rest of the incantations.

"...Path! Fireball!"

He launched the fireball, but most of the bats made it into the sewer.

BOOM

The fireball exploded and greatly damaged the entry way. Sungjin flew to the front of the sewer to look at it. It was very small.

It would hardly fit a human being, or even Cain.

Welp. Sungjin returned to the front entrance of the castle using the Magic Carpet filled with disappointment. The Hunters watched him return.

"Did you manage to catch him?" Giovani asked.

Sungjin knocked on the cube next to him and replied, "If that were the case, this guy would have said something."

Sungjin glanced at Peng Long. Because of his arrow, the Count had been able to get a bigger head start.

I can't really tell him off, though, since all he wanted to do was help.

Sungjin shook his head and entered the castle. The other Hunters followed suit. The interior of the castle was dark.

Dominic looked over to the cube and said, "Operator, I still have that lantern from the cemetery, right? Please take it out for me."

You don't need it... Sungjin thought to himself, but he didn't say anything. He didn't want others to know this was already his second time experiencing everything. While the Hunters were busy trying to light up the lanterns,

TI TA DII~

From the dark, a violin and other classical instruments began to play an orchestral song. At the same time, the lights in the castle came on. On the first floor was a large corridor.

The previously pitch-black ceiling was now brightly illuminated by chandeliers.

DAA~ RAA TA DA~

The classical music continued to play in the background while

"Hahahahaha~"

"Hohohohoho~"

Unnaturally laughing pairs of men and women appeared. The men wore suits, and the women wore fancy dresses. The couples danced to the tune of the music, but each of them wore strange-looking masks.

The Hunters' faces had various emotions displayed on them. Dominic muttered,

"This Chapter... just what..."

It had been written in the Information sheet, but it was still odd to experience it first-hand. Sungjin addressed the Hunters.

"Don't be put off by them, stay alert."

And in a moment during the middle of the song, suddenly

BANG

A loud smashing of the keys of the piano could be heard, and the music stopped playing. Sungjin turned to the Hunters and informed them, "Okay, it begins now. I will take care of most of them, so try to hunt safely."

KEE TA TAAN~ TA TA TAAN~

The elegant and graceful music was replaced with an eerie screechy sound. The dancing couples threw away their masks all at the same time.

"Ugh..." One of the team members gagged upon seeing their faces. Behind the masks were deathly white faces, with fangs showing from their lips. Their faces twisted into a wicked grimace, and they began to screech. "KYAA!"

"You're supposed to bait one of them at a time and fight them, but..." Sungjin muttered something. He held the Moon Spectre and Blood Vengeance like a cross and charged alone into the narrow corridor. The well-dressed vampires also came charging towards Sungjin.

Unlike the other kinds of undead, these were extremely fast. But there was no way these Vampires could match the power of Sungjin who was wielding Legendary Tier swords in each hand.

With each swing of his sword, heads, arms, and legs were cut off. While Sungjin charged onwards through the corridor like a hurricane, a few stragglers began to attack the other four Hunters.

"Wait! Here they come! Careful!" Giovani came to the vanguard and raised his shield. Dominic raised his spear, and Peng Long nocked an arrow. But,

"Taha!" Mahadas dashed forward and kicked one of the Vampires. He broke the chin of a female Vampire in a single blow.

He turned to face the male Vampire and said, "Overheat."

With the command, the gauntlet he wore glowed bright red. Using the bright-red gauntlet, he landed a punch exactly on the vampire's diaphragm.

SPLAT

A strange sound erupted; a sound that was difficult to imagine that it could come from a human being.

WHEEZE

The Vampire let out a strange sound of agony. When Mahadas pulled back his fist, a large hole had been punched through the Vampire's stomach.

Giovani, who had been tense, lowered his shield. Dominic and Peng Long also relaxed their weapons for a moment.

"Taha!" Mahadas began to hunt the multitude of Vampires with incredible speed and power. The Korean ahead of them already formed a mountain of Vampire corpses. The three remaining Hunters glanced at each other.

They understood deep inside that this Raid could probably be cleared with just the two of them. But Peng Long began losing arrows towards the vampires in the distance.

Giovani and Dominic saw that and also prepared their weapons.

"Uryah!"

They charged towards the enemies.

*

Guard Dominic swung his spear around, and couldn't help but feel that this Chapter was very strange. *The Chapter is one thing... but the teammates, especially those two...*

Just surviving from Chapter to Chapter was a struggle. Had been a struggle. It had been nice to get high contribution percentages, but survival came first. He had fought hard for the sake of his own survival first, and contribution second.

But there was something very different with this Chapter: the Korean teenager who charged onwards, slicing off limbs of Vampires like a human tornado using two swords, and the monk who beat the monsters to a pulp using his fists.

Between the two of them, he had to work hard to scrape together contribution points. He was also part of the top 0.01% of the best Hunters among humanity.

No matter how strong the allies are, they cannot gift contribution points... Dominic's weapon was a spear. It was a weapon designed to fight enemies from behind the cover of the tank. But right now, the tank, Giovani, wasn't able to get any points either.

The Korean and the monk were rushing ahead killing everything in sight, which rendered the defence and ranged support unnecessary. Peng Long had been able to try and get some contribution by shooting enemies far into the distance, but Dominic had no such ranged abilities. After considering his options, the only solution he could come up with was to charge ahead with his spear, even if he had to put himself at risk.

A Vampire whose jaws had been shattered was wandering about in front of him.

"Yaaah!" He charged forward and stabbed at the Vampire's head with his spear.

STAB

With a piercing noise, the Vampire died without even being able to let out a cry. He felt a rush of adrenaline upon hunting the undead.

What if... my teammates aren't strong, but it is the enemies that are weak? Dominic thought as he charged towards another Vampire.

***

After killing a single Vampire with his spear, Dominic scanned the hallway for another lone Vampire.

There.

He took his spear and charged forward once more.

"H... hey!" Someone shouted at him from behind, but he ignored it. If he didn't do something, he would be left with no contribution points to speak of.

"Don't worry; I am also skilled," he answered.

"Endless Needle!" shouted Dominic as he clashed against the Vampires. He aimed for the neck and stabbed with the spear.

"Kyaa!" The Vampire tried to dodge the spear by tilting its head, but the weapon suddenly split into dozens of spears.

And one or two of them pierced through the Vampire's neck.

"Kuh!" The Vampire grabbed the newly formed holes in its neck and fell to the ground. Dominic had now taken two down and was feeling more confident.

He searched for additional targets.

Luckily, he found a female Vampire wandering by herself in the distance. It turned to look at Dominic and screeched. "Kaa!"

"So he must have been your partner", thought Dominic and cast a spell.

"Flying ball of flames, Fire Bolt!"

The Fire Bolt he fired was aimed at the Vampire's feet. The Vampire jumped high into the sky. But that was what he was aiming for.

It would be easier to target enemies in the air.

I shall send you with your partner.

He watched the Vampire in the air to time its landing and have it land on the spear. However,

"Ugh" He felt piercing pain on one of his legs. He couldn't move his feet. He looked down to see.

The Vampire he thought he had defeated earlier had stabbed his ankle with its long nails. It was still alive, despite the holes in its neck.

Dominic opened his eyes wide. But despite the pain and the surprise attack, he shouldn't have taken his eyes away from his other foe.

"Kaaa!"

The female Vampire that dodged the Fire Bolt earlier was now upon him. He turned to look at her. She was descending faster than he had anticipated.

They can fly? His realization came too late. The Vampire was already past the spear tip. Dominic tried to take a step back, but his feet were held down by another Vampire.

The Vampire flew into his embrace, ten claws scratching his back open.

"Aaah!" He screamed out loud in agony due to intense pain, but it was not over yet. The Vampire clamped down on his neck and drew blood.

"Ack..." His vital organs were ripped open, and the blood supply to his brain stopped. Dominic felt faint, and he started losing consciousness. But before he passed out,

"Pa!"

A sword came flying from somewhere and pierced the Vampire's head. The hands holding Dominic loosened up.

"Haa!"

The sword came flying back and cut through the neck of the Vampire sucking his blood. The head fell off, and along with it, the fangs holding onto his neck.

"Ta ho!" Mahadas appeared and kicked away the head of the Vampire holding his leg. He caught Dominic as he was about to fall over. "Are you alright?"

"Kyaa!" A crowd of Vampires tried to take advantage of the situation by surrounding them, but Giovani appeared and blocked them with his shield. Meanwhile,

PEW

Peng Long's arrows pierced through one of the Vampire's arms. Giovani pushed the Vampires back with his shield and axe.

While Giovani was buying time, Sungjin appeared out of nowhere and severed the heads of all the Vampires like the wind.

The surviving Vampires were finished up in moments, and the battle was over for now.

Giovani looked over to Dominic to scold him for running ahead alone. "I told you to..."

But he stopped himself once he saw Dominic's ashen face.

*

Once Sungjin was done dealing with the last Vampire, he returned to the other Hunters' side. At the center lay Dominic. Sungjin inspected Dominic's state.

Why did he overdo it?

He had been able to save Dominic thanks to 'Telkron – Jester's Gloves,' but his state looked dire. He was bleeding from his ankle and neck profusely.

If I was even a little bit slower... he would have already died. But... if he got bitten by a Vampire...

Mahadas recited an incantation. "By my authority, close the wound and remove the pain, Heal!"

A white light spilled out of his hands and covered Dominic's injuries. His wounds disappeared wherever the light touched.

Sungjin pursed his lips and gazed at him. *He still uses White Magic...*

Mahadas was no tank, but because he fought without a weapon, he had to fight at the very front lines, resulting in him getting injured often.

So in the previous life, Mahadas had used various spells of the White Magic such as recovery magic, and buff magic. It was a wise decision.

Thanks to Mahadas's magic, Dominic's condition improved. But his state was still strange.

"Are you alright, Dominic?" asked Mahadas.

Dominic finally spoke, "I feel fine, but... something's weird... I feel dizzy."

Sungjin asked the operator while watching Dominic. "Operator, how long does 'Blood Curse' last?"

[Blood Curse, duration is 30 minutes.]

Peng Long asked, "Blood Curse?"

Sungjin frowned. Peng Long's reaction reaffirmed his suspicion. The information sheet did not contain any mention of the Vampire's bites.

Information sheet? Where's the info? Sungjin had come to distrust the information sheet for this reason. Although it was informative, it always redacted few key information necessary to complete the Raid.

Sungjin was about to open his mouth to explain the effects of the 'Blood Curse,' but Mahadas calmly asked the Operator, "Operator, what is the Blood Curse?"

The Operator gave an explanation in her usual expressionless tone.

[Blood Curse (Debuff): Duration 30 minutes. Lower all stat points by 30% for the duration of the curse. Once the time runs out, the curse kills the target, and the target is reborn as a Vampire.]

Giovani whispered, "Kills... my God. Is there no cure?"

Peng Long replied, "I checked every item in the consumable shop, but I've never seen anything that reverts curses."

Sungjin shook his head. "This is not a poison; it's a curse. Does anyone have 'Remove Curse' or 'Scroll of Remove Curse'?"

Everyone's eyes grew large. It was probably their first time hearing about a curse. Dominic's eyes lost their lustre as he fell into despair. Everyone fell into silence.

Sungjin thought about it for a moment. *Remove Curse... Soldamyr said that he couldn't use White or Green schools of magic...*

There was no immediate answer. But, there was still a way. The only way available to them. Sungjin told them immediately. "Even if we don't have 'Remove Curse,' there is still a way to save him. The only way."

"How?" asked Mahadas.

"Complete the Raid before the 30 minutes are up. As you all know, if you get teleported back to the Black Market, all your injuries go away."

Everyone nodded at his words. Even if one took an otherwise fatal wound, if they were to be teleported to the Black Market, all their wounds would disappear as if nothing had happened.

But there was a problem with this method as well.

"Operator, how much time is left until the Raid is over?"

[1 hour 19 minutes and 4 seconds.]

Everyone turned to stare at Sungjin, thinking *so it's impossible after all.* None of them had ever experienced being teleported back early; they had always been sent back when the time ran out.

Even if we don't hit the time limit, if we reach 100% completion for the Raid...

Sungjin was about to say, but he decided against it. Instead he said, "I will do my best to save him, so please trust me. Giovani."

"Yes? What?" Giovani answered in panic at being called out.

"Please protect Dominic. Even though his stat points were decreased, you two should be able to keep each other safe if you two work together," explained Sungjin.

"Ah, got it." Giovani's helm moved up and down twice.

Sungjin now looked over to Peng Long and Mahadas. "You two, hunt with me. As fast as you can possibly manage."

The other two men nodded as well. They hadn't had a chance to speak properly, but they already understood his strength; they trusted him.

"Let us hurry, then." Sungjin pointed towards the elevator on the far side. Within the elevator was the same circular formation as the castle entrance. "Please go stand on them."

Everyone took their spots. Once all 5 of them took their place, the elevator began to climb. Even if one of them died, they had to carry the corpse and place it on the slot in order for the elevator to continue moving.

This part was written on the information sheet, although it didn't help improve their chances of survival.

CLANG CLANG CLANG CLANG

The elevator made worrisome noises as it began to climb. Sungjin was thinking about various things as the elevator moved up.

Will I be able to kill the hidden boss and find the secret location within 30 minutes? I can try, but...

Still, there were two things going right for the team.

First, was that the monsters were not spaced far apart like in Ahenna's forest or the Kutan Desert. They were all gathered up in the same floor. So all they had to do was clear each floor as fast as they could and kill 'Count Dimitri' and the hidden boss within the thirty-minute time frame.

Second, he had decided to bring Treasure Hunter this time rather than Master Hunter. He would be able to find both of the hidden elements of this Raid faster than any previous Raids.

Of course, the thirty-minute window was extremely difficult to overcome. Sungjin glanced at Dominic. His face was very pale.

If 30 minutes are not enough... then with my own hands... Sungjin reviewed his options while having such thoughts.

Keep Romance of the Three Kingdoms for the hidden boss. I may have to face the hidden boss alone. Then the only other thing I could use to reduce the time spent is...

Sungjin took out Cain's wooden figurine and Soldamyr's golden lamp. He threw the figurine into the air and rubbed Soldamyr's lamp. Soon,

"Woof woof!"

"Did you summon me, master?"

Two loyal summons appeared before him. The others stared at Sungjin out of surprise.

Ding!

Meanwhile, the Elevator reached level 2. Level 2 was the Spider room. Due to the large amount of giant spider webs laid out, trying to clear the room normally would take considerable time and effort.

But this time was different. Sungjin ordered Soldamyr. "Soldamyr."

"Yes, master."

"Burn them all."

At his command, Soldamyr began an incantation. "Eternal Flames of Hell!"

Blinding light and heat formed in Soldamyr's hands, and the Spiders in the room turned towards the elevator. One or two began to make their way towards the elevator, but it was too late.

"Inferno!"

The ball of fire left Soldamyr's hands and quickly spread to everything it touched, setting them ablaze.

"Kiiii~" High-pitched screeches of the spiders filled the air as they cried out in agony. Several spiders ran amok across the room while on fire. It was a scene straight out of hell.

While the other Hunters were afraid to make a move,

"Let's go, Cain."

"Woof!"

A lone man and his trusty wolf ran into the room.

***

Peng Long took a glance behind him. The room was littered with corpses of spiders. Spiders that were burnt to death, sliced to pieces, head kicked in and bitten to death by a wolf.

Giovani rebuked him from ahead. "Hey, what are you doing, Chinese man? Get on."

Peng Long looked forward again. The other four Hunters, the Genie, and the Wolf were all in the elevator waiting for him.

"Ah, ok."

Peng Long then took his spot on the elevator.

CLANG CLANG CLANG CLANG

Once all the Hunters were in place, the elevator began to rise again; the metal scraped against the walls.

While the elevator was moving, Peng Long glanced at Dominic's face for a moment. His face was as pale as death, without any hint of vitality. The Vampire's curse seemed to have sucked not only the Stat Points but also his motivation.

It was understandable; he had 30 minutes left in his life with the clock ticking away.

SNIFF SNIFF SNIFF

Suddenly, the large wolf went around the elevator smelling everyone. Peng Long glared at the wolf.

336

Ever since Ahenna's Forest, where he had almost perished upon being bitten by wolves, he had come to hate them unconsciously. The Korean Hunter then issued a command.

"Cain, settle down."

With one command the wolf obediently walked over and sat next to his feet like a tame puppy. Just a moment ago the Wolf had been ripping the Spiders apart like a ferocious beast.

He sure is loyal to his master.

While Peng was lost in thought, Sungjin suddenly spoke to him, "Mr Peng Long."

"Ah... Yes?"

"Do you have any abilities that allow you to fire multiple shots at once?"

Peng Long thought for a moment before replying. "Well I can use Split Arrow. I..."

He began to try and explain to them verbally, but instead, he stopped and opened up the status window of his bow to simplify things.

Dragon's Claw Bow – Bow of Johan
Heroic Bow – Strength A Dexterity B

Active Skill
Split Arrow (III)
After the initial arrow hits, several magical arrows are fired in the same general area. Cooldown 5 minutes.

Dragon's Eye (III)
Fires an audible arrowhead to sense enemies out of the line of sight. Cooldown 5 minutes.

Bow wielded by the leader of the legendary Four Great Thieves, Johan.
It is said that the effectiveness of the bow greatly depends on the wielder.

"It's like this."

Sungjin read the status window briefly and nodded. "Then when I give the signal, shoot as many arrows as you can into the suits of armor."

Peng Long tilted his head. *Hmm? Which suits of armor?*

Peng Long wanted to ask, but Sungjin already turned his head towards the Genie and gave him instructions.

"Soldamyr, prepare your Chain Lightning."

"Understood, Master."

While Peng Long was still out of it, the elevator stopped moving. Ding!

Accompanied by the bell, the elevator doors opened. Unlike the first floor where they had been greeted by dancing couples and music, and the spider swarm on the second floor, the third floor was dead silent.

In the long corridor, there was nothing but rows upon rows of empty suits of armor placed on top of mannequins.

"What kind of room is this? Where are the enemies?" Giovanni asked.

Peng Long thought to himself, *"How did that man know that the next floor will have suits of armour?"*

Peng Long also doubted that the man would answer his questions.

Sungjin gestured to him and said, "Ok, begin shooting. Aim to hit as many enemies as you can."

Enemies? Peng Long was filled with questions, but he decided to act as he was asked to. Starting with the 'Blood Curse,' Kei knew far too much. Even details not displayed on the Information sheet.

Peng Long looked up at the ceiling. High above, a chandelier was glistening where it hung.

That should work.

He aimed for the chandelier and shouted, "Split Arrows!"

His arrow accurately hit the chandelier, and once it struck, dozens of magical arrows appeared and scattered all over the room. It hit most of the suits of armor standing in neat rows.

"Intruders detected."

"To Arms."

"Defend the master."

The mannequins wearing suits of armor came to life, brandishing their weapons. Their speed wasn't all that impressive.

Giovani readied his axe and shield. But Sungjin held him back.

"Wait for it... Wait for it."

The suits of armor came alive and began marching towards the elevator in a single file, perfectly in sync with their footsteps.

"Just a bit more..." Sungjin waited just a bit longer, and then he gave the Genie the signal.

"Soldamyr."

The Genie immediately chanted an incantation. "Murderous thunder, jump from foe to foe!"

At the same time, Sungjin shouted out the same incantation as the Genie.

"Murderous thunder, jump from foe to foe!"

Sparks of energy began to gather in their hands.

"Chain Lightning!"

"Chain Lightning!"

A blinding light shot out from both sets of hands and flew towards the approaching army. The suit of armour in the front was hit and was lit on fire, while the lightning continued to jump from suit to suit. Those hit by the lightning fell one by one.

Only a few survived the attack and were left standing on the far end of the room.

"Let's go!"

The heavily armoured enemies looked very tough, but due to the fact that they had already taken damage from the lightning bolt earlier, they were easily broken by even Giovani and Dominic's attacks.

The third floor was cleared in the blink of an eye. The Hunters quickly boarded the elevator and took their places.

The elevator began to climb again.

*

Sungjin searched his memories. *What was on the fourth floor again?*

He remembered. It was Frankenstein's Monster's room. It wasn't very fast, so it didn't prove to be very threatening, but it had such high HP that it took forever to kill.

I think last time we attacked it nonstop for close to 10 minutes.

The Frankenstein's Monster felt like a mini-boss. In fact, in terms of HP, it had more health than any other enemies Sungjin had fought so far; even greater than Count Dimitri himself. It was inevitable that fighting Frankenstein's Monster would take a bit of time.

Sungjin looked down at his two swords, Moon Spectre and Blood Vengeance.

I guess it wouldn't be bad to test out how high my stats really are.

But,

"Ugh..." Dominic held his forehead and began to moan. There was no time to waste. He had to try his hardest to pull through. Sungjin turned to Soldamyr.

"Soldamyr, do you have any debuff magic that lowers the enemy's defenses?"

"Of course," answered the Genie.

"Then use it right away on the enemy that will appear."

"Acknowledged."

Sungjin turned to the other Hunters and said, "Please give me a hand with the next one. Attack it with everything you've got."

Peng nodded, Mahadas gathered his hands into a prayer and answered. "Certainly."

Ding!

The elevator stopped, and the bell rang. The fourth floor was a laboratory. Unfamiliar tools and unknown chemicals lay all over the place.

And at the center was a giant, who stood still with his eye closed. Once the Hunters entered the floor, the strange contraption surrounding the giant began to move.

It injected strange chemicals into the giant's chest, and sparks of electricity zapped its head. "Kraugh!"

"Let's go!" Sungjin yelled as he dashed forward.

Soldamyr chanted a spell, "Fragile body, broken will. Weakness!"

A strange black light appeared over the monster's head.

PEW

Peng Long's arrow hit its head dead on, but Frankenstein's Monster wasn't something that would die with just that. Sungjin ran in brandishing his dual swords.

"Haa Yaah!" He ran in shouting.

"Taho!" Mahadas came flying in with a kick. Sungjin's swords impaled deep into the monster's chest, and Mahadas's kick landed square on its chin.

*

CLANG CLANG CLANG CLANG

The elevator began moving up again. Sungjin looked behind him. Frankenstein's Monster lay there bloodied and in pieces.

This time it took about... a minute?

Last time with all five Hunters it had taken almost ten minutes, but this time it ended much quicker. Sungjin looked down at his swords. *The damage is on a whole new level compared to last time.*

The other Hunters wouldn't know, but Sungjin could tell the difference after having fought Frankenstein's Monster the second time.

I really might be able to complete the Raids by myself.

Sungjin took a look at the people around him.

Like a true monk, Mahadas showed no change in his state; he was standing peacefully.

But Giovani and Peng Long's expressions looked grim. Even though the Raid was progressing well, they looked concerned.

Sungjin thought to himself, *"It must be because of the contribution level".*

He understood their feelings somewhat. If it were something like the desert or the cemetery where he could go alone, they wouldn't be able to tell just how much contribution Sungjin was taking. But from beginning to end, the party members could directly see just how much Sungjin had taken for himself; watching 70-80% of the contribution points being monopolized right in front of their eyes must have felt very threatening.

Even if they were weaker than Sungjin, these people were all within the top 0.01%; some of the strongest representatives of Humanity. They knew by experience that if they failed to grow stronger now, they will die for sure later on.

The cause of why Dominic had acted rashly wasn't difficult to guess.

But it isn't as if I could afford to simply stop my growth.

This was a dilemma, and Sungjin was fully aware of the implications. Becoming stronger meant weakening his allies, and in most cases indirectly getting them killed. Becoming moderately stronger was better for his teammates, but Sungjin had become immensely powerful in the last five Raids.

Even Mahadas, who had survived until the late game in the previous life, was having difficulty squeezing out any respectable amount of contribution points. Whereas, without Sungjin, he could have potentially gotten as much as 40% of the total.

And this side effect could only grow worse over time. The rich grows richer and the poor grows poorer. Just like in reality.

The strong takes the larger share of the contribution and grows even stronger. Back on Earth, Sungjin had been part of the poorest of the population. But here, he was part of the richest... No. He was simply the richest one of all.

Once again, Igor's words echoed in his mind. *Isn't this just like how the world works?*

Sungjin bit his lips. Igor was definitely a vile man, but his words continued to stick in Sungjin's mind. Sungjin shook his head. He decided to erase Igor from his memories.

This is the last time I monopolize all the points. Using the points from this round, I will obtain 'that item' from Darker than Black... and this won't happen anymore.

He would clear the boss together with the team but leave the trash mobs alone for the others to take. And for himself, he would hunt enemies while jumping from Raid to Raid. With this method, the current dilemma will naturally resolve itself.

This game is structured this way.

Sungjin replied to the memory in his head. *Just because the structure is retarded does not mean that I have to act like one as well.*

Sungjin steeled his heart. This was the last time he was going to be manipulated by the system. Starting with next Raid, he would freely travel between dimensions.

Ding!

The elevator bell rang as the door slid open. This was the fifth floor; the final level. In front of them, stood a well-dressed Count Dimitri, waiting.

[Warning! Boss Monster]

[Thousand-Year Count Dimitri has appeared!]

***

Count Dimitri waited for them, dressed up in a fancy suit. And like before, he greeted them in an overly polite manner. "Congratulations for making it to the top. Did you enjoy the events I had prepared for you?"

Sungjin didn't have time for idle chat. "Pa!"

He threw the Blood Vengeance towards the Count. It was thrown right on target, but once it almost reached the Count, he burst into a cloud of bats and dodged the sword.

He could hear the Count's annoying laughter from the swarm of bats. "Hahahahaha!"

"Haa!" Sungjin recalled the Blood Vengeance. The bats flew towards the podium and reformed into a human shape.

The Count grinned mischievously as he commented, "My, my, how eager... It seems as though my servants weren't able to provide a satisfactory entertainment for you all."

The Boss drew his rapier. "Then, as the Master, I will be personally entertaining you all."

Count Dimitri was a difficult boss to defeat. The annoying bat transformation, his immense speed, ability to cast magic, high intelligence, and the blood sucking ability made him a formidable opponent.

If he managed to grab one of the teammates even once, he would become fully healed and empowered.

Sungjin had to kill him before he had a chance to bite one of Sungjin's teammates.

And so he charged towards the Count, brandishing his two Legendary tier swords.

Count Dimitri waited for Sungjin to approach with his rapier. The Count must have thought he could contest Sungjin with his weapon. But for the first time, the Count's confident smile crumbled.

CLANG CLANG!

In just two strikes, the rapier was knocked out of his hands. He took a step back with eyes wide open.

I won't let you escape. Sungjin prepared his sword and slashed at the Count. But the feedback on the sword felt strange.

BANG

Along with the sound, the Count turned into bats and flew away. Meanwhile, the Count shouted an incantation. "What is real is fake and what is fake is real! Illusion!"

Suddenly the swarm of bats multiplied. They flew higher into the air before splitting into four parts and landing on four corners of the room. The four swarms assumed human forms once more. There were four Counts now.

The others fell into a panic. Sungjin first returned to the group of Hunters; it would be annoying if one of them were bitten. Sungjin addressed the team.

"Damage dealers, it's nice if you can attack, but it is more important to avoid being bitten. Especially Giovani, please stick close to the team and protect them."

"Got it," affirmed Giovani.

"Soldamyr, do you have magic that can be used to differentiate the real from the illusions?" asked Sungjin.

"You can always set it on fire to see if it turns to ash," suggested the Genie.

"Ah... right..." Sungjin's reply was thick with disappointment.

Soldamyr bowed his head to apologize. "I apologize for not being able to use White Magic..."

"No, it's fine. Just pick one of them on the right side and fire a spell at it."

"It will be done, Master."

Sungjin looked down next and spoke.

"Cain, you take the one on the left. I'll ring the bell."

The wolf affirmed with a short bark.

"Finally... everyone else, please cooperate against that one back there."

"Ok." The four Hunters answered together.

Once Sungjin was done giving out instructions, he counted down.

"3, 2, 1, let's go!"

Sungjin took out the Manyata from his pocket and rang it as he charged towards the Count. He didn't know if this was an illusion

"Incinerate everything in your path! Fireball!" Soldamyr shouted an incantation.

Cain snarled as he flung himself at the Count.

"Taho!" Mahadas charged in with a shout.

Sungjin slashed at the Count but his body seemed to shrivel, then fell apart in half before disappearing.

Illusion! Which one is real? Sungjin looked around. Soldamyr shook his head. Cain was also left alone in his corner. The only one remaining was the one behind the others. The four of them were all looking up towards the ceiling.

Sungjin followed their gaze and found the Count hovering over them; he was reciting an incantation.

"Steel-cutting blades of wind! Wind Cutter!"

Several green blades appeared at the end of his fingers and flew towards the Hunters.

"Get behind me!" Giovani raised his shield and tried to protect the Hunters behind him, but he wasn't fast enough.

PI PI PIT!

Several blades were blocked by the shield, but others found their mark on Peng Long.

"Ugh..."

The magical blades cut through his armor and left him injured. Sungjin ran towards the last remaining Count.

"What is real is fake and what is fake is real! Illusion!"

But the enemy rose back in the air and cast his spell before splitting apart again.

"Grrr..." Sungjin ground his teeth together. The Count was an irritating enemy to fight. The other Hunters gathered up without having to be told by Sungjin. Even one victim could restore and empower the Count.

The Count finished splitting into four again.

"Master, the time has run out."

"Woof! Woof woof!"

His two summons announced their time was over.

Ah...

Ten minutes must had elapsed since they were summoned. Cain returned to his wooden form, and Soldamyr returned to his lamp. The options had shrunk now.

Mahadas, take the left, Dominic take the right, Giovani and Peng Long take the one in the back would have been great to be able to say, but if even one person got bitten, the situation could only grow worse. Sungjin decided to change his mind.

He was feeling rushed due to Dominic's condition, but he decided to take it cautiously and address this situation calmly.

I feel sorry for Dominic, but I'll have to take my time and handle all four on my own.

Trying to rush this one could cause an unintended casualty. Sungjin made up his mind and was about to jump into action when he noticed blood.

He saw drops of blood in the room. It wasn't splattered all over the room, only in certain locations.

Where did it come from? Sungjin searched his memories. The first time he faced the Count before the castle earlier, he had thought that his sword brushed up against something. The Count could have been injured at that time. No, he must have been injured by that strike.

All the illusions had a cut on their left arm. And there was only one which still had blood dripping from it.

That must be the real body.

Sungjin whispered to Peng Long, who stood next to him. "Peng, blood."

Peng Long understood him with just those two words. Sungjin charged at the Count right away. Unlike last time, it seemed to have been taken aback.

The Count recited an incantation. "Stiff muscles and cramped legs. Slow!"

Sungjin's movements slowed down slightly, and the Count immediately retreated into the air and turned into bats.

"What is real is fake and what is fake is real! Illusion!"

He didn't seem to understand how Sungjin was able to tell the fake. Even after the bats split into four, one of the swarm was still dripping blood.

"Peng!" Sungjin shouted, despite being slowed down.

Peng drew his arrows and yelled, "Split Arrows!"

His arrow flew straight and true. It landed on one of the bats of the swarm, and many magical arrows appeared nearby, piercing all the bats around it.

Sungjin ran through the dead bats falling out of the air and returned the Moon Spectre back into the sheath. The moment he saw the bats resume human form he yelled, "Deathly Wail!"

"KYAAAAAA"

For a moment, the Vampire let out a cry of agony matching the tune of the screech of Sungjin's skill.

*

Giovani had just barely regained his sanity after a few moments of trembling in fear. He was slightly embarrassed, but the feeling went away quickly.

"D... Die!" Dominic was stabbing his spear in the air while hallucinating.

"Eeek!" Peng Long was running amok in the distance. Mahadas had his eyes closed in meditation. Giovani scanned his surroundings to search for the Vampire and Sungjin.

But the Operator gave an announcement.

[Boss 'Count Dimitri' Cleared!]

[Returning to the Black Market in 1 hour 2 minutes and 45 seconds.]

He saw Kei in the distance swinging his swords to shake the blood off of the blades before returning them to his sheath. Giovani saw the Count's beheaded corpse lying at Sungjin's feet. He breathed a sigh of relief.

But Kei came up to him and said, "Let's go. 15 minutes has already passed... so we should have close to 15 minutes remaining. There isn't much time to waste."

Giovani was surprised at his words. Dominic's complexion continued to grow paler, so something had to be done. But he still had a question. "But... where are we going?"

To that, Sungjin replied, "Ah, that's right."

Kei clapped once when he realized something and turned to speak to the Operator.

"Operator, I'll use the Treasure Hunter active once. Please give me a hint about a secret place or a hidden boss."

[I will first inform you about the secret place in the map.]

"What is...?" Giovani began to ask, but Sungjin cut him off and put his finger on his lips.

"Shh..."

The Operator began to speak in a similar manner to how she gives warnings.

[A wandering merchant from lands afar,]

[Climbed the mountain carrying his treasure.]

[Finding a castle, he celebrated in joy.]

['Master of that castle will pay for my treasures.']

[But the only thing awaiting him at the old castle.]

[Were grotesque monsters and beasts, so he ran.]

[But he was soon caught and turned into a cocoon.]

The Operator's explanation ended, and Giovani turned to look at Sungjin with even more questions than before. But then Sungjin suddenly began to talk to himself.

"Wandering merchant from afar... Turned into a cocoon..." He muttered. Then Sungjin opened his eyes wide and began to walk towards the door. "Let's go!"

Everyone was completely out of it. But they didn't have a choice but to listen to him. The Hunters all took their spot in the elevator, and it began to move again.

CLANG CLANG CLANG CLANG

The elevator noisily made its way down. Meanwhile, Mahadas, who had been quiet until now, respectfully raised a question. "Excuse me, but... what is it that you are trying to accomplish?"

Sungjin answered his question. "Ah... This is a type of side quest which gives you a treasure as a reward."

"Treasure?" Peng Long showed heightened interest at his words.

"Yes. You'll see when you get there. I think you all are very lucky. That merchant... his personality is a bit... well, it should prove to be helpful."

Giovani then turned to ask a question. "What do you mean by helpful?"

Instead of answering the question, Sungjin said something else while drumming his fingers over his lips. "You were all worried about getting low contribution points this round, right?"

Giovani, Peng Long, and Dominic all flinched. It was a sore topic to all of them.

Sungjin continued to speak. "The guy we're about to meet will make you all a great deal. All of you should be able to get something good out of this."

"Treasure is treasure, and a deal is a deal... but what's going to happen to me?" Dominic asked.

Sungjin glanced at him. "Ah... Now that you mention it... it might get solved rather easily..."

Dominic tilted his head in confusion. "What do you?"

At that moment,

Ding!

The elevator rang and they returned to the 4th floor at the Frankenstein's Monster's room. In order to go down, they had to cross the room to the other elevators on the other side.

Sungjin quickly made his way across the room as he spoke. "Please quickly follow me. And trust me, you won't regret it."

Giovani remained curious about what he meant. "Where are we going anyway?"

Sungjin answered, "She said cocoon earlier right? We're going to the spider's room on the 2nd floor"

***

Ding!

350

Along with the sound of the bell, the five Hunters arrived on the 2nd floor. The room still smelled of burning flesh. Sungjin took the lead and surveyed the room.

"Everyone, please search for a cocoon. There should be one hidden away somewhere around here."

The four Hunters began searching the surroundings. This was their first time looking carefully around the castle. They hadn't been able to earlier due to the time limit.

Cocoon... where could it be? Sungjin used the Blood Vengeance and the Moon Spectre as a prod to check areas covered by spider webs. But there weren't very many spots left. Spider webs were very flammable, and the entire room had been lit at some point.

Eternal Flames of Hell! Inferno!

The spell Soldamyr had cast a few minutes ago was mighty to behold. It had caused collateral damage far exceeding what is possible with Fireball; turning the entire room into a scene from hell.

Sungjin was worried. *Did... we accidentally kill him?*

He combed the whole floor, praying that he was wrong.

Finally, Giovani called out to the others. "Hey, guys, look here!'

Everyone rushed to his side to see what he had found. There was a small waterway. A small gap was put in between the stone to allow the water to flow freely.

The waterway flowed across the room and was designed to drain out of the room through a dark opening blocked by vertical metal bars.

"Operator, lantern," called out Peng Long. He took out the lantern from the cube and checked inside the opening.

"A sewer..." Sungjin recalled the small sewer he had seen while chasing the Count's bats.

"Please move aside." Sungjin pushed the others aside and used his two swords to slice open the metal bars of the waterway.

CLING CLANG

Once the bars were removed, he made his way through the opening. The others followed suit.

351

The interior of the sewer was larger than expected. There was not a single drop of water on the walls or ceiling, only sticky webs which only seem to increase the further they went in. It was an uncomfortable place, where sticky, invisible webs would adhere to the face. But this gave Sungjin a sense of certainty.

This is it. We found it.

The webs continued to get thicker and thicker. Sungjin had to use his swords to cut open a path and continue inwards. And deep within the webs was a gigantic cocoon.

It was a little smaller than a human being, but it matched the mental image of the merchant he had in mind.

It's most definitely that guy from before. Sungjin grinned as he cut open the cocoon. Inside was an unconscious Ratman. The operator gave an announcement.

[Congratulations.]

[You have discovered the Hidden Merchant Ruff Han.]

A rat found in a sewer... How fitting. While Sungjin was thinking so in his mind, the other four Hunters were surprised.

"Hidden Merchant?" asked Giovani.

"Is it talking about the Ratman over there?" pointed Peng Long.

Sungjin slapped Ruff Han across his cheeks twice. Not enough to hurt, but enough to snap the Ratman awake. Ruff Han blinked twice as he woke up.

"Ugh... No. Nooo!" Ruff Han began to scream as if having a nightmare. He then turned towards Sungjin and stammered.

"What? How did you... where... What about the spiders?"

Sungjin ignored him and said, "This is the second time I have saved your life. There are no more spiders. Now hand over the 'good stuff' you promised me last time."

Ruff Han blinked a few more times. He looked at Sungjin, and also at the other Hunters present.

"Ah... So that's how it is. Well, thank you, since you did save me..."

And then he turned around. There was a smaller cocoon behind him. The ratman ran up to the little cocoon and gnawed away at the spider web there. Within the cocoon was a cube that was a little different from the ones that followed the Hunters.

He lifted that up and said, "Well, then... As a reward for saving my life, I will sell an item to each of you. Of course, it will be much cheaper than the prices you'd get in the Black Market. But, since this is a special discount, you can only buy one item each. Got it?"

Once he was done explaining, he began to take out items from the cube one by one. The Hunters concentrated on the merchant's hands. He took out a large variety of goods.

Gloves, shoulder pads, shoes, helm, necklaces, staves, axes, swords... the Hunters picked them up one by one to check the specs. Peng Long was the first to find an item he liked.

Kaodum -Shooting Gloves of the 'Hunter of the Dark'
Heroic Gloves Defense 10%

Passive Skill
Focus Fire (III.) – Each third hit against the same target deals 300% of normal damage.

'Legendary Hunter of the Dark' Vyen's Shooting Gloves. It is said that her hands never wavered while aiming an arrow towards her enemies.

"How much is this?"

"Ah, that's worth 4400 coins in the Black Market. But I will sell it for 1600 coins, which is less than half that price."

Everyone turned to listen to their conversation.

"Please let me get this. Operator, check out please."

Ruff Han and Peng Long put their cubes together.

"Alright, transaction complete."

Ruff Han handed over the Archery Shooting Gloves. Peng Long received it and said, "Equip."

Once the gloves appeared on his hands, Peng Long smiled. He must have liked the gloves a lot. After all, he had just bought a Heroic tier item for the low price of 1600 coins.

"Then we're done with the archer... Anyone else?"

Giovani and Mahadas began looking earnestly through the items in front of them. The only ones who didn't get into the shopping mood were Sungjin and Dominic. Sungjin had a good reason. In order to buy the item from Darker than Black, he had to save his coins.

Dominic just waited slightly off to the side. He just wanted the shopping to be over quickly. It was understandable.

Each moment the others spent shopping was cutting away at his remaining life. Sungjin glanced at Dominic before asking Ruff Han.

"Hey, do you have any item that can remove curses?"

Ruff Han responded, "Ah... if you need curse removal..."

He rummaged through his rucksack. From within, he pulled out a luxurious necklace with a white-diamond center-piece.

Innocence – Angel's Blessings
Heroic Necklace

Passive Skill
Magic Defence (II) – Receive 20% reduced damage from all sources of magic.

Active Skill
Purify (V) – Curses, fears, petrification, and all forms of status effects and debuffs are removed. Cooldown 10 minutes.

Snakes avoid those with angelic innocence

"But this is a little expensive. It's almost Legendary-tier item among the Heroic tier. I assure you that this is a very good item."

Sungjin nodded. 5th-tier active skill, and an excellent passive. If anyone had no choice other than to buy it, it was Dominic Spencer.

"So how much is it?" asked Sungjin.

"2600. This is worth 6300 coins at the Black Market."

The item was being offered at nearly a third of the original price. Sungjin had thought that Dominic would buy it without hesitation. 2600 coins was a cheap price to pay for one's life. But Dominic hesitated. "...2600..."

"What's wrong?" asked Sungjin.

Dominic answered, "To tell you the truth... I don't have enough money. 2600 coins..."

Everyone turned to look at him. Dominic lifted up his spear as he continued.

"This spear... I had been saving up for it and bought it as soon as I could afford it. It took almost everything I had earned so far to buy it. So...I am now left with only 1800 coins..."

Everyone froze. Sungjin quickly thought about it in his head.

2600... I have that right now, but...

Sungjin couldn't afford to spare his coins right now. The Item he needed to buy from Darker than Black would likely need all the coins he had currently, plus most of what he would receive from the end of this Raid.

The item was not a bad one by any means, but Sungjin already had the Basilisk's Eye. Innocence was not good enough to justify swapping Basilisk's Eye for it. Sungjin glanced at the others.

It was then that Mahadas spoke up. "I will buy the item, then."

Everyone turned to look at him.

"This Purify Skill, can it be used on others?" asked Mahadas.

Ruff Han nodded and answered his question, "Of course."

"Then please allow me to purchase it. I will pay 2600 Coins."

The transaction was over quickly. Once Mahadas equipped the necklace, he placed his hands on Dominic's forehead and said, "Purify."

The diamond necklace glowed for a moment, and the hand touching Dominic's forehead began to glow as well.

It was an extremely fitting image; a monk with his hands basked in purifying white light, healing another.

"Ooh." Peng Long and Giovani couldn't help but exclaim at the sight and watched with their mouths open.

But instead of Dominic or the hand, Sungjin was staring at Mahadas. *Skilled... does not hesitate to sacrifice himself to help others.*

Color returned to Dominic's face. The 'Vampire's Blood Curse' had been lifted. Dominic faced Mahadas and Sungjin and knelt, he put his hands on the ground and bowed deeply in the eastern style.

"Mahadas and Kei, both of you have saved my life. I vow to repay this debt someday."

Sungjin indifferently received the thanks. "Sure."

To be honest, he didn't think it was possible for Dominic to ever repay him in any form.

Mahadas gathered his hands respectfully, befitting that of his status as a monk, and replied magnanimously, "It was no big thing. If you truly wish to repay me, then please, do an act of kindness for others. I would be satisfied with just that."

Dominic was now no longer under a time constraint, so the group no longer needed to rush. 1 hour was plenty of time to search for and kill the hidden boss. The shopping continued.

Giovani was torn between buying a pair of steel greaves versus a silver axe and finally decided on the former. It was the type of greaves that fired rockets to allow long-distance jumps.

It can be used to escape when surrounded by enemies, or rush to an ally's aid when they're in danger.

Ruff Han's sales pitch won him over immediately. Dominic asked for and bought a ring worth exactly 1800 coins.

Although the ring didn't provide nearly as much protection from spells as Mahadas's 'Innocence', it was better than nothing.

In the end, the only person who did not buy anything was Sungjin. Before he closed up shop, Ruff Han offered him an item.

"Although you think poorly of me, I do have to repay my debts... so here you go."

He muttered as he pulled out an item from his bag. What he handed over was not an item, per se, but a Mystery Pouch.

"Someone completed Ancient Stories of the East, so the net worth has gone down a bit, I guess if you get one of the 'East' components, you can consider it to be a bust."

Ruff Han returned all the display items back into his sack and then stood on all fours. "Then until next time! If there is another!"

He disappeared into the sewers.

***

Once Wandering Merchant Ruff Han ran away, the Hunters left the smelly sewer and returned to the 2nd-floor room.

Giovani, who was first to leave the sewer, found a spot without webs to sit and took off his helm. "Whew... I guess this Chapter is pretty much done."

Peng Long caressed his new gloves as he replied, "It was hectic for a while, but there were no casualties. Everything turned out okay in the end."

Dominic Spencer thanked the remaining two Hunters as well. "I am sorry... my rash actions inconvenienced you two as well."

The men shook their head and denied being troubled.

"No, it wasn't bad at all."

"All's well that ends well."

Sungjin was last to climb out of the sewers and briefly stared at the men conversing with one another. It was a rather heart-warming moment. But it wasn't over yet; there was still the hidden boss remaining.

Sungjin first placed the 'Mystery Pouch' in the cube before addressing the other Hunters.

"Excuse me, sorry to bother you all while you are resting. But there is one more hidden element remaining in this Raid."

Everyone turned to stare at him.

"It's called the hidden boss... as the name would suggest, it is a secondary boss hidden somewhere on the map. I am planning on going back to search for it. Does anyone want to come with me?"

Giovani asked in response, "Hidden boss?"

"Yes. Hidden bosses are stronger than regular Raid bosses. It should be hidden in the castle somewhere," replied Sungjin.

"But... is there a point to seeking it out?"

Sungjin answered simply, "Killing the hidden boss grants bonus points and coins for everyone. Also, it increases contribution level."

The other Hunters looked among themselves. They had greatly benefited from the Wandering Merchant Ruff Han encounter, but their contribution levels were still extremely low.

Peng Long asked Sungjin, "So... is our help necessary?"

Sungjin shook his head. "No, it isn't necessary; I should be able to beat it alone. That being said, I am not going to refuse if anyone decides to help..."

Sungjin dragged out the last word before he continued. "Hidden bosses are typically extremely dangerous, so I can't guarantee your safety. I don't know how it looks like or how it attacks; I don't know anything about it."

Sungjin's words made all the Hunters pause to reconsider. It wasn't an exaggeration to call hidden bosses a gamble with your life.

Sungjin spread his arms wide as he said, "Feel free to act as you please. You are under no obligation to help out. Even though it'll be tricky, I can manage alone. If you decide not to help out, you can stay far away in case I die."

Mahadas moved closer and said, "I have decided to tackle any challenge that comes my way. I don't understand what the point of these Raids is... but through fighting, it could lead to some sort of revelation."

Sungjin nodded. A fighter at his skill level would not be a hindrance. Peng Long raised his hands.

"Aye. I shall come as well. Supporting from a distance can't hurt."

He was right, it wouldn't be bad at all. If he kept a good distance and attacked from afar, Peng Long had very little to be afraid of. The ones who would have trouble were the tank and the melee DPS, Giovani and Dominic.

Giovani wasn't happy about the prospect of facing a second boss. His facial expressions screamed, *Why not just go to the Black Market as is?*

Dominic seemed without enthusiasm, probably due to his near-death experience. Sungjin addressed the two men. "The two of you are welcome to stay behind and rest here. The other two, follow me please."

But Dominic picked up his spear and replied, "No, I owe my life to both of you. If I could be of even a little assistance, I will gladly do it."

Since Dominic declared his intentions to go along, Giovani must have felt nervous about staying behind as he chimed in, "Well, I'll go along as well. I don't know about combat, but if it's just helping to find something..."

And so, for the first time since the restart, all five Hunters left together to hunt the hidden boss. Sungjin addressed a question to the cube.

"Operator, I want to use the Treasure Hunter active. Tell me the clue to find the hidden boss."

The Operator recited the second hint.

[Loyal knight of the count]
[renowned on the battlefield]
[betrayed and beheaded]
[not even death broke his will.]
[unwilling to let go of the reins]

[he circles the castle, searching]

[to find his head and return to battle]

Sungjin looked around at the other Hunters after hearing the hint. Everyone looked confused. Sungjin gave a request to the Operator.

"Operator, one more time."

The Operator repeated the hint, and once again the Hunters all contemplated the meaning.

"Beheaded..." Giovani was first to speak. "So it's something of a headless ghost?"

Peng Long replied, "I feel that 'unwilling to let go of the reins' is the key."

Mahadas gave his thoughts. "Circling the castle... isn't that the most important part?"

After listening to all the Hunters' thoughts on the matter, Sungjin suggested, "In that case, should we take a look around the castle?"

The others agreed and they began moving.

Once the men came to a conclusion, they took the elevators back down to the ground level. All the Vampires who had been dancing in the hall had turned to ash.

The Hunters walked past the ashes and came back outside. Once they passed the two zombie dogs laying outside, everyone suddenly remembered something.

"Headless coachman!" Giovani was first to yell it out.

"Ah, you're right!" Dominic shouted in agreement. The five Hunters cautiously exited the castle gates. The carriages were still standing in the same spot where they had left them.

There was a horse-drawn carriage which had brought them to the castle at the beginning. The Hunters slowly approached the carriage.

A horse stood in place breathing out mist in the cold night air, and a coachman was sitting on the carriage, still holding the reins.

"Hold on." Sungjin had the Hunters wait behind him. He pulled out his two swords and approached the coachman. The headless coachman did not respond.

Sungjin was about to try poking the coachman's arm with the 'Moon Spectre,' but the Operator gave a warning.

[Warning.]

Sungjin took a step back and prepared for battle.

[Attacking a non-hostile life form will cause penalties from the Raid Rewards.]

It was a different warning message than what he had been expecting. It was just like the time he was trying to fight Wandering Merchant Aindell.

Are we wrong? Sungjin began to doubt himself. But he then heard a droning voice.

"Sir Hunter?"

He was missing his neck, but Sungjin could hear someone speaking from the general direction of the coachman. It was a voice of a ghost.

While Sungjin stiffened up, the headless coachman asked, "Did you kill Count Dimitri?"

Sungjin answered him honestly. "Yes, I beheaded him..."

The otherworldly creature before him laughed happily. "Beheaded... Ka hahaha! So in the end... just like me..."

Betrayed and beheaded.

He had the same background story as the hint; in other words, he was most definitely the hidden boss. Only, it was unclear how to stop him from being non-threatening.

Sungjin wasn't sure what to say to the coachman, so he stared at him. But it was the coachman who asked him the question.

"Excuse me, but... did you happen to see my head in the castle? Please find my head. I cannot return to the battlefield without my head..."

"Ah, got it." Sungjin returned to the other Hunters after receiving the hint.

"Everyone, did you notice any heads inside the castle? A severed head?"

The group members racked their brains.

"Is there anywhere they might have preserved a severed head?" asked Sungjin.

Giovani slapped his knees and replied, "Now that you're asking, remember the 3rd floor? All of those suits of armours? What if the head was hidden in one of them?"

Everyone nodded at his suggestion. The full plates of armours would work as hidden places, and indeed the Hunters had not searched through them.

It wouldn't be strange if one of the helms held a severed head. The Hunters returned to the castle ruins.

With the exception of Mahadas, the other three Hunters didn't look very happy. Having to repeatedly search the castle was probably bothering them.

Regardless of how they felt, the Hunters rode the elevator back to the 3rd floor, the ground covered in suits of armours.

"Let's split up and look through the fallen helms," said Sungjin.

Everyone began looking for helms for a severed head.

"All empty here."

"Here as well."

"All empty."

There were no results. Every helm was searched through, but not so much as a hair was found. Sungjin cradled his head and thought carefully.

"Head... Severed head..."

No matter how hard he thought, this room wasn't it. There was no head.

The 1st floor was filled with Vampires who turned to ash after being beheaded... the 5th floor only had the Count. The 2nd floor had spiders, the 3rd had suits of armour, and the 4th floor only had Frankenstein's Monster...

Sungjin paused. A thought occurred to him.

Frankenstein's Monster's head.

Frankenstein's Monster was basically a flesh golem created by stitching together corpses and parts of several people. Sungjin gathered the Hunters.

362

"Please follow me."

He led the Hunters to the elevator and returned to the 4th floor. He inspected the monster they had defeated earlier.

He pulled down the shirt of the monster and saw that the neck had been stitched onto the body. Upon close inspection, the colour of the skin where the neck was stitched was different than the rest of the body.

It was gruesome, but it wasn't the right time to be creeped out. WOOSH

Sungjin sliced through the stitches in one swing and beheaded the monster. He held the head and returned to the elevator where the other Hunters waited. Happy that he had found the key to the hidden boss, Sungjin smiled.

The Hunters stared at him with distaste. *"I thought he was an oddball but good at heart... but he's actually just a weirdo after all!"* they probably thought of him. Sungjin didn't care.

Once the Hunters returned to the 1st floor, Sungjin stood in front of the castle gates. He turned around for a moment and addressed the others.

"Please prepare yourselves. Those of you who don't want to participate should return first to the 1st floor."

Once he was done, Sungjin took the head to meet the headless coachman. "Excuse me, but is this..."

Before Sungjin was even done speaking, the ghost of the headless coachman shouted, "Yes! That's it! My head! Quickly! Return it to me!"

Sungjin held the Moon Spectre with his right as he returned the head to the coachman.

Once the coachman was reunited with his head, he didn't immediately stick it back on his body, but held it his hands and laughed loudly.

"Ahahahahaha! My head! MY HEAD!"

His head emitted green light, and the laughter started to come from the head instead.

"Ahahaha! Come! To battle!"

The headless coachman held his head in one hand and pulled out a long sword that had been hidden on the horse, then destroyed the carriage in a single blow.

Sungjin put his left hand inside his vest upon witnessing the coachman's actions. He was preparing to use the Romance of the Three Kingdoms. The Operator gave out a warning.

[Warning! Hidden Boss]

[Dullahan Knight Besgoro has appeared!]

***

As soon as the hidden boss Dullahan appeared, Sungjin deployed the Romance of the Three Kingdoms. There was no need to drag on the fight. The content of the book revealed itself.

Sungjin wasted no time reading it out loud. "When the Minister of the State, Dong Zhuo, decided to take her to the Mei Citadel..."

It was then that the knight shouted, "Let us go, my steed! Shadow Run!"

"Hee!~" The horse stood up on its hind legs and let out a mighty cry that reverberated in the surrounding.

"She intentionally..." Sungjin was forced to pause while reciting the verses from the book. When he was interrupted, the book automatically closed itself.

Damn!

Romance of the Three Kingdoms returned to the front cover, and Sungjin looked back towards the Dullahan. The Dullahan was rapidly riding into the distance at an unbelievable speed.

Sungjin quickly shouted, "Swift Paw!"

The claws emerged from his boots and he sprinted. But, although he was running at ten times his normal speed, Sungjin was unable to close the distance.

Swift Paw's active period lasted just 30 seconds, but the Dullahan continued to speed away.

What the... how the hell am I supposed to catch up to this guy?

Sungjin checked ahead and saw that the path was curved slightly to the left.

Wait... Sungjin stopped running and pulled out the Magic Carpet. "Flight."

He soared into the sky and checked where the Dullahan was running off to. As he thought, the knight was running in a huge circle, with the castle as the center.

Count Dimitri's castle was quite large, but due to the Dullahan's speed, the Knight was finishing up the first lap around the castle in a very short time.

The Hunters were standing around at the entrance with their weapons in hand, lost as to what they should be doing.

"Where did that thing go, Kei?" asked Giovani.

Sungjin explained as he returned to the Hunters. "He's coming back. He's running a lap around the castle."

And just like he said, the Dullahan came into view from the other side of the castle. Sungjin took out the Romance of the Three Kingdoms again.

But the book stubbornly refused to open, as if secured by chains and locks. The Operator gave an announcement.

[5 seconds remaining until 'Declamation' is available off cooldown]

What?

The Dullahan's head shouted, interrupting his thoughts. "Soldiers! To me!"

At his command, dozens of ghost cavalrymen appeared behind him. Each of the ghost soldiers held a weapon while riding a horse. One of the Hunters muttered, "My god..."

Sungjin put the book away and returned to the inside of the castle gates. Standing directly in the path of the galloping cavalry could only result in death.

"Ahahaha! Cowards! Attack! Go bring me their heads!"

The Dullahan Knight issued orders to his soldiers. Soon, the ghost horsemen entered the castle walls. The Hunters, waiting inside, met them head on.

"Come at me, monsters!" Giovani shouted raising his shield.

"Yaa!" Dominic braced his spear.

"Taho!" Mahadas punched the head of the oncoming horse.

PEW

Peng Long wordlessly let loose bolts at the oncoming cavalry. Sungjin also faced off against a horseman. It came charging straight at Sungjin with a lance.

But it was no match for him.

WOOSH

In one strike, both the horseman and the horse's head were severed. The horse continued forward and ran into the wall, scattering into dust.

Sungjin scanned the surroundings for the Dullahan, but he could not find him. Only a small portion of the cavalry had entered the castle gates.

While the other four Hunters were fighting against the cavalry army, Sungjin used the Magic Carpet to fly into the air. He saw the Dullahan Knight running in the distance, drawing the same circle around the castle.

Sungjin concluded that the main body of the army did not enter the gates. Returning to the gates once more, he prepared the Romance of the Three Kingdoms again.

I will do it this time.

Sungjin began reading the words. It was different from last time. But he didn't have time to ponder the reason; the ghostly cavalry army was almost upon him.

"As Cao Cao asked, those from Heibei are not used to naval combat; riding ships gave them sea sickness. Is there anything we can do to solve this problem? To this, he answered, 'if you tie the boats together, it will reduce the shaking and be just like walking on land.'"

As Sungjin calmly read out the verses, the cavalry grew ever closer; He was moments away from becoming a pancake.

But Sungjin decided to trust the book and continued to read the verses until the end.

"Cao Cao slapped his knees and shouted, 'You are the answer to my prayers, Pang Tong!' "

Once Sungjin was done with the declamation, the book automatically closed itself and returned to his embrace. The Operator gave an announcement.

[Seance of Pang Tong Activated!]

[Passive Skill Rapid Cast (IV) and Increase Mana (II) enabled.]

[Active ability Link Trap (I) is available for instant cast.]

Sungjin wasted no time, immediately casting the active skill. There was no doubt this hero had been chosen for this very reason.

"Link Trap!"

Chains appeared before the cavalry army, and their speed visibly fell; from the speed of a runaway train to that of a crawling baby.

Sungjin rode the Magic Carpet and rose into the air. There were lots of enemies and the point of a 'Strategist' was to cast magic.

Once he climbed high enough, Sungjin recited an incantation.

"Incinerate every..."

But a ball of fire already gathered in his hands. It was the effect of Rapid Cast. Sungjin immediately understood and acted accordingly; He began rapid-firing spells, alternating his hands.

"Fireball!"

"Fireball!!"

"Fireball!!!"

"Fireball!!!!"

"Fireball!!!!!"

"Fireball!!!!!!"

Once he had fired six fireballs, the Operator gave a warning message.

[Low Mana]

Sungjin finally stayed his hands from firing another shot. The ghost cavalry was nearly stuck in place, moving at a snail's speed.

BOOM BOOOM BOOOM RUMBLE RUMBLE

Six balls of fire landed on the ground, and the ghost army was reduced to ashes. The only thing standing after the fires had subsided was the Dullahan Knight.

[10 seconds until the end of Seance. 9,]

The Operator began a countdown, but it didn't matter. Sungjin pulled out his two swords and hopped off of the Magic Carpet.

The Dullahan moved the hand holding his head to look back and forth. The head emitted green flames as he cried out loud, "How can this be? My cavalry! You knave!"

The Dullahan Knight swung his sword towards the approaching Sungjin, but the Link Trap dulled his movement.

Sungjin easily dodged the blow and used his Moon Spectre to sever the hand holding the head and Blood Vengeance to sever the head of the horse, Shadowrun.

Shadowrun was beheaded and turned into dust. Only the one-armed Dullahan remained. He had no weapons remaining, nor a horse.

Sungjin walked up to the knight to deliver the final blow. But green lights began to emit from the head, and he heard the head recite an incantation.

"Awaken and become my slave!"

From the first words, Sungjin knew what the knight was trying to do; he also had this spell memorized. The knight must have wanted to use the spell to resurrect his fallen soldiers.

Sungjin had no reason to allow him to finish his magic. Sungjin pointed at the knight with both of his hands

"Pa!"

His two swords flew out of his hands and cut away at the remaining arm, and also his neck.

"Haa!"

Once the swords passed him, Sungjin cast the return spell. The swords sliced apart the head on its return trip and flew straight into his hands.

The Operator gave out an announcement.

[Hidden Boss The Dullahan Knight Besgoro cleared!]

Sungjin looked down at his swords. He had been planning on swinging his swords in the air to remove the blood, but there was not a single blood stain on the blade.

I guess he was a ghost of sorts. Sungjin grinned as he sheathed his swords again. Every enemy had been killed. Sungjin was planning on returning to the other Hunters' side, but then he saw the others staring at him with mouths hanging open.

"Pang Tong[4]... so you're the Master Hunter? Kei?" asked Dominic.

He couldn't deny it. Treasure Hunter Sungjin raised his arms and answered, "I wasn't trying to hide it, per se."

The Hunters were unable to look away from Sungjin.

"How did he get so strong?"

"Magic... how did he rapid fire so many at once?"

"That book... how is Romance of the Three Kingdoms obtained?"

Sungjin was considering how to respond to the others when he was interrupted by the Operator's announcement.

[All enemies slain.]

[Beginning reward distribution.]

Once reward was mentioned, the Hunters were finally distracted.

[Monsters Slain. Zombie Watchdogs: 2. Vampire Nobles: 20. Giant Spiders: 30. Living Armour: 15. Frankenstein's Monster: 1. Total 6000 points.]

[Boss Monster Slain: 'Thousand-Year Count' Dimitri: 750 points.]

[Hidden Boss The Dullahan Knight Besgoro: 750 points.]

[Final Point count: 7500. Distributing points.]

First up was Dominic Spencer's reward. Due to being bitten by a Vampire early on, he hadn't been able to rack up many points.

[Your contribution is 3.0%. 225 Stat Points, 225 Black Coins awarded. Raid Clear Bonus 2000 Stat Points and 2000 Black Coins awarded. Distributing 2250 Stat Points and 2250 Black Coins.]

It was a low amount, but he didn't look upset. He just considered himself lucky to be alive. Next up was Giovani. Due to Sungjin and Mahadas's strength, he hadn't gotten many opportunities to fight as a tank.

[Your contribution is 5.7%]

Next was Peng Long. Thanks to his long-ranged attacks he was able to rack up more points compared to the two before.

[Your contribution is 8.2%.]

Mahadas excelled in attacks, but by using magic and items to support his team, he racked up lots of contribution points from this round.

[Your contribution is 12.2%.]

Last up was Sungjin.

[Your contribution is 70.9%. 5318 Stat Points, 5318 Black Coins awarded. Raid Clear Bonus 2000 Stat Points and 2000 Black Coins awarded. Item effect 'Additional 10% gained' activated. Distributing 7318 Stat Points and 8050 Black Coins.]

8050 Coins...

Sungjin calculated quickly in his head. Even though he had allowed the other Hunters to take a few contribution points away from him, he had enough money left to buy the item from Darker than Black.

That's good.

While Sungjin was breathing a sigh of relief, the Operator continued to speak.

[And now we will distribute the items.]

***

The item rewards were next, starting with Dominic.

[Spider Silk Mantle]

[Recovery Potion – Medium x2]

Dominic, who hadn't had anything draped over his back, immediately equipped the mantle. It appeared to be at least Rare tier, and he seemed to be satisfied with it.

Next up was Giovani.

[Vampire Slayer's Axe]

[Recovery Potion – Medium x2]

He picked up the axe and muttered,

"This is so much worse than my current axe... time to sell..."

Next in line was Peng Long.

[Arugo – Frankenstein's Monster's Ringer's Solution]

[Recovery Potion – Medium x2]

Peng Long lifted up the item.

Arugo – Frankenstein's Monster's Ringer's Solution
Heroic Belt – Defense 5%

Passive Skill
First Aid (I.)
Once HP drops below 10%, the belt automatically injects Recovery Potion into the bloodstream.
Cooldown 20 Minutes

Ringer's Solution attached to Frankenstein's Monster. It is so large that it is the perfect size to be used as a belt on a human being.

It wasn't a bad item. Drinking a recovery potion in the middle of combat was difficult to say the least. The health recovered by the automatic system could be the difference between life and death. But,

"Hmm... this is a tank item."

As Peng Long suspected, it was meant to be used by tanks.

"I'll just sell it at the auction."

As soon as he declared that, Giovani immediately ran up to him.

"Peng, sell that to me!"

"You want to buy it? For how much?"

"Give me some discount. I spent a lot with the Ratman earlier and don't have much left."

"You just received the Raid reward a moment ago!"

While the two men were haggling, the rewards moved onto Mahadas.

Mahaeen – Frankenstein's Monster's Hard Flesh
Heroic Shoulder pad – Defense 36%

Passive Skill
Living Skin (III)
Recover 2% of total health per minute

Skin from Frankenstein's Monster's shoulder region. It automatically regenerates upon taking damage.

Mahadas equipped the item right away. The green skin from Frankenstein's Monster's shoulder wiggled its way under his clothes and made its way to the shoulders. It was great that the item was not visible from the outside.

Last was Sungjin's turn.

[Blood Sucker – Vampire's Ring]
[Besgoro – Dullahan's Head]
[Shadowrun – Ghost stallion]
[Spellbook – Illusion]
[Recovery Potion – Medium x4]

Sungjin was reading the messages when the Operator gave out another announcement.

[Congratulations! You have obtained the Legendary item Besgoro – Dullahan's head!]

Sungjin picked up the items that fell before him. The first item to catch his eye was Besgoro – Dullahan's Head.

It was a Legendary item, but the skull emitting green flames was still a strange item to behold.

[Last but not least, you will be awarded titles earned in the Raid.]

Everyone received one title each. The title Sungjin received was,

[Summoner – Familiars summoned through 'Spiritual Link' will last 10 minutes longer.]

So not having this title equipped means that the bonus is only 5 minutes.

This title wasn't all that great for now, as it only granted an additional 5 minutes to Soldamyr and Cain's active time. It would probably be more useful once he was able to increase the number of summons available to him via Spiritual Link.

Well, there's no downside to having more titles available to me.

Sungjin checked the item he received, starting with Besgoro's head. The Operator opened up a status screen.

Besgoro – Dullahan's head
Legendary Helm – Defense 70%

Passive Skill
Ghost Vision (IV) – Enables low-light vision.
Substitute Chanting (II) – Chants the incantation of the spell being thought of on behalf of the caster. Cooldown 1 minute
Chat (I) – Consult Sir Besgoro, who has a wealth of knowledge from countless battles.

Active Skill
Frenzy (VI) – Increases attack speed by 10% for each hit against the enemy. 1 minute duration, 20 minute cooldown.

Legendary Hero Besgoro was well renowned on the battlefield, but met a terrible end. Whispers of his grudge can be heard from his head.

Sungjin frowned while reading the status screen. "It's a helm?!"

The skull was covered in green flames. And yet this ghastly thing was still considered a helm. The specs were undoubtedly good. High defense rating and great skills, both passives and active.

With the exception of 'Chat (I)'. Sungjin swallowed once and said, "Equip."

The skull grew large enough to accommodate Sungjin's head, and then jumped on top of his head. Once it was on, Sungjin's vision changed dramatically. Despite being dark out, he could see as clear as day.

So... This is ghost vision...

Sungjin turned his head left and right. When he saw Dominic, Dominic jumped back in surprise. "Wah!"

Sungjin touched the helm covering his head as he asked, "Is it... weird?"

Dominic replied, "No... I mean... it's intimidating rather than weird..."

Dominic is probably right, thought Sungjin as he felt the skull. Suddenly, he heard a familiar voice from above.

Hmmm. Are you my new master?

Sungjin looked up in surprise. But there was nothing there. But this time he heard the voice from behind.

Where are you looking? It is I! You are wearing me.

Sungjin kept a neutral expression as he continued to feel the exterior of the skull. "...Mister Besgoro?"

Yes, that is my name. Although, I have peerage, so call me 'Sir' instead of Mister.

This was probably the passive skill Chat (I). It appeared that the only person who could hear the voices was Sungjin. Mahadas worriedly asked Sungjin, "Is the spirit still haunting you?"

"Yes. *My grudge cannot be washed clean with just my death. Curse you, Dimitri!*" said Besgoro.

"Count Dimitri is slain. I have severed his head."

I know. You told me. You've done well, good job. He deserved to die!

375

Sungjin recalled the Operator's hint from earlier. *Betrayed and beheaded.*

Anyway! He accused me of plotting a rebellion! No such thought had occurred to me at all! In fact, I was planning on joining his family as a son-in-law!

"Son in law?" asked Sungjin.

Yes, by marrying the Count's daughter. She had fallen in love with me. So I asked for her hand in marriage. But once he heard that, he falsely accused me of treason and had me executed.

"So that marriage... sounds like he was against it."

I stood on the battlefield fighting for his honour and clan for 40 years!

Sungjin couldn't help but feel that there was something strange about what had been said. "Did you say 40 years?"

Yes. I have killed so many in the name of the Count. So many...!

"How old were you when you asked for her hand in marriage?"

Hmm... I believe that I was 52 years old then.

"And the Count's daughter's age?"

20...

Sungjin couldn't help but blurt out, "That's totally criminal!"

Why? If I dedicated 40 years of my life, letting me have his daughter is fine, right?

"No, wrong. Totally not fine."

Sungjin glanced at the others. The other four were staring at him.

"What a shame..." Their eyes seem to say.

Sungjin slapped the skull on his head and said, "Okay, I got it. Count Dimitri is dead, so let go of your grudge and pass on."

But I want to roam the battlefields once more.

"Then shut up"

Fine. Call me when you're in battle.

He finally stopped chatting.

But I'm never going to call you... thought Sungjin before moving on to check the other items. The next item was a ring with a bright red ruby. Strangely, the colour of the ring resembled blood.

Blood Sucker – Vampire's Ring
Heroic Ring

Passive Skill
Life Steal (II) – Steal health for 2% of the damage dealt by physical attacks on hit.

Ring imbued with the power of Vampires.
Count Dimitri had the power of this ring injected directly into his blood by someone from 'far away.'

It was a simple and easy-to-understand item. It only had one skill, but the effects were unimaginably powerful. Especially since Sungjin's offensive power was off the charts.

The last item was a small round coin. On it was minted an image of warhorses.

Looks just like Mapae[5].

Sungjin picked up the coin to inspect it.

Shadowrun – Ghost Stallion
Heroic Summon

Passive Skill
Spiritual Link (Shadowrun) – Summons a Legendary Stallion who can run continuously without rest. 10 minute duration.

Besgoro's steed. After the death of its master, the stallion continued to serve its master in death.

It was another summon. It would synergize well with the title he had earned this round. Sungjin flipped the coin into the air. From midair,

"Houhynhynm~" With a loud noise, a ghostly stallion appeared next to him. Of course, someone couldn't help but speak up.

Of all the many stallions I have ridden on, he was the best! Ride him! You'll find no better mount!

Sungjin climbed on top of the horse. Despite being a ghost, it made a great mount. Sungjin wanted to try running a lap around the castle like Besgoro had done. But, the Operator's announcement interrupted him.

[Returning to Black Market in 1 minute.]

I should try out the stallion next time. Sungjin climbed down from Shadowrun.

What? Why aren't you galloping away on him? Besgoro asked.

Sungjin replied, "There is only 1 minute left. I wanted to say goodbye to my teammates before we go."

Sungjin first addressed Dominic.

"Stay well, Dominic. I am glad we could save your life."

"Thank you, Kei. If we meet again... I will definitely be of help."

Next was Giovani and Peng Long... but they were too busy haggling.

"3500"

"3000"

"3300... I won't sell below this."

"Let me buy it for 3000."

"No, I will not sell it for 3000. I'll get a much better price at the Auction house."

"We fought and worked together side by side through a Raid. We're comrades!"

"That's why I discounted it to 3300!"

They were busy quarrelling. Sungjin passed them and spoke to Mahadas. He had displayed impressive combat prowess as well as a commendable attitude and mind set towards others.

Sungjin offered a handshake. "It was good working with you, venerable Mahadas."

Mahadas returned the handshake and smiled. "No, you were the benefactor, Kei. You've worked hard for our sake."

"Then until next time we meet."

Mahadas gathered his hands into a prayer. "As our fate and karma allows."

[Returning to the Black Market in 10 seconds. 10,]

The operator's countdown began. Peng Long and Dominic haggled up to the last few seconds fervently, and finally, they pressed their cubes against each other's.

Meanwhile, they both turned towards Kei to say their goodbyes.

"Thanks, Kei!"

"See you next time!"

Sungjin waved his hands towards the other Hunters.

[3, 2, 1, 0]

He was teleported away to the Black Market.

Chapter 13 – Black Market Sixth Shopping

The first thing Sungjin did once he arrived in the Black Market was to check how many coins he had in total.

"Operator, how many coins do I have?"

[10900]

"Hmm."

"We received new shipments! Please come and check them out!" One of the vendors tried to grab his attention, but Sungjin paid no attention to him. The item he wanted to purchase at Darker than Black would cost 10,000 Coins. He only had 900 coins in excess.

There's nothing I can get with this.

Sungjin thought of going to Ninety-Nine Nights straight away, but he got an idea. *There's the Wandering Merchant's Mystery Pouch.*

He hadn't had a chance to open it yet.

"Operator, can you retrieve the Mystery Pouch for me?"

The Operator handed Sungjin the item. Once it was in his hands, Sungjin thought about it for a moment. *I might get a Legendary... Crafting material, eh?*

Currently, the Ancient Stories of the East Romance of the Three Kingdoms was already complete. Once the Unique Legendary item was complete, receiving another material pertaining to it lost all meaning and would become a redeemable coupon with the value of 500 coins to be exchanged at the Black Market.

That's if the 'Roulette' lands on one of the volumes of Ancient Stories from the East...

The losses of opportunity would be unthinkable. It wouldn't be any better even if he got Ancient Stories of the Middle East or West. From what he was told by the previous owner of Romance of the Three Kingdoms, the Declamation skill worked independently of the item used, and could only be cast 1 time a day.

In other words, even if he gathered and crafted another book, it would be useless. And although the ingredients for each book would initially be worth 5000 Coins, if someone managed to gather and complete the book before he could sell it off, those pieces would drop in price to 500 coins each.

I hope I don't get any book pieces...

Until now, the total number of Pouches he had seen being opened were three; two by himself, and one by Serin Han. And of those, all three had contained book volumes.

If he was guaranteed to take a loss; it was better to go in with no expectations at all. Sungjin held the Pouch in silence for a while before he finally made up his mind.

I won't open it. I'll just put it out on the Auction floor.

That was probably for the best. For those who already owned the books, the item held no real value anymore. But on the other hand, it could prove to be useful to other Hunters. Taking others into consideration, it was the right thing to do to make it available for other people.

Sungjin headed towards the Three Achi Brother's Auction house.

"Welcome, esteemed Hunter!"

Sungjin first asked them, "Did Manta get sold?"

The middle brother answered him back. "No one placed a bid last night and so it was withdrawn."

As I thought... magic hasn't really caught up yet with the general populace.

"Should we cancel the auction?" asked the pigman.

"No, no. Please continue to make it available on the floor."

"Okay, understood."

Sungjin then showed them the mystery pouch and said, "And please put this up for auction."

"How much would you like for us to sell this item for?"

Sungjin took a moment to consider.

If a book comes out, each one is worth 5000 Coins... if East comes out, only 500...

Anyone who understood the true value of the Mystery Pouch would know that the pieces of Ancient Stories of the East were already worthless.

I should make it cheaper than 5000... But not too much lower than that.

Sungjin replied, "Put the starting price at 3000, and buy out at 4000 please."

This price seemed fair. It was an item with gambling element built in, after all.

If they were to pay 4000 coins up front and then receive a favourable outcome, they would be satisfied with the purchase, and if they pay 3000 coins but were still disappointed, at least it wouldn't be too big of a loss.

Once Sungjin was done with his business, he left the Auction house and headed towards Ninety-Nine Nights.

*

When Sungjin arrived, Cain was baring his fangs and growling towards something. The place he was facing was the stables; stables which now held his mount, Shadowrun.

It was a stable that was always vacant, but thanks to 'Spiritual Link' the stable had finally received an inhabitant.

Sungjin reassured Cain as he gently tried to calm him down. "Oh, Cain, please don't do that."

Cain stared at his master. Sungjin glanced at Shadowrun. There were food and water filled at the trough before it, but it didn't seem to have touched any of it. Sungjin extended his greeting towards the ghost stallion. "I look forward to working with you too."

Shadowrun snorted in a low tone.

Responding to the horse, Cain resumed his growling.

Cain was completely on guard against the horse. Even though they were both beasts, he didn't seem to like the fact that it was a ghost type.

Sungjin returned his gaze to Cain and said, "Ahh Cain, don't do that. You should make friends."

Cain turned to look at him again. He didn't seem to want to do so.

Sungjin couldn't help but say, "Oh well, let's go eat for now."

Cain let out a bark and obediently strolled into Ninety-Nine Nights. Sungjin followed behind him and entered the inn.

Sungjin was greeted by Dalupin and Genie Soldamyr, who were waiting for him inside.

"Welcome back"

"Thank you, Dalupin.

"Good work today, Master."

"You did well today as well, Soldamyr"

Dalupin approached Sungjin and asked, "What would you like to eat for dinner today?"

*

Sungjin was laying down. He had eaten dried sellfish, sharkfin, swallow nest soup, and other varieties of Chinese course meal in bulk; he wasn't moving anytime soon.

I should go to bed early tonight if I want to wake up early tomorrow...

Sungjin glanced outside. It was already dark out, long past sundown.

I wonder if anyone placed a bid on the Mystery Pouch.

And exactly when he thought of that,

KNOCK KNOCK

Dalupin knocked on the door. Sungjin opened the door for him as usual. And as always, Dalupin brought him a piece of paper and greeted him courteously. "Are you getting a good rest?"

"Yes, thanks to you."

Dalpuin handed over the paper and said, "Here is the information page for the next Raid."

Sungjin accepted the sheet and answered, "Ah, thank you."

But Dalupin had another piece of paper. "And this... this is a receipt from Time is Money Plan."

Sungjin accepted the receipt.

Receipt – 3400 Black Coins

The item you placed on the auction, Mystery Pouch, has been sold. 3400 Black Coins was paid by Head Hunter.

Place the receipt into the cube to instantly redeem the amount.

Sungjin was surprised to see Head Hunter as the purchaser, since he already knew one such person.

"Thank you, Dalupin. There's one other thing I need your help with."

"Please tell me."

"Please wake me up at four thirty."

"Understood. Please have a good rest."

Sungjin sent Dalupin away and read over it again.

...Did she buy this?

It was likely that there were other Head Hunters in the world, but buying a Mystery Pouch so decisively, he was nearly certain it must have been her. But...

No, forget it... The chances we will meet again are less than 10%.

Becoming attached to any random Hunter could only bring more pain. He had experienced it time and time again. He gazed at the receipt one last time before shoving it in the cube.

[Received 3400 Black Coins.]

Sungjin walked out to the balcony as he listened to the Operator's voice. In the distance, he could see the lights coming from the Black Market.

I guess somewhere out there, another Hunter is seeing this view...

In another dimension, in another alternative Ninety-Nine Nights, other Hunters lived and breathed. But the only time the Hunters could interact with one another was during the Raids.

Even though he had Spiritual Links with his summons, he could never meet another Hunter in the Black Market.

Hunters had to put their lives on the line to fight, but it was also a battle against loneliness. Sungjin let out a long sigh while staring off into the night.

"Haaah…"

It was then

[Attention Please.]

[Head Hunter has succeeded in completing the Legendary Ancient Omnibus One Thousand and One Nights]

[All other copies will be destroyed, and the owners will be refunded by 500 coins.]

Sungjin froze. One Thousand and One Nights; Arabian Nights. This was undoubtedly Ancient Stories of the Middle East. Sungjin couldn't help but recall the woman with long flowing hair. He thought to himself.

Serin… I guess our chances to meet again are higher than 10% after all.

Sungjin turned away from the balcony. Behind him was a full moon.

*

Sungjin climbed down the stairs back to the main floor. Dalupin came to see him off. Soldamyr was inside his lamp.

Once Sungjin was outside, Cain barked and ran after him.

"Cain, don't follow me. I'm going 'there' again."

Cain didn't listen and showed that he was going to come no matter what.

"Ok, fine, I guess you can walk with me till the entrance or something…"

Shadowrun watched him from the Stables. Because he was a ghost type, he apparently did not need sleep.

Sungjin put Ninety-Nine Nights behind him and headed towards the Black Market with Cain by his side. He headed towards Darker than Black. Once he reached the corner where Darker than Black was located, Cain stopped walking and sat down.

Sungjin wasn't sure, but the man seemed to inspire fear in others. He took the shape of a man, but he was most definitely not a man.

"I'll be back, then."

Sungjin said to Cain before entering the area. The stairway down was as dark as ever, but Sungjin was able to clearly see without trouble, thanks to Besgoro's Ghost Vision.

Sungjin unhesitatingly entered the darkness and entered the bar within. Inside, he saw the Hidden Merchant.

"Second visit already. Welcome," said the man.

Sungjin approached him. "I have come to buy the item we discussed last time."

The Merchant took out a small marble from his coat.

"Here it is, the Trollseeker Marble. 10,000 Black Coins."

Sungjin didn't hesitate. "Operator, pay."

The Merchant handed over the 'Trollseeker Marble' to Sungjin and said, "As the name would suggest, it allows you to forcefully enter a Raid where a troll has appeared. In exchange, you need to recharge its power. The recharge fee is a thousand coins each use. Got it?"

Sungjin nodded. It was the same information he had heard last night.

"If you don't have the money you can't use it. Just be aware."

Sungjin replied, looking straight into his eyes, "That won't be a problem. I am confident that I will be able to make more than a thousand coins each time I use it."

The man grinned widely, revealing his white teeth and asked, "Is that so?"

Sungjin thought as he held the Marble.

Equip Adjudicator and hunt trolls in other Raids, and put the items I get on the auction house... That should earn me at least 1000 coins per jump.

He would cut away Trolls, who obstructed the growth of other Hunters, as he empowered himself at the same time.

Except... keeping Adjudicator active...

That was the only part that was bothering him; he would need to keep Adjudicator activated as long as he planned to go Troll Hunting. He could neither use Master Hunter nor Treasure Hunter titles.

The Hidden Merchant spoke to him breaking his chain of thoughts.

"Why are you looking so troubled? Do you believe that you are restricted to a single title per round?"

It was as if he read Sungjin's mind. When Sungjin turned his head towards the merchant, the merchant continued, taking another item out of his coat; a star-shaped item with a whirlwind drawn in the middle.

"Star of the Nameless. It is an item that allows you to change your title at will."

Sungjin's eyes opened wide. The Merchant grinned again, revealing his white teeth as he laughed.

"Did I not tell you when you first came? If there is something you want, ask me."

Sungjin couldn't help but reach out to try and touch the item. The Merchant then muttered something, as if reciting verses from a holy book.

"He who searches for answers finds questions, and he who searches for questions finds answers."

***

Sungjin touched the star's whirlpool design. The Operator opened up the information screen.

Paranova – Star of the Nameless
Legendary Amulet

Active
Rename (I)
Change your Title. Cooldown 10 minutes

For some, Name is everything. For some, Name is nothing.

"How much is this?"

The man raised two fingers up. "Twenty thousand."

Sungjin stared at the star for a moment. Even though the star was held in place, the whirl design seemed to spin on its own, as if Sungjin was hypnotized.

20,000...

Considering that Legendary items could be bought for just ten thousand, it was an item of immense value. Even Sungjin's most expensive item, Romance of the Three Kingdoms, was worth 15,000 coins in component costs. But here was an item being sold for 20,000. The item effects were unbelievably useful.

Every 10 minutes I can change my title to use the full effects of each title... If I were to change my title according to situation...

Sungjin kept the item in the back of his mind. Even if he were to receive a generous amount of Raid rewards, it would still take two more Chapters until he could gather enough coins to purchase this item. The man knew that as well.

"Well, you won't be able to get it now, but... just know that this kind of thing exists."

The man returned the star-shaped item back into his suit. Sungjin stared at the man for a second. This man was on a completely different level compared to other vendors and merchants.

Sungjin got an idea. "Well, then... Is there any way for me to be able to stay in contact with other Hunters?"

The man fell silent for a moment to consider Sungjin's words. He then replied, "Tell me more about what it is that you want to do."

"For example... I met someone in a previous Chapter, and I have become good friends with them. I would like to be able to meet them or at least be able to send and receive messages with them."

"Hmm... That's difficult to accomplish. Especially in 'this world'... You probably know that already."

The man turned to look at the cube behind Sungjin as if to indicate the Operator.

"Communication between Hunters is strictly forbidden unless you happen to meet each other during the Raid..."

"So, is it impossible?"

The man raised his pointer finger and shook his head.

"No, there's no such thing as impossible. It's just... in order to overcome the structure of this world, you are in need of the Power of God."

"Power of God?"

"Yes. The Power of God."

Sungjin tilted his head at the words of the man. The merchant continued to explain.

"Well, Power of God isn't nearly as fancy as it sounds. The Power of God just refers to the holy ability to create something out of nothing. The Power of Creation."

He continued with his out of the world explanation. Then

"For example..."

He took out something from within his pocket.

"Something like this?"

It was a glass bottle. It was cut into a precise shape, and there was some sort of fluid contained within.

"What is it?" asked Sungjin.

The merchant answered, "Touch it. As you already know, touching is free in the Black Market."

Sungjin placed his hand on the bottle.

Jasepit – Holy Water of Baptism
Mythological

Active Skill
Baptism (I)
Imbue the title of 'The Chosen One" to the target.

I am the grape tree. You are the branch.

Mytho?

Even though Sungjin had been the longest-surviving human in the previous Raid, this was the first time he had come across a Mythological-tier item. And the active skill was shocking, to say the least.

Forcefully change the other person's title to The Chosen One...

The bizarre active skill was something Sungjin couldn't even imagine to have existed. So he touched the glass bottle again. It looked like an ordinary glass bottle, but it gave the strange sensation that his skin was sticking to it.

"How much is this?"

To his question, the merchant gave another question rather than an answer. "How much do you think it is?"

When Sungjin couldn't answer, he laughed and said, "Just one."

*

"2000 to Strength, 2000 to Dex, 1000 Endurance, 500 to Magic Power, and the rest to Mind Power. Apply."

[Applied.]

"And... equip title, Adjudicator."

[Equipped.]

Finally, Sungjin picked up the black spellbook in front of him.

Spellbook – Illusion
7th Circle Black Magic

Create perfectly identical mimics.
The number of illusions is based on the user's Magic Power.

Soldamyr gave a tip from the side. "It is a spell that is heavily influenced by Magic Power. Most mages use this spell as a way to buy time to shout incantations. But you, who are proficient with the blade, should be able to utilize it offensively."

Sungjin nodded. "Memorize."

The spellbook burned up in black flames. Next item to check after the spellbook was the information sheet.

"Information on Tahrakhan Plateau"

Sungjin picked up the sheet and the piece of toast sitting next to it and walked out of the Ninety-Nine Nights. He sat on the rocking chair placed in front of the door and watched the sunrise.

He held the bread in his mouth, toasted with egg on top, for over a minute without moving.

Finally, Soldamyr spoke up. "Are you... uncomfortable, Master?"

"Ah? Mmm..." Sungjin finally bit off the first piece before responding. "No... I was just lost in thought."

"Then I'll be returning to the lamp. Please call for me if you need my assistance."

Soldamyr returned to his lamp, and only Cain remained by his side. As if understanding what Sungjin was going through, Cain sat next to him motionlessly.

Sungjin petted his head as he continued to think.

Darker than Black... it was even crazier than I imagined...

Definitely... Someone else's thought interrupted Sungjin inside his own head. It was Besgoro's voice.

Sungjin asked him, "What? Did you see it too, grandpa?"

I am not your grandpa. I am a Knight. Call me Sir Besgoro.

Geez, you're just a ghost, why are you so uptight? Thought Sungjin. "Okay, Sir Besgoro. Were you able to watch the whole thing?"

Anything you can see, I can see. Anything you can hear, I can hear.

It was an unwelcome revelation.

I should keep it off of me when I don't need it.

Sungjin thought to himself as he replied, "What do you think it is? That place? That man?"

I'm not sure... even I, a ghost, find him very peculiar. Actually, is he even a man? Is he even human? Or a ghost? But not the same. He was closer to something like... closer to the Devil or God.

The man was definitely a mystery, in many ways.

"Well, whether or not he is the Devil or God... he does seem to have the items I need."

But why did you feel those items are necessary? I can see the argument for the star, but what about that holy water? Where are you going to use that for? Asked Besgoro.

"...It's for marking the people I need."

People you need?

"Yes. Strong, but also trustworthy."

The ghost began to laugh at his words. *Heh ha ha ha ha ha*

It was a ghastly laughter which echoed in Sungjin's head. He decided to ask, "Why are you laughing?"

Such a thing does not exist.

Sungjin closed his mouth; he also knew what Besgoro was telling him. After all, he had experienced it first-hand. Besgoro continued to speak.

Well... Kind people, those who are eager to help others, that's good and all. But power does not gather around them. It is far more likely for them to have their power taken away. He who is strong has sapped much strength from those around him.

Sungjin paused and remembered for a moment.

Serin Han, Mahadas.

And then he answered, "No. That is not always the case."

Of course not. There are always exceptions. But the majority will be like that. Trust me. I have roamed the battlefields for 40 years. I have met countless allies, and I have watched most of them die.

Sungjin silently listened. Besgoro's 40 years of combat experience was something he could relate to.

But in the end, the ones who survive are those who are strong, who became strong by ruthlessly and mercilessly taking and stealing from everyone around them. Those who monopolize every resource they can take, said Besgoro.

Sungjin disagreed. "You must believe so because you've spent your whole life on the battlefield. The place I've come from is a little different."

To which, Besgoro gave a short reply. *It's the same anywhere.*

And with that said, Besgoro finally went silent. Sungjin shook his head briefly, trying to disperse the negativity the ghost had been trying fill his head with.

He had a flashback. To Serin Han, Igor, Mahadas, people he met in the previous life, the final ten members.

Araujo, Ryushin, Nada, Umkhuba, Ilich, Hildebrandt, Shunsuke, Mustafa, and... Edward.

Each and every one of those members were incredibly powerful people. Masters among masters. In luck and in skill. Rightfully described as 'Those Chosen by the Gods.'

Sungjin was the best swordsman of them all, but in terms of his overall strength, it wasn't very high compared to the other nine members. The only problem with the nine masters was the pride befitting of their enormous talent. He still remembered their conversations.

I will do the next one.

No, it will be me.

If you're fighting over contribution level, cut it out.

Shut up. Do you have any idea what happened in the last Raid when he tried to solo the boss?

In the end, they had been wiped out. Truth be told, the reason why the team got wiped out was not due to lack of stat points or ability; each of the members overflowed with power.

The party was wiped out due to their inability to cooperate. Sungjin lowered his gaze down to the ground. He could see his two swords, Blood Vengeance and Moon Spectre. He then had a thought.

I am probably the strongest in this timeline. After all, I've done a 100% clear on every Raid.

Of the nine others who were in the final parties, he had had some who he could get along with, and others he could not. And of the final few, there were those who 'let their team get wiped out.'

Sungjin stood up. *Star of the Nameless and Holy Water of Baptism; I'll buy them both and create a brand-new final ten members of my choosing. And with these new teammates, I will see to the end of the Final Raid.*

After he made up his mind, he took out something from within his jacket. It was a ring. It was a simple ring, made of an ordinary metal.

Only, that it looked peculiar. It was made to look like two wires were twisted around as it created the bend. Sungjin lifted up the ring and inspected the status window.

Helix Ring – Ring of the Warlord
Heroic Ring

Passive Skill
Reign (I)
Receive 1 White Coin from those who, knowingly and of their own free will, kiss the ring.
Those who kiss the ring receive a permanent 10% loss to all future Raid coin rewards.
Can only be used once per person.

Between the two stairs, he lay and sang freely.
Holding the crown, the new king has returned.

It was an item he had paid 3000 Black Coins to purchase. Sungjin recalled the conversation from earlier.

Just... one?

Yes, just one. But, it's a different type of currency.

Sungjin had never heard of a White Coin. At least, not from his memories of the previous life.

I don't know what it does yet, but... Sungjin made a fist and stood up.

I will obtain these things and rise as the new power and establish my rule over the Raids.

Thinking of what he was going to do next, Sungjin returned to Ninety-Nine Nights. The sun gradually rose higher and higher into the morning sky behind him.

Afterword

Oppatranslations

Thank you for reading. This was our very first translation project when we started our career as translators, and we are finally able to bring it to Kindle and soon Audible. It was quite a task translating it to the English language as it was written originally in the Korean language which brought its fair bundle of challenges such as different grammar structure, lack of dialog tags, use of certain elements such as onomatopoeia etc. The author and the team hopes that you had a pleasant reading experience.

You can write to us at oppatranslations@gmail.com

Notes:-

[1]HP is 10x Endurance, MP is 10x Mind Power

[2]Murim- This is korean version of cultivation/kung fu genre. He's standing on the club as shown in chinese movies.

[3]Battle of Changban Historical background:
The Battle of Changban was a battle fought by warlords Cao Cao and Liu Bei in 208 in the late Eastern Han dynasty. Three legends spawned in this battle.

Liu Bei was in a retreat, running away south, after finally convincing the master strategist Zhuge Liang following the occurence known as the Three Visitations. Soon after accepting Zhuge Liang's Longzhong plan (long term strategy to attack and capture the Imperial Capital), Liu Biao (who had been protecting Liu Bei from Cao Cao) died and was succeeded by Liu Cong, who immediately surrendered to Cao Cao without telling Liu Bei. This is why by the time Liu Bei found out and began the retreat, Cao Cao's gigantic army was already marching upon his city.

Loved by the people, they decided to follow him, and the peasants initiated a voluntary exodus to follow their lord, with their numbers running into several hundred thousands. This is the first legend of Battle of Changban.

Cao Cao at the time, commanded the Mongolian Cavalry division and rode hard day and night to catch up with Liu Bei. Liu Bei, moving slowly with hundreds of thousands of peasants which included elderly and children, could not move fast enough, and were eventually caught. This is the Battle of Changban. During this battle, most of Liu Bei's followers were caught, killed, or swore loyalty to Cao Cao. Most of Liu Bei's family were captured by Cao Cao, to which one of his heroic generals, Zhao Yun, charged head on against the gigantic armies of Cao Cao.

Liu Bei's men shouted that Zhao Yun has abandoned his lord, to which Liu Bei refused to believe. Lo and Behold, from within the middle of the Cao Cao forces, Zhao Yun returned with the infant son (Liu Bei's Heir) and Liu Bei's main wife, both rescued from captivity. This is the second legend of Battle of Changban. According to legend, Liu Bei throws away his son and casts him to the ground, angry that he nearly caused him the loss of a great general and a hero and Liu Bei's other wives attempted suicide by throwing themselves into the well, so that they don't burden Zhao Yun with having to protect them all.

The third legend- During the retreat, Zhang Fei (the sworn brother) of Liu Bei, decided to form a rearguard with 20 cavalrymen, blocking the main bridge across the River to buy Liu Bei and the final few surviving followers time to escape from the battle. Zhang Fei is a legendary warrior himself, and he alone, with just 20 men, were able to block the bridge and defend against the entire might of the Cao Cao army until Liu Bei could escape.

After killing dozens of enemies, including several generals, he made the legendary shout "I am Zhang Yide! Come battle me to the death!" to which Cao Cao's army's morale broke and they retreated, no longer daring to fight him. Left alone, he and the men destroyed the bridge and retreated to Liu Bei's camp. The passage that Sungjin read out loud is actually from the real 'Romance of the Three Kingdoms' where it describes Zhang Fei's legendary defense of the bridge.

[4]There are two very different but linked scenes mentioned in the text.

First one is about Dong Zhuo and Diao Chan. Specifically, the scene where Diao Chan is taken to the Mei citadel.

Diao Chan is one of the most famous fictional characters that appeared in the Romance of the Three Kingdoms. To end the tyrannical rule of Dong Zhuo, which was destroying the Han Dynasty, Wang Yun asked his adopted daughter to create strife between Dong Zhuo and Lu Bu (Legendary warrior).

She is first betrothed to Lu Bu, who becomes entranced by her beauty, before she is then introduced to Dong Zhuo, who immediately takes her away to Mei citadel; site of untold savagery and debauchery where Dong Zhuo kept his large harem. Lu Bu is outraged and later kills Dong Zhuo. This plan is called Linked Trap.

The text Sungjin actually finished reading out loud is the scene where Pang Tong tricks Cao Cao to use a flawed strategy.

Pang Tong, at this point, was already a world renowned strategist and tactician. Pang Tong was working with Liu Bei and Zhuge Liang to bring down Cao Cao. Pretending to join Cao Cao as a strategist, Pang Tong gave Cao Cao the idea to tie boats together with steel chains so that the ships will stop rocking, and place the planks above the chains where the boat meets so that the men could freely run from one ship to another as if walking on land.

The idea worked. Soldiers no longer had sea sickness. However, it greatly slowed down the progress of the ships to a crawl, especially at bends.

Emboldened by the apparent success of chaining ships together, Cao Cao attacked deep into the Sun Quan territory where he was without cavalry support.

At night when winds were favorable, Zhuge Liang launched an attack with unmanned boats filled with oils and torches which lit the chained ships on fire upon impact. Unable to pull away due to chains and planks linking the ships together, the whole of Cao Cao's great fleet went up in flames, burning a large portion of his army alive, and drowning most of the survivors. Stranded in the marsh and river-filled Sun Territory without a proper navy nor seamen, Cao Cao was forced to retreat. This is the famous battle of Red Cliff.

Pang Tong's great strategy which led to Cao Cao's defeat at the battle of Red Cliff was also called Linked Trap.

[5]The item called Mapae (Horse Requisition Tablet), was used by secret royal inspectors during the Joseon Dynasty to requisition horses and soldiers from local stations; it gave them authority equal

to the highest rank in government with which they could dismiss anyone from office, including Governors (highest official rank) in the name of the king if they were found to be corrupt. It has the connotation of being associated with justice and rightful authority.

www.ingramcontent.com/pod-product-compliance
Lightning Source LLC
Chambersburg PA
CBHW051517250626
47156CB00001B/129